praise

GOING DUTCH
BY JAMES GREGOR

"*Going Dutch* involves a graduate student with an aversion to honesty: Richard is openly gay, but when an unassuming classmate, Anne, helps him write his dissertation, eventually taking over the project entirely, he enjoys the plagiaristic convenience of her company too much to tell her he's attracted to men. As the dueling vectors of his life threaten to collide—one, in which Richard is happily dating a man named Blake, and the other, in which he and Anne seem the perfect picture of upper-crust heterosexual romance— Richard justifies his lies as 'a kind of settling of scores with his past,' as though his sexuality were a debt of which he's owed relief."

—*NEW YORK TIMES*

"A book of deceptive ambitions, a breezy page-turner that, every few pages, slides in an observation that inspires some combination of laughter, mortification, and admiration. A witty and perceptive examination of contemporary social mores, you'll tear through this tale of a thoroughly modern love triangle. A comedy of manners for the (very) modern age. . . . A dizzyingly satirical tapestry of the absurdities of contemporary urban life and love. . . . *Going Dutch* is also just really, *really* funny."

—*ENTERTAINMENT WEEKLY* (A Best Debut Novel of 2019)

"A charming, well-observed debut. While the plot and the characters and the relationships in the novel are deeply engaging, what stuck out to me even more was Gregor's writing itself. [Gregor's] mix of old-fashioned style and contemporary setting makes *Going Dutch* an incredibly fun read, even in its most tragic moments, when Richard is at his most infuriatingly resistant to change. I can't wait to see what Gregor writes next."

—NPR

"A sardonic, procrastinating PhD candidate gets close to a classmate and questions his own sexuality in Gregor's excellent debut. Filled with pithy secondary characters . . . Gregor's on-the-nose depiction of New York liberal intelligentsia makes for wonderful satire. This marvelously witty take on dating in New York City and the blurry nature of desire announces Gregor as a fresh, electric new voice."

—*PUBLISHERS WEEKLY* (Starred Review)

"*Going Dutch* is a sharp, endearing update of the love-triangle rom-com, and Gregor's depiction of millennial New York is masterful. It's an exciting debut, and will leave you eager for more. . . . When we look back on the canon of modern dating-while-living-in-New-York escapades, *Going Dutch* will stand out as a vivid portrait of a life and time that—for many—feels almost too familiar. It's bleak out there. But at least the brunch is good."

—*BUZZFEED* (Most Anticipated)

"If you need your main characters to take the moral high road, this one isn't for you. But if you're into existential questions, *Seinfeld*-level awkward-dating scenarios, and a little dark humor: Start reading."

—GOOP

"*Going Dutch* is a feast for the senses. I found myself totally enthralled by its rich language and whip-smart observations. But the characters sparking off of one another—that is what kept me furiously turning the pages, hungry for more. [A] glorious debut novel . . . a smart and sometimes sardonic tale of queer couplings in the era of Grindr, obnoxious foodie culture, and millennial boredom."

—*CHICAGO REVIEW OF BOOKS*

"A directionless grad student finds himself at the center of a bisexual love triangle in debut novelist Gregor's charmingly melancholy Brooklyn rom-com. Of course . . . Richard's double life must come crashing down, which it does, spectacularly. A deeply kind novel—all three characters are rich and complicated and human—[brimming with] biting observations of modern urban life."

—*KIRKUS REVIEWS*

"Gregor's debut novel is a carefully observed story about desire, love, and dependence in contemporary New York. Readers will be swept up in Richard's life and love triangle, even as they wonder if he has any idea what he wants."
—*BOOKLIST*

"*Going Dutch* is a hilarious and relatable story that shows great promise for Gregor as a novelist. It plays around with the tropes and clichés of love triangle stories and twentysomething arrested development stories in a fresh and engaging way. It's a perfect snapshot of academic and romantic life in the '10s that will hopefully resonate as time passes. After all, while some of these dating sites and apps will potentially fall into obscurity or be consigned to the digital mausoleum that all defunct sites and programs fall into, there will always remain that anxiety and allure that comes from branching out and trying to develop oneself as an adult, whether it involves writing about centuries-old literature or just figuring out the best place to get dinner on a Friday night in Brooklyn."

—LAMBDA LITERARY

"Comedic and captivating . . . Gregor] lays bare the protagonist's, and our own, motivations: how we are drawn to another person; how, consciously or not—and often for the wrong reasons—we become bound up with that person; and how we sometimes fail to make honest and authentic choices, due to cultural forces or personal baggage. It also raises the question of whether sexual attraction is destiny, and whether emotional intimacy can sustain a relationship. At the novel's center lies a mystery more complex and elusive than that of desire and identity: what makes two people want to be together?"
—*THE GAY & LESBIAN REVIEW*

"In this intelligent, entertaining and elegantly written novel, James Gregor pulls off something many psychological novelists aspire to and few achieve: he convincingly captures the thinking of a character who earnestly sees himself as sympathetic, even as he behaves terribly. Without being intrusive, Gregor makes the reader see what his protagonist Richard can't—the way unexamined shame and insecurity drive his actions (and nonactions). Never have I read a book where I so badly wanted the smart, well-meaning but benighted hero to get a good therapist, ideally one as insightful as the author himself."

—ADELLE WALDMAN, national bestselling author of
The Love Affairs of Nathaniel P.

"Be it the horrors of online dating, the absurdity of academia, or the dicey interplay of gender and class, I'm convinced there's nothing that escapes James Gregor's attention. *Going Dutch* is more than an assured debut—it's a novel packed with so much sly wisdom and charm that it'll leave you reeling. I devoured this book, and you will too."

—GRANT GINDER, author of *Honestly, We Meant Well* and
The People We Hate at the Wedding

"Every once in a while a novel of simply unremitting goodness lands on your front porch and *Going Dutch* is one of the best of the best. James Gregor is a generous, funny, easygoing natural and this book sheds much light on how we live and love now."

—GARY SHTEYNGART, *New York Times* bestselling author of
Lake Success and *Super Sad True Love Story*

"*Going Dutch* is my favorite kind of novel—smart, insightful, and brimming with sly humor. James Gregor explores the complexity of contemporary life with honesty and welcome cynicism, while still allowing for the possibility of love. This novel left me edified, entertained, and eagerly waiting to see what the author comes up with next."

—STEPHEN McCAULEY, author of *My Ex-Life*

"In this satisfying, plot-driven, and utterly adult novel about a bisexual love triangle, James Gregor has created a bitter black comedy set in the trenches of dating both on and off-line in twenty-first-century New York City. *Going Dutch* is trenchant and kind, witty and devastating. As a debut work of fiction it is a knock-out."

—CHARLOTTE SILVER, author of *Bennington Girls Are Easy*

GOING
DUTCH

a novel

JAMES GREGOR

Simon & Schuster Paperbacks
New York   London   Toronto   Sydney   New Delhi

Simon & Schuster Paperbacks
An Imprint of Simon & Schuster, Inc.
1230 Avenue of the Americas
New York, NY 10020

First Simon & Schuster trade paperback edition July 2020

SIMON & SCHUSTER PAPERBACKS and colophon are registered trademarks of Simon & Schuster, Inc.

For information about special discounts for bulk purchases, please contact Simon & Schuster Special Sales at 1-866-506-1949 or business@simonandschuster.com.

The Simon & Schuster Speakers Bureau can bring authors to your live event. For more information or to book an event, contact the Simon & Schuster Speakers Bureau at 1-866-248-3049 or visit our website at www.simonspeakers.com.

Interior design by Alison Cnockaert

Manufactured in the United States of America

1 3 5 7 9 10 8 6 4 2

Library of Congress Cataloging-in-Publication Data
Names: Gregor, James, author.
Title: Going Dutch : a novel / by James Gregor.
Description: First Simon & Schuster hardcover edition. |
New York : Simon & Schuster, 2019.
Identifiers: LCCN 2018044382 (print) | LCCN 2018058927 (ebook) | ISBN 9781982103217 (ebook) | ISBN 9781982103194 (hardcover) | ISBN 9781982103200 (trade pbk.)
Subjects: | GSAFD: Love stories.
Classification: LCC PR9199.4.G738 (ebook) | LCC PR9199.4.G738 G65 2019 (print) | DDC 813/.6—dc23
LC record available at https://lccn.loc.gov/2018044382

ISBN 978-1-9821-0319-4
ISBN 978-1-9821-0320-0 (pbk)
ISBN 978-1-9821-0321-7 (ebook)

To my parents

"Inward successes, yes. But what does one get from such as these? Do inward acquisitions give one food to eat?"

—Robert Walser

ONE

Richard looked out the window. April, and he was sure he could identify in the faces of the passing students a certain late undergraduate mood: the weather having turned sweet, exams just finished, and you're preparing for whatever plans you've made. A summer internship or humanitarian junket. But in the meantime you feel accomplished and blamelessly lavish your days on nothing: afternoon drinking and smoking pot, watching shirtless guys play Frisbee, walking amid the blooming magnolias.

"Why have you not submitted anything?"

The intrusion of Antonella's sympathetic but firm question made Richard feel like a child poised for a lecture.

"I'm blocked," he said, nodding morosely. "I just go in circles."

"There are tricks I can suggest."

Across her forehead a glossy fringe of brown hair was cleaved asymmetrically, and she wore a gray cashmere turtleneck tucked into Adidas track pants. On the desk there was a plastic container full of untouched salad, one black splash of balsamic dressing down the side. Its sweet smell was filling the office.

"What do you have in mind?" Richard asked.

"Acupuncture, therapies, mind games maybe," Antonella said. "Have you ever tried standing on your head?"

1

"That could work." For a moment he looked thoughtful. He clasped his hands together in his lap. "On the other hand, it all might get better tomorrow."

A doctoral student in medieval Italian literature—ostensibly—Richard Turner had done little in the past months to deserve the title. It was a significant change. Not too many years ago—he was twenty-nine now—he'd been a cultivated, slightly pedantic undergraduate, someone for whom a high GPA, prizes, bursaries, and glowing reference letters came easily. But lately he'd found himself blocked and unable to write, and in the face of this mystifying impotence, whose source he could not identify, all his efforts at maintaining a long-cultivated identity of academic competence and dependable accomplishment had taken on an air of pointlessness. Yet his solvency depended on remaining a student, and so he continued to show up faithfully at the library and to meet Antonella, his supervisor, in that cluttered office where they were now sitting.

He felt like an impostor, an actor playing a previous self. Still, he decided, given that so few students continued to bother, had ever bothered, to study what she taught, Antonella would be invested in retaining as many of them as she could.

But her face stiffened.

"I will have to write the letter soon, Richard. I cannot in good faith write it without seeing any work."

"I understand," he murmured.

His tuition and living expenses were covered by a fellowship from a family of degenerate industrialists with a deep presence in his hometown—the MacLellans or the MacLennans, he always mixed up the name. The long-dead patriarch had wistfully forgone a career as a professor of literature in order to accrue vast wealth, and had set aside a portion for the advancement of humanity, in the manner of Alfred Nobel.

For the money to flow, the foundation required written updates from an academic supervisor every six months. Richard pictured the reader of these letters, no one he'd ever met: some loafing male heir, one of a group of scattered dilettantish progeny who dressed in Balenciaga and ran flailing subsidiaries, scrolling absentmindedly through his phone at a Michelin-starred restaurant as he scooped pâté onto a fussy square of toast. Richard had always felt a condescending superiority to this handsome specter, the same sort of condescension, mixed with envy, that most of his academic colleagues felt toward alarmingly rich people.

"There are others who could use the money," Antonella said, her crossed arms indicating a disinterested concern for the student body at large, the numberless deserving beneficiaries, while the vaulted eyebrows over her dark, clear, slightly amphibian eyes made her affection for Richard plain.

He should have been much further along. Most of his immediate colleagues had graduated or moved into postdocs, a mellow encampment he'd also once considered his rightful destination. Instead, he was still auditing the occasional seminar, purporting to move forward with a thesis, but he hadn't written anything in months, the end was nowhere in sight.

"Will they continue to pay?" Antonella asked, her apprehensive voice becoming jarringly conspicuous in the quiet room.

"I don't know," Richard said. "I was going to ask you that."

"I'll delay as long as I can."

"And I'll get something to you as soon as *I* can."

For the rest of the meeting, in a welcome but abrupt change of subject, they discussed their summer plans. Antonella would be returning to Italy for a wedding, an event she was not exactly looking forward to. Richard imagined he'd probably end up at some beer gardens. Otherwise, the summer was vague. He hoped to get a lot of work done. If he could manage to interest himself in any of the material he was supposed to be interested in, that is. None of it compelled him the way it used to, for whatever murky, idling reason.

"I'm rooting for you," Antonella said, smiling again. "You'll come out in the end."

For a moment he imagined that she would reach out and embrace him, but she didn't move.

"Thank you," he said, standing up.

"See you soon, Richard."

He went outside and paused in the sun, waited as the students, changing class, whirled around him in energetic streams.

AS HE TOOK THE train back downtown in a fresh white shirt under a pilling blue sweater, and wearing the tennis shoes he had cleaned using Windex, Richard wondered if the guy he was going to meet would resemble his OkCupid profile pictures. People so often didn't. The challenge of presenting oneself on-screen, widely considered a prerequisite for a full life in the early twenty-first century, flustered many, including Richard. There was either too much self-promotion of a flavorless, unoriginal kind—the guy in front of the Parthenon or the Eiffel Tower—or a depressing lack of artifice: "obligatory body shot" in the speckled bathroom mirror; the guy smiling beside a buffet, wearing a shapeless suit, his arm around a woman who looked like his wife. One of Richard's fantasies was telling the love of his life that he'd signed on to the website *on a whim*, after *yet another* disheartening date, *and there you were*. But like all fantasies, it derived its power from its robustly chimerical nature, its palpable utopianism and unreality.

The train swayed.

Did Richard resemble his pictures? He was good-looking enough, he supposed, just shy of six feet, wavy-at-a-stretch black hair, peaches-and-cream complexion, lips he would have preferred substantially fuller. Physically on the broad but skinny side, he wore eyeglasses that were a cross between aviators and Gustav von Aschenbach. His youthful face and at times stuffy sense of dress were two characteristics that pushed his likely age in opposing directions.

"You're, like, simultaneously twelve and forty," an old boyfriend had once told him.

Richard looked up and scanned the jammed subway car as a woman pushed past in search of a seat. A few feet away, there was a harassingly good-looking Latino guy dressed in smooth black athletic clothing, wearing earphones, staring at the floor. A preoccupying thought had him confronting a void of inattention with the most beautiful scowl.

Richard envied people whose faces naturally descended into such hard cohesion, bestowed as he'd been with open, boyish, defenseless features. Enough guys did, thankfully, find him cute, but not necessarily mysterious or *hot*; he didn't have that distilled facial architecture that plunged people into fits of despair and longing. The guy with the earphones was probably a model or an actor.

Whenever Richard went out into the city, he usually recognized at least one guy from the websites and apps he was on and could recall details from their profiles, lovelorn or hopeful as they might be.

He had a very good memory and almost instant recall—at least when it came to men. Out at the Boiler Room or some other bar, peering through the dingy amber light at the impatiently aslant bodies in line to buy a drink, he knew that the guy wearing the shredded denim shorts was *HORNY KEWL AND MELANCHOLY*, and his favorite thing was *BEIN NAKED WITH PEOPLE I LUV.*

There were so many beautiful boys in the city, and they did so many beautiful things. A hematology resident, for example, whose grandfather bought him Barbie dolls every Christmas, sat across from Richard at Starbucks, one leg flopped over the other, with a bitchy expression and a caramel Frappuccino; a boy with a gold Afro lay sprawled on the steps of Low Library, James Baldwin in hand, ignoring Richard's attempts at eye contact. *My mother says the universe will bring him to me,* the boy had written under *THE MOST PRIVATE THING I AM WILLING TO ADMIT.*

When Richard went on dates with them, they became arguably more than strangers but broadly less than acquaintances. Coffee enthusiasts, secondhand bookstore employees, painters, urban gardeners, grant writers, sous-chefs, asset managers—Richard met them for drinks in Brooklyn, lower Manhattan, and sometimes Queens. They were in the main decent and polite. They ordered a second drink, went to the bathroom, and returned to nurse the inch of water formed by melting ice cubes. Richard did the same. They parted—that night or the next morning—with a hug and a smile and a promise to be in touch.

Who knows, Richard thought, as he entered Café Grumpy and saw Blake standing at the counter—a largish, cheerful-looking white guy, dressed with an inconspicuous competence in jeans and a button-down shirt—maybe this time will be different.

"Hi," Blake said, with a smile on his face and an open-handed wave. "Richard?"

"Blake?" Richard reached out to shake Blake's hand. Blake's other hand was wrapped around an iced Americano. "Nice to meet you."

Richard was already taken aback, detecting what seemed to be genuine enthusiasm in Blake's voice. Was Blake actually *looking forward to the date?* Most guys in New York were fidgetingly impatient to skip preliminaries, to get wherever they wanted to go, whether it be marriage, sex, or somewhere in between. Then again Blake, though an administrative assistant by trade, was an actor by profession, so maybe he was just good at faking it.

"I hope this was a convenient place to meet," Blake said.

"It's great," Richard replied, poised to outline the essential flexibility of his schedule but then deciding to hold back those details for the time being. "I come here whenever I'm in the neighborhood."

They left the café and went walking on the High Line. There were small, hairy tufts of green at their feet, architectural birdhouses to their left, and condominiums looming in. On one side, the Hudson swept past.

"I was sure I was going to be late," Richard said. "The subway stopped for like, ten minutes just before Thirty-Fourth Street."

"The subway is in free fall. Everything is."

"You think?"

Blake nodded.

"I'm going to make an outrageous claim," he said.

"Go ahead. I love outrageous claims."

"Taxation is a crime. All politicians are criminals."

"Well, that's not so outrageous," Richard said.

"Government is a farce."

Blake shook his handsome, swarthy head, an earnest smile on his face, as if he could see the idolized anarchist future just beyond Richard's shoulder. Under a gray cardigan he wore a dark green gingham shirt, his body invitingly soft and hairy.

"No government at all then? This is good," Richard said. "Usually we surround ourselves with people who just back us up in our own opinions."

Richard's political views, when mildly articulated, tended to favor the indebted welfare states of Europe.

"That's because we're lazy and tribal," Blake said, with docile conviction, staring out at the sparkling water. The April mist, which had blanketed the city all morning, was beginning to lift.

The majority of the interests represented on the website where they had exchanged messages at first seemed predictably progressive and benign—riding bikes, drinking whiskey, organic gardening—but the omnipresence of Ayn Rand, that avatar of selfishness, in Blake's profile and so many others, struck a discordant note.

People actually read this shit? Richard thought.

Initially dismissing it as a fringe movement, he was forced to revise his opinion as her name proliferated, appearing on countless profiles under the headings *FAVORITE BOOKS, MUSIC, FOOD ETC.* or *WHAT I SPEND MY TIME THINKING ABOUT.* It was so common, in fact, that it had inspired a small countermovement of aghast leftists. Unfortunately, the principals of this countermovement were not as attractive as those whom they attacked. It was undeniable: the Ayn Rand aficionados were fucking hot.

And probably rich, Richard thought, though with Blake he couldn't quite tell. Was his apartment some counterintuitive structure in an implausible corner of the borough, the opaque potential of which

Blake had been the first to discern? The kitchen a pinched triangular space with parquet flooring, an array of fatigued appliances on the counter? Did he sleep in a double bed?

"Long trip?" Blake asked, probably wondering the same things about Richard, probing for clues in his clothes, his shoes, and his manner of speaking.

"It's not that far from here back to Brooklyn," Richard replied.

"I bet I'm farther out than you."

"Where exactly are you?"

Blake was reluctant to give his neighborhood a name, as online there was fierce disagreement as to where its borders truly lay.

"It's a bit of a walk to the subway from my place," Richard said, also deliberately vague. "But there are some nice brownstones along the way."

"Do you like the neighborhood?"

"It's okay."

Aside from getting on and off the subway together, Richard interacted with the other residents of his neighborhood only when he entered the local bodega to line up for a cheap and substantial made-to-order sandwich. Among the dim begrimed shelves of Doritos bags, marshmallows, and ramen noodles, he tried to strike a pose of belonging but not possession; he smiled when he made eye contact— sometimes the other people in line smiled back at him, and sometimes they didn't. That was okay. It was like that with the women who ran the laundromat around the corner. They were never nice to him, made him wait forever when he needed change or detergent, just talking among themselves in Spanish, and with his conflicted sense of his own right to live in the neighborhood, he certainly didn't blame them.

"It'll be a whole different place in a year or two," Richard said.

"How do you feel about gentrification?" Blake asked.

"Not sure."

"I'm not sure either," Blake said, smiling bashfully at the ground.

Blake's hand—its thick, blunt fingers and chewed-down nails—dangled by his side. Richard imagined them walking hand in hand, as in a commercial about marriage equality, vacations, or pharmaceuticals.

"Men used to have sex over there," Blake said, pointing west toward the formerly dilapidated piers that stretched out into the Hudson. Richard knew that the area had once been something quite different from what it was now, with its yards of peroxided blond hair, hordes of rich tourists, and prominence in guidebooks. What gay man in New York didn't? He had a hardcover black-and-white coffee table book on the subject. In one chapter, men were photographed fully copulating among the jagged spikes of decaying wood, or strolling blithely in leather jackets, naked from the waist down, through decrepit, spectral industrial spaces.

"Now it's just tourists," Blake said. "Late capitalist gourmands."

Blake seemed to be in the familiar posture of struggling in a stylish dead-end job and floundering creatively, or resolutely indifferent to his inner life and living in a transitional neighborhood for cachet. In any case, he was cute. Richard felt a lurch of attraction every time they brushed against each other.

He cautiously thought back to the advice his best friend, Patrick, had recently given him. *You have to be pickier.*

They'd been drinking beer at one of the interchangeably squalid bars they went to on weekends, standing beside a retro arcade game, surrounded by young men tapping at their illuminated screens in the soggy collusion of sweat and denim shorts. "No more secondhand bookstore employees, painters, whatever. I'm all for independence, but this city is a Golgotha," Patrick warned.

"But I thought New Yorkers were like, notoriously single people?"

"That was before Bloomberg turned everything into a park and criminalized soft drinks."

Richard was unsettled at the memory of these words: he didn't himself have a nerve-racking, high-yield job in finance or law, or even a nerve-racking but low-yield job such as working in an art gallery. He was in graduate school, okay, but not for anything in vogue like urban planning or public health.

Blake glanced over and smiled.

"Did you have a busy week?"

Should he pretend to be run off his feet, or radiate a sense of calm availability?

"Not too bad."

"I had some auditions this week, on top of work," Blake said. "Apologies if I'm a bit demented. This is my fourth iced coffee of the day."

"Did the auditions go well?"

"I think so. One of them brought back some funny memories."

They passed a small outdoor café, fluttering with activity, and Blake related an anecdote from his adolescence, something about a hunky chemistry teacher and a narrowly avoided scandal. As he did so, Richard fished in his memory for an experience of his own that might appeal to Blake. He considered relating his first encounter with Ayn Rand: reading the slim fable *Anthem* in high school English class one day, while the rest of the students worked through *The Catcher in the Rye*, but decided against it when he realized that Blake was talking about his relationship with his parents.

They hadn't helped him realize he was gay; he'd spent his late teens and early twenties in a "sexual darkness."

"My twenties were sexually dark too," Richard said.

Blake smiled.

"But it's gotten much better," Blake continued. "I think they were just confused. They've come around a lot in the last few years. I'm lucky. Now they're supportive."

Blake began talking about dating girls in college. Richard looked over the railing toward the miscellany of buildings that flocked to this part of the island—some billowed, some pierced; it was a playground for famous architects. A group of guys, laboriously tanned and muscled, moved down the street, chatting loudly and gesturing in broad, confident whorls. Richard didn't have a "group of friends," only ornery but devoted individuals in a variety of pursuits—teaching English in foreign capitals, learning violin making, studying yoga on a banana plantation—and he envied those who seemed to belong to a unified pod that spread itself five abreast on the sidewalk, sharing gossip. As it was, the majority of his friends were too indebted to afford gym memberships, though some among them managed to wrangle free Bikram yoga classes in exchange for washing the floor after all the sweaty bodies had lifted off.

Blake touched his hand.

"Hey, what's so interesting over there?"

"Nothing. Sorry. Want to have dinner?" *Take me out for dinner*, Richard meant. He'd finished the last of the Raisin Bran in the middle of the night, munching tactfully at the dark kitchen counter while his roommate, Leslie, snored on the nearby sofa. The cupboard was empty now. But Richard knew that Blake was unlikely to come through. Going dutch was, not just between two men, but among everybody now, the norm.

"Somewhere around here?"

"Sure," Richard said. "I'm easy."

A yolky suggestion of ozone blanketed New Jersey, couples drifted past holding hands, and tourists took pictures of the big concrete hotel.

"What kind of food do you like?"

"I have eclectic tastes," Richard said, resolved to seem as open-minded as possible, and not wanting to bracket off any potential dinner opportunities with Blake.

"My friend is a sous-chef at a place in my neighborhood," Blake said. "He said he'd get me pan-roasted fluke at a discount."

Richard was hopeful again.

"But I don't know if he could do it for two. I'd pick somewhere cheaper"—Blake smiled compassionately, tilting his head—"but I really need to eat something decent tonight."

Richard nodded. "I understand."

They went down a flight of stairs to street level. Richard followed behind Blake, eyes on the black sickle of his hairline, the tag of his cardigan erect against the green collar of his oxford shirt. These dates always failed. It was a predictable script: a few hours of milky diplomacy, siblings and sleep patterns and diet touched on, before parting ways with a hug that was not exactly disingenuous but certainly performed, as if wishing each other courage in the next phase of the battle, which was the continued search for love, later to ignore each other in public if they ever crossed paths again. Then back to his apartment, back to sitting cross-legged on the bed with his laptop and a tub of lime sorbet, trying to view his life in a positive light.

"Actually, I think I know a place," Richard said.

They stood on the corner, facing each other, about to part.

"What kind of place?" Blake asked, perking up skeptically.

"It's not pan-roasted fluke, but it's good."

Blake thought for a second, then said: "Okay."

Buoyed by this successful maneuver and the temporary rescue of the date, Richard led Blake south down a sidewalk thronged with dog-walking couples. No one knows that we just met, Richard thought. We could be in a long-term relationship. Any one of these people might think that Blake had chosen *me* from among the countless eligible young men of New York City.

Richard wanted to belong to that group of young men who were chosen.

When they arrived at the restaurant, Blake peered through the window as if into a condemned building. "What's an egg cream again?" he asked, climbing into the booth.

Did this mean Blake was a recent arrival to New York, lacking that period knowledge? He'd been evasive when Richard asked him how long he'd lived in the city. People could be so touchy about that question.

"It's milk and syrup added to carbonated water," Richard said.

"What are you getting?"

"The garden salad or the Caesar salad," Richard said, scanning for something cheap. "Probably the garden salad. You get whatever you want."

"You're going to make me fat and happy."

When the waiter came over, Blake ordered the shrimp Scampi. It was three times the price of the salad. Richard was someone who never ordered a dish more expensive than the host's, even when exhorted to do so. At the same time there was something agreeably carnal about Blake's shameless appetite.

"Eating is a very cerebral and academic experience for me," Blake said after the waiter left. "I love to think about food connected to history, psychology, sex, and gender . . ."

"So, when you eat a hot dog . . ." Richard said.

"Hot dogs? *Hell no*," Blake said. "Do you know what's in them?"

"Okay, fine," Richard said. "Veggie, wheat burger, whatever. You're besieged by the linguistic, historical, religious, etcetera of the burger."

"Okay, you have been listening," Blake considered, with a smile.

"What about just, you know, a taste sensation?"

They bantered in this vein for a while, until the food arrived. Blake glared at his dish—a morass of oily threads under a squall of Parmesan cheese.

"I'm blaming you if I get sick," he said.

"I'll nurse you."

"You better."

Richard's salad went quickly, and for several minutes he tried not to watch Blake consume the shrimp.

"Are you watching me eat?"

"Sorry," Richard said, taking a sip of water, which he'd been nervously doing ever since they arrived. Now he needed the bathroom. He excused himself, and as he made his way across the diner, peopled by a mix of old ladies, dissipated rent-controlled locals, and nostalgia-oriented transplants like himself, he wondered if Blake was husband material. His *LAST ONLINE* always indicated a reasonable time of day, unlike the majority of profiles, which, especially on those weekends Richard came home in the middle of the night, were usually active at some desolate hour: 2:46 a.m., 3:57 a.m., 4:21 a.m. Richard imagined the owners of the profiles in their bedrooms, lonely insomniacs, their frustrated return home from yet another disappointing night out; waiting alone with a collapsing buzz on the grimy subway ledge for the train that wouldn't come; the pitiless white light in the cars that decelerated frequently between stations; the walk home at the end of the journey through dark and empty streets.

He imagined Blake pulling an elegant maneuver and paying for the meal—standing there beside the booth when he returned, as though to assist Richard with his coat, not meeting Richard's eyes because he wouldn't want to draw attention to the payment, with a glimmer of demure masculine capability in his expression.

But the bill was still there when Richard got back, and Blake was staring out the window at two muscular men in tight V-neck T-shirts—tempting the still fickle spring weather—who were walking arm in arm. For such a supposedly solitary city, where everyone either was a lonely neurotic who lived with a dog, or blew most of their paycheck on therapy, analysis, or rent, New York could at times feel as if it was the exclusive domain of couples. And children. Every day there were more children.

Richard took out his wallet, trying to mask his disappointment with chivalry.

"Only a five-dollar tip? I thought the waiter was a nice old guy."

"I just think tipping is getting a little out of hand though, you know?" Richard was flustered by Blake's insinuation of cheapness. "It seems like every six months it goes up by, like, five percent."

"Shitty job though."

They left the diner and soon reached a basketball court surrounded by a fence. Sweaty men moved back and forth over the artificial ground. Richard was unsettled by what had just happened. So was Blake just rigorously egalitarian in his dating practices? As the sky began its parabolic exit, he imagined their future together as a scrupulously calibrated transaction of equals, a continual updating and canceling of accounts, until the ledger effaced itself.

These moments, as the next stage of the date was decided, were always filled with pressurized speculation. Richard glanced at Blake out of the corner of his eye. He at least wanted the entanglement of their arms, the cozy liaison of an easy silence, to walk along the Hudson with him, serene in the high-strung city. He didn't want to go back to his apartment alone.

"It's such a nice night," he said, looking up at the pink clouds and risking an optimistic note.

"I hope your nice night continues," Blake said.

"Are you leaving?"

Blake nodded, and Richard's heart—whatever it was that could sink—sank.

"Well, we should do this again sometime."

"I have your number," Blake said.

"You should use it."

Blake leaned in and kissed him on the cheek.

"Ciao!"

Richard watched as Blake hurried down the street and disappeared around a corner. For a moment, he stared at the empty intersection. A truck careened through.

So that was it? Another extended hand left hanging in midair, but no overcoming of particularities, no conquering of idiosyncrasies, no alliance made? He turned and started walking toward the subway.

On the ride home, in the intimate scrimmage of the shaking car, his sense of loneliness was alternately charged and deflated, belittled and aggrandized, by the presence of so many other people. A homeless man snored at the other end of the car, a nebula of smell keeping others away. A child ate a chocolate bar with a hypnotic expression, his mother's eyes red from crying. Richard felt a shivering sense of defeat at what he was going back to: the dark apartment, the ziggurat of plates in the sink, his faraway roommate, Leslie, on the couch, the empty bed. It seemed foolish and unjust to be moving in that direction, when Blake was maneuvering through the streets behind him, drawn somewhere else, free again, set loose in the potential and marvel of the city.

TWO

Richard went back to campus the next day. Calmly lit by muted sunlight, all throughout the library people seemed to be making great progress with whatever they were doing. Richard sat in one of the glazed wooden chairs, his thoughts crawling. He was supposed to be writing about Pier delle Vigne, the Sicilian court poet whose suicide had inspired Dante to transform him into a bleeding tree in Canto XIII of *Inferno*. But hadn't the great Austrian philologist Leo Spitzer said everything there was to say about that?

Richard clicked open the homepage of the *New York Times*. He checked the weather, and the price of a pair of sneakers. He dragged the throbbing cursor indolently back and forth across the glowing screen.

He decided to go back to Brooklyn and try working there.

As he walked down Broadway toward the subway, Richard spotted another doctoral student from the department up ahead. Her name was Anne and she was standing beside a table of ratty used books, lorded over by a man with Coke-bottle glasses and a gray ponytail. She had on sturdy tweed pants and a shapeless maroon sweater, and she wore large, circular black sunglasses.

Looking for an escape, Richard slowed his pace. Anne, also a PhD candidate in medieval literature, but with a slightly different focus, had been inviting him to lunch ever since they'd discussed collaborating on a paper a few weeks back. The initial gesture had been Richard's, when they'd spoken at a departmental wine and cheese, bonding sarcastically over a hole in the wall and the general disrepair of the facilities.

"I thought this university was supposed to be well endowed," she'd said, giving him a preposterous heavy-lidded wink.

Painful joke aside, Anne was well known for her ferocious intellect and Richard had been struck by the idea that a professional association with her might resuscitate his sputtering academic career. She was always publishing in the most prestigious journals—if it was still possible to call those types of journals prestigious—and there had recently been a call to submit papers for a conference taking place in Montreal. Coauthoring would be easy: her interests were close to his own, only substantially more radical and compelling.

But the routine was getting expensive. Numerous times over the past month he'd found himself sitting across from her at exorbitant restaurants in various parts of the city—though mostly on the Upper East Side (they took cabs there), where she'd spent part of her childhood. The restaurants were often checker-floored, and traversed by haughty waiters in tuxedo collars. Swept up in farm-to-table and other Brooklyn-centered dining trends, to the degree that he could afford to be swept up in them, Richard had all but forgotten that these formal white-tablecloth restaurants existed. Barely able to afford anything and feeling underdressed, he often ordered only a single bottle of Perrier. Sometimes the waiters would glare down at him as if they considered this an outrage.

The last time Anne had invited him to lunch, he'd accepted but then blown her off an hour before for a Grindr rendezvous.

A FRIEND IS IN CRISIS, he'd texted.

I HOPE EVERYTHING IS OKAY, she'd replied. **LET ME KNOW.**

Afterward, feeling an unexpected swell of guilt, he'd gone into an overly elaborate description of this phantom crisis, then asked to see her again as soon as she was free.

Part of him found her annoying; another part was curious to observe her. There was something both needling and captivating about her that he couldn't explain. The other week, he'd gone to watch her teach a class. Before an audience of callow undergraduates, she transformed, emitting waves of musky, indeterminately foreign glamour. Gesturing wildly under a forest-green cape, she expounded on the book the students had been assigned; then, pacing from one end of the cramped room to the other, she digressed on the subject of humility, a trait she clearly felt most of the students lacked. She wore bangles on her wrist that made a punitive rattling noise. For misusing the term "stream of consciousness" in an oral presentation, she lambasted a young girl.

Richard found himself strangely excited by her presence in the classroom. It wasn't attraction exactly, but he felt the blurred outlines of that category. The possibility that she would address his discernible but unacknowledged sexuality played a part in it. This potential disclosure—of something both laughably obvious and titillatingly ignored—gave their interactions a weird and alluring sense of pressure. She was stubborn and bullish in her feeling, ignoring all signs of potential failure, but this sprang from a mind that was impressively retentive and refined.

Was Richard scared of genuinely becoming attracted to her? She wasn't even pretty, and he was gay. But then, his heroic dedication to the male body—all of his screensavers were Mapplethorpes, for instance—and his rigid indifference to the female body, had begun to seem passé. Once a kind of calling card, the fact that he was attracted to men wasn't particularly novel anymore. Yet it was *men* he was attracted to; *masc* men if he was being honest, though he knew that was deemed *problematic*. Still, for reasons unclear to him he'd felt unable to rebuff or even to clarify her overtures.

He turned down 109th Street.

"Are you trying to avoid me?" Anne called out to him. "Sometimes I run after people when they do that."

"Of course not," he said, trying, by an abrupt torquing movement of the head, to make it look as though he hadn't seen her.

"I'm buying a Russian dictionary." She walked over and showed it to him. "There's no point reading Anna Akhmatova in translation."

"Ah."

He was distracted by a muscular deliveryman lifting a FedEx box through a doorway.

"Come over for lunch," she said. "I live nearby."

"But you don't cook."

"Of course I do. I just *prefer* restaurants."

They began walking, and Richard was incredulous. Was he *actually* going to her apartment? This was the height of absurdity. It was like the first time they'd spoken, on the way out of the Italian Department, during those sticky, thudding days at the beginning of the semester.

"I can't believe not a single one of them has read Auerbach," she'd said, complaining about a class she was TA-ing and stumbling to keep up with him—she was barely five feet tall, curvy and slightly plump, with a reddish, boyish pixie cut—as she gave a clotted group of smokers, gathered by the door to escape the rain, a nasty look. "You should read that before college, don't you agree?"

He'd nodded more enthusiastically than he meant to.

"If you want to get anything out of your college experience, that is."

As they crossed the harshly streaming traffic of Broadway, he glanced at her, sighing inaudibly. At least she wasn't one of those medical or law students whom he always seemed to get stuck talking to at parties, or one of those calamitously thin hipsters who chewed his ear off about their boring critical theory papers. Why was he always transmitting signals he was unaware of?

"My roommates might be home."

What did she mean by that? He wanted to laugh out loud.

"I have some pork buns left over from the weekend. They're even better after a day or two in the fridge."

They took the elevator up four floors and walked down a dingy corridor. Anne opened the door to her apartment. It was a jagged collection of rooms the color of old margarine, like other graduate housing Richard had come across in the neighborhood.

Richard followed Anne down the narrow hall.

"I hate that we have a television," she said.

"There's a television at my place too."

A grainy sweetness floated in the air.

"That's the smell of vegan chocolate cake in case you're wondering."

In the kitchen two women, probably in their midtwenties, dressed identically in gray hoodies, navy-blue aprons over jeans, and red Swedish wedges, stood amid spoons and a torn bag of flour. They were engaged in vehement conversation.

"*I'm* going to sleep out on the field," one said, a bag of sprinkles in her hand.

"*I'm* going to drape a banner from the roof," the other replied, leaning into the open fridge.

They were almost identically tall and robust, and wore bandanas in their hair, one red and one yellow, over pale, waxy faces.

"Oh look, it's Liz Taylor," the one with the sprinkles said. She licked a thick glob of icing from her finger.

Anne snorted and raised her sunglasses onto her head. Richard turned his face toward a beaten stack of books on the windowsill, *The Fourth Wave* and *Veganomicon* among them.

"This is Richard," Anne said. "Meet Erin and Alicia."

"There's going to be a series of protests on campus," Erin said to him. "Are you going?"

"I don't know anything about it."

"You should really stay informed," said Alicia. "It's *important*."

"I *am* informed."

"About what?"

"About a lot of things."

"Oh, you mean like, who's the most important bald man in the Western canon?"

"Right!" said Erin, leaping on this. "Or like, how many teenage boys did Plato deflower? The *important* stuff."

"To some people," said Anne, "Plato's erotic life is of the utmost importance."

She got some pork buns out of the fridge. As they spun in the microwave, she led Richard into her room, offering him a seat at her desk, a broad mahogany thing dauntingly out of place in the mangy apartment. He noticed a shelf of old porcelain makeup dishes and glass figurines. On the walls there were black-and-white photographs of a parched landscape.

"I drove across the Peloponnesus last year," she said. "I went with a really wonderful older woman friend. The men were frighteningly aggressive."

"Really?"

"They would just bark at us in Greek. Obscene things, I'm sure."

"I thought you spoke Greek."

"*Ancient* Greek. Not the dialect currently in use at gas stations on the outskirts of Thessaloniki."

Richard shifted his attention to the bookcase.

"So what's up with your roommates?" he asked.

"Oh *them*," she said, leaning against it. He turned away slightly, as though intrigued by her Loeb Classical editions. "Don't worry about them. *Wannabe* lesbians."

"I don't care," said Richard. "I don't even know them."

On the other side of the room, there was an abstract painting on the wall. He walked over to get a better look. It was a swirl of black ink on a white background. "My sister is an artist. I come from a family of depressive, intellectual women."

"Does she exhibit a lot?"

"Yes, in the mental institution where she lives."

The microwave binged. "It sounds like they're ready," he said, with an anxious speed.

As he stepped into the kitchen, Erin and Alicia launched into an abrupt and self-consciously spirited discussion as though a moment before, they had been in a posture of attentive surveillance.

"What this all comes down to is, the school needs a stronger environmental policy," Alicia declared, pulling a Pyrex tray of black material out of the oven.

"Are you aware of the fact?" said Erin, offering Richard a piece of cake. "That there are no composting toilets on campus?"

He shook his head.

"How about you, Anne?" said Erin. "Are *you* going to the protest?"

"No."

"Why not?"

"Because I'm not interested in feeble gestures."

"We'll see how feeble it is when I throw an egg in the president's eye," said Erin, and the two young women erupted into laughter.

Anne rolled her eyes as she took the pork buns out of the microwave. She put two each on a plate, but instead of taking a place at the kitchen table, where Erin and Alicia were sitting, she walked back into the bedroom. Richard followed, feeling the eyes of Erin and Alicia on his back. He sat near the door. Was it was more awkward to leave the door open, or to have it closed?

Sitting at her desk, Anne looked at him and mouthed *sorry*. She shook her head, gesturing in the direction of the kitchen.

"Don't worry about it," he said quietly.

"Aren't these even better reheated?"

"They're very good," he said.

He ate the pork buns slowly—they were extremely hot. As soon as he was done he said he had to be going.

"You do?" she said, clearly disappointed.

"Unfortunately."

"Okay."

As Richard followed her to the front door, he said bye to Erin and Alicia, who were now on the couch. They waved with unreadable expressions on their faces.

"We didn't get a chance to discuss our paper," Anne said in the elevator.

"That's okay," he said, too relieved to be out of the apartment to much care, at that point, about the paper.

They stood on the front steps of the building.

"Next time," she mused. "They have a habit of hijacking the conversation."

"You're pretty verbal yourself."

"There are two of them."

"How did you meet each other?"

"We were put together by the housing office. That was a few years ago and now—*dot-dot-dot*—we're friends. I stay because they're here. I'd move out otherwise. Sometimes we're hard on each other, but it's just kind of our style. We really love each other."

"The whole Elizabeth Taylor thing?"

"That's one thing they do—make annoying comparisons."

"Well—it's good to be friends with your roommates, I guess."

Anne nodded.

"Are you friends with *your* roommates?"

"I just have one," Richard said. "We don't really talk."

"I'm sorry to hear that."

"I'd move out if I could."

There was a heavy silence. She cupped his bare elbow, her small hand soft and warm. "Lunch Tuesday? We'll get back on track with the paper?"

"Okay."

She strained on her toes to reach his cheek. He bent down and she kissed him.

"I had fun today," she said blushingly, her words like pale legs exposed to the sun after a long winter.

"Me too," Richard said, smiling, surprised by his own fervor.

"Bye."

She went back inside.

THREE

"He was tall, skinny, chest a bit concave. Total white supremacist body."

Richard nodded. It was later that night, and he was at the loft of an independently wealthy hairdresser and amateur playwright named Toller. He'd been to parties there before, accompanying Patrick and Patrick's newish boyfriend, a Latvian gallery assistant named Valdes, who had moved to New York to go to art school, and metamorphosed from a socially peripheral figure into a caustic, haughty, and nocturnally adventurous bon vivant. Valdes was famous in art school for his Adderall-fueled finger-painting marathons. Tall, blond, and broad-shouldered like Patrick, Valdes wore turtlenecks, gold jewelry, and jean jackets on which he'd affixed numerous opalescent brooches. He traveled in a pack with two glossily handsome, stout undergraduate brunettes named Barrett and Amir, who occasionally worked as go-go boys at bars in the East Village.

"No, but they often do," Barrett continued, in his soft Maryland accent, pouring another glass of champagne.

"Often do what?"

"Have orange hair."

Amir, who seemed impatient to speak—he and Barrett were always in competition for the floor—began describing the way he came out to his mother.

"I said I wasn't sure, and she was like, well if you're not sure don't tell anybody! And *I* said, didn't you notice when I got a subscription to British *House and Garden*? This was a while back, I'm proud to say. People still had subscriptions to magazines then."

"My mother was *far* more satisfyingly melodramatic," said Barrett. "She said I feel like I just discovered you have terminal cancer."

They all laughed.

"So then I got my head shaved, and whenever I knew she was around, like in earshot, I'd make gagging sounds."

Toller's friends were mostly younger than Richard. They could be really annoying, but they were also energetic and witty, and some of them had amusing stories to tell about famous people in the city, in whose lives they played subaltern roles involving email management and food preparation and disturbingly intimate access to the sordid personal affairs of their bosses.

Richard left their conversation when a muscly, ponytailed boy caught his attention near a table covered with vivid-looking sashimi. Richard slurringly asked the boy's name and then showered him with compliments about his clothes and lips. The boy had a vaguely Quebecois accent.

"It's from the thrift store," the boy said when Richard pointed to the mesh tank top he was wearing. His name was probably Benoit, though it was hard to tell with how loud the apartment had become. "Beacon's Closet."

"Pardon?" Richard said, using the pretext of incomprehension to lean closer and inhale the arousing scent, evergreen mixed with sweat, which lifted from Benoit's armpits. Even in mesh form, polyester didn't breathe.

"Never mind," Benoit said, indicating with his thumb and index finger that they should go into Toller's room. Patrick was already there, sitting on the edge of Toller's bed, watching Valdes raffishly snort a line of cocaine.

Benoit attempted to engage Patrick in conversation, but instead of responding directly Patrick said, "Have a line."

Slightly dumbstruck, Benoit sat down beside Valdes and proceeded to loudly inhale, at which point Valdes stood up and walked over to where Patrick was now standing. Richard took the open place beside Benoit, all along watching Valdes approach Patrick. If he couldn't have Patrick's attention, Richard supposed having this athletic specimen beside him was not a bad consolation prize.

"Patrick is so funny," Benoit said, sniffling as Richard partook in the line. "I've never met anyone like him."

"Sure," Richard said, rubbing his nose and abruptly deciding to abandon this unresponsive Francophone, as Valdes started manhandling Patrick in the corner. Richard turned away from this irksome display and walked out into the main loft area to join Barrett and Amir, who were sitting on a sofa on either side of the flushed and sweaty Toller. His peroxided hair flattened against his forehead, Toller fixed Richard with an accusatory stare.

"You didn't bring anyone?"

Richard shook his head.

"Doesn't anyone ask you out? You have an understated masculinity."

Richard tried not to smile too widely. He had often been mistaken for a girl when he was younger, notably into puberty, and his perceived position along the gender spectrum at any given moment was never far from his mind.

"I invited someone tonight, but he's not coming."

Twenty-four hours after their date Richard had sent Blake an ill-advised flurry of texts, not a single one of which Blake had responded to.

"You met online?" Toller said.

"Yeah."

"There's your answer."

"Don't be a Luddite," Barrett said. "It makes you sound old. Everybody meets online. My sister met her husband online."

"Maybe for gay guys, it's fine. But girls? No chick should have to do it. No chick should be reduced to the hunt and peck," Toller declared with an ersatz air of authority.

As far as his own luck dating online went, he said—he was the romantic-slash-bourgeois type, it was important to keep in mind—his encounters had mostly been dull.

"I've been on four dates in the last week," he said. "The first guy was beautiful, but he kept going on about the appendectomy he got in Paris. The second and third were too political—one on the left and the other on the right—and the last guy told me outright that, though he thought I was interesting, my complexion was"—he used his index fingers for quotes here —"too milky, too feminine."

They were all listening intently.

"But of course, I'm not surprised when a date doesn't amount to anything," Toller continued. "Profiles don't give you an accurate idea of a person. If you meet someone out in the world, their personality comes out in drips and drabs—if they're not totally basic, that is—and it's all just more palatable."

"Every date can be dull," Barrett said, his lustrous brown curls spilled messily but perfectly on his head. "Especially the ones that start out in real life."

They all nodded.

Richard thought it possible that the gadgets involved in contemporary dating made it easier for someone like him, a misty introvert who didn't do well exposed and put on the spot at bars, to approach other guys. Since it was just a message on a screen, there was minimal gumption required and the sting of rejection was reduced. On the other hand, the thrill and magic of meeting someone in person—but *was* it thrilling and magical?—was gone.

"You haven't convinced me," Toller said.

"That's on you," Barrett said.

Richard tried to imagine Toller in the ubiquitous profile poses—shirtless in the kitchen, pretending to nap in freshly washed sheets, squatting in some fastidious urban weight room—but found these poses difficult to reconcile with the odd, preposterous hairdresser and heir, patron of emaciated young men, who roosted in front of him.

Barrett and Amir, on the other hand, entered effortlessly into these molds. They both had beautiful faces smoothed to a poreless glisten and got frequent mani-pedis. They worked out with obvious expertise. Richard pictured them scampering down the beaches of Fire Island in tiny swimsuits, posting shots of themselves to Instagram, going inside to drink and cook up some delicious meal, before a night of orgiastic sex with an appropriate third.

"I hate the idea of being displayed on-screen, trying to prove your worth," Toller said. "People passing by leaving comments." He paused for effect. "Like dogs marking their territory."

"But there's a lot of possibility if you keep going, statistically," Amir said.

"Statistically I never meet anyone and I never fall in love," Toller said. "Barrett says it's because I don't bother. I choose to believe him."

Barrett nodded.

"All I want," Amir said. "Is to be tall and naturally fit and never age, and have a big dick."

Patrick was suddenly dancing with Benoit, who raised his hands into the air, undid his ponytail, and fluffed his hair out.

"Don't worry," Barrett said, turning to Valdes, who was staring at them. "Patrick loves you the best. Apparently you're the only person who really listens or something."

I'm the one who really listens, Richard thought peevishly. He was hit by the vexing image of himself as Patrick's scribe—monkish, self-denying, and oratorically competent—recording Patrick's escapades from the fringes of the party and then, over yogurt and mimosas the next morning, recounting them to him all over again. Their conversations consisted mostly of Patrick speaking and Richard listening. Patrick was oppressively happy. He'd told his Evangelical grandmother, with whom he was close, that he was gay, then had a string of brief but meaningful affairs to celebrate. He was spending his latest academic stipend with a thrilling rashness, on shirts and cashmere ties; he told Richard that he could *hang clothes* from his cheekbones. It had amused him to no end one night when, squeezing out of a crowded, narrow bar, a punkish-looking girl in black leather ankle boots said to him in a robot voice, "Tall blonds must pass." Patrick was socially brilliant, and Richard had always felt that he didn't measure up, except as a kind of secretary.

As if sensing these thoughts, Patrick abandoned Benoit, who was dancing fiercely with his eyes squeezed shut and fists in the air, and came and stood beside Richard, who was now sitting on the sofa.

"Where's your date?" Patrick asked.

"He didn't text back."

Patrick's eyes seemed to slide out of focus. Afraid of being mundane, Richard went for the dramatic gesture.

"If they ever find my body and say 'he loved life,' you have to tell them it isn't true, because it isn't."

"Don't be melodramatic. There's always hope."

Patrick sat down on the arm of the sofa. Staring down from a reassuring height, he began to recount the story of a couple he knew whose route to a successful marriage, begun on a dating site, had been marked by the flaky, noncommittal slalom of online and real-life interaction, a tortuous route whose destination turned out to be a solid and loving partnership, and residence on the top two floors of a brownstone.

They both joined the website around the same time. The initial gesture was his.

"Hi," he wrote in a message. Patrick lowered his voice in an oafish manner to imitate this hapless straight man. Among his phalanx of talents, Patrick was a vivid mimic, and Richard, who was now smiling, always felt affectionately indulged when Patrick performed for his benefit.

The recipient of the message read it on her phone as soon as it arrived, but she did not want to give the impression that she was hovering desperately, waiting for a message, so she waited thirty-six hours to reply.

She wrote, "Hi."

Patrick's voice became high-pitched and vaguely midwestern to capture her.

The hapless straight man read the message on his phone when the Q train entered the liminal zone of reception on the Manhattan Bridge. His instinct was to reply but when he considered the amount of time it had taken for her to reply, he decided to multiply the time it had taken her to respond by one and a half, and then reply. He would reply in fifty-four hours.

At which point, he wrote: "How are you?"

Over the next several days he checked the website compulsively on various devices, but no messages came. But then—it was a week later—he checked the website on his phone when he was in the bathroom at work and there was a message from her.

"I'm good. And you?" she wrote.

Basking in the message, he waited in the stall for an extra minute. When he returned to his desk, he worked on his reply. There wasn't much to do at the office; he worked on it all afternoon, rewriting it a dozen times.

The next night, while out with a friend who was visiting the city, he thought he saw her at the solar-powered taco stand in the neighborhood. But he pretended not to see her, as the etiquette of contact in the real world had not been discussed, and he had not yet responded to her message. He spent the night with his back to the entrance, an awkward maneuver, now and then stealing glances behind him. She also had her back to him, deliberately too, it seemed.

A few days later, while out eating dumplings, her friend asked her how dating was going. She rolled her eyes and said all the men in the city were flakes. Her friend rolled her own eyes in sympathy and they both dug into their dumplings. Soup shot out.

I've had enough, she said. I'm going to get rid of my profile.

But after the meal she secretly, a bit unconsciously, decided that she would leave the profile where it was, because she still held out a faint hope that a nonflake would send her a message and maybe a new life would bloom from the seedling of a kind or flirtatious phrase.

When the appropriate amount of time had passed, he decided to send his reply. It was four words long, just as her previous message had been.

He wrote: "Not bad. Working hard."

When she read the message on her phone at the grocery store, she had to think for a minute to remember who it could be. The attempt to remember distracted her. When she realized who it was, she shook her head and walked out into the street, inadvertently stealing the head of lettuce she had cradled in one arm.

They ate that head of lettuce the first time they had dinner together.

"What's the point of that story?" Richard asked, frustrated at the futile hopes Patrick had momentarily inspired in him.

"I don't know, maybe that love can spring from ordinary circumstances. Anyway, I feel like it's your MO to go for guys who are emotionally unavailable."

"Thanks for saying so."

Richard felt the warm pang he always did when Patrick expressed a sympathetic anger about his emotional life. It was like that charge he got when a stranger or acquaintance unexpectedly praised him for some casual, tossed-off remark he'd made about a work of art or a person, and suddenly his sense of his own worth abruptly expanded. Who else could he rely on to go to bat for him in that cold, antagonistic landscape of handsome, determined young men?

Patrick offering judgment and advice on Richard's life—and cooking for him—had been the thrumming heart of their friendship for years now: Patrick the advisor, Richard the beneficiary of this advice, Patrick the intercessor, Richard the court stenographer. It was one late afternoon at the end of October, in their fourth year of college, when they'd gone for some of the metallurgically bitter coffee at the Architecture Café, that Richard abruptly realized he was in love with Patrick. Patrick said the summer had taught him that he was still negotiating his identity, and this made Richard feel better, because if someone so stylish, so strangely enchanting, with such deftly orchestrated gestures as Patrick was still *negotiating his identity*, perhaps Richard didn't need to worry so much about it himself. On the other hand—Richard concluded later with declining optimism, after they had parted with as chaste a hug as ever—this could likewise mean he had a long road in front of him, a road whose length he'd stumble alone and vainly in search of his "identity," while Patrick found happiness with others like himself: confident, direct, capable people who just *were* who they *were*. Whatever happened, Richard would find himself alone.

"Are you going to be all right here?" Patrick asked. "I'm leaving with Valdes and Benoit."

"You're leaving with *both* of them?"

Patrick nodded, grinning. Richard's feeling of reassurance vanished.

"You might actually change your life with some conversation," Patrick said, as Barrett and Amir went to refill their drinks. "You could do this too, you know. You might actually meet someone."

"Maybe if I get an eyebrow ring," Richard said, and waved his hand in a grotesque imitation of Barrett's flamboyant hand gestures.

Patrick bent down to tie the shoelaces of his black high-tops, and handed Richard his champagne, which Richard promptly drank.

"You have to stop judging people," he said, his face near the floor. "Do you *seriously* hate them so much?"

Patrick stood up again and leaned against the wall with an aura of brightness around his face. He smiled out at the dancing crowd.

"If that's the case, you might as well just go home."

"I'm falling asleep anyway," Richard said, feigning a yawn.

Patrick threw up his hands in frustration and walked off. When Richard entered the guest room to get his jean jacket, he found Toller lying facedown on the bed.

"Is Patrick leaving with Benoit?" Toller asked.

"Yes."

"Goddamn it! It's that fucking ponytail. It works every time."

Outside it was humid and there was an uncanny hush to the block. Furry, sluglike things—what were they called?—littered the sidewalk. Richard wanted to feel diva-ishly exhilarated by his exit, but instead he merely felt sheepish, and also nervous to be alone in that still quite industrial part of Bushwick, with its shuttered repair shops, desolate lots enclosed by fencing, and the occasional livery cab that pulled up, honked interrogatively, and sped away.

As he reached the end of the block, he could feel the onset of one of those schmaltzy waves of introspection that sometimes hit him when he'd had a lot to drink and was traveling alone on a nighttime sidewalk. The sour taste of champagne lingered in his mouth, and he acquiesced to the reflection that he was yet again leaving a party *alone*, heading to bed *alone*, from all possible vantage points *alone*—alone in the crowded city of great possibility. For a moment he indulged this cozy gloom, until it abruptly fermented into a headache, accompanied by regret that he'd argued with Patrick.

At the bus stop he opened a dating app and loaded a gingham of torsos onto the screen of his phone. He was immediately drawn to *Kind, Courteous, and Horny*—according to the GPS the third-closest person to him at that moment, trumped only by *Kenneth_bulge,* a sweetly smiling brunette, and the backside of *SimpletonNYC. Kind,*

Courteous, and Horny had an orange beard, pierced nipples, and hiero-glyphic tattoos along his flanks.

Richard's phone shook as a message arrived.

Love to blow you man.

He scanned for a backlit figure in a window, lunar screen glow revealing a jawline from which a cascade of orange beard merged with the luxuriant body hair *Kind, Courteous, and Horny* claimed with pride. But all the surrounding buildings were dark.

Thanks bud.

Anytime man!

A bus arrived and Richard climbed on board. He found a seat at the back. As it heaved forward, he imagined Patrick in a taxi, lazing in the attention of his admirers who would soon be naked, the lights of the city swept behind them; and then himself, walking home through dark and empty streets, returning to the roommate who would keep him awake all night, the cackles of street-level libertines, the predictable but irresistible postmasturbation ennui.

Richard had to admit that Patrick did try in his way to help, despite his increasing romantic distractions. His latest scheme was to prod Richard into therapy in order to demolish the blocks that prevented him from finding a decent boyfriend and working on his doctorate. Patrick was himself seeing a therapist—this service was free for students at the university—but was someone whose "issues" had never enfeebled his day-to-day confidence, or his ability to stay out all night and hook up with guys, occasionally date them, and then move on with little sign of damage. Puzzled at the obvious asymmetry and bias of therapy itself, Richard wondered what the point was. So you sat and talked to a stranger? He imagined confessing to a rotund man who represented a parody of a Viennese psychoanalyst. The man wore a monocle. Richard was convinced his desires and anxieties would seem routine and unsurprising once he articulated them out loud, like a bird launching out of a tree, having a heart attack in midflight, and then falling to the ground with a heavy thud.

Patrick was probably right—not about therapy, Richard considered himself too intelligent for that, but about a boyfriend. If he found a decent man, an *emotionally available* man, they could move in together to alleviate some of their mutual financial woes; people did it all the time. They built a life in common, took on the challenge of the city as one entity.

Most of the time it seemed like a dismal joke to search for another kind of life in the transactional indifference of the streets, like looking for consciousness in the head of a mannequin. But then in certain optimistic moods Richard could feel woozy with choice and sympathy, almost telepathically generous and porous. Contrary to the sensation one had at rush hour in the subway, the city was essentially benevolent in its crowded human bounty, its opulence and plenitude. The streets gushed with young men on their vibrant way, zealous platelets in a bloodstream. The blind statistic of so many anonymous faces hid the potential for a jarring recognition, an extraordinary conferment of attention, the tidal blur resolving itself into one determined stare that picked you out of the crowd.

FOUR

Anne had followed up by text to cement their working lunch date, and on the following Tuesday Richard was sitting on a red banquette, watching three older male waiters as they drifted in a disintegrating choreography of semicircles across a room covered in yellow wallpaper. A saxophone played in the background and gilt mirrors, several reflecting Anne, hung on the walls.

Richard hadn't slept well, and he felt acutely the dry challenge of making conversation. They didn't know each other well enough just to indulge whatever mood they might be in, and silence, it went without saying, was far from Anne's default mode.

"Do you think Antonella gets those pants in New York?" she asked, her third or fourth attempt at igniting a sustained dialogue between them.

"Naples," Richard said, feeling guilty that he wasn't trying harder. "I noticed that kind of style when I was there—that sort of . . . top-of-chic, bottom-of-chic thing."

"I like it," she said.

"Really?" he replied doubtfully.

"I think it's unique."

"Unique?"

Anne made a grimace of joking reprimand.

"Don't get me wrong, I think Antonella is beautiful," Richard said. "But she needs to stop smoking. It's aging her skin."

"The tanning also plays a part."

"She *tans*?"

"She invited me once. Can you imagine? I'd incinerate."

"That's practically assault, with your complexion."

They both laughed.

"I've never thought about what Antonella does in her free time," Richard said, his eyes wandering back toward the kitchen.

"She has a boyfriend."

"Oh yeah, I think I met him once. Dima—he's Ukrainian, right?"

"Yup—more of a bro than you'd expect."

Richard had tried to gossip about Antonella before, but those attempts had mostly fallen flat. Initially reluctant to descend to the level of base, hedonistic, and gleeful speculation over the life of their advisor, Anne had held back, laughing when Richard dished but not adding substantially to the conversation. But as they'd spent more time together, she had begun to supply anecdotes—first skeptically, as if conceding to the well-placed point of an intellectual adversary, and then jumping in zestfully, finally even initiating the gossip herself. She could probably tell that Richard liked to talk about other people. He in turn wondered if it was a relief to dispense with her demure, professorial air. There must be a retaliatory pleasure in it, the upstart attacking the mentor, though he doubted that Anne would ever articulate it that way or admit to it.

"You should come and see my new place," Anne said, as if this naturally followed.

"You moved?" he asked, startled by this sudden new tack in the conversation. She hadn't mentioned her intention to move at all the last time he'd seen her. That was only ten days ago. Had it all been on a whim? Did she make a call and a swarm of movers descended to liberate her from the depressing graduate school apartment, an experiment in communal living that she had brought to a merciful end, a brief indulgence? He wondered suspiciously if she had relocated to Brooklyn, perhaps even to his neighborhood.

"I had to get out. I felt like I was playacting for the benefit of Erin and Alicia so they wouldn't criticize me."

"Okay."

"They kept calling me a free-speech fundamentalist. And I really didn't want to do their dishes anymore. There was no dishwasher, of course."

Richard nodded, but he was confused by her new attitude toward Erin and Alicia. During his recent visit, she had seemed devotedly if grousingly attached to them, while they had clearly been skeptical of *him*. Perhaps she had cut them loose in order to move closer to him.

"No dishwashers in those apartments," he said, shaking his head, trying to remain focused. "What do those two study again?"

"Erin is in epidemiology and Alicia works on cyber-bullying."

Richard coughed.

"Here we are," said a tall bald man in a white shirt who had arrived with their food. A goat cheese salad was lowered to the table. Richard leaned forward and sniffed, hungrily riveted.

"Thank you," Anne said to the waiter, who nodded and walked away.

"There's a gym and a pool in my new building," she said.

"Really?"

Of course, now that there was no one else in the apartment, there would be no one to observe them there together. It would be the freedom, or the captivity, of privacy.

Richard realized he had his knife and fork in hand.

"And a sauna."

"A sauna?" he said, attempting a tone of analytical disengagement. "Very nice."

"Made from Japanese fir trees."

He put down the fork and passed a hand surreptitiously over his belly. He was still essentially thin, but he had not been to the gym in some time, conscious all the while that you were essentially invisible in New York without muscle tone.

"We can have a lazy Saturday."

"What's a lazy Saturday?"

"Drinking coffee, reading the paper, doing laundry."

So she wanted him to come over and get in the sauna.

"After five there's usually no one in the pool."

"Much nicer that way," Richard considered, ambivalently.

"Isn't it?"

Eating these meals together had made him wonder if Anne, despite her encircling intelligence, was largely unaware of how other people perceived her. It was like one of those illnesses, suitable for description in long magazine articles, in which you did not recognize the face of someone you'd known your whole life, or could only see the left half of things. She did not sense, perhaps, or she did not acknowledge sensing, indifference, instead launching forth unbidden to fill the void of disinterest. It was a dynamic that held in the seminar they were currently taking together. A collective stupor came over the room when she spoke, a tremendous daze in the eyes of their colleagues, despite her frequently brilliant commentary. One day a few weeks earlier she'd been sick with the flu, and in her absence, the mood in the seminar, taught by a visiting professor from the University of Palermo, changed instantly and noticeably. The professor only barked at one person, a timid brunette, and this was not because of any preposterous reading of the text, but because the brunette's phone rang during the lecture. Several fellow students, previously silent back-row spectators oppressed by Anne's eloquence, rose into the vacuum like dolphins surfacing in a grotto.

It also seemed that Antonella, whose thesis Anne claimed to admire deeply—Antonella called it "Disemboweling Leopardi" with a discharge of scornful laughter—felt irked by Anne's presence and treated her with hauteur and stinting respect. Richard would see them walking together through campus, up stairs of somber stone and through clumps of backpacked students, Antonella's chin in the air and Anne stumbling to keep up. In the classroom Antonella rarely made eye contact, disavowing the scholarly connection that was evident beyond the walls, preferring instead to stare at a point slightly above Anne's head when listening to a response or replying to a question. She would exhaust all possibilities before conceding to Anne's raised hand, scanning the class and imploring a response from the other faces, despite knowing full well that Anne's comment would be the most articulate, thoughtful, and profound.

The other students enjoyed Antonella's open distaste; an unspoken complicity existed between them against Anne's luminous intelligence. Perhaps it had something to do with the scarcity of the jobs for which they would all be competing. Anne effortlessly navigated the scraggy complexities of the language while the rest of them stepped tentatively forth, despite the advanced nature of their degrees, growing more frustrated and entangled with each new concept. Her Italian was more fluent and elegant than the Italian of those in the class who had grown up in Italy, or with Italian parents. She made none of the modern concessions to speed or efficiency, but spoke instead in the coherent mahogany outbursts of a philologist.

"The sauna sounds nice," Richard said, at the same time reflecting that for him saunas—whether of the YMCA or the bathhouse variety—had always, whether in reality or just in his mind, been a charged male space where women did not figure at all, let alone prominently. Anne must somehow realize this, he felt certain, and her blindness, her willful ignorance, was strange if gallant. It was like an animal, born blind, that struggles to its feet and instinctively wobbles forward, not cowed by the challenge of the darkness it confronts.

The waiter came and filled Richard's wineglass to an appropriate level, but as soon as he left Anne grabbed the bottle and added more.

"I really should work this afternoon," he said, putting his hand over the glass.

"It's a good vintage," Anne said, batting his hand away and continuing to pour. "It's the price of a good vintage anyway. You should think about coming over for a lazy Saturday."

Not knowing whether the meal was paid for or not, Richard was unsure where to apply the emphasis in his words. He felt he should speak in the effacing tones of gracious acceptance, while at the same time he worried that Anne would detect this grateful register, realize he expected her to pay, and abruptly clarify the terms of the meal.

"Toasted, please," Anne said when the waiter came to the table with another basket of bread. "I always take my bread toasted."

Could he ask her outright whether or not she planned to pay? Richard raised the wineglass to his lips and sipped.

"There's this very good Italian place that just opened near my building," Anne said. "Their veal meatballs are superlative. We could order in."

Richard lifted a crumb of goat cheese to his mouth.

"I'm always up for a superlative veal meatball," he conceded.

"How is the salad?"

"It's good," he said. "Like I said, you have great taste in restaurants. You have great taste in general."

He chewed demurely.

"That's kind of you to say."

Richard was beginning to feel buzzed, but at the same time no more confident. The wine wasn't settling him the way he wanted it to. A growing tension attached itself to every word he uttered; each second mixed the anxiety of his frozen degree with the anxiety of the end of the meal. It was all heightened by the fact that, late that same morning, a message from Antonella had arrived indicating forfeiture of the money if the foundation didn't receive a response within a week. Richard was worried that Anne would bring up the lazy Saturday again; he felt that in his present circumstances he could only accept.

The waiter cleared the plates. Richard shifted in his chair.

"What are you working on?" he asked.

"*De vulgari eloquentia*," Anne said, relishing the pronunciation of the Latin.

"What about it?"

"Well, Dante advanced an important aspect of his linguistic theory in that work: the human need for language. It was a necessity because, unlike with the angels, our thoughts are not instantly and readily available to each other of their own accord."

What a relief, Richard thought.

"'Therefore,'"—she made quotation marks with her fingers—

"'in order to communicate their mental conceptions to one another, men had to have some kind of rational and sensory sign.'"

"Is that a direct quote?"

"Yes."

"You have a phenomenal memory."

"It's nice to talk to you," Anne said, leaning forward, her knife and fork poised in the air. "Good conversation is almost impossible to find now. I feel that way sometimes, anyway."

"I think you can still find it," he said. "But thank you for saying so."

The main course arrived.

"Bon appétit," she said.

Richard began to carve his chicken, while Anne took a small bite of her duck. He observed her movements, which were quick and fastidious but also tentative. It was as though she kept them in a halfway kind of state, so that they might be quickly disowned and replaced should the need arise. The effect was oddly charming.

"When I worked at my father's firm, I had to talk to the dullest people in the world," she said. "Client meetings, the small talk, it was awful."

"You worked for your father's firm?"

"I did."

"What kind of firm was it?"

"Biotech."

He started out as a professor of biology, she said, and then he discovered a way to make certain mammals infertile by shooting them with darts, in the process amassing a considerable fortune. The Canadian government now wanted to buy a stake in his company, establish a fleet of vessels equipped with special cannons. It was a more humane way to control the burgeoning population of Arctic seals, for example, than to club them to death. The Russians were interested too.

"I got hooked on golf when I worked there, because of the meetings," she said. "Isn't that strange? I don't like it, but I'm good at it. It's the same with math."

Richard nodded, imagining her with a piece of chalk, like Einstein in front of a blackboard covered in hieroglyphic symbols. This seemed more appropriately rigorous and unfathomable than learning a Romance language, though he didn't know if she'd ever taught math. She never went into detail about her past, evoking it instead in large arcs, like a great billow of postmodern glass over a crowded lobby, peopled by strangers she wouldn't discuss. He didn't even know how old she was. He suspected that she was only a few years older than he was: there was something theatrical about her maturity. But it was also possible that she was forty-five, or some other, similarly extravagant age. Between them there was often the reserve and decorum of two people communicating across a generational divide. She walked and behaved with a tenured nonchalance, which at the same time was artificial, as though it had been learned in a literal fashion and not through accumulated experience.

She would probably want to play the professor with him; he often felt that she did, as if she was practicing for an imminent, glorious phase in her career. Her formality hinted that she could be drawn into a kind of mentorship role, that she would be disposed to help him if she felt that what they were doing was educational, leading him to a better version of himself, adding to the world's store of knowledge.

The waiter came back, firmly and evenly offering dessert.

"You should have the chocolate soufflé," she said.

"Is it good here?"

"That's what he'll have," she said. "He'll have the chocolate soufflé, and I'll have the crème brûlée."

Richard watched as the waiter disappeared into the kitchen.

"Crème brûlée," he said. "I haven't had that in years."

"Then you should definitely try some of mine."

Aside from the fact that she was clearly attracted to him, she would probably *want* to swing her intelligence like a scythe through the overgrowth of his research, to clarify a mass of lurking, abeyant, and potentially useful or at least elegant knowledge. It was her great talent after all.

"My father is in the city this week. We're going to play a round of golf early tomorrow morning."

"Sounds fun."

She shook her head.

"I don't get along with my father."

"I'm sorry to hear that."

She shrugged. During her childhood, she said, he had mostly been absent while he laboriously experimented and built his company. Her mother meanwhile was occupied with various therapies designed to address a case of borderline personality disorder— medications, magnets that changed the polarity of the brain, spa treatments, and spells at ashrams. At base, her mother was a flake and her father a rationality zealot, a biological determinist convinced his children's genes would push their personalities to fruition. For him, nurture was irrelevant, and from a certain perspective this had been a great relief.

"He mostly left us alone. We had a few nannies."

The dessert arrived, and Richard immediately took his fork and sliced down through the cake, into the hot dark lake beneath. He waited for Anne to resume speaking, but she didn't. When he looked up, she was staring trancelike into her glass, as if a fly had drowned in it. She abruptly consumed the remnants.

"Should we get another bottle?"

"It's the middle of the day."

He imagined the thwarted, self-loathing mood that would descend on the afternoon if he continued drinking.

"You're right. We shouldn't."

"This is delicious though. Thanks for recommending it."

"You really do have some interesting articles to your credit," she said, which struck Richard as a lucky tack in the conversation, perhaps *too* lucky. Maybe their thoughts, like the thoughts of the angels in *Paradiso*, really *were* available to each other of their own accord. Or perhaps *his* were available to *her*. It was a horrifying idea.

"I read a few of them," she said. "But where are the recent ones? I couldn't find any links."

"They're out there somewhere."

"Don't be bashful."

"I'm not, really."

He blushed despite himself, a result of the wine and his nervousness.

"I've heard you translating with Professor Caputo. You have a nice accent. Who did you work on?"

"I did some modern stuff, and one Guinizelli."

"Send something to me."

"You would read it?"

"Of course."

"I don't know. I'll have to think."

"Everything needs editing. There's no shame in it."

"I have to reach certain conclusions first."

"What conclusions?"

"I think I have obstacles in my personality."

"I'm very good with obstacles," Anne said. "I *do* suffer from chronic fatigue syndrome."

"We'll see."

"Maybe you should be out in the world. Academia will kill you. Besides, there's a market correction coming. A lot of schools will disappear soon."

He frowned.

"But *you* want to be a professor."

"Oh, it suits me."

"What about your father's company?" he asked. "You never wanted to do that?"

She shook her head.

"I don't want anything to do with it."

"It was that bad?"

She fixed him with an excavating stare.

"My father started the company with his best friend, another scientist at the university," she said. "Then that scientist, his name was Gerhardt, had an affair with my mother."

"Oh, God."

"Gerhardt was like a second father to me. Or a first father, really."

"That sounds terrible."

"The divorce was messy. But I loved Gerhardt," Anne said.

As a young man, with his young wife, Gerhardt had been in a car accident. It was night; a deer crossed the road. The ditch was unforgiving and his arm was crushed. Over time most of the flesh seemed to disappear; the nerves died. It was more like a kite that he carried around, tucked beneath his other arm. As a young girl, this arm had inspired feelings of compassion and defense in Anne.

"My father had to keep working with him even after everything came out about the affair," she said. "There was too much money involved."

The restaurant had largely emptied out; the waiters milled around, pretending to be patient. Richard wondered what his face looked like, if he was maintaining an expression of careful focus. A part of him was honestly intent on Anne's story, even sympathetic; another part had lifted up to the ceiling and was looking down at them both, like a chimpanzee on a branch, distant, instinctual, cool, asking if it was such a good idea that he was there, despite what he needed from her.

But it wasn't as if he could stop her and say, I think this is too much information; I'm not sure what you're getting at by telling me about your childhood and your parents' divorce; don't you have someone else you can talk to? He really wasn't such an asshole. He didn't want to be a person who fled from honesty, who recoiled from forthright confession, who had no time for genuine human difficulty and judged people inadequate if they weren't at all times productive and competent, like some animatronic Manhattan professional.

Now she was talking about—was it a tennis match?

"Gerhardt was thrashing my father, even with one arm," she said.

Somehow this event had led directly to the discovery of the infidelity, and the ensuing divorce.

"I was the one who found them," Anne said, briefly describing herself as a little girl wandering outside of a log cabin, a fragrant bed of pine needles, standing at a window and glimpsing Gerhardt and her mother wrapped around each other as if scratching at fleas.

Richard could see her drawn away by this decisive anecdote, just as he would have been. In its shadow, his problems felt trivial. Her life had obviously been bigger than his. He frowned. Was it too embarrassing to ask her for help to write a simple paper on Guinizelli after this tale of infidelity?

Then it dawned on him that *this* was partly why he was here: she needed his help. Not just his help: his presence, his conferment of attention, corporeal evidence that he had chosen to sit and listen.

"After that we took up golf," Anne said. "My father and I. We never played tennis again."

They could help each other. Everyone was vulnerable to periodic bouts of system failure. There were moments where doing what was expected of you seemed insurmountable, the most grotesque challenge, and you wondered how other people managed just to live. If he wanted something in return for listening, there was nothing strange or cynical in that. Friendship was more transactional than most cared to admit. It was a struggle to be alone with problems. Besides, the sympathetic part of him, or maybe it was the gossipy part, wanted to know how she had turned out the way she did.

So he listened.

"My father never really got over it," Anne said. "His life is just an orbit around the insult, some years the circle grows larger, others smaller, but it never goes away."

Now there was something tranquilizing about her voice. Richard was after all accustomed to the voluptuous complaining of female friends—the warm reprieve of dialogue turning to monologue, his feline withdrawal into the posture of immune observer snugly focused on the cantankerous life across the table, his own life cozily withheld and protected, like an object you hide surreptitiously so a guest won't ask to borrow it, or a cake you don't mention, so as not to share it. He'd been in a variation of this situation many times before.

But he knew that Anne would not let him remain quiet and evasive about his own past for long. It was not a place he particularly wanted to revisit, not because it had been traumatic but because it was now revealed to be completely ordinary: the small town in Maine, with its dentists and asset management firms in gabled houses off main street, wooden signs flapping in the wind. He didn't want to describe the preserved nineteenth-century buildings housing little gift shops and bakeries, and the boat-building festival that happened every summer, and how it was always cloudy and chilly in his memory, covered in a clear Plexiglas rain that never ceased to fall.

It all seemed intolerably maudlin: the easy friendships with girls and the wanting to connect with boys that marked his adolescence. The oddly formal lengths he went to to declare his belief in the ideal of privacy, so as not to have to reveal who he truly was: in retrospect it was weird and silly. He saw himself walking along the sidewalk as a closeted teenager, heading home from school to watch *Cabaret* or *Paris Is Burning*. At the time it had been heroic; now it just seemed miserable and pathetic.

There had been no great crisis or climax. When he came out, his parents accepted him. He was the only child of Terry, a patent lawyer, and Angela, who taught French at a local college, both now semiretired. They were indulgent, liberal-minded, Unitarian Church members. They had happily welcomed him back into the house after college and his wandering spell in Europe. He cringed at the specter of how banal it would all seem to Anne.

"Have you had enough to eat?" she asked.

The waiter was there with the bill. Looking back and forth between them, he held it in the air like a feather.

"That's for me," she said.

Richard quietly exhaled with relief.

"Thank you," he said as they left the restaurant and entered into a warm breeze. "I feel like I'm always saying thank you to you. You're always doing things for me."

"I think it's the other way around," she said, her voice unexpectedly placid after the rancorous tale she'd just told. But as they walked toward the subway, Richard felt he was expected to say something, perhaps a summing-up, though he had no idea what that should be.

When they reached the entrance, Anne paused at the top of the stairs, looking down into the station as if into a dark pit, grimacing.

"Are you okay?" he asked. He felt like he was also asking himself the same question.

"I'm not," she said, shaking her head. "I'm really not."

"What can I do?"

"Can we keep walking?"

"Where should we go?"

"Let's go to the park. I need some air."

They walked the few blocks to the park. When they entered, Anne moved with a silent, focused aimlessness. Joggers and dog walkers streamed around them in a blur of Gore-Tex and nylon. They wandered and wandered; she was seemingly lost in her own thoughts. Richard wondered how long this would go on. The buildings stared down at them from above the tree line with Easter Island solidity and composure. When they passed a bench near the eastern edge of the park, Anne indicated she wanted to sit down.

"What's up?" Richard asked finally, trying to tamp down his impatience.

"I don't want to become like them," she said.

"Like your parents?"

"Mmm."

"It's not going to happen," he said, hoping to quell what he feared was a new upsurge of emotion.

"I'm afraid there's something bigger pulling me that way. Something too big and vague to fight or even to see."

"It's not true. You have choices."

"I'm not sure."

It was the first time that he had heard her express uncertainty, except about some abstract philosophical issue, and even then she usually came down on one side or the other.

She asked him to tell her something that would equalize the air between them. He said he wasn't sure whether he could do that.

Actually, what they were doing reminded him of that scene in *The Idiot*. Had she read it? A group of aristocrats recount to Prince Myshkin the worst things they've ever done. One man describes grabbing a woman's simpering lapdog and throwing it out the window of a moving train.

"But Dostoevsky is a hard act to follow," Richard said as a breeze blew across his face, making the comment feel more dramatic.

"That's true."

She squeezed his fingers, and he looked at her small pink hand as if it were an oddly brave bird that had dared to land on him.

"It's almost as hard as Tolstoy," she said.

"Almost."

He smiled.

"This is why my career is so important to me," she said. "It's something that my family has nothing to do with. I control things. Nothing depends on them. It's where I can get away from that company and my father. He wants me to take over." She paused. "And that would be the end. Maybe it sounds strange, but my life would be over. I don't think I would survive."

"It doesn't sound strange to me, Anne. You don't belong there."

"No."

"You're a born scholar."

"That's sweet of you to say."

"You can go anywhere with it. I'm sure."

She nodded but didn't reply. Of course she already knew she could go anywhere with it. That was obvious to anybody.

"Do you know about the Clio Prize?" she said. "The department gives it out—to a paper written by a graduate student. If you get that, you're basically guaranteed a position somewhere."

"You'll get it. You'll win it."

"I don't want to go to Nebraska."

"Why ever not?"

"Ha. Right?"

They watched a fluffy group of West Highland terriers trot past. The sky had grown clear and sharp. Her mood was lifting, and Richard sensed an opportunity.

"I might have to leave."

"I've kept you long enough," she said.

"I mean—I might have to leave the city . . ." He trailed off.

"What do you mean?"

She turned to look at him.

"I haven't met a deadline in months. Antonella is threatening to cut off my funding."

At the very least he would be suspended when she wrote her letter to the foundation, or failed to, and the money stopped.

"You can't leave New York."

"Who said 'You can't go home again'?" he asked.

"Thomas Wolfe."

"You *can* go home again. You can go home and get *stuck* there."

"It's too expensive here," she said, shaking her head slowly and, in doing so, scanning the hyperprosperity that formed one latitudinal border of the park. "It's inhuman."

He wondered whether she sensed the irony in what she was saying. Did she condemn herself as part of that inhumanity?

"It's the fault of people like my father."

He doesn't live in New York, Richard thought. But then again, neither do a lot of people who own property here.

Anne stared at the turreted apartment buildings like a sad revolutionary. Richard hoped this would not be her entire reaction, a pointless commiseration about the inequality that surrounded them, as though it was ground they really needed to cover again.

"You're not leaving," she said, taking his wrist in hand.

"It feels like a foregone conclusion now."

"Nothing is a foregone conclusion."

"I don't know."

She looked down at the wet grass.

"What can we do?" she said, and he shrugged. "What are you working on now?"

"Well—" He brightened, trying not to be too obvious about his ulterior motive. "The Guinizelli, but I've got nothing."

"I can help you."

He looked at her with a timid expression. "Really?"

"We'll start right away," she said.

"Anne—"

"There's not a chance I wouldn't. Please don't take this the wrong way, but it's easy for me. I have more than enough material. I always overproduce."

"It's too much."

"It's not. I said I would, and I will."

He paused as if deliberating.

"Well, um, could you look at the paper I'm working on then? It wouldn't be a big commitment. I'm just having some trouble finding the through-line."

"Of course."

"Maybe if Antonella saw that I could finish, she would give me some breathing room."

"That's what we'll do then."

"I respect your work and I would love . . . your advice."

Something inside him teetered. He wanted to leap forth and recoil all at once.

"It will be *fun* to work together," she said, smiling now.

"Yes it will," he said, excited. "This is so generous of you, Anne."

"It's nothing."

He smiled.

"Tonight, we'll go to the library. Bring your notes. Bring whatever you have so far. We'll figure it out."

She was such a sweet, generous person, he thought. No one in his life, not even Patrick, treated him like this.

"You don't know what a relief this is."

FIVE

With her index finger, Antonella pointed to a stapled sheaf of papers on the desk.

"This is very good, Richard, very good."

Behind her head, a screen of plants filled the window.

"Let's see." She picked up the papers, scanned a page, and read aloud:

"'The difficult nature of the problem of language in Dante's time is evident in his claiming superiority for the Italian *volgare* in one theoretical work—*De vulgari eloquentia*—while doing the same for Latin in another—*Il Convivio*. The resolution of Dante's equivocal stance on language should be sought for not in theoretical works but in the *Commedia* itself, where he employs the Italian *volgare* to go beyond even the models of antiquity, written in Latin, from which he drew inspiration.'"

Richard nodded, though he had lost all sense of whether Anne's words were insightful or merely pompous.

"When can I see more?" Antonella asked, with a previously absent level of excitement in her voice.

"Soon."

"And you are going to apply to the conference in Montreal? Anne knows the details."

Prudently considering how to respond, he paused. "We've had some discussions along those lines."

"What changed?"

"Maybe it's the weather," he said, looking past her now at the budding campus, green beyond the window. "I've been feeling better. My head is clearer."

He and Anne had worked together in the library for the past three days, crafting the paper from which Antonella had read aloud. He was still reeling from watching Anne's nimble mind roam through the unkempt hamster cage of his research—collecting and stockpiling still-edible morsels, trimming rancid bits from salvageable parts, and sweeping away what was clearly dead. Assuming they would do this together—an equal partnership—Richard had at first made spirited, sincere efforts to contribute, and sensitively Anne had responded with an enthusiastic openness, taking his points into account. But in the end she'd accelerated away from him and discarded most of his suggestions. He had to admit that she had done most of the work on her own. But this was only their first time working together. A more balanced arrangement would emerge, he was sure, as they both got their bearings.

"It seems to me to be the way forward," Antonella said. "I've sent the letter to the foundation. The money will arrive soon. I'm sure you're relieved."

"Very much." He exhaled. "Thank you."

She smiled her slightly parched smile. "I'm happy this was resolved. I think you have turned a corner."

After his meeting with Antonella, Richard went to see Patrick for lunch in the student union building. They ate there sometimes despite its obdurately soulless decor, its odor of soya sauce, and the often enraging lineups for the ATM. If they felt they could afford it, they ate elaborate salads or moist veggie burgers immersed in condiments with elaborately milky coffee, and if they were feeling particularly broke, Richard ate a squashed tuna sandwich and Patrick ate nothing.

Patrick was deep in conversation with Barrett and Amir when Richard arrived. Richard sat down with the intention of being silent throughout the lunch, but this primed audience, assembled by Patrick and now at his disposal, made it so that he couldn't keep himself from trying to mention the ridiculous thing he was going to do that night— join a protest on the lawn, and sleep outside in a tent.

"It's important to keep going out," Amir said. "You can tell if you have chemistry with someone. Even if I think someone is cute, I still swipe away out of ennui."

"*Ennui?* If someone is cute, I'll invite them over," Barrett said. "That's why I get more action than you."

"You've always gotten more action than me."

"Let's talk about the real world. You have to know where to go. Urge is good for the bathroom scene, but the drinks are watered down."

"I'm going to sleep outside on campus tonight," Richard said.

"I think the Boiler Room is the worst for fatsos," Barrett said, charging over Richard's words and completely ignoring his perturbed face. "But Eastern Bloc is worse for sweat."

"No Urge is worse for sweat!"

"Those bars are all the same," Richard said. "It gets boring."

"What gets boring?"

"I mean, they're not interesting after a while," Richard said.

"Do you even know where to go?" Barrett said.

"Give me a break," Patrick said.

It was unclear whom he was addressing.

"Whatever," Barrett said. "This city is lame anyway. I can't wait to get out of here."

"And go where?"

"I don't know. Maybe London, maybe LA."

Richard looked away and saw a young woman drizzling vinegar on her French fries, a beatific look on her face.

"It's not so bad here," he said.

Later in the afternoon, he went to the protest and found Anne sitting on the ground, resentfully cross-legged. Beside her, Erin and Alicia sprawled on their stomachs, a furry plaid blanket beneath them. They were eating rice cakes slathered in peanut butter and writing slogans with black markers on cardboard placards. Around them, gaunt young men mingled with girls dressed in cascading vintage garb.

"Welcome to the conclave of our future leaders," Anne said. She was wearing black sunglasses, which seemed to be growing larger with each meeting.

Richard sat down.

"Here," said Erin, handing Anne a placard. In black marker it said *My Grievance:* and then a blank space.

"What's my grievance?"

"Oh, I figured you could just pick one," Erin replied.

Anne dropped it on the ground and stuffed her hands into her pockets.

"It's weirdly cold," she said. "Why? Couldn't you have chosen a warmer day?"

Alicia unwound a thin pea-green scarf from her neck and handed it to Anne, who draped it on her shoulders begrudgingly. People were setting up tents nearby.

"Is that where we're sleeping?" Richard asked.

"No, we're sleeping there," Alicia said, pointing to a listing green tent that was entirely too narrow to house the four of them.

"We won't fit," Richard said.

"We're going to be up all night anyway. I've got a list of prepared chants," Alicia said.

They sat and watched students pass by in the declining light.

"Was this a good idea?" Anne said.

"I don't know," Richard whispered. "But we probably shouldn't leave now."

She shrugged. "Probably not."

Richard surveyed the scene. There was no one in earshot. "How's your father?" he asked.

"My father left for the Vineyard or somewhere else dangerously close to marine life," Anne replied, sounding indifferent.

"Are you okay?"

She smiled at him. "I'll be fine. Did you bring anything to read?"

He shook his head.

"I brought Erwin Panofsky. I love that era."

"Me too," Richard said, pleased that she had decided to talk about something other than her family.

In his theory classes, he said, all the books had these beautiful titles—*A Thousand Plateaus*, *The Transparency of Evil*, *Totality and Infinity*—but the content never delivered the aesthetic bliss they seemed to promise.

"There are some important points if you dig around, though. It's not all nonsense. Want a cookie?"

That was one of the interesting things about Anne's mind, Richard thought: despite her intermittently old-fashioned air, she was open to new ideas; she didn't dismiss out of hand what was novel, but she was nonetheless grounded in what had come before. Most other doctoral candidates, while intelligent enough, were naively dedicated to whichever explanatory discourse, whichever style of thinking, was currently in vogue. Didn't they realize that in time it would be shown to be hopelessly limited, if not laughably wrong? Every discourse eventually was. In the end, you had to conclude, it was all a lot of fashionable bullshit.

"What kind?"

"They're from Levain Bakery."

She reached into her bag and pulled out a gigantic cookie in a paper sleeve.

"Thanks," he said, taking the cookie.

It had felt a tiny bit brutish and cheap to accept Antonella's praise earlier, when it wasn't really his to accept. Until his own capacities returned, he could—he would—say yes to Anne's help to move past this fallow period. It wasn't going to be easy, it was going to be hard on his ego, to sublimate himself to her. Part of him wanted to tell Anne how good Antonella thought the paper was, but then again she didn't *need* the praise. She already had a lot of success in her life. And it wasn't as if under normal circumstances he couldn't do what she did. He'd been accepted into the program after all. System failure happened. He just couldn't see the point of all this sometimes, and then he'd start wondering why he hadn't gone into artificial intelligence or that kind of thing.

Because he wasn't good at math, that's why.

He decided that the next paper on which they collaborated, he would do better. He would show Anne that he had valuable ideas to contribute.

Erin came over and demanded to know if there was any sparkling water leftover.

"We've been yelling all night. We're *very* thirsty."

"We'll go to Morton Williams," Anne said. "But someone will have to watch our stuff."

"And *who* is going to do that?"

They walked out of the gates onto Broadway and crossed the street toward the glowing windows of the supermarket. Inside, lines of expressionless people inched forward, pressing their cards against black boxes and then grumpily stuffing produce into plastic bags. Richard heaved a twelve-pack of bottled water into the cart.

"It's so wasteful," Anne said. "And for a *climate change* protest."

Richard shook his head.

"I hope they're reimbursing you for this," he said.

"Are you kidding?"

When they got back, Erin and Alicia were standing on milk crates, leading a chant. Occasionally a spectator would approach, inquire as to the cause behind the protest, and be rudely rebuffed. Richard eyed the tent with increasing nervousness.

They arranged the snacks and water into neat piles.

"So how did it go with Antonella today?" Anne asked. "You haven't mentioned anything."

"It went well."

He was annoyed all of a sudden that she'd brought it up. And in public, no less.

"See? All you needed was a fresh set of eyes." She patted him on the knee. "You had some very good ideas."

"Nice of you to say."

"Anyway," she said, leaning toward him with a cozy expression on her face. "We're not going to let you move into your parents' basement."

He smiled. "I certainly hope not."

Around midnight, they went to bed, rolling out their sleeping bags and lying in the tent, heads on their backpacks. Erin and Alicia and the rest of the protesters finished their chants and began playing Broken Telephone in a circle outside.

"I wish I could brush my teeth," Richard said.

When Anne didn't respond, he tilted his head to look at her. It was dark, but he thought that her eyes were closed. He had expected her to initiate conversation. He had expected her to be a person, like himself, hassled by nighttime anxieties. Evidently she was not; she had begun to snore.

Still, even if it was as mute logs, they *were* sleeping beside each other in the same shared, narrow, confidential space. He felt suddenly disappointed that she was asleep. Also, a tinge of resentment she'd left him to face Erin and Alicia alone.

When they entered the tent a few minutes later, they made no effort to be quiet. But their flurried arrival did nothing to disturb Anne's slumber. Erin squealed. Alicia made honking noises. She got on all fours and neighed like a horse.

"Liz snores!"

"Let's get it on our phones!"

Richard pretended to be asleep.

"We know you're awake," said Erin.

It felt, it sounded, like a threat. He tried to imitate REM sleep, shifting his eyes around.

"Stop faking," Alicia said.

"Yeah, quit it."

They sounded drunk. Had they been drinking? He couldn't smell alcohol.

"Oh hey," he said. "Yeah, I'm awake."

"*Oh hey*," Alicia said, making fun of him.

"Of course you're awake," Erin said. "How could you sleep with this trombone beside you?"

They cackled in unison.

"I can't believe this," Alicia said. "This is *too* perfect!"

"All is revealed," Erin mused.

"I'm so excited to tease her about it!"

"No, we shouldn't tell her we know. We should just, like, quietly imitate her whenever she walks by."

"Move over," Alicia said, teasing.

"I'm as far as I can go," Richard said.

He pushed against the side of the tent.

"I'm just kidding," she said.

It was three in the morning when he looked at his phone again. He was hot and stiff. Beside him, like a Greek chorus furtively tranquilized by a doomed protagonist, all three of them were snoring. Moisture gathered on the canted nylon walls. He struggled out of the sleeping bag and then out into the dark, zipping up the tent quickly behind him, as though securing a predator.

Indifferent to their protest, whatever it was, the patrician campus was still. Anne would probably be upset when she woke up and found him gone. Erin and Alicia would snicker all day, doubting his commitments, making inferences about his politics. He turned on his heels and started walking.

If Anne was upset, that was something she would have to deal with; she had to admit that it was one thing to go out for lunch, another thing entirely to ask him to sleep all night in a tent, squashed in with her dubious friends. She was helping him, but this favor had all been a bit much. Perhaps a piece of his anger stemmed from the fact that she had abandoned him in the tent with Erin and Alicia, that he needed her in that situation just as he did with Antonella.

He was mouthing an argument, coddling a lump of guilt like a small infant it was imperative not to wake. He went down into the subway, and after a long wait, the train finally arrived. He found a seat and hardly moved during the entire floridly lit, heavy-gravity crawl home.

S I X

What a chore it must have been for Patrick to have a needy best friend when he was a new resident in an emotional and erotic paradise. Since falling in love with Valdes—if he was really *in love*—Patrick was in the habit of being grotesquely late. And even when he did show up, Richard was always on the lookout for signs of hesitation and impatience, like a detective perched with binoculars at the window of a rented room. He was convinced that Patrick came only grudgingly to hear his repetitive tales of romantic frustration, or just to marvel at the bitter telemetry Richard brought back from excursions into the dating pool, Patrick having climbed out of that pool himself.

It was Saturday morning, two days since the protest and the abortive night in the tent, and the weather had made another one of its benevolent early-summer leaps—T-shirts prevalent and eager crocuses visible in the grass. Richard yawned as he entered the warm cave of Sloppy, a coffee shop close to his apartment. Still not having fully recovered his lost sleep, his eyes were dry and he was craving the pastoral taste of their dark roast.

He wondered whether he should buy Patrick his coffee. But the coffee was liable to be cold by the time Patrick arrived. He was prob-

71

ably lolling in bed with Valdes at that very moment, whining about how he didn't want to leave, the sheets in a warm tangle.

Patrick could get his own coffee.

"Hi, Richard!"

Courtney, one of the Sloppy baristas, waved from behind the bar.

"Good morning, Courtney. How are things today?"

"I'm okay, Richard," she said, in her characteristically frantic, ambivalent tone.

The Sloppy baristas were infamous for their habit of roaring over and complaining about obliterated relationships, badgering you to attend an improv performance, or joining you, when all you wanted to do was to drink your coffee in peace and read the paper, the moment you sat down at one of the tables with a small square prosthesis of cardboard fastened to one leg.

"A cappuccino, please, Courtney. I'm considering a sandwich, but maybe for later."

Or maybe not, he thought, as he looked at the chalkboard. Despite the air of naïveté that prevailed at Sloppy, their prices, already vexingly astute for the gentrifying neighborhood, had definitely gone up.

Richard tried to be detached about it. He'd woken up in a good mood, and he wanted to prolong it as long as possible. The beautiful day, teasing out flowers and grass, tactfully disrobing the inhabitants of the city, helped a great deal. Moreover, that morning the money from the foundation had come into his bank account, indicating happy receipt of Antonella's letter. It was the sort of efficiency you didn't expect in a nonprofit.

"I'm happy to see you, Richard," Courtney said. "I'm putting you on my gratitude list for today."

"I'm glad to be there," Richard said.

Courtney was a fixture of the surrounding blocks. She had long chestnut hair, aeronautical arms and legs, and rode around waifishly on a vintage Peugeot bike. Today she wore an undershirt and disintegrating acid-wash jean shorts. Her engagement to Craig, a fellow barista at Sloppy, had recently ended when Craig moved to Seattle to get into tech, despite having learned to count with wooden beads. Since his departure, Courtney had been spontaneously but reliably bursting into tears as she prepared the vegan sandwiches that figured heavily on Sloppy's menu. You could see nervous customers watching to make sure that none of the tears fell into the beds of avocado and tempeh for which they were impatiently waiting. If the crying jag persisted, she went outside and sat on a bench. Once or twice Richard had taken a place beside her and she'd wept on his shoulder. She claimed she was going to have Craig's baby, but her belly never grew.

Sloppy often felt utopic: the diversity and stylishness of the clientele, the quality and ethics of the coffee, the brownstones across the street, and the occasional vintage Mercedes-Benz sedan that appeared at the curb and just sat there, gleaming, absorbed in its own sublime mechanical prowess. It was a feeling usually punctured by the disgusting clogged toilet and the fact that they were always out of key ingredients. A rat had once died under the floor and was not removed for several days. Then again low-key celebrities frequently came in and let their adopted children crawl around on the ground. They arrived in Volvos or hybrids and acknowledged you as a fellow regular.

Cappuccino in hand, Richard went to the back and found a table. Around him freelancers leaned into their computers with slumped intensity. He checked his phone. There was still no sign of Patrick.

Before Patrick had got together with Valdes, he was often the first to arrive at Sloppy for their afternoons or mornings of caffeinated bitching. Wherever they happened to be, Patrick and Richard found a coffee shop to colonize together. They had been friends since meeting in a study-abroad program in Rome when they were both twenty-one. Learning a Romance language had seemed practical then; less than a decade later, it was without question a demonically frivolous act. But in those promising early days they had memorized their vocabulary together and gone to discos in Testaccio, to anarchist bars in San Lorenzo, and to the slowly crumbling lavatories and baths once enjoyed by the murderous politicians whose busts filled the city. Above his bed in Piazza Bologna, Richard pinned a postcard of Albert Camus that read *There's no shame in preferring happiness*, which Patrick laughed at. But then Patrick rescued him from penury after his grant money stubbornly failed to materialize. He searched out the address of the Ministry of Foreign Affairs and rode with Richard on a series of buses to the diplomatic section of the city, a region of long, unforgiving boulevards without sidewalks. The ministry was a marble edifice protected by numerous bored security personnel. When a pleasant elderly woman in one of the vast offices professed her ignorance as to the money's whereabouts, Patrick demanded it be transferred into Richard's account immediately, which it was.

In the years that immediately followed their undergraduate degrees, they'd stayed in intimate but intermittent touch without actually seeing each other. Patrick, having put Europe sensibly behind him, settled in New York to continue his education while Richard returned to loaf around the continent on a grand tour, his own tenuous version of Goethe's *Italian Journey*, teaching English and nannying or manning the night shift at a hostel. Long weeks of silence were broken by the arrival of text messages or emails in which Patrick bemoaned his "boring existence" in which he was "anxiously preoccupied with handing over my life to the next terrible generation"—Patrick went through periodic but intense bursts of wanting to procreate—and declared that he'd "had the urge to meet up with you lately in some random city, dressed to kill, and destroy people with our side eyes." Like many of his friends in that period, Richard felt, Patrick's life had begun to assume an increasingly solid romantic and professional structure, something his own just stubbornly refused to do.

After Europe, full of the alarming dread of comparison via social media —"compare and despair"—Richard had returned home in a fog of gloom to live with his parents and regroup in the town where he'd been raised, which was just a swelling on the lip of the ocean, a small northern place where the phrase "all the world's a stage" did not quite apply. Full of envy at Patrick's life in New York, Richard spent a despairing year living in his childhood bedroom, which in his absence had been turned into an office and storage space. On the shelf there was a selection of paperback novels and a VHS tape with *Princess Diana's Funeral* written along the spine in black marker. He got a job at an independent bookstore on its last legs and when, naturally, it closed, his parents began reluctantly filtering money to him through an old bank account he'd had since childhood, but that stream of cash had then been diverted to support a new habit of taking cruises up the Pacific Coast to Alaska—intellectual cruises where famous writers and physicists gave lectures.

It had been Patrick who suggested that Richard try his hand at graduate school, with the claim that it was an easy bridge for the moderately intelligent, and a last refuge for the neurotic and antisocial now that bookstores and video stores were vanishing and libraries turning into glorified Internet cafés. It was exciting to think they'd be living in the same city again, not too far from where they'd gone to college.

Patrick helped Richard find the apartment and move in, and before Valdes entered the picture, they developed a nice routine. Most nights around ten o'clock Patrick would bike over from his apartment on Willoughby Avenue. Richard would eat Kraft Macaroni and Cheese Dinner or something equally glutinous while he waited, and when Patrick arrived in a jean jacket, his blond hair strikingly windblown, they'd close themselves into Richard's room, put on Eurythmics, and Patrick would roll a joint. Then they'd escape the apartment and walk the arboreal streets of Clinton Hill or Prospect Heights, pleasantly high.

Richard's first months in New York had been a time of stamina and optimism. Almost every night of the week he went out to destinations chosen by Barrett, Amir, or Toller, all of whom he'd met through Patrick. They in turn had dozens of energetic and fashionable friends who were frequent recipients of tickets and invitations to openings and sample sales. The nights felt stirring, romantic, and full of potential.

But it was a routine with an inevitable expiry date. People were pairing off, not least Patrick, who still came out at night with whomever he happened to be dating, but who would soon disappear forever into a comfortable domestic bivouac, Richard was certain. Some nights—just as these new couples did—Richard would have preferred to stay in with pizza and Netflix. There was also the matter of being able to get any work done in the hungover days that interspersed these sparkling nights.

Coupling off in New York proved more frustrating and desolating than he had predicted. His attempts to date boys, these blind lunges toward happiness, soon predictably unsuccessful attempts at raw human connection, and the emotional hypothermia that followed led him to endorse the slogan, which floated around on the Internet and on

Hallmark cards and in drunken conversation at the end of the night, that friends really were the *most* important relationship in your life, a conviction maintained despite mountains of evidence to the contrary in the form of married couples and nonmarried couples, couples with children, the agitation for the right to marry and adopt children, the number of guys on the dating sites and apps who wanted a husband, the waves of superiority that washed off couples, and the envy Richard felt toward those who didn't have to go home at night alone and log on to their dating profiles at some stark hour. And then on top of that there was the obvious insincerity in profile names like *norushfortheone* and the radiant candor in names like *waitingforthemiracle*. But despite all that, Richard decided to try to believe it was true, and not just a comforting deflection intended for those who, like himself, couldn't seem to get themselves into a relationship.

He was tired of feeling inferior and cast off, so he would change the terms of the debate, or game, whatever it was. But it was difficult when you were the only one who seemed to want to believe it. He was destined to find himself on the other end of a café table, it appeared, perpetually waiting for Patrick instead of some doting boyfriend.

The bone crack of fractured china fragmented through Sloppy as Courtney dropped a plate onto the floor. Richard felt newly annoyed at Patrick's lateness, but also a growing need for him to be there, to sit beside or across from Patrick in that room of not-quite-strangers.

Where was Anne? Probably by herself too. Was she thinking about him? Anne did not leave you on perturbed standby, he reflected. She made you feel like *you* were the focus, not an incidental feature of the environment. Patrick wasn't about to drop Richard, but the ambient threat that it *could* happen, and that if it did happen, it would be Patrick who did the dropping and not Richard, Patrick who was pulled away by some other more exciting thing and not the other way around, lent him an attractive menacing quality that was impossible to achieve consciously, Richard knew.

Anne was earnest and reliable and even if, by some inconvenient evolutionary tick, earnestness and reliability weren't as attractive as the threat of abandonment, or a muscular physique, there were certain qualities you had to force yourself to value. In the long run it was for your own good.

She was like eating your vegetables, or quitting smoking, or going to the gym.

Windswept as ever, Patrick finally appeared. He came and sat down with a cappuccino in hand, carrying an attractively beat-up leather messenger bag.

"You're not that late this time," Richard said.

"What do you mean?"

There was a pause as Patrick arranged himself. Richard chose not to clarify.

"I'm sorry," Patrick said, turning to Richard. "How are you?"

"I'm all right."

"I don't think we ever *really* discussed that date you went on . . . a while back. Tell me what you did again?"

The date in question was now several weeks old, but Richard still felt immediately the warmth and comfort that came with being the sole focus of Patrick's attention.

"His name was Blake. We went for a walk on the High Line and I bought him dinner."

"Where?"

"At a diner."

"Did you sleep with him?"

Richard shook his head.

"A kiss, even?"

Richard thought for a second.

"No, we just hugged," he said.

"And he never responded to your texts?"

"No."

Patrick nodded thoughtfully.

"There's your answer," Patrick said, as though reading a thermometer.

"What do you mean?"

"You took him to a diner."

"I wondered if that was a bad idea. You can't live on that kind of food," he sighed. "I don't think that men see me as a provider."

"You're not a provider."

"Do you think it's something innate, or can it be learned?"

"It's totally innate."

"I thought you'd say that."

Richard was overcome by gloom. His various handicaps—using credit cards that came in the mail attached to suspiciously cheery letters, not bothering with his taxes, not knowing how to make a tuna melt—had in the past been an amusement to his friends, and to himself the sign of a fine, original mind, too preoccupied by abstract thought to find its way to the kitchen or the bank. Now, as houses and marriages and children were being contemplated, and sometimes actually *acted upon*, these charming dysfunctions were taking on a more ominous aspect. He wasn't eccentric and intelligent anymore, but flaky and incompetent, not original and endearing, but blundering and doomed. Doomed, that is, to be alone.

Patrick sipped his cappuccino, scanning the other tables.

"Maybe I should change my 'Wants Kids?' answer to 'yes' instead of 'undecided,' " Richard said.

"Good idea," Patrick said. "If you don't want a kid, you're a curiosity, you're obsolete."

"But I have a right *not* to want children."

"I know you do, but don't *say* that. People who are ambivalent about children are supposed to have great careers to compensate."

"I just want someone there when I wake up on Sunday. Sunday *fucking* Sunday."

Or Saturday, he thought. That morning, he was quite certain—despite the preciously conjured biosphere of south Brooklyn in which it took place, with all its percolating coffee, gently stretched sailor shirts, tennis shoes, lives made up of a baffling potion of accomplishment and leisure—would have turned to an abyss of boredom and disappointment had Patrick not been able to meet him. All the accoutrements, the trappings, the dishes of citrus donuts and caramelized bacon, Schwinn bicycles, vintage Mercedes-Benz cars, the beautiful people in perfect jeans, would not have been sufficient to prevent it. Being there actually made it worse, Richard decided. It was the contrast between him and them, himself and the people on the street who seemed fulfilled. If he had been somewhere bland, unremarkable, ordinary—like his hometown—he might not have felt it so acutely. But here what amplified it on weekend mornings was the absence of potential in the place that was supposed to contain the greatest potential of all.

The line from Dante came to him. *There is no greater sorrow than to recall happiness in times of misery.* There is no greater sorrow than to feel like a horny loser in Brooklyn. There is no greater sorrow than to feel ugly and unstylish in Williamsburg . . . something, something.

Yes, on the weekends he wanted someone there in the morning when he woke up, a warm body, a young man who might stay instead of springing from bed and bounding out the door in a flash of impatient emancipation.

"It *is* nice to have someone there on Sundays," Patrick said, a dreamy look in his eyes, as if reading Richard's mind.

He would know, Richard thought, taking out his phone and clicking open Grindr. The faces and torsos and crotches loaded as the locator sent its sensory shock wave over the surrounding blocks. Below his picture, a blue-eyed brunette wrote, *True confession: I haven't been in love for years. I always fall for the ones who don't give a shit.* A moment later, a picture of his buttocks arrived.

They went outside and sat on one of the wooden benches, which were as wobbly as the tables inside, and Patrick lit a cigarette. He explained that he was considering modifying his dissertation again, after reading the autobiography of Alexander Herzen, the nineteenth-century Russian liberal. Herzen had a best friend named Ogarev, a fellow student at Moscow University. Herzen described one of the most important nights of his life when, as an adolescent, he went walking with Ogarev on the Sparrow Hills overlooking Moscow. They were both secret liberals. This was in the midst of the post-1825 crackdown, after the Decembrists, free-thinking aristocrats, had been crushed and disbanded. Herzen and Ogarev embraced each other and vowed to sacrifice their lives to the struggle.

"That's very romantic," Richard said.

Of course, Russians rushed into love, especially nineteenth-century Russians; they threw themselves under trains for it. Is that what he should have done, declare his feelings for Patrick in a dramatic gesture, instead of hanging around in this courtly suspension, like a medieval troubadour who sings but never touches, like poor dead Guido Guinizelli himself?

Perhaps in a Russian love story by now they too would have embraced each other and vowed to sacrifice themselves for something, perhaps for each other (political struggles not being Richard's thing, exactly).

"It *is* very romantic, isn't it?" Patrick said.

The political stuff was all well and good, he continued, but the unarticulated dynamics of the friendship between Herzen and Ogarev were distracting. Were those two lovers? Or maybe it was just one of those confusing nineteenth-century-style male friendships where they expressed their love ardently but it was platonic? Or perhaps one of those English boarding school things, where it was sexual but only as a kind of prelude to the more real, valid, legitimate heterosexual love that would lead to a family and establishment in society?

"I think all of that sounds great," said Richard. "You could turn it into a book. Queering Russian politics or whatever. The academic presses would go gaga for it. Just throw in some Foucault."

"How's *your* writing going?"

"It's getting better." Richard looked at the ground when he said this. "Slowly."

"What changed?"

"Oh, a few things."

Patrick was a problem in this whole situation, one that had been until then fairly easy to ignore because they didn't see each other as often anymore. When Richard had begun having lunch with Anne, Patrick immediately jumped to the conclusion that she was yet another kind, hapless woman with a crush on a gay man. With this in mind, Richard decided that it was best not to disclose Anne's assistance. Patrick would think it ridiculous, or possibly cruel, that they had continued seeing each other.

To the uninitiated, Patrick could come off as some kind of feckless urban decadent, a tall amoral partier with a cigarette-ravaged voice— it was his natural voice—who didn't care passionately about much beyond the tawdry personal sphere, but this was far from correct. While he was less outwardly political than many of their contemporaries— Patrick's outer politics were now largely confined to signing petitions online and watching Al Jazeera—he was in a sense very *inwardly* political. Despite his cynicism about a great many things, he still believed in the sacred inviolability of scholarship, the way some people still believed in the sacred inviolability of money, religion, or even art.

They were very honest with each other—at least it felt that way, though how could you ever really tell? Patrick did most of the talking. This reduced the difficulty, Richard supposed. And there were many things they *could* talk about.

He'd had no trouble telling Patrick that he couldn't get his work done, for instance; he had not felt an ounce of shame about revealing the apathy and blurring that came over him as he tried to interest himself in the material that was supposed to be his career, although Patrick's response had not been what Richard expected or what he needed. Patrick told him he was probably just lazy, or indulgent, but otherwise he hadn't bothered probing far into the problem, just *Okay, that's not good.* There was no condescension dressed up as sympathy, but there was no assistance either. Now that Patrick was living this swamped but electrified life in New York, and had Valdes to think about, he expended much less effort trying to solve Richard's problems. Considering this, Richard felt resentful.

Just then Courtney emerged from Sloppy, a crumpled pack of

Marlboro Lights in hand. This saved Richard from explaining to Patrick what exactly had changed.

"I hate morning sickness," Courtney said, taking a seat beside Richard.

"It's the afternoon," Patrick said, clearly annoyed at her arrival.

"Afternoon sickness then."

"When's it due?"

"*It's* two months along."

Patrick blew smoke in her direction, eyeing her flat belly skeptically.

"I can't tell."

"I'm lucky that way," she said. "I'm an ectomorph."

"Me too," Patrick said.

Richard nodded, agreeing with these assessments. It was a taxonomy used often on some of the dating sites he frequented, and he was becoming well versed in it.

Patrick motioned toward the cigarette in Courtney's hand. "You're smoking?"

"I hear some judgment from you. Judgment is a trigger for me."

"It's supposed to be."

"I just take a puff once in a while. When I'm stressed."

"Pregnancy isn't easy these days," Richard said, attempting conciliation.

"When was it ever easy?" Courtney said, lighting the cigarette. She inhaled once, exhaled pleasurably, and then stubbed it out under her sandal. "Your roommate came by the other day, Richard. He's a sweetie."

"Leslie?"

"He gave me a really big tip, like, *huge*."

"You know what they say about guys who leave big tips," Patrick said.

"He sat and talked to me for a while. He was sweet and he listened."

"Hard to believe," Richard said.

"I guess he's had a tough time? He had a bit of a smell, but you know, that's just the human body."

Richard knew the smell she was referring to—the greasy off-gassing of his long, dread-locking blond hair, combined with the odor of whatever it was he kept in his room that he never disposed of. After plunging into a depression following his comprehensive exams, Leslie was on an extended leave, with a blank ferment in his eyes that made you want to avoid confronting him about anything.

"Surprise, surprise," Courtney said, stuffing the cigarettes into her pocket. "Pasquale is watching. I better go."

Pasquale was the owner of Sloppy, an enigmatic figure in cargo shorts and Birkenstocks whom no one knew much about, except that he had once been exonerated of a grave crime in his home country. He was standing at the window now, watching them.

"Thanks for listening, guys. Have a good day."

"There's no baby in there," Patrick said once Courtney was gone.

"I know, but she gives me free coffee sometimes."

Patrick lit another cigarette. He relayed that he had gone dancing with Toller and the boys the night before. Out of all the people there—an illegally smoky, underground storage space—Patrick had been the tallest. Standing in the middle of the dance floor, lasers and lights raking his face, he'd hopped from foot to foot and rotated his head with a contemptuous sneer. *Aren't you the king of the castle?* Toller had screamed, and spanked him as he danced off to the bar to get more drinks.

"Doesn't he creep you out?" Richard asked.

Toller's appearance—his prematurely wrinkled face under peroxided hair, his lurid hands with their embossed network of veins—made Richard uneasy. "I mean, doesn't Valdes get jealous?"

"When we're alone he usually just sits on the sofa and rambles. I go through his closet. He *does* creep me out sometimes."

"Did he try something?"

"I'm big enough to sort of bat him away if he comes too close. But he didn't get the chance. We went back to the loft and he got into a fight with Barrett and they sort of fell down the stairs. Toller tore his jacket. He was limping around moaning that it was Gucci, and like, showing everyone the label."

Patrick said that Barrett had broken his ankle, but that he'd been too drunk to realize it until he woke up the next morning with a swollen leg. Richard was overcome with a familiar jealousy. If only he was an equal member of this group of young men who were so passionately attached to each other, instead of floating out on his own, tethered to them only by Patrick.

"I'm quitting therapy," Patrick said.

"Why?"

"It's too obvious. I can see exactly what the therapist is doing."

"What's he doing?"

"He's trying to link my present-day problems with a distant father and an overbearing mother and oh, I don't know, it's all such a yawn."

There it was: Richard hadn't even *started* therapy yet and Patrick was already finished.

"Sounds old-fashioned," Richard said, trying to retaliate somehow against Patrick but not having the right words and feeling too deflated to be effective.

"Whatever. I feel good these days. I'm having a lot of fun," Patrick said, and Richard nodded.

The barometric gloom, which had briefly lifted, settled on him again. It was foolish to expect any indulgent reassurance from Patrick, any sentimental or tribal preference; pointless to wait for a reprieve from the judgment that lurked, its snout to the ground. Yes, Patrick cared, but his concern revealed itself as a feature of his own invulnerability, an invulnerability he clearly thought Richard should simply take on himself. Commander Patrick made no concessions, Richard thought bitterly. His appraisal of any difficulty was always rational and proportional, the advice sensible and brutalizing. Instead of extending a hand to lift you onto the boat, he tossed out a life jacket and observed your technique. How many times had Richard wanted to scream at him, *I know what I should do, but can't you see that I'm miserable?* He knew that Patrick would consider any such declaration laughably dramatic and maudlin.

"I'm glad you're having fun," Richard said.

Patrick tossed his cigarette to the curb.

"I have to go," Patrick said. "Valdes is waiting for me."

SEVEN

Looking for a temporary solution to his immovable low spirits, Richard texted Anne two days later. Predictably, she was free. They spent the morning in the library, working on another paper, Anne so thrilled by their collaboration that she kept whispering loudly, nearly hissing.

"We're like monks copying manuscripts while the barbarians roam outside," she said. "On their phones."

Not so loud, Richard thought, gritting his teeth. He glanced around the crowded library, eyelids flickering with paranoid annoyance. What if Antonella walked in? Couldn't she be quiet?

"Yes, everyone should be reading Petrarch," he said with an edge to his voice.

Either not hearing or not acknowledging the sarcasm, Anne merely nodded.

When she left for one of the distant bathrooms, he was happy for the temporary peace. In her absence, he passed the time by clicking through a dating app. The inevitable tapestry of longing and disappointment filled the screen of his phone. The closest guy called himself the *Butt Police*.

'Cause I'm lookin' at your REAR!

Butt Police was only fifty feet away. Richard glanced around the library again, in search of a horny Cycloptic eye peeking out at him from behind a bookcase. Maybe someone wanted a hand job in the Chinese History section. But no, just like always, everyone was intent on their work except for him.

The next-closest guy was called *Size Queen. Girth wins!* he wrote.

Richard closed the app and inspected Anne's belongings, the taut silver wall of her computer screen, behind which the thinking happened. Signs posted around the library detailed recent thefts. He would karate-chop anyone who approached, or give them a hand job.

He was feeling increasingly sarcastic and bored. Despite an earlier resolution to tip the balance of work back in his direction, today was going just like the other days had gone: he made suggestions, Anne debated and considered them for a minute, batting them around like a dead mouse, before dropping them conclusively.

They weren't *that bad*, he thought, disgruntled.

She did praise him, he had to admit. She said that he could certainly do what she was doing. Whatever blockage he suffered from would surely afflict her at some point, and then she would come to him for the same kind of help. It was a mutually beneficial exchange, just a bit deferred. She sent him to faraway stacks to retrieve volumes by John Freccero, Elena Lombardi, and Benedetto Croce. Attentive, he was like a good assistant, ensuring she had water or coffee or snacks, which he went out to purchase with her credit card. And though Richard was convinced their arrangement was symbiotic—or, at the very least, that Anne didn't care if it was or wasn't—he nevertheless felt a sense of lurking worthlessness that threatened to eat away at this magnanimous conclusion.

But offsetting this feeling was yet another, an elusive sentiment somewhere between affection and desire, a movement that he felt in her presence, and a needling, distracting urge to know where she was, to keep tabs on her. It was a newly hatched feeling, a hazy yearning that tended to crowd out whatever annoyance or resentment he might have felt.

Anne returned from the bathroom, smiled at him, and went back to work. He watched her type with a gathering momentum, now admiringly, if not a little jealously, wishing he could join wherever it was she was going.

They stayed at the library for several more hours, and then went to a Vietnamese restaurant downtown for a late lunch. Anne said she wanted new sunglasses, so afterward they walked around the Lower East Side and SoHo looking in boutiques. Despite visiting a dozen places, she didn't find anything she liked. By four o'clock Richard was sick of the groups of shoppers and harried tourists crowding the sidewalks.

But he was also drawn into this comfortable and intimate annoyance. They hadn't spoken in over half an hour and it didn't seem to matter. They walked in a dazed, complacent silence, every once in a while bumping into each other, and each time it happened, he wondered if they might continue on like that, stuck together.

When meeting a friend or a loved one in Midtown or the Financial District or any other especially imposing section of the city, Richard sometimes got the feeling of a barely pulled-off heist of human closeness, of snatching something tender from the obdurate, unyielding air, the thickets of skyscrapers and the imperturbable density of concrete. The city could feel infinitely warm and welcoming, it wanted to endorse his presence, and yet he was the cold fish, the one who couldn't accept its lavish gifts.

Maybe if it had been up to him, and there were no consequences, he would have found himself somewhere else, at Urge or Eastern Bloc or another small gay bar. Then again, after the sputtering doggy paddles across the dating pool, which always left him shivering and cold, it was a relief to spend time with Anne. Just the few hours they'd passed together that morning in quiet, concentrated production had cast a calm and therapeutic air over the rest of the day. Anne's energy was jarring but invigorating, an inconclusive mix of maturity and immaturity. She was like a child let loose in the restraint and focus of an adult. But she was also like a mother who hands you a heavy towel and squeezes you after you've wrapped it around your shoulders, telling you to dry your hair because you lose heat through your head. At odd moments he found himself enchanted. As they stopped at a red light, he wanted to reach out and touch her face, stroke her hair. He caught himself glancing at her breasts. Perhaps it was for no other reason than that she was so novel, she was so unlike everyone else. Despite the epic and touted diversity of its population, the people he met in New York, the inevitable cul-de-sacs, one's career or one's social circles, could end up being dishearteningly similar.

They began walking north, and then Anne turned west. He followed without asking where they were going, but the destination became clear when she said, "You still haven't seen my new place."

"Oh, right."

"It's close by. We can stop and rest for a minute."

Since their meal in the French restaurant, several weeks ago now, Anne had not brought up the lazy Saturday proposal, but the details were still vivid in his mind: the gym, the pool, the sauna made from Japanese fir trees where he would be expected to disrobe.

As they traversed a narrow, shaded street he caught her reflection in a window: the dogged pout of her thin lips, the red curls puffed into a rampant yet controlled cloud, the bright blue shirt and black sunglasses she wanted to replace.

"I didn't mention this before," she said. "Erin and Alicia are staying with me while their apartment is fumigated."

"Why is it being fumigated?"

He already knew what the answer would be.

"They had bedbugs."

"You're not worried they'll bring them to your place?"

"What am I going to do, let them sleep on the street?"

In the lobby of the building, a doorman played a game on his phone at a thin glass desk.

"I'm still sort of moving in," she said as they stepped into the elevator.

They got out on the eleventh floor and walked to the far end of the hall, where the scent of a pungent flower lingered. The apartment was spacious, and minimally decorated. It was big enough that the kitchen had an island. There were cardboard boxes stacked in a corner, and a curtain was folded over the back of a chair.

Anne sniffed the air suspiciously.

"What's that smell?" she said loudly, as if she'd been waiting to accuse somebody of something and had found her opportunity.

The odor was familiar to Richard, yet he couldn't place it. They entered the large, comfortable-looking living room, full of sunlight.

His eyes adjusted, and he made out Erin reclining on the midcentury sofa, the first time one of those sofas had looked even remotely comfortable to him. Her pose was an extreme and studied, almost degenerate, relaxation. She could have been feeding herself grapes. As it was, she was reading a book.

"Erin, *what's* that smell?"

"The usual."

"Please open the windows if you're going to cook."

She didn't answer.

"Erin," Anne repeated. She was interrupted by the opening of the front door.

"Is it ready?" Alicia said, coming into the apartment and closing the door behind her. She had a bag of sprinkles in her hand.

"I hope you didn't pay for that," Erin said.

"Of course I didn't. I never pay for anything at Whole Foods." Alicia turned to Anne. "You haven't touched it, I hope?"

"Touched what?"

"Our cake."

"I wouldn't touch it with a stick."

"Look what the cat dragged in."

Richard waved limply.

"Still solving world hunger through Neoplatonism?"

"This is the best nondairy cream I've ever tasted," Alicia said, removing a bottle from a pocket in her cardigan.

Richard followed Anne into the kitchen, relieved to escape the abrasive chorus of Erin and Alicia. She opened the door to a large fridge. Inside, it was clean and white-walled as a laboratory, empty except for several bottles of Gerolsteiner water and a block of salted butter. On the wall beside it was affixed a chalkboard with a grocery list and an interrogative sentence in Spanish written across it.

Anne retrieved one of the bottles, took two glasses from the cupboard, and proceeded into her room. Richard followed, making sure to leave the door open a foot or two. The black-and-white photos of Greece had been remounted on the new walls; the abstract painting—

the swirl of black ink on a white background—had resumed a central position among them. On the bed, a single pristine pillow with a tasteful floral watercolor sat atop a large feathery comforter.

"Do you like this neighborhood?" he said, looking out the window at the leafy West Village street below. People were passing along the sidewalk with big white shopping bags.

"There are lots of tourists."

"And cupcakes."

She poured him a glass of fizzing water.

"Are you hungry?"

"I'm good."

"You're sure?"

He nodded.

"I never eat them," Anne said. "The sugar gives me a headache."

She got up, opened the window completely, and sat down again, this time closer to him.

"It can get loud with the window open," she said. "But I try not to use the air conditioner, for energy and environmental reasons."

"I like the sounds of people on the street."

"Sometimes they make me feel lonely."

"I think the noise of the city is comforting."

"I wanted to ask you something," she said. "My father's place on Martha's Vineyard is going to be free next month. I thought it would be fun to get out of the city. It's going to be so *humid* here, and the breeze is lovely. We could get a lot of work done."

Richard pictured them together in this opulent, hypothetical cottage, alone and with nowhere to go. He tried to lift the image up above his own flooding worry, like a man plucked from a rooftop before a large wave consumes it.

"I'll have to check my schedule." He swallowed. "But I'll let you know as soon as I know."

"You don't have to give me an answer now."

They both nodded. Something in the room deflated, and they were silent for a moment.

She turned toward him, and with the thumb and index finger of one hand lifted the glasses off of his face. With her free hand she removed her own and put his on.

"You're blind."

Staring at the blurry floor, he nodded.

"You look so different without the glasses," she said.

"You think?"

"With them on you're kind of, like, a child and an adult all at once."

"And without?"

"Just a child."

"Ha, okay."

"No, no," she said. "With them on you're kind of like some teenager who has become a professor too soon. It's your smooth pink skin."

He laughed.

"And these glasses," she said, handing them back to him.

He put them back on.

"I . . . can . . . see!"

She smiled, patting him on the knee.

"Just let me know whenever you can about the Vineyard," she said. "It would be fun."

Richard couldn't think of what else to say, so he just nodded, pretending to adjust the glasses. He wanted to stand up, but he felt that standing up would be insensitive, so he remained sitting.

It was a relief when Anne got up herself and walked over to the window. Feeling that it was perhaps prudent to mark a line in the sand, he asked, "Are you seeing anyone right now?"

She looked at him as if he'd said something ridiculous. "*Seeing anyone?* I'm not seeing anyone."

"It's tough to date in New York," he said, shaking his head, which felt exceedingly unnatural, like a bad performance.

Anne frowned, but didn't say anything. "Have you tried going online?" he continued, tumbling forward in this line of inquiry.

"No." Her voice was flat.

"One in five marriages begins online now," he persisted, hearing himself as if from a distance.

"To think those Stasi-types in California know what makes two people love each other," she snapped.

"You shouldn't dismiss it," he said.

"Why not? It's so robotic."

"There's always the possibility."

"Do you *actually* connect?"

"Lots of my friends met their significant others that way," Richard said.

"The modern world is so stupid."

"Your profile would be great." He felt that he could not stop now. "You're so articulate."

"I hate the Internet. Let's talk about something else." She turned her head toward the door. "Do you smell that? What are they doing out here?"

She walked out of the room. He stood up and followed. A plate of chocolate cake between them, Erin and Alicia were sitting on the sofa in the living room.

"It smells like something is burning," Anne said.

"We're not burning anything."

"What are you doing then?"

"We're comparing antidepressants."

"I'm surprised the fire alarm didn't go off."

Anne opened a window. Richard just stood there as they stared at him.

"Which antidepressants are you on?" he asked.

"Erin is on Lexapro. It targets ruminating."

Alicia was on something that made her jittery but did not prevent orgasm.

"Are you *really* talking about this?" Anne said, rolling her eyes.

"What *should* we be talking about?"

"Yes, please enlighten us, O Mistress."

"Not all of us have your 'inner resources,'" Alicia said, making air quotes and affecting a matronly accent.

"You're right," Anne said. "I don't know what I'm talking about."

"Did she really just admit that?" Erin said, turning to Alicia with an astonished expression.

They giggled.

"I don't know what I'm talking about even though my family has been single-handedly bankrolling GlaxoSmithKline for a generation."

Richard looked at Anne, and then at Erin and Alicia. They had a bulky agility and unity against which it was hard to maneuver. An abrupt and aggressive solidarity struck him.

"Did you get the school to implement the environmental policy?" he said, his voice ballooning slightly with a defensive grandiloquence.

"What? Oh, *that*. We've moved on to more important matters now."

"What could possibly be more important than that?" he declared rhetorically.

As if conscious now of a new adversary, they paused and appraised him. Behind them, Richard noticed again the chalkboard with the sentence scrawled in Spanish, question marks at either end.

"One of the question marks is supposed to be upside down."

"Do you speak Spanish?" Erin asked.

"No, but everyone knows how to punctuate a Spanish sentence."

"That's a pretty privileged thing to say."

"And who, exactly, is *everyone*? Do *you* speak for them?"

"And whom do *you* speak for?"

"*Lo siento*," Alicia said, and burst into laughter.

They smirked, as though itching to continue the argument, but also as if it was merely a test to recruit him to their debate team.

"Want some cake?" Erin asked.

"Actually, I should get going."

"We made tons. You can take some."

"I'm good, thanks."

"I'll walk you to the subway," Anne said.

"Stay here with us," Alicia said. "He can figure it out on his own. He's not a child."

"I need some fresh air," Anne said.

They took the elevator down and went outside, not talking. The evening was balmy and superb; the humidity had dissipated. Sometimes the city was so perfect.

"How can you live with them?" Richard said finally, shaking his head, as they made their way down the block.

"I like having someone else in the apartment," Anne said as they turned a corner.

Richard didn't say anything in response.

"Thanks for pointing out the incorrect punctuation," Anne said. "It has been bothering me for weeks, but I'm not allowed to say anything."

"What do you mean, not allowed?"

"They say I'm too critical. We came to an agreement that I would try to tone it down."

Richard rolled his eyes.

"You don't see them when we're alone. They're not so bad."

Anne said that she considered Erin and Alicia—she always thought of them collectively—one of those skeptics you keep close, an abrasive confidante who turns you into a sleeker, more illusionless version of yourself. They usually compensated for their testy carapace with a generosity and an occasional tenderness, a more expansive self that reminded her of those irascible genius protagonists of hospital dramas who have no bedside manner, yell at patients and condescend to colleagues, but who ultimately have the most profound humanity of all and find ways to cure incurable diseases.

"*God,*" Richard said at this gentle tirade.

"I'm making it sound worse than it is."

She was comforted by their presence. She had always been surrounded by autocratic women, felt the undertow of their moods—her mother's initially glum and then ecstatic persistence as she broke from Anne's father, her sisters and the adolescent mutability and insomnia that had leveled into professional accomplishment in one and in the other accelerated and detonated. It had a certain abusive and touching familiarity. Erin and Alicia were intimidating, yet reassuring.

Staring at the ground ahead as they walked, Richard nodded. He could admit that they had a certain charm. Their truculence reminded him, in a roundabout way, of Patrick, of the way he and Patrick would swiftly ally themselves against a common target if they were in a certain kind of belligerent mood. Richard remembered, as an undergraduate, giving an oral presentation in an anthropology class when a self-righteous and impudent boy accused him of "cognitive imperialism." From the back of the room, a previously unnoticed Patrick sprang to his defense, decrying the boy's "jingoism" and "Il Duce tactics." At which point, with tall, striking young Patrick on his team, Richard had been seized by a hawkish confidence. Over the next minute, they'd unleashed a volley on the poor boy that intensified until the professor stepped in to admonish them for using words like "nonsense" and "ridiculous" to describe the opinions of their fellow student.

Remembering, Richard smiled.

"I thought I wanted to live alone," Anne said, looking away. "But to be honest I was kind of relieved when they got bedbugs and had to move in. If they weren't living there," she said, "I'd be alone."

Richard nodded again but declined to add anything.

"Anyway, you need to write up the bibliography for the conference," Anne said, tapping him on the arm. "I'll send you the links. It's best if you're familiar with the sources, in case Antonella asks."

As they came to the end of the block, she detailed her method for the proposal: splitting the work into distinct but interrelated areas, such that they could plausibly act as collaborators without setting off alarm bells. Richard had contributed essentially nothing, but he figured he could give himself a pass again, if it meant a free trip to Montreal. It had been so long since he'd left New York. The last time had been to visit his parents, but that was over six months ago now. They were largely distracted by the blandishments of semiretirement anyway, and he hated to return, even for a night, to that bedroom that had become a storage space.

"Make any changes you want," she said.

"I doubt there will be any changes to make, Anne. I'm sure it will be perfect."

What had been bothering him about their collaboration—its entirely lopsided character—suddenly seemed less troublesome. Antonella was placated, and there was money in his bank account. What was there to complain about?

He swallowed.

"I'm looking forward to seeing Montreal," she said, smiling.

"I've read articles in *GQ* about the food scene."

The entrance to the subway was suddenly across the street.

"I'll let you go here," she said.

"Okay."

"And sorry about today," she said. "It felt like things took an odd turn."

"Don't apologize. I hope it wasn't my fault."

She shook her head, kissed him on the cheek, and squeezed his hand. Then she went around the corner and he waited for the light to change. The street was briefly a fabric of steel as a garbage truck sped past, then the previous medley of bank, salon, supplement shop, and bank was reasserted. Richard crossed the street. As he stepped onto the curb Erin and Alicia emerged from the Duane Reade directly in front of him, a container of Häagen-Dazs visible in a plastic bag swinging from Erin's wrist.

"We must have taken different routes," he said, eyebrows raised.

Alicia stepped forward.

"Whatever you're doing with Anne, be careful."

"What do you mean?"

"She's always falling for guys like you."

"*I'm* into guys."

"*Duh.*"

"Just, you're nothing special, okay?"

They turned and walked away, leaving Richard fastened to the ground, his limbs tingling. He was both enraged and pummeled. He didn't know what to do. Stand there and wave his hands in the air like a lunatic?

He turned and hurried down into the subway, his brow furrowed angrily.

Erin and Alicia didn't give anything to Anne. They gave her nothing, in fact, except a kind of condescending pressure. Why did they want to shove everyone into such a small, desperate, and separate space? You had to resist petty, ideological people like that. He would text Anne before bed just to say good night.

EIGHT

The Amtrak Adirondack train paused at the edge of Canada. For two hours customs officers, with pugnacious blankness, roamed the aisles, inspecting passports and demanding to see the last fifty debit transactions of a Ugandan woman.

When the train rolled forward again, the landscape was green but stark, a thin fuzz of spring accrued on trees and fields. Soon highways roped into knots and tall buildings appeared on the horizon.

"It's not that big," Anne said, craning her neck to look out the window as a cityscape gathered nearby. They were moving across a bridge, stretched over a wide slate river. "It used to be very Catholic here, but they beat back the church. Families of twelve children—that kind of thing."

There was a humping rhythm as they entered a tunnel.

"I don't know anything about it," Richard said, which wasn't entirely true. Though he'd let Anne take care of the accommodation, train tickets, and registration for the conference, he had done quite a bit of research around the restaurant scene—other people cooking him food gave Richard such a sense of security—which he'd heard described as one of the best in North America. There were a number of places he planned to suggest: one establishment where, in a saucy version of surf and turf, they stuck a lobster into the mouth of a pig, another where they served oysters on an old radio.

The train lurched to a halt. Passengers sprang from their seats and retrieved their bags. Anne's belongings were in a green leather weekender. Richard's luggage consisted of two canvas totes, one covered in flowers, the other advertising a jam from New Hampshire.

"This place looks worse than Penn Station," he said as they walked along the platform. The weekender swung cheerfully at Anne's side. It occurred to Richard that he could offer to carry it, but he did nothing with this thought.

"Nothing tops Penn Station except Port Authority. At Port Authority there are actually ghosts."

"Only four lines," Anne said as they looked at a subway map. "That should make it easy."

Commuters waited on their phones, having conversations in French, reading, or staring off into space. The next train wasn't for seven minutes.

"This has been a very long day," Anne said. "Let's take a taxi." The words rang beautifully in Richard's ears.

They sped north up an avenue lined on either side by shops and restaurants, staring out the windows like children.

The apartment was on a residential street of two- and three-story brick town-house structures. On the opposite side of the street there was a soccer field. Young men with muscular legs changed direction frequently and abruptly, yelling in Spanish. Richard followed Anne up a twisting exterior staircase that led to the second floor.

The initial impression of the rental was discouraging. A dark hall led to a kitchen and Richard walked into it with the feeling that he would encounter cobwebs. The cupboards were painted an ailing green and the floor seemed to sag. In one of the upper corners, something had recently gushed down from the ceiling—there was a rough gathering of plaster, like skin that had healed badly after a vaccination.

"Welcome to the Four Seasons," he said.

"Their rating is going down," Anne said. "*Down.*"

"I second that."

With a more focused sense of something not being right, Richard surveyed the rest of the apartment.

"Where's the other bedroom?" he asked.

"It's a one-bedroom," Anne said.

"Is there a foldout?"

He glanced into the living room, but he couldn't tell whether the grim tumuli of the sofa was equipped with the hoped-for feature.

"The bed is queen-sized."

He paused, looking at her, his eyes affably but hesitantly wide.

"Oh, right. But I don't want to crowd you."

Anne had an expression of mounting disarray on her face. She was going through her bag. She stopped what she was doing and looked at him.

"Sleep in the bed," she insisted.

Imagining the nocturnal cluster of their two bodies, he smiled tightly. "Sure. Lots of room."

He watched her as she walked across to the counter.

"Look at this."

It was a bottle of red wine with a pink ribbon tied around the neck, with a note from the owner of the apartment. She picked it up.

"Let's open it," Richard said, happy at the appearance of this tranquilizing agent.

"Right now?"

"Why not?"

The sun was beginning to set. Wineglasses in hand, they stepped through a door off the kitchen, out onto a small deck that overlooked a disorganized garden.

"The bed isn't bad," Anne said. "It's comfortable. I sat on it."

"Great," Richard said, smiling blandly and nodding. "An uncomfortable bed would really ruin their rating."

He took a large sip of wine.

"I wonder if all the houses look like this one inside."

"I wonder," Anne said, putting the glass to her lips. "Too bad for them."

They drank most of the bottle. By the time ten o'clock came around they were both quiet with fatigue. They took turns in the bathroom. Richard had forgotten pajamas, which for a moment had him panicked. But the wine was having a settling effect, and when he came into the bedroom, the light was already off. A slight glow from the window showed Anne lying on her back, the sheet up to her neck, staring at the ceiling.

"It's comfortable," she said.

Richard removed his clothes. In the dark, his white briefs seemed to glow.

To his relief, she did not move when he got into bed beside her. He closed his eyes and resisted the urge to open them again. He worried that if he did, he would see her staring at him, and they would have to reckon with their proximity. Whenever he shifted positions, he did so with an onerous consideration. He only realized that he had fallen asleep when he woke up in the middle of the night and heard an animal skittering across the floor above his head. Without his glasses on, the room was blurry in the dark, the streetlamp beyond the window a buttery blot. The smell of cigarettes drifted in through the open window. He was aware of Anne getting up and leaving the bedroom, the flushing of a toilet, and her return.

It was morning the next time he opened his eyes; sunlight saturated the thin curtains. He got up and put his clothes on. Out in the living room he pulled the curtains aside. On the street below a woman passed by, muttering to herself and holding a shattered mirror. He opened the window. A misty spring warmth hung in the street.

He went into the kitchen and poured himself a glass of water. Anne emerged from the bathroom in a cloud of perfumed steam.

"How did you sleep?" she asked.

"Fine."

He rubbed his eyes, his body aching in the aftermath of keeping straight and circumspect all night, of having avoided an unintentional annexation of her half of the bed.

"You're a heavy sleeper," she said.

"I guess so."

If not through an open-eyed surveillance while he slept beside her, how had she arrived at that conclusion?

They had breakfast at a nearby café, and then took the subway to the McGill campus, an obstacle course of backpacked students. At the end of a paved drive there was a pillared building with a green copper roof. A red and white flag palpitated on a cupola, against a backdrop of hardening blue sky. Two shirtless guys played Frisbee on the grass.

"Bulletproof glass was invented here," Anne said. "I read it on Wikipedia."

"Huh."

They went into a library, made with the thick concrete of another architectural era. A large poster board on an easel indicated the conference was being held upstairs.

They took an elevator up one floor. Beside the entrance to the conference room there was a curly-haired blond guy with a pink snub nose in a black T-shirt and jeans.

"It's fifty dollars each for registration," he said, with friendly authority. "*Canadian.*"

Anne handed the guy some cash and they walked inside. They sat down beside each other at the head of the conference table, and Richard arranged his face into an expression of scholarly vehemence. Anne had printed off a sheet for him to read from. They were introduced, and then presented in fluid counterpoint. Sections were arranged to seem extemporaneous, to give the impression of sudden insights, as though their real-time dialogue had led them out to new, previously unknown suburbs of analysis. Richard recognized three points he had made about Boccaccio in a discussion they'd had on the train. This made him feel better about his participation in the event. Anne smiled at him and nodded. Afterward the small audience clapped.

They sat dutifully through several other presentations before breaking for lunch.

"What did you think?" she said as they stood up.

"I liked that one guy's reading of Machiavelli."

"Counterintuitive. A peacemaker?"

Outside, the sun was high and bright. They put on their sunglasses.

"I included your points about Boccaccio and Pasolini," she said as they walked through the campus. "I'm sure you noticed."

"Thanks."

Even when she was being generous she couldn't help the inadvertent condescension, he thought. He chose not to focus on it.

"They were relevant," she continued.

"Relevant might be a stretch, but I appreciate you including them."

"Where should we go for lunch?"

He scrolled through a list in his head. The Ritz was just a few blocks away, and had recently been colonized by a celebrity French chef. Perhaps that was too shameless. He opted to let Anne decide and press his own agenda at dinner.

"We'll find something."

On the crowded sidewalk of Saint Catherine Street their moods wilted.

"Everything looks terrible," she said.

They gave up and chose a sushi restaurant that proved disappointing, which Richard thought was a waste, as if Anne were somehow to blame.

After several more hours of presentations, they decided to look around again in the hopes of eventually finding something better for dinner. A few blocks east they went into a secondhand bookstore. They browsed, visited a coffee shop, and then descended out of curiosity into the brightly lit, air-conditioned underground corridors of the shopping district that lay beneath the downtown. Young men in gray and black singlets and bulky high-top sneakers gossiped in groups and walked hand in hand with tall young women wearing dark sunglasses. A global cast of retail workers looked on with boredom.

Outside again, a pleasant light filtered down through the trees; Richard felt like he was in South America, though he'd never been there. They walked, enjoying that particular pleasure of being with another person and not feeling compelled to break the silence.

"Do you think you could move here, if the government ever became too extreme?" Richard asked eventually, imagining a scenario in which they didn't return to New York but continued to live there as exiled scholars, new lives in that decrepit but cozy apartment, working on their French.

"It's already too extreme."

"You could have a nice life, I bet. How is your French?"

"It's good," she said.

"Why did I even ask?"

They walked to a grassy park pinpointed by a tall statue of a winged woman. Nearby a group of nerdish-looking young men pretended to do battle with makeshift swords.

"I think it would be invigorating to move to another country," she said. "Abandon your past—that sort of arc."

"Shed your identity and become a new person? Is that even possible for you?"

"Why wouldn't it be?"

A PARTY WAS THROWN that night for the conference attendees. It was a motley assemblage of academic-looking types in ties, round glasses, and long, hip-hugging sweaters. When they arrived, Anne fell into conversation with one of the organizers, and Richard wandered around, listening in on knots of people. Pot smoke gray-braided the air. He entered the kitchen in search of a drink. There were bowls of guacamole along the counter, beside torn-open bags of corn chips.

The blond guy with the pink snub nose, the conference sentry, was at the sink washing dishes. Waiting to be noticed, Richard stood behind him.

"Great presentation today," the guy said finally, looking over his shoulder.

"Oh, thanks," Richard said. "Do you usually wash dishes at parties?"

"I'm trying to sober up. I'm supposed to *drive*."

"Is there anything to drink in here?"

It had been a pleasant day, and Richard's confidence was unfurled and plumed.

"I can make you a gin and tonic. That's all that's left."

"I've been drinking beer, but okay."

Splashing equal amounts of the two ingredients into the glass, the young scholar prepared the drink. Richard took a sip and almost gagged.

"That's robust, thanks. I'm Richard."

"Hi, Richard. I'm Jay."

"Thanks, Jay."

They shook hands.

"Want to have a cigarette with me on the fire escape?" Jay asked.

Richard smiled at this unexpected invitation.

"Sure."

The level of Jay's drunkenness became evident as he moved irregularly out the window.

"Put your foot there," Richard said. Jay paused in a long, uncertain foot-to-foot arc, half inside and half outside the apartment. "There you go."

Holding on to a crusty metal grating, Richard climbed out after him. He looked up at the mountain, a hump in the middle of the city. On top, an enormous crucifix glowed.

"It's sort of flat for a mountain," he said. "It's very Catholic here, right?"

"I think so," Jay said. "I'm not from here."

"The food is good, though?"

"There's a Scandinavian café a few blocks away. You can get cod-fish poutine. How does that sound?"

"Good, I guess."

"What have you been eating?"

"Nothing spectacular," Richard said, thinking with regret that he hadn't yet succeeded in getting Anne to take him to any of the note-worthy restaurants in the city.

"Really?"

Richard shook his head, then leaned leftward to kiss Jay.

Jay stepped back defensively but smiled. "Can I rinse my mouth out first?"

"Sure. Whatever works."

"Back in a second."

Jay flopped into the kitchen and went out the door. Richard fol-lowed him inside, propping himself against the fridge, puffed up by his own intrepid moves. He awaited the trajectory of the next few mo-ments in a state of hazy acquiescence.

The door opened again and Anne came in.

"Where did you go? I've been looking all over." She squeezed his arm. "I'm having a good time. Do you need a drink?"

She had an empty glass in hand with a slice of lemon in it.

"I'm good," he said, holding up his noxious gin and tonic. He laid his arm across her shoulders. "Meet anyone interesting?"

"Simon—who presented on Tasso. He's charming, but kind of goofy."

Her eyes were foggy and glimmering.

"Did you get his number?" Richard asked.

Anne frowned.

"Why would I get his number?"

"To call him."

She removed Richard's arm and went toward the counter.

"I'm not going to call *him*. Is there any more guacamole? I've been sent to find it."

Jay came back into the kitchen.

"I'm ready." He noticed Anne and smiled. "Oh, hey. Great work today."

"Ready for what?" she said, looking back and forth between them.

"Anne is on a mission for guacamole."

"There are more avocados over there," Jay said, demurely using his hand to stifle a burp.

Richard consumed the last metallic dregs of his drink and coughed.

"I can make you another but let's go outside first," Jay said. "It's getting hard to breathe in here."

"Why are you going outside?" Anne asked.

"To smoke."

"Then I'll join you," she said.

"You smoke cigarettes?" Richard asked.

"Simon does. I'll go get them."

Anne left the kitchen, and Jay led Richard back out to the fire escape. When they were both standing in the open air, but in the dark, shadowed like homosexuals in a rendezvous of an earlier era, Jay smiled broadly and kissed him.

Richard interrupted their contact by putting a finger to his lips.

"Can we get to the ground from here?" he asked quietly, looking out over the railing.

"We can climb down the fire escape," Jay whispered.

One behind the other, they descended to the sidewalk. A group of partygoers were smoking beside the front door, a wig of smoke stretched over their heads. Richard and Jay decided to split a cigarette. Halfway through the cigarette, Anne emerged from the doors behind them.

"Where did you go?" she demanded. "I looked for you on the fire escape."

"We decided to come down here," Richard said, making up this excuse on the spot. "We didn't feel safe up there."

"You didn't hear me? I've been looking for you."

"We came down here."

She looked at Jay.

"Thank you for organizing the party."

"I didn't organize the party."

She turned and began walking, a small, decisive body moving swiftly down the block.

"Where are you going?" Richard said.

She didn't answer.

"Sorry," he said to Jay, tossing the cigarette to the curb. Jay watched it wheel through the air and scatter sparks. "I've got to go."

Richard hurried and caught up to her at the end of the block. She was quick on her feet.

"What are you doing?"

"Why are you apologizing to him? You left *me* all alone."

She walked with her arms tensed by her side, like a child about to pummel someone ineffectually.

"You were talking to Simon. I thought you were talking about Tasso."

"I didn't want to talk to *him* about *that*."

The street was deserted. Their argument reverberated against the reticent jowls of darkened storefronts. Richard was embarrassed.

"I wanted to talk to you."

"I wanted to talk to you too," he said, but even as he hurried along beside her, he was skeptical of his own pursuit.

She didn't respond. They went in silence for another block.

"It didn't seem so," she said finally.

When they arrived back at the apartment, Anne went into the bedroom and closed the door. Richard stood in the kitchen, his hands hanging limp like dead fish against his thighs. He sat down at the kitchen table, opened up his laptop, and compulsively refreshed his email and some newspapers, but he didn't absorb anything.

After a few minutes, he walked over and tapped on the door to the bedroom.

"Can I come in?"

There was no answer. He slowly pushed open the door. Anne was lying in bed in the dark, a porch light from across the yard split into sharp slats over the dune of her body. He removed his shirt and pants and got into bed beside her.

In the morning she had already left for the second day of the conference. Richard's head pounded. He stepped out of the bedroom with a salacious feeling of disclosure at being in his underwear in the apartment of a stranger, mixed with an awareness that a hangover was being tuned in his brain and would soon play like a Bartok concerto in the nursery of a sleeping baby.

He sent Anne a text:

YOU LEFT WITHOUT ME.

There was a croissant on the table, dry and armadillo-like. He drank two glasses of water, and then got back into bed with the croissant, but he couldn't fall asleep. In the adjacent backyard, a man watered the garden and sang to himself. Richard got up and left the room again and sat on the sofa in his underwear, surveying the grimy apartment with a sense of dissipated consternation.

An hour later, Anne texted back.

YOU WERE ASLEEP.

HOW ARE YOU? he responded immediately.

She sent an emoticon indicating a headache.

ME TOO, he wrote back. **HOW DID YOU SLEEP?**

NOT WELL.

ME NEITHER.

When nothing further came, he wrote again:

CAN I TAKE YOU OUT TO LUNCH?

He suggested Chinatown, because Chinatown would be cheap.

OKAY. WHEN?

They met at the edge of the neighborhood an hour later. The sun was driving and acute. Wearing dark glasses, they walked in a ponderous silence.

"I'm disappointed you didn't come today," she said finally.

"You could have woken me up."

"I thought you were invested in all of this."

"I'm hungover, that's all. I drank a lot last night."

"But you know how important this is to me," she said.

When something was important to her, did that mean everyone else's life had to flatten out and disappear? Did everyone have to be good? Was he not allowed to get drunk and sleep in if something was important to Anne?

They chose a restaurant at random. When they sat down, she sighed heavily.

"We're both in fantastic moods, aren't we?"

Richard scanned the menu. The curtain over the window jerked limply.

"We'll feel better when we eat something," he said, not looking up.

"You didn't miss much this morning," she said. "Anyway."

"I'm sure you asked some devastating questions."

"Maybe," she said.

She described an example of the mediocre command of the literature she'd detected in one of the conference participants.

"Mostly I couldn't be bothered though."

"Probably better for them."

Soon they were plopping greasy pieces of duck into their mouths. For dessert they had bubble tea. Richard paid the bill. With the exchange rate significantly in favor of the American dollar, it was negligible. They strolled through the neighborhood, going from store to store. Anne spotted a pair of satin slippers. Richard bought them for her. Then he bought himself a key chain attached to a small pagoda. She saw an embroidered fan she liked and he bought that for her too.

At the Old Port they bought iced coffees and walked down to the river.

"I feel like I could drink an endless cup of coffee right now," he said. "I feel like I have a hole in my stomach."

"Me too. Thank God we don't have to make small talk."

"Thank God."

He laughed and looked at her, and wanted to squeeze her.

They linked arms, walking in a zigzag pattern out of the Old Port and through a neighborhood of seedy commercial strips. They were dazed to be somewhere uncharted, anonymous claimants to the block along with the actual residents of the city.

They passed into a gay area of the city, indicated by a series of pillars in rainbow colors above the entrance to the subway station and signs for "Le Village." Richard noted to himself the same hoary retail that he had seen elsewhere: a store that specialized in crochet; a shawarma place; a French bookstore; a travel agency whose door was plastered with rhapsodic descriptions of the Danube. Men in singlets and shorts made prolonged eye contact with him as they passed. It was a silent pleasure—a pleasure he did not voice—to have his attractiveness endorsed and acknowledged on the streets of a new city.

Anne pointed to a store window.

"You would look good in that sailor shirt."

"Too many middle-aged women wear them."

"You think?"

"I'm always afraid I'm going to run into a rich seventy-two-year-old woman on her way to the golf course who is dressed exactly like me."

"Unlikely."

"You never know. When I'm a middle-aged woman, I'll dress like a middle-aged woman," he joked.

She squeezed his arm. Another man went past, gawking boldly. She pulled at the hem of her shirt, fanning herself.

"I didn't realize it would be so hot here."

"It's not the Arctic," he said.

"I didn't think it was."

"Do you want to go back to the apartment?"

"Not yet."

"What should we do?"

Anne thought for a moment.

"Let's go swimming," she said.

"Where are we going to do that?"

Richard thought of the lazy-Saturday proposal, an offer he had never taken her up on.

"I was reading about a pool in one of the guidebooks. It looked beautiful. It's not far," she said, already heading toward the subway.

"What do we do about swimsuits?"

"I'll buy us some there."

They went for several stops, found their way to the pool and an adjoining shop that sold athletic gear. Richard picked out a pair of boxy shorts.

"We're in another country," Anne said, lifting a red Speedo off the rack.

Richard shook his head.

"But it's my treat."

"I don't know," he said, taking the swimsuit in hand.

"Abandon your past."

It was a ludicrous proposal, but oddly enough he liked the idea of being voluptuous and exposed in the suit while Anne watched.

Without waiting for an answer, Anne took the swimsuit and went to the cashier.

At the pool, Richard emerged from the changing room feeling like the protagonist of a public-service self-esteem campaign.

He held a towel over his crotch and kept his eyes on the ground. Anne was in an athletic black one-piece. They went to a corner of the pool deck and spread out their belongings.

"We have to put sunscreen on. I'll put some on you first."

Richard lay down on his stomach. Casting his head into shadow, she knelt beside him. He felt a cold squirt on his back, her hands moving in concentric circles, ranging up and down his back, the length of his legs. She worked the lotion between his toes and over the soles of his feet, her touch supple but direct. For a moment Richard thought—what luck it was, to be one of the organisms that is taken care of and not devoured.

He got up and she lay down on her front. He smoothed the sunscreen into her shoulders, then around into the scoop of her back, gliding down her legs, greasy and bright, to her feet. Her body trembled.

What am I doing? he thought, and almost stopped himself. All the people splayed around the pool, with their glistening skins and dark sunglasses, were sure to think that he and Anne were a couple, if they cared to think anything about them, or maybe some of them noted his swimsuit and thought differently. Why did that matter? He could get a raging sense of claustrophobia when a woman, one of his female friends, was affectionate with him in public, when he felt he was being blocked off from some more authentic kind of attention. It was almost a political sense of indignation and entrapment, like someone deprived of an education. They were shutting him off from his potential. But why was it more authentic? *Was* it more authentic?

"I think that's good," she said.

Their arms brushing together, he lay down again, eyes closed. At the edge of his perception a baffling conversation, accented French spoken too quickly, spun in place like a whirlpool, alluring and incomprehensible. The sun anointed his back and he felt dazed. They lay there for some time. Finally Anne got up and stepped into the pool. Richard watched her go and then stood up himself, starkly vertical. From the water she watched him, her attention indiscreet, the water heaving leniently around her waist.

He stepped into the water and submerged himself. The cool of it mitigated a headache that was beginning to knot at the back of his head. He went forward under the water, surfaced, and floated away from her. The swimsuit breaking the surface, he drifted on his back. Their movements felt free and arbitrary, but also immaculate, as if choreographed from above. She breast-stroked in a curve around him.

When their eyes met, she splashed him with water.

A line of athletic young men, in a mirage-like procession, their rippling silhouettes crammed into swimsuits even smaller than Richard's, passed by en route to the competition pool. Richard turned onto his stomach and watched. Anne looked over, and they both gawked.

RICHARD CONTINUED TO FLOAT in his odd mood. After returning to the apartment in a taxi, a shower, and another taxi to the restaurant, he felt vacant and serene, rinsed of worry and initiative by the long day in the sun. The menu at the restaurant Anne chose for dinner was like the preamble of a serial killer experimenting with animals before making the leap to humans. One dish consisted of a pig with a fork driven through its skull. Richard opted for a pig's foot stuffed with foie gras. Anne ordered the magret de canard.

Anne's dish arrived in a can. The waiter turned it upside down and the glistening food slid out and fell in a wobbly tower onto her plate. It made Richard think of dog food.

"Do you think we got sunstroke?" he said, cutting into the foot. "I feel out of it."

"I'm okay."

"I should drink more water."

He took another sip of wine.

"Want to try this?" Anne said.

"Sure."

He leaned forward and bit the tendered meat from her fork. Outside, the occasional car rolled past on the cobblestoned pedestrian street, like a tank in the warfare of the evening.

"You looked great today," she said, smiling. "I hope you don't mind me saying so?"

"That's delicious. No, it's fine," he said. "I mean, whatever."

There *was* something intolerable about her saying so—unbearable in its candor and exposure. For a moment they ate with concentration, the artfully displayed food steadily decimated.

"You looked great too," he said. "Is that okay to say?"

She did look great—it was that end-of-the-summer-day disheveled blooming sheen, her hair extra springy and curly, the tanned scoop of her exposed chest.

"I haven't reached a definitive conclusion."

"Well, let me know when you figure it out."

Richard looked for his water glass, but it was still empty.

"I bet you killed it at the conference today," he said, feeling himself slip into a new gear of intimacy. "I bet you annihilated *everyone*."

"Do you have to put it that way?"

"You like a more peaceful rhetoric?"

He felt as though they were on a stage somewhere.

"Maybe I don't. I bet I did kill it, with my questions. I guess I'm the . . . *annihilator*."

She snorted.

"That's your new nickname."

"I know I'm strong," she said, more seriously now. "I'm stronger than my family. I'm stronger than my father. I've always had to be."

"You're stronger than me."

"I don't know. We're strong in different ways."

She poured more wine into his glass, and then into her own.

"I'm not strong," he said.

"Why should strength be the measure of anything?" she said.

It wasn't exactly the response he was looking for.

"Right," he said.

She laughed—her normally serious, erudite face curled under a childish steam of emotion. With the napkin she wiped her eyes. He wasn't exactly sure what she was laughing about.

"There's some enormous basilica here that looks like an Italian futurist temple," she said. "I want to see it."

"Let's go."

"Did you grow up with religion?" she asked.

"Not really."

"You didn't go to church?"

"Once in a while," Richard said. "My parents are like, orbiting Unitarians. They're out there . . . I don't even know if they believe in God. I think they believe in St. Anselm's proof for the existence of God."

"It's abstract."

"No, the opposite. It's more, like, clambakes and picnics, that kind of thing. The best part is, the church has this yellow Jeep Cherokee with 'Love' painted on the door with a rainbow underneath it. Whenever I visit they want me to ride in it but I always say no. I think they drive it as penance for any awkwardness when I came out."

His whole body shrank. For a moment, he couldn't raise his head from the plate. It was the first time he had stated this outright in her presence, shifted the information from the liquid realm of unvoiced context to hard syllabic life. He looked up slowly. Anne was gazing into her wine with a mild but inscrutable expression.

"And my father likes the singing," he said, by way of conclusion, choosing to leap, almost coughing out the words.

Anne nodded, though it might have been in agreement with one of her own thoughts.

"I envy religious people," she said, her previous tone unchanged. She was still looking into her glass. She took another sip.

"When they're not killing each other," Richard said, deciding to move along in the conversation with her.

"Even when they *are* killing each other," she said quickly and brightly, now looking up at him with a smile.

He smiled back.

"You're enjoying that wine," he said, his voice excitable. He felt quite drunk now.

"Yes I am," she said, cheerfully. "And so are you."

She seemed not to want to pursue the topic. He would follow her lead. He decided to keep drinking the wine, and to encourage her to drink too.

The sliced-up ruins and smears of their plates were taken away. For dessert Anne had lemon meringue pie, and Richard something called milkshake XXX. Then the waiter brought digestifs, followed by espresso. Anne paid and they left the restaurant.

"Let's get another drink," Richard said when they were standing on the street.

"Good idea," Anne said. They started walking. "We're going to feel terrible tomorrow," she said breezily.

"I brought aspirin," Richard said, extending his arm and taking her hand, and then winding them down the street toward a bar that was attractively disgorging people onto the sidewalk.

Along the block of iron staircases that plunged gently from stone facades, the innards of the restaurants were exposed. They went into a wine bar and huddled together on a banquette, squished in with others.

"That shirt," Richard said, nodding with endorsement as he brought the glass to his wine-stained lips. "It looks great on you. You should wear it more often."

"You like it?"

She looked down at the shirt.

"It's a nice cut."

"A low cut," he said.

"It is."

Anne laughed. They had to scream into each other's ears to be heard, and they kept brushing their lips against each other's cheeks and ears.

When they left the wine bar, they made their way to the curb in search of a cab. Richard steadied himself against a tree.

"Can you flag down cabs here?"

"*I* can," Anne said, theatrically stepping out onto the street. She stuck an arm into the air and, like magic, a taxi stopped.

Air poured in through the open windows of the speeding cab. Anne nuzzled against him, her nose in the crook of his neck, while the radio blared in French. They giggled and whispered to each other.

"I love the accent here," she said.

"I can't make it out."

When they arrived and climbed up the stairs, their drunk legs heavy on the wooden slats, Anne pushed Richard from behind, her hand cupping one of his butt cheeks.

"Be careful," she said.

"You be careful," he said, laughing. "I might fall on you."

"You're not that heavy."

"I'm *heavy*."

Suddenly, they were unpeeling their clothes, toppling into the bedroom. They got into bed and Anne struggled up onto Richard's chest, her groin like a frame above his torso. She kissed him on the mouth, a kiss that was more expert and adroit than he'd expected. A bolt of current surged through his lower body. They were both sweating and the room was stifling. Then his hand was sliding inside her pants, and she reached to unbutton his fly, once again with a confidence and competence that surprised him, and took out his cock. Like a group of dancers clumped in a hot, loud room, searching for space, his thoughts lurched from stasis to glee and back again. He thought of an article he'd read about cows getting squeezed before they are slaughtered, that it calms them and preserves the meat. Increasingly unskillful and enthusiastic, they burrowed toward each other. As her mouth moved down his body, each thought seemed shadowed by a barometer that measured its strangeness, importance, and intensity. But the barometer kept offering up disparate readings, flares of frenzied energy and inertial dips.

He seemed to be moving and then he was still; he was floating and he was falling; he was trapped and he was free.

NINE

Back in New York, several days passed and Richard heard nothing from Anne. He was surprised by the feeling of bitter neglect, the swollen rejection that finally shrank to a sore lump of regret. He didn't know if he should write to her first. A restless confusion came over him. Was she embarrassed? Did she feel differently about him now? There had been no awkwardness or regret afterward. She had even complimented him on his sexual skill. Despite their awful hangovers, the train ride back had felt light and oddly uncomplicated, as if now that the important matter had been settled with no catastrophe in its wake, the world still functioned, and there was a new, straightforward momentum to things.

In Montreal her body had been delirious and happy, feral like a small zebra hopping around a lake that has finally replenished at the end of a drought. The evidence that she had not been touched in a long time, her scrambling maneuvers and chaotic breathing, mixed themselves with a natural refinement, a composure and prowess, and the erect, tensile but soft antennae of her empathy, like headlights sweeping up and down his body, assessing its needs and tailoring her behavior to his own. She was lonely, desperately so; but so was he. And now there were scratches on his back.

In this grumpy negligent aftermath, he attempted to distract himself by cleaning, reading, making ultimatums about not going on the Internet, and taking walks. Avoiding the humped specter of Leslie on the couch, he bought cigarettes and smoked out the window of his bedroom. Now that it was early June, the panels of spring sudsy and transparent, the streets were filling with pugnaciously underdressed young people looking for patios and beer gardens. They passed below the window in their shorts and sleeveless T-shirts, unaware of Richard's eyes angled down on them, like a lonely old man as he waits for his popcorn to inflate in the microwave, the black elaborate tattoos spiraling out on arms and backs, absorbing the sunlight.

This morbid rhythm was broken when Patrick invited Richard over for brunch. Brunch was always a rescue of sorts, Richard thought, whether it was from the confusion and regret of a hangover, the intolerable presence of a roommate, or just the general despair of Saturdays. Brunch at Patrick's apartment—eggs Benedict or burritos or lox and bagel, or some leaning peppery construction accompanied by mimosas and croissants from down the block—was also one of their long-standing routines. Now that Valdes was in the picture, however, they hardly ever kept to it. Still, Richard didn't begrudge Patrick his warm exclusionary weekends in bed with his boyfriend. He too would have abandoned his best friend to a cold-cut sandwich, bowl of cereal, any beggarly survival-mode food, for just that.

Patrick was standing at the stovetop, whipping eggs, when Richard arrived.

"I'll be using a whole clove of garlic," he said by way of a greeting.

A cool organic odor drifted in through the window from the shaded garden below.

"Oh, fun," Richard said, sipping the last watery inch of the iced latte he'd picked up at Sloppy on the walk over. He'd bought one for Patrick too, which Patrick accepted with a hug. The *New York Times* was spread out on the table. Patrick always got a paper copy of the weekend edition. His loyalty to print was charming, if perhaps uncharacteristically quixotic.

As he sat down, Richard glanced at the predictably depressing headlines, but his head wasn't in the news today, if ever it was. Entering the apartment, he'd been struck by how strange it was to come here, into Patrick's kitchen, and not to tell him about Anne, to rely on the arbitrary and precarious barrier of his own silence. Patrick was sensitive to withheld information; it was like having a polygraph machine as a best friend, which naturally made things hazardous. Richard knew that Patrick would think what had happened a moral abnegation on the scale of a Russian novel. Why was it that Patrick usually saw Richard as an aggressor, attributing to him the agency and power that Patrick himself possessed? Was it possible that Patrick saw it as flattery?

Maybe if Richard could be more like what Patrick thought he was, he might gain a greater foothold in his life. There had to be some maneuver, some final gesture in a series, that other people knew about and employed to organize things, to make everything fall into place.

Or maybe it was just a convenient way for Patrick to esteem his own behavior.

"Do you want the rest of my latte?" Patrick asked, still whipping the eggs. "I've already had too much coffee."

"Sure."

Richard took it and hauled through the straw. There must be a psychoanalytical category for people like Patrick, for people like Anne, he thought, and the spaces they took up in your life. He felt a pang of neurotic excitement, a tense expectation whenever he thought of Patrick and his competence, and he wondered if Anne had any equivalently ambiguous experiences from her college years, any shadow figure on whom she projected so many possibly fictitious or pointless yet compelling romantic and sexual hopes. It didn't seem possible. She was too direct and also too aloof. The image that prevailed of her life before Richard knew her was a solitary figure in a grand library, shoeless and curled up in a chair, with a plastic bag of carrots at her fingertips. A grand celestial light formed above her, a glowing gash, as if the sky and then the roof had opened so a saint could descend and tell her that she belonged there. Her destiny was to be the lonely seeker of truth, and she nobly accepted.

Now Patrick and Anne both walked through Richard's mind, like visitors at either end of a vast estate, their footsteps echoing in cavernous rooms. There had been the night in college Patrick had first offered to come and cook Richard dinner, and the exchange that had ensued upon Patrick's arrival to the studio, which at the time Richard considered very chic, due to the staggered black-and-white postcards of movie stars, dead writers, and retro bodybuilders affixed to the walls.

"Do you have a mixing bowl?" Patrick had asked.

"No."

"Do you have butter?"

"No."

"Do you have salt and pepper?"

Thanks to a nearby market, and the fact that Patrick loved impressing people with his cooking skills, the meal was rescued. Patrick quelled Richard's anxiety by dismissing his lack of basic ingredients with a nonchalant shake of the head and reframing it as an enviable and ecologically responsible lifestyle. But Richard knew that his incompetence had been exposed. Though for the rest of the evening Patrick behaved without noticeable deviation from his usual cultivated and placid distraction, stretching his sinewy body across the bed and flipping through Richard's books, flexing his vascular hands, speaking with attractive precision, shortly after that evening they stopped hanging out.

In the weeks that followed, with the penumbra of the meal lending his surroundings a chiaroscuro frailty, Richard studied the withering stream of communication, Patrick citing the workload in preparation for his qualifying exams and other onerous application requirements for various doctoral programs. Richard went over what had been said in text and email, clicking away, attempting to ascertain why Patrick had detached, with a sinking feeling noting the elongating delays between texts that were distilling quickly into negligent monosyllables, like grains of salt left at the bottom of a jar.

Did Patrick perceive relative poverty or incompetence in the walls checkered with postcards, in the bed barely off the ground, in the old electric teakettle, rusting on the bottom, that left a brown ring on the table if you forgot it there for any length of time?

You're not a provider. It was Patrick's instinct to flee from all ineptitude, if not from the incipient feelings that he must have sensed coming from Richard.

They'd come back together at the end of the year, immediately before graduation. Richard was still bruised by what had happened—the damage throbbed, buried too deep to massage—but he couldn't react any other way than to forgive Patrick and step back into friendship. Without even realizing it, he'd decided that he wanted Patrick in his life no matter what. Patrick said that he regretted they hadn't seen more of each other, now that they would no longer be living in the same place. It was a sad time to reunite, as immediately after, Richard went back to Europe, to wind up in residence at a hostel, and Patrick migrated a few hundred miles south to the city.

Today, they were living in the same place again, and Richard had discovered to his dismay that, along with this geographical reconstitution, he was back where he'd started with Patrick: jealous every time Patrick began dating someone new, relieved every time the relationship ended. Obviously, Richard was still in love with him.

Perhaps things would be different with Anne in his life. It changed you when someone picked you out of the crowd, and whatever else Anne did, she *saw* him. Patrick would be sure to notice this transformation. She'd said in Montreal as they lay naked together that for months before they'd spoken she'd had him under observation, as he moped around with a messenger bag cutting into his shoulder, his open, bewildered face hit with sudden shards of thought as he made his way among the library stacks, the hydraulic sway of his supported chin as he hunched over an open book, sighing and distractedly freeing sandwiches from cocoons of Saran Wrap. When she walked through the department, she sometimes heard him translating with Professor Caputo—Richard's reedy voice more masculine than she would have surmised from his face, his accent northern-sounding because he couldn't roll his *r*'s. She observed Richard staring at men in his vicinity, smiling at them when they looked up or if he caught them in some private tick or small accident, like tripping or dropping something on the floor and not bothering to pick it up—the conspiratorial edge he could give his smile when needed. She'd seen him holding doors for elderly black women and attractive young freshmen of all genders, their gratitude prompting a nod or their indifference leaving him stranded in his own pointless hospitality. He smiled at unfortunate rejects, locked eyes with overweight people, and gave change to the homeless who wandered through campus or buzzed at its fringes. He was always eating things out of plastic bags. She saw him go regularly for a colossal dripping pepperoni slice at Koronet Pizza, walking toward it wearing expectation on his face or emerging with a haze of tomato sauce still clinging to his mouth.

From a certain angle, the level of her attention was morbid, unsettling. But did he really want someone to be *lukewarm* about him? Maybe it was creepy and obsessive; maybe it was moving.

It was a kind of devotion, and given that he hadn't heard from her since they'd returned from Montreal, it might have diminished, disappeared. Did she no longer want him now that she'd had him? Women weren't supposed to be like that; it was supposed to be different from the terrible hardness that arose when only men were involved.

"I might have used too much salt," Patrick said.

He brought the omelet to the table and Richard inhaled forcefully, trying to overcome a feeling of internal disorder.

"It smells delicious."

"You want ketchup?"

"Please."

Patrick sat down and cut into the omelet. He said that he'd been writing on the topic of superfluous men, those enervated Russian aristocrats of the nineteenth century. He was attracted to the idea of spending your life in glamorous dissipation after having been defeated in your higher cause, a great excuse to give it up if you survived, but with the memory of your noble initiative still shining in your mind, testifying to your essential gravity. Patrick had once worked at a refugee resettlement center in San Francisco, but his political commitment had softened in the intervening years, to the relief of Richard, who did not enjoy having his moral turpitude constantly pointed out to him.

When they were finished eating, they went out onto the balcony to smoke, staring down at a gnarled fig tree and the disheveled garden that enclosed it. Patrick said he'd heard a rumor that the landlord, a nineties club kid named Paul Michael, was planning to gut the building and sell it. In the process everyone would be kicked out.

"Our parents lived in small, crummy apartments expecting to move into houses as they got older, while we live in small, crummy apartments with the expectation of continuing to live in small, crummy apartments."

Richard laughed. "It's too bad. This place has so much charm."

"It's a dump," Patrick said, taking a drag of his cigarette. "But I'd be sad to leave. Lorna was a total fluke."

"Yeah, and looking for an apartment is hell. Unless you move to Baltimore. Are places in Baltimore still cheap?"

"No idea."

Richard had recently seen a Tumblr page in which a new arrival from Albuquerque cataloged the ghoulish spaces she'd come across in her search for a room in New York. In one, the ceiling was only five feet high, and the rent was fourteen hundred a month. Another was a concrete-walled room in a basement that resembled an interrogation chamber and was summarized with the eerie phrases "For single male working," "with door for privacy." Their college friend Jeremy shared a studio with a muscular recent immigrant who sat in the lotus position while wearing lime-green bikini briefs, observing to various telephone interlocutors that he was a streetwise Praetoria boy who used his posh accent to intimidate rich Jews.

"It doesn't matter," Patrick said. "I'm moving in with Valdes anyway."

They were the words that Richard had long dreaded. He saw immediately what would happen—not just the end of their Saturday brunches, but the definitive end of everything. Living with Valdes in a distant neighborhood—in *Manhattan*, no less—Patrick would disappear physically from his life, though they would probably still text, and from then on Richard would eat Saturday breakfast, all breakfasts, alone: emptying the dusty remains of a box of Cheerios into a bowl of milk, spreading butter on toast if he remembered to buy butter, drinking burnt coffee, eating an occasional Pop-Tart while Leslie snored on the sofa.

Richard looked at Patrick. He had the urge to disclose all of the details of his time with Anne, to pour them over Patrick's head like a bucket of ice water and make him shiver in his exclusion. He could be swept off his feet and disappear into a life of glamour and sex just as easily as Patrick could.

But Patrick wasn't about to be brought to his knees. It was the tactical tragedy of it all. Such a sudden disclosure would do nothing except reinforce a sense in Patrick of Richard's endless unreliability, the impression that he moved through life chaotically, without logic or planning. You did *what*? Not to mention the fact that it would mean Richard was taken, that their lives now pointed toward other people and therefore away from each other.

"Don't you think it's a bit early to move in together?" he said.

"No, I think it makes sense at this point," said Patrick.

Richard slipped his phone out of his pocket and texted Anne a smiling emoticon. He couldn't come up with a sentence fast enough. He suddenly felt he *had* to communicate with her, receive some signal.

The cigarette went out and Patrick handed him the lighter. Richard clicked it violently.

"*Fuck.*"

"Relax," Patrick said, taking the lighter and holding it to the cigarette. The flame rose before his taut, determined face.

Richard inhaled and looked down at the phone in his hand. The irritatingly active device, with its constant fondling for your attention, was always disturbingly silent and still just when you needed it to light up. Where *was* she? So it seemed that Patrick was leaving him. Was she doing the same?

Richard wanted to toss the phone into the garden, get into a car, and leave the city.

"Why don't *we* move in together?" he said.

"That's a terrible idea," Patrick said placidly. "Our friendship would never survive."

"You don't think?"

Patrick shook his head, and Richard inhaled the cigarette too forcefully. He leaned against the railing, looking down at the ground below. For a moment, he felt like he might be sick.

TEN

The following evening Valdes was curating a performance on the Lower East Side. Inside the entrance to the building, there was a metal donation box on a plastic concession table, surrounded by glossy copies of various art publications. Richard recognized the volunteer manning the donation box. *Communications Director at the Narcolepsy Network.* He was one of those guys who stated his occupation outright on his online profile. Richard had sent him a message about a week ago, but no reply came back. As they passed the table, he avoided eye contact.

Inside there was a sea of gaunt young men in athletic, feudal-looking clothing. A heavy synthesizer chord issued from an invisible musician, and then a girl with a sharp dome of blond hair emerged.

"Are your phones working?" she said into a microphone. "Because Mercury is in retrograde, and it's really fucking up my service . . ."

Two figures dressed in red leotards and enormous plastic sunglasses joined from the wings. They gyrated and kicked in uncoordinated fashion.

Well, Richard thought, *The Rite of Spring* probably felt stupid back then too. After the performance they waited in the sweaty crowd while Valdes greeted well-wishers and answered questions. Patrick ran into someone he knew and Richard was left standing to one side, listening in on the conversation. He had the unsettling impression that all the young men in the room were poised to fall into an orgy from which he would be excluded.

"I can't tell if they liked it," Valdes said, in his slight Baltic accent, as they walked to the subway, Richard thinking all the while that he could have saved two subway fares if he'd skipped this risible performance. He was always trying to economize by purchasing single tickets and not an unlimited pass, but he usually ended up spending more in the end. It was a lesson he might have learned.

"Who cares what they think?" Patrick said, kissing Valdes on the neck.

"Can *you* write the review?"

"You'd regret that."

They went down into the subway and emerged on the other side of the river in Bushwick. The sky had begun to pinken, the air was mild and soft. Soon they arrived at a blackened, garage-like structure. Two bouncers chatted and ignored a line of young men, who mostly stood courageously alone with the glow of phone screens on their soft, bearded skin. Now and then the young men looked up, locked eyes with each other, and looked away again.

Inside they encountered perspiring dancers who stared narcotically at the floor as spastic lights flashed over their faces. They found Amir and Toller standing around a small table. Nearby, Barrett danced opposite a muscular boy in a tank top, both of them twitching with earnest self-absorption. Richard was pleasantly stimulated by the chaos and incoherence of the scene.

Gesturing toward the crowd, Toller screamed into Richard's ear.

"I'm starting to think arranged marriages are the way to go!"

"Really?"

"They cut passion out, and someone else does all the work!"

"But don't some people find passion in them as well? If they're lucky?"

"That's not the point! If you're more friends, but just have sex to reproduce, you're less likely to break up."

They danced for a few songs, and then went up to the roof to smoke. Across the river, the skyline of Manhattan shone persuasively. Richard wondered where Anne was, in among the archaic computer bank of the gathered buildings. He imagined her on a sofa, in childish patterned pajamas, watching Netflix; naked, floating in a bathtub, her pelvis rising toward the air with the longing of a bubble as it bursts, eyes closed and the dull immensity of silence in her ears.

"Someone slipped this into my pocket," Amir said, holding up a gum wrapper on which was written, in a spidery blue script, *I DON'T CARE* and a phone number.

"It's what you call *meeting in person*," Barrett said.

"It could be true love," said Toller.

When they went back down to the dance floor, Richard was promptly waylaid by a group of large, hairy, gregarious men. As the group disintegrated and he made his way toward the bar, someone grabbed his shoulder. The grip was provoking, like a declaration of commitment in that room where an alert neutrality prevailed.

He turned around. The hand on his shoulder was attached to Blake, his erstwhile date from the High Line. Looking stoutly appealing in a white T-shirt and black jeans, Blake stood there with a grin on his face that was disarming in the sea of impervious faces.

"How *are* you?" he screamed in Richard's ear.

Richard didn't immediately register the question, but he felt a leap in his skin.

"How are *you*?" Blake repeated.

"I'm good!" Richard said, smiling. The room abruptly glimmered. "I thought nobody came here anymore!"

Blake wrapped his arms around Richard's torso, and Richard responded in kind. They were knocked back and forth by passing bodies.

"Have you ever Eskimo-kissed?" Blake asked.

He closed his eyes and rubbed his nose against Richard's nose, then stepped back, his hand brushing across Richard's crotch. Richard felt a rotation in his mind, as though he was being turned away from everything that had recently been happening in his life and, from what he could see in Blake's eyes, toward the uncomplicated chemistry of two men in a state of happy horniness.

"I was hoping I'd see you again."

"Me too!" Blake said. "Yurrrr hot!"

Then you should have texted me back, Richard thought. But in that scatterbrained age of utter flakiness, what was the sense of pointing *that* out?

The song changed and the beat turned frenetic and aggressive, like a bucket of rocks thrown over the crowd. The crowd threw their arms in the air, beating back the assault. Blake dragged Richard in among the bodies and they dug out a small, airless pocket. It was comforting, and not unsexy somehow, that Blake, with his earnest and spirited moves, was an even worse dancer than Richard. His arms and legs swung out in spastic arcs, like a primitive android imitating its clumsy human progenitors. A tall, beautiful Asian guy in a ball cap gave them a nasty look. Then an impish white guy with a jutting disc of brown hair leered close and screamed "*Husband material!*" at Blake before dancing off.

"We're not very good dancers," Richard said when the music briefly lulled.

"That's okay," Blake said, his hands upturned and fingers spread apart, beckoning Richard toward him. Richard stepped forward and found himself in a quick damp embrace, their stubbly cheeks roughly stuck, the hard lump of Blake's crotch against his leg. For a second their belt buckles caught, and then scraped apart.

Richard wondered where Patrick was. Had Patrick noticed that someone had chosen Richard, if perhaps just for a moment?

"I'm wearing a jockstrap tonight," Blake said into Richard's ear, which struck Richard as both hilarious and seductive. "It's not as comfortable as I'd hoped."

"Are you really wearing a jockstrap?"

"Yup."

"Planning on some football later?"

They hugged again, and Richard reached a finger down under Blake's belt and caught one of the thin pieces of fabric that cupped Blake's buttocks. He tugged and Blake grunted.

All of a sudden Richard felt their blended desire to fuck like a clenched fist that needed to smash through an obstacle before it could rest. He smiled to himself, his lips grazing Blake's earlobe, as he imagined them trying to leave the club with their crotches stuck together, four-legged, conjoined at that place that in the moment seemed to matter most.

He was so drunk, the music was so loud; he felt they might dissolve into the pandemonium. He caught sight of a few men standing alone, flummoxed outsiders engaged in a restless audit of the fringes, a longing scrutiny. He felt sympathy for them; he felt like they should just go for it.

The music decelerated and grew quiet.

"Do you want to get out of here?" Blake said.

Their first, seemingly discarded date appeared now like a prolonged case of mistaken identity. It had been two other people, or Blake behaved as if it had. Or maybe this was the night they would have spent together, time had cycled back on itself, and tomorrow would shimmer with déjà vu.

The interregnum was part of the choreography; the teasing absence was the out-of-body prelude to this warm, thumping, in-body resolution.

"Yes," Richard said, as if he could never answer quickly enough.

Blake took his hand and led him out of the crowd.

"Bye-bye!" Amir said with a wink as he saw them brush past.

The end of the night—leaving the club, waiting for a car, climbing the stairs to Blake's apartment—would be a flickering shade, Richard imagined. In his recollection there would be enjoyable, outlandish blurring. As they broke free of the crowd and made their way to the door, he thought he was saying goodbye to Patrick when he waved at someone tall and blond. There was a brief spark of nasty pleasure at this confusion and neglect. He told himself it might have been anyone and he didn't care, though of course he wanted it to be Patrick, a witness to the confirmation that he was leaving and he wasn't alone.

THEY WENT BACK TO Blake's apartment, their knees touching in the car, heavy and quiet with expectation. The night had turned cool. There was a garland of mist around the streetlights.

In Blake's apartment, they walked and then blundered through the kitchen and into his bedroom. Blake dove to kiss with a lunging, arcing tongue, which is what Richard liked; he was disappointed by dainty kissers, guys who paused to say "not so much tongue" or made similar protests. Once Richard had even burped in a screenwriter's face in the aftermath of such a comment. It wasn't intentional, but there had been a willed and Freudian quality about it.

They were standing by the bed, kissing, and now Richard was kneeling in front of Blake, and Blake had his fingers in Richard's hair.

Richard always paused—it was probably too quick for anyone else to notice—before he undid a zipper and a cock rose to meet him. It always took on the cliff-edge, indulged, spoiled aspect of waking up on a holiday when you were poised for gifts or at least a different kind of attention. When a final compatibility was established—Richard was versatile but preferred to top—he could settle or launch into what was happening. But it was the question of how to do it without talking, which he preferred.

He liked to be a little forceful, and this had confused him with Anne; he hadn't known how forceful he should be. The literal mechanics were of course not mysterious but the qualities of the symbiosis they were trying to achieve, because it had felt like they were groping toward something beyond the mere thudding contact of their two bodies, had remained perceptible but out of reach. It was more complicated than this.

They struggled, as if arresting each other, into Blake's big, comfortable, fresh-smelling bed, which felt like an island of hygiene in the messy room. Part of Richard just wanted to hug Blake all night, to squeeze him, and to maintain contact with his every warm inch, not even to bother with artful mechanics. The intensity of the feeling surprised him.

The next morning when he woke up painfully early, as he usually did after a night of drinking, Richard was horribly thirsty. He propped himself up on an elbow and surveyed the room. In the previous night's darkness, he'd had a vague but strong sense of its disorder. The morning light revealed a topsoil of clothing and documents covering the floor. On the dresser, deodorants, shampoos, and empty coffee cups formed a dim, rippling horizon.

Blake slid into the declivity between them. He appeared profoundly asleep, with the waxy perspiring tint of a body struggling to process large quantities of alcohol. A drop of saliva fluttered at one corner of his mouth. Two symmetrical rings of black hair swirled out on his soft pectorals.

Richard nestled his fingers in the hair of Blake's chest. Blake shifted and swallowed. He opened one eye.

"Oh God, why are you awake?"

His voice was gravelly.

"Can I say something?" Richard said.

"You're already talking," Blake replied, his eye closing again.

"That was fun," Richard said, fondling Blake's nipple.

Blake exhaled audibly through his nose.

"Go back to sleep," he said, his face settling into a still, bearded mask.

Staring at the ceiling, Richard lay down beside him again. He knew he would be unable to fall back asleep in that unfamiliar bed, his body touchy and resentful after the stew of beer and cocktails he'd consumed only a few hours earlier.

Anyway, it was better to leave early than late. He rolled over and looked at Blake.

One of Blake's pectorals twitched, likely at the beginning of a dream. Richard softly poked it.

"On your profile, the *gym* was high on your list of favorite things."

Blake groaned.

"Everyone's profile says that."

"I'm going to give you your space back, okay?"

Blake opened both eyes. "You're welcome to stay."

"I have to go."

"Okay."

Blake slid his hand around Richard's waist, rolled over, and kissed his belly. Then he groaned again and swung out of bed. He put on some clothes, while Richard did the same.

They walked to the front door.

"Can I say something else?" Richard said.

"You really like talking early in the morning, I take it?"

"I thought you weren't interested after our first date." Worried that he was being too candid, Richard nevertheless pressed on. "When I didn't hear from you."

"It wasn't you."

Blake rubbed his eyes.

"That's good to hear," Richard said.

Blake slid his hand around Richard's waist.

"It was work."

"Oh, work."

"And then, I'd left it so long, I felt sheepish," Blake said, more alert now. "I was afraid you wouldn't write back. I don't like rejection."

He smiled as he said this.

"Nobody does," Richard said.

"Are you getting an Uber?" Blake asked.

"The subway."

"You're taking the subway? That's brave. I couldn't face the subway right now."

Blake told him the quickest route, and they hugged for a long moment.

"See you?" Blake said.

"See you soon," Richard said.

Words in these moments were full of a hunger to be away. Whether to eventually return, it was not clear.

Richard stepped out of the apartment and Blake closed the door gently behind him.

AN HOUR LATER RICHARD arrived back at his apartment, his eyes fizzing and dry with fatigue. When he opened the door he was startled to find Courtney, the barista from Sloppy, perched on the sofa, wearing a green flannel button-down shirt that was too big for her.

"Hey, Richard."

"Hi, Courtney." He closed the door behind him, speaking quietly. The sun was beginning to rise over the buildings across the street. "What are you doing here?"

They stared at each other, and Richard abruptly noticed that it was Leslie's shirt Courtney was wearing. Possibly his socks too.

"I'm meditating. Where are you coming from so early?"

"Why is it so hot in here?" he said, ignoring her question.

"Not sure. Oh, we made muffins, if you want one." Richard's nerves pulsed with irritation at the word "muffins." "Long trip?"

"Um, yeah. The train stopped for like ten minutes between each station."

"Leslie and I spent all yesterday baking together."

"That's nice, Courtney. Well, I'm going to bed."

"We'll be cooking breakfast soon if you want to join."

"Maybe I will, maybe. Depends on when I get up. Thanks for the offer."

"Sure thing. Sweet dreams, Richard!"

Richard went into his room and closed the door. Almost immediately, Courtney and Leslie started clattering around the kitchen, laughing and dropping things on the floor. He undressed and slid into bed, the specters of Anne, Patrick, and Blake scampering away in the brambles of his fatigued mind, like lost, big-eyed does. It was comforting to have them all there. Trying to hold them in place, he closed his eyes and lay still.

ELEVEN

WHERE ARE YOU?

Richard texted Anne when he woke up, feeling like someone in the aftermath of a hurricane who had declined to heed the evacuation order.

So recently sticky and sweaty, his body had dried into a state of fusty peacefulness and ache. It would be nice to maintain this feeling, the olfactory and muscular evidence of his time with Blake, he thought. But he was desperate to shower. And his head throbbed.

Having sent the text, he hid his phone for a moment in the folds of the blankets, as if he could forget that it was there. Several impressions vied with each other. There was the familiar, mundane guilt of a wasted morning, which Richard had become used to since the appearance of his writer's block. There was the excitement of having slept with Blake, the residual static of value granted to his limbs by the devoted attention of another person. And underlying all this, a startling current of guilt, mixed with a desire to know immediately where Anne was, a need to make contact.

The phone quivered in the blankets. He fished it out.

I'M AT HOME, Anne wrote. **WHAT'S UP?**

DON'T BE COY.

I'M NOT BEING COY.

WHY HAVEN'T YOU TEXTED BACK? he asked with some hesitation.

There was a pause. No answer. She was better at these games than he would have predicted.

He waited a moment, then asked:

WHAT ARE YOU UP TO TONIGHT?

She was busy having dinner with her father that evening, but the following night, she said, Richard should accompany her to the opera.

The next day and a half passed in an unfocused blur of his romantic prospects. Richard was relieved when it was time to go into the city and meet Anne at Lincoln Center.

It was a production of Mussorgsky's *Eugene Onegin*. They met in the plaza and went inside. In her black sheath dress and red patent-leather pumps, Anne looked like a threatening young lawyer. Wearing a blazer and jeans, Richard made a more earnest impression.

They walked down the aisle toward their seats, and then turned their bodies sideways to preserve the knees of the elderly, early-arrived spectators who made up the majority of the audience.

"I love a capricious nobleman," Anne said with an air of satisfaction.

Taking his seat, Richard surveyed the space. The background was a lush purple forest. A quilt of fallen gold leaves covered the stage.

"Thanks for inviting me," he said. Then he paused. "Honestly, I thought I might not hear from you."

Anne looked surprised.

"Of course you were going to hear from me."

"You don't usually go so long without being in touch."

"I was busy," she said. "I had things to do. My father was here."

He smiled. "You were just trying to string me along."

"Oh, sure. I do have a life, you know."

"Of course I know."

"I wanted to give you space," she said, with an air of reflection. "I wanted you to have time to process."

"It didn't feel like space. Well, okay, it felt like *empty* space."

She squeezed his arm. "You could have written too."

"I did."

"Eventually," she said, with a slight exhale.

He sighed.

"Is this a stupid text standoff thing?" he asked.

"I guess it is. Let's not fall into that."

The lights dimmed and puffy figures ran around the stage in heavy costumes. Richard was still unable to summon an enthusiasm that, through years of trying to appreciate opera, had always eluded him. Soon Anne was snoring. Why did she want to go to the opera if she found it dull? She could be so strange, Richard thought, getting annoyed. Maybe she had been up all night working.

At one point she opened her eyes and they stared at each other, then she closed them again. A whiskered man in a navy blazer sighed haughtily beside her, draping one leg over the other. When the lights came on for first intermission, she woke up and sat bolt upright.

"Let's get out of here."

"It's only the first intermission," Richard protested.

"I want to walk around. I love Midtown at night."

"But it's so humid."

She got to her feet.

"Let's have a drink—maybe at Petrossian. I'm not responding to this production."

"I can tell."

"We can come back another time."

"Fine," he said, shaking his head.

In the lobby, a young man in a skinny dark-blue suit with a Rasputin-like beard helped an elderly woman in a Chanel jacket through the doors. His eyes moved up and down Richard's body with the lag of appetite and pursuit.

They went outside into the heavy air.

"Sometimes I wish I smoked," Anne said, looking at a man in a leather jacket lighting a cigarette beside the fountain. "I like the smell."

She wrapped her arm around Richard's waist. Traffic noise bloomed around them and a glow filled the plaza.

"I smoked pretty regularly in college," he said.

"You smoked *regularly* in Montreal if I remember."

He put his arm across her shoulder.

"Should we go to Petrossian?"

"Let's just walk."

They went down Broadway toward the blocky eruption of the Midtown skyline. Nocturnal pedestrians ambled by with their hands in their pockets. A woman walked two West Highland terriers on a leash, speaking on her phone as the dogs sniffed a bench.

At Columbus Circle, dressed in neon T-shirts and high-top running shoes, a group of teenagers tapped their skateboards against the pavement. Richard stared into the arboreal reaches of Central Park, commanded now by cairn terriers and Bernese mountain dogs, strollers and joggers, as it once had been by rapists, drug dealers, and junkies, or so they said. He imagined himself reflecting back on this humid scene from the future—their awkward distribution across the clammy traffic island, the dark spangle of the skyscrapers, the park tamed but still potent with metropolitan promise and mystery—and erasing the fatigue, boredom, and clumsiness.

"What's up?" she asked.

"Nothing, really," he said. "Just thinking about what Central Park used to be like."

His phone buzzed and he slid it out of his pocket.

HOW ARE YOU TONIGHT? Blake asked.

"Who is it?"

Richard didn't look up.

"My father," he said, invoking a man who, in fact, never texted after eight o'clock in the evening.

"Oh, hi to your father. How is he?"

"I think he's bored."

"Yeah?"

She put her hands in her pockets.

"He's just wondering what I'm doing."

"What are you going to tell him?"

"The truth."

She was standing close. He moved away slightly, to hide the screen.

"Have you ever mentioned me to him?"

"Have I ever mentioned you to him?" Richard repeated, frowning and looking up at the upper floors of a nearby building. "Sure."

"I'd like to meet him."

"My parents never come to New York."

"We should go and see them. I want to see where you grew up."

"I don't want to go home. It's just . . . trees."

"You're being testy."

"There isn't much to do. And my parents would be there."

Richard could almost feel the odd, suspended dynamic that would settle on such a trip, like an episode of some neurotic comedy whose humor springs from an unwieldy, weekend-long social embarrassment: the wrinkled-forehead politeness, his parents' tolerant confusion as they tried, in private, to reason out what was going on, to discern the contours of the relationship before them without offending or "judging," wondering if their guests wanted to sleep in the same bed but not wanting to ask, while at the same time not wanting to presume.

"I thought you had a good relationship with your parents," Anne said.

Richard shrugged.

"I do, I do. It doesn't mean I want to go home."

He put the phone back in his pocket, not wanting to get caught up in a texting back-and-forth with Blake at that moment, an exchange Anne would surely notice.

"You don't want me to meet them?"

"I didn't say that."

His phone buzzed again. He pulled it out and glanced down. It was Patrick this time.

PARTY AT TOLLER'S. GET HERE NOW. I WANT TO GIVE YOU A BIG KISS.

Richard smiled.

"*That's* not your father," Anne said.

"It's Patrick."

"What's going on?"

"He's saying hello. He got back from Boston today."

She rolled her eyes and looked away.

"What's wrong now?" he asked.

She didn't answer.

"Should we call it a night? I'm tired and you're not in a very good mood," he said. The guilt he'd felt the previous morning in bed, in contrast to the rank comfort of his body, was now almost completely gone, and the prospect of Blake looming somewhere in an unidentified corner of the city, writing him messages, and the fact of Patrick demanding his presence from across the river at Toller's loft, made him feel impatient and corroded his generosity.

"We could watch a movie," she suggested.

But the idea of watching other people move around on a screen was unappealing when his own life was so rife with potential action.

"I think I'll head back to Brooklyn," he said.

"You're leaving me?" she said, with a pained look.

"You don't seem very happy with my company."

"We were having a nice time. Let's stay out."

He inhaled.

"Do you still want to get a drink at Petrossian? I don't want to watch a movie."

"Maybe." She was looking up at a building. "Let's keep walking for a bit. It'll clear our heads."

"Okay, but I don't want to be interrogated."

"I wasn't interrogating you," she snapped.

As they went along Central Park South, Richard was overcome by the urge to flee. He glanced over into the humped, thistled vacuity of the park, saw himself scrambling over the mossy rock and vanishing into its black, pastoral depths.

"Let's get away from that thing," Anne said. They were approaching the beaming white cube of the Apple Store on Fifth Avenue. They turned south and paused in front of the window at Bergdorf Goodman.

"That's beautiful," she said, pointing to a rose-colored Valentino crepe de chine dress.

"You would look good in that."

"I am too short to wear a dress like that."

He beat back a flare of exasperation.

"All right then," he said, enunciating primly.

She grabbed his hand and squeezed it. "You know what I just remembered?"

"Nope."

"Our night in the tent."

"The protest?"

He felt his phone buzzing again.

HEY STRANGER! Blake wrote. WHAT'S UP?

"Is that Patrick again?"

"Yes."

She let go of his arm. She glared at him as he concentrated on his phone.

"Do you have feelings for Patrick?"

"What are you talking about?"

Of course Richard knew what she was talking about. He knew that she noticed him checking out guys on the street. It was obvious they were both captivated by the same exemplary, specimen-like young men—they had similar tastes, he suspected—striding down the block, which of course happened often in Manhattan, though their shared appreciation had never quite been expanded upon.

"Your voice changes when you talk about him."

"No it doesn't."

"I've asked you several times if I could meet him."

Richard tried to think of a response, but nothing came.

"Do you talk to him about me?" she said, sounding pained again.

"Why does that matter?"

"You don't want to introduce me to your friends. That hurts me."

"That's not true."

"You've met Erin and Alicia. I haven't met any of your friends."

"Erin and Alicia live with you. That's different."

"You're making an excuse."

"Honestly?" he sighed. "I'm afraid you won't like each other."

"You think he wouldn't like me?"

He saw the sting in her face. "I didn't mean it like that. That didn't come out right. It's more that you wouldn't like him."

"If *you* care about him I will like him. I will *try* to like him."

His phone buzzed again.

ARE YOU COMING OR NOT? Patrick wrote.

A second later:

?????????

"Don't look at your phone while we're talking."

"I don't know what you want me to say. Why are you acting like this?"

"You're being rude."

His phone buzzed again.

IT'S NOT COOL, Patrick wrote. **THAT YOU'RE IGNORING ME.**

This was followed by a text from Blake:

HI.

"There's a party," Richard said, feeling assailed. "It's happening right now. Do you want to go?"

"Where?"

"Brooklyn. Patrick will be there."

"Oh God, really?"

"You just said you wanted to meet my friends."

"Am I actually welcome?"

"Do you want to go or not?"

The thought of her walking off alone, amid the anonymous late-night shoppers and scrutinizing tourists, both pleased and distressed him. In his annoyance and fear, he felt the urge to dismiss and repudiate her, to send her off on her own. At the same time, he wanted to comfort her.

A young man and a young woman were kissing several feet away.

"I hate public displays of affection," Anne said rancorously.

"Let's get out of here then." Richard raised his hand to hail a taxi.

THEY RACED DOWNTOWN AND over a bridge, not talking. Richard stared at his phone and Anne turned her face sourly out the window. Manhattan leapt forth to one side as they turned onto the Brooklyn-Queens Expressway.

COMING! Richard texted Patrick. CAN I BRING A FRIEND?

THAT GUY YOU RAN OFF WITH THE OTHER NIGHT?

So he did notice, Richard thought.

NO, A CLASSMATE, he replied, immediately questioning that moniker.

When they arrived at Toller's loft, they found Toller, Amir, Barrett, and Patrick sitting on the couches. Richard led Anne across the room to make introductions, but when he tried to formally introduce her to them, the boys just nodded sparsely.

Patrick explained the rationale of the party. Barrett and Toller had been fighting for at least a month, at first playfully and then more genuinely. Barrett said that Toller played bad music at his parties, and that he was "sick of gyrating like a dreidel until his hair was about to fall out." Toller retorted by calling Barrett a spoiled brat, and in turn Barrett accused Toller of being "old." Several abrogated parties later, it was clear that they were dependent on each other—Barrett had no comparable space to take his friends, Toller no one to invite to his parties. To celebrate the renewal of their friendship, as well as to welcome Patrick back after his trip to Boston to look at postdocs, they were throwing this party. There was a male model in a jockstrap present to serve drinks.

"Check out the bulge on that guy," Patrick said to Richard and Anne.

Patrick smiled at him. The young, curly-haired man waved back.

"I think I would have preferred drinks at Petrossian," Anne said.

No one acknowledged this comment. A light machine attached to the ceiling fired kaleidoscopic rays at the dancers in swift, precise volleys.

Patrick vanished to field excited greetings and hugs.

"I'm getting a drink," Anne said to Richard. "Do you want one?"

"Sure."

She went off to the bar. While she was gone, Richard watched the dancers. When she came back, she had two glasses in hand. She gave one to Richard—it was a gin and tonic—drank hers quickly, and went back for another.

Maybe it's better if she gets drunk, Richard thought. She won't notice how they treat her. Or she will, but I won't.

Beyoncé came on the speaker and Barrett, Amir, and Toller ran to join the small clump of dancers in the middle of the loft.

When Anne returned again, she said: "Did you notice that none of them asked me a single question?"

"You didn't ask them anything either."

"I'm the guest."

"Everyone but Toller is a guest here, technically."

They looked on as Barrett, Amir, and Toller bobbed in an arrhythmic cluster at the edge of a mass of happy dancers.

"I hope you're not planning to dance," she said.

"What's that supposed to mean?"

"I'm not insulting you. I just don't want you to leave me standing here by myself."

"You wanted to come."

"I wanted to go to Petrossian."

"We had to go somewhere."

She crossed her arms. A moment later, she rested her head on his shoulder, and he cocked his head impatiently.

"Are you falling asleep?" he asked. "Do you want to go home?"

"Do you want me to leave?"

"I didn't say that."

"This is moronic," she said.

Perhaps it would be more difficult to integrate her into his life than he'd ever imagined. They were like two ornery stray cats sitting on a wall, maintaining a peevish distance from each other, commenting bitterly on whatever transpired, and then disappearing into a dark space to copulate.

"This is *not* moronic," he said. "Everyone is having a good time."

Barrett appeared beside them, bathed in his own sweaty effulgence.

"What's it like out there?" Richard asked cheerfully.

"That guy in the lime-green tank top won't leave me alone. It's like, I do not appreciate your unibrow, okay?"

"Don't be mean," Richard said with a chiding smile.

"Are you having fun?" Barrett asked Anne.

"Not really."

"Why don't you have another drink? Then it won't matter."

"Good advice."

She went back to the bar.

"Bit of a wet blanket, that one."

"She's just tired."

"Who is she again?"

"A friend from school."

Toller and Amir appeared.

"Should we get out of here soon?" Barrett said, looking around with a contemptuous sneer. "I don't know about this crowd."

"You can't *leave,*" Toller said, his eyes wide with exasperation. "You're one of the *hosts*."

"Where's Patrick?" Barrett turned to Richard. "He loves you the best, you know?"

"Did he say that?" Richard asked, feeling an involuntary spring at this remark, like a dog intercepting a Frisbee. Anne returned with her drink.

"He and Valdes are fighting," Barrett mused, almost optimistically. "It won't last."

Anne raised an eyebrow.

"Really?" Richard said.

Patrick hadn't told him that. Why not? Richard had always thought of himself as having privileged access to Patrick's inner life, and the idea that he did not dismayed him. At the same time, part of him was atavistically comforted to know that Patrick and Valdes were having relationship issues.

The song changed.

"Ooo, I love this," Barrett said, and he darted off.

Richard watched as his broad, glistening back disappeared among the other dancers. As Anne again placed her chin on Richard's shoulder, he was seized by a desire to flinch and let her topple to the floor.

"Where's the bathroom?" Anne asked.

He pointed to a far door.

"Don't go anywhere," she said, handing him her drink.

When she was out of sight, carrying her drink and taking cat sips, Richard went to look for Patrick. He was impatient to find Patrick and talk to him, perhaps to comfort him. But when he passed the crowd, Barrett grabbed his arm and pulled him in. The music separated into sharp, discrete notes and fused into a charged ascending crest. Some-one's hand brushed his crotch. Richard closed his eyes and swung his arms in the air.

"Where's Patrick?" he said when the music paused.

"I think he went outside to talk with Valdes."

Richard squeezed out of the crowd and walked over to a window, scanning the street below. A few feet down the block, in the humid air portioned out by bent branches and a heavy canopy of leaves, like a grouping of hands spread out one on top of another in a communal gesture of support, Patrick and Valdes were getting into a cab. The door slammed shut and Richard watched as the cab accelerated down the block and turned a corner.

"What are you looking at?" Anne said, coming up and standing beside him.

"Nothing. I just needed some fresh air."

"It is kind of stuffy in here."

"Are you okay?" he asked, still watching the cab.

"I'm fine, I guess."

He turned toward her.

"Should we go?" he said, feeling resigned now to the diminished emotional possibilities of the party.

He rested his chin against the top of her head.

"You don't want to see your friends?" she asked.

"Let's go."

Anne smiled at him.

"Okay."

She ordered an Uber and they went downstairs. The night was cool and still but for the muffled vibration of the music emanating from Toller's loft.

As they waited, a group of guys, large young men in polo shirts, their arms a sequence of veiny bulges, appeared on the opposite sidewalk and crossed the street toward them.

One of the group stared at Anne.

"You look like the kind of art school chick I'd like to fuck," he said.

"I'd fuck your dad," she replied immediately.

"My dad's dead."

"Yeah, but he's still got the biggest dick."

The guy paused, a look of stark but forgiving confusion on his face. He stepped forward—Richard tensed but did not move—and embraced Anne.

The embrace lasted a long moment. Her arms hung at her sides, but then she raised one hand and briefly patted the young man's broad back. When it was over, the group moved off without a word. The Uber arrived.

"Are you okay?" Anne asked Richard, getting in.

"Yes," he said, not knowing what else to say, feeling he should be the one to ask her how she was. So he did. "Are *you* okay?"

He closed the door behind him as Anne looked out the opposite window.

"I'm fine."

"That was impressive," he said quietly. The car began to drive.

"It all happened very fast."

"You were so poised."

"It wasn't that bad," she said, squeezing Richard's leg. "You're not traumatized, I hope?"

"No, I'm fine."

Richard's mouth seemed to dry out completely as they made their way back to her apartment, and with it any words he might say. Anne didn't appear particularly interested in talking either. For her it had to be the full, radiant quiet of triumph, he thought, but for him it was like admiration mixed with the aftermath of a scolding, a failing.

They went immediately to bed, but just to sleep.

"Good night," she said, rolling toward the wall.

"Good night."

TWELVE

Three nights later, in restaurants all around the city, dinners came to an awkward conclusion.

I didn't have wine.

I didn't have an appetizer.

Let's split it seven ways.

You added cheese and bacon though.

Stomach contents were taken into account, and generosity was improbable even from generous people. The bulky arrival of debit machines in the hands of aproned waiters signaled that genteel discussions among friends—even lovers—would turn flinty as the pleasant energy of the evening dissolved in an acid bath of addition and subtraction. Sometimes the diners did the calculations themselves on a napkin or the back of the check, then parted quickly outside, impatient to get home, put on the next episode of the latest network series, and forget the petty end of the meal.

Around eight o'clock, Richard walked along DeKalb Avenue on his way to meet Blake at one of the lackadaisical but expensive restaurants, where babies breastfed by candlelight, scattered throughout ever-greater swaths of Brooklyn.

Blake was waiting in the vestibule when Richard arrived. They greeted each other with a smile and a kiss. Soon they were seated and handed menus.

Richard scanned his menu in a slight confusion. Nothing immediately stood out in this curio cabinet of flesh and bone. A mooning straight couple sat a few feet away—an alabaster redhead with ringlets, and a sensitive ursine type in a plaid shirt. They had arranged their plates beside each other in the middle of the table in order to share what they'd ordered: citrus donuts, pancakes, some sort of smoked-meat hash. It was breakfast for dinner.

"Do you have any favorites?" Richard asked Blake finally. "I can't decide."

"They change the selection every week depending on ocean currents."

"Ah," Richard said, as if this had been clarifying, which it hadn't.

"The steak," Blake said, when the waiter arrived. "Rare."

"The steak for me too."

A hunk of meat seemed like a safe bet.

"And the plate of grilled wild sardines for the appetizer," said Blake. "And more bread."

"To drink?"

Blake spent a long moment examining the wine list. Richard smiled up at the tall, shaven-headed, gorgeous young waiter in a gesture of commiseration. The waiter's face looked like it naturally descended into the clinking shield of an intimidating scowl, but also he was doing little to mask his annoyance. Of course, with a face like that he could get away with it.

Blake finally came to a bottle that was to his liking.

"You should have ordered something different," he said when the waiter left.

"I was following your lead."

Blake nodded. "It's not a big deal. I'm just OCD about sampling as many dishes from a menu as possible." He smiled. "Next time."

"Next time" made Richard feel cozy, despite the slap on the wrist of Blake's disappointment.

"That makes sense," Richard said. "So, how's work? You said things were busy the last time I saw you."

"I need to tell you something about work," Blake said.

"What's that?"

"I *am* an actor, but I don't work in administration. I'm really a lawyer."

Was this some kind of coquettish game? If so, Richard was not, in his first gut reaction, too disappointed by the turn it was taking.

"Okay, but you are, or you're not, an actor?"

"No, I *am* an actor, in my spare time. I'm in an amateur Tennessee Williams troupe."

"I love Tennessee Williams!"

"Tell me about it. One of the highlights of my life as a young fag was seeing Jessica Lange play Blanche DuBois."

"No!"

"Yes."

"What made you lie?"

"It's sort of a test. You know—are you still interested if . . . ?"

"You think I'm a gold-digger?" Richard said, smiling.

"And that wasn't my apartment."

"What are you going to tell me next—that's not your real face?"

Blake pretended to peel off a mask.

"No, this *is* my face."

"That's good. It's a good face."

"Thank you. I was renting out my place on Airbnb. That was a friend's place. I'm not that messy."

"Good. That place was a disaster."

"And I'm into literate guys," Blake said. "I don't know, 'creative' guys"—he used his fingers to indicate quotation marks. "Guys who read, who are thoughtful. I always worry they'll think I'm lame if they know I'm a lawyer."

"It's the opposite," Richard said. "It's definitely a plus. My father is a lawyer."

"I know. It's just one of those silly irrational worries we all have."

"My turn," Richard said. "*I* wondered about the food we ate. What you thought about it."

"The diner, you mean? Well, I wouldn't want to eat there every day."

"No, no, of course not," Richard said, shaking his head.

"A healthy body and a healthy mind are essential," Blake said, with intentional pomp. "It's the Spartan ideal."

"Throwing babies over cliffs too, I think."

"What about naked wrestling?" Blake quipped.

"That's the Athenians," Richard said. "So where do you *really* live?"

"I have a studio here, in Fort Greene."

"You own it?"

Blake nodded, and Richard felt a mixture of trepidation and satisfaction. Blake's tone of responsibility, and his ownership of property, suggested that he took to heart the task of secure and adult living. Whether he expected that same seriousness and ability in a partner was the question that naturally followed.

Blake said that his building was old, with beautiful crown moldings, which helped ease the blow of its many deficiencies. It was a stalemate of gentility and neglect. He'd made valiant advances with hanging plants and wicker chairs inherited from his grandparents, but was routinely outflanked by bad plumbing and clever rodentia. When he left the confines of the apartment and went out onto the street, a leafy curving omission from the area grid, he liked to pretend that his own building was erased completely—an orgiastic wrecking ball turning it to rubble.

"What about *your* place?" Blake asked.

"It's really nothing," Richard conceded.

"Whenever you're ready."

"I'll let you know."

Blake smiled, and Richard wondered if he could convince Leslie to vacate the sofa, even for an hour.

"How long have you been there?" Blake asked.

"Two years."

"I never want to leave this city," Blake said. "It turns you into a different person."

Richard wondered if Blake was one of those people who thought New York had once been better—who idealized its squalid past, burned-out buildings, cheap rent, and creativity. Or was he a sunny optimist, in love with statistical data, pleased with the influx of foreign billionaires and the new pedestrian zones and landscaping, and eye-rollingly dismissive of those romantics who felt the soul of the city had been lost? By sensibility, Richard was drawn to the first group; but of course, at this point in history it was obviously to the latter group that the future of the city belonged.

"I could never move back home," Blake said.

"Me neither," Richard said. "My hometown is like a graveyard. Does your family ever visit?"

"My parents are coming for my birthday."

The grilled sardines with frisée arrived. Looking thoughtful, Blake took one between his fingers and chewed the flesh off the bone. Richard ate one too, and then promptly washed down the invading flavor with a gulp of wine.

"I'm sure *you're* the good son," Blake said, leaning to one side and pretending to vomit. "I can just tell. *Sweet, dependable*."

"Dependable?" Richard said, thinking back to Patrick: *You're not a provider.* "I don't know about that."

"My parents haven't met many of my boyfriends, except Luke. But they didn't know he was my boyfriend at the time."

"Who was Luke?" Richard asked, feeling retrospective jealousy at the mention of this figment of a person.

"His parents were Christian Scientists who made this huge anti-abortion placard and paid to have it installed on the side of the highway. It was a baby in a big yellow sac—I guess it was supposed to be a uterus—with a hand creeping up behind it. Luke would come over wearing an oversized wool coat. He'd have on a sparkly dress or something underneath that he got secondhand. We'd put on the *Paris Is Burning* DVD and try to vogue, but neither of us had any sense of rhythm."

"I love that movie."

"Yeah, everybody does. Anyway, Luke needed rescuing. So I rescued him, for a while."

"How old were you?"

"Fourteen."

"Your parents are really progressive then?"

"Progressive enough, I guess."

After school, Blake said, he would get a ride to Luke's house in a wood-paneled Dodge Caravan, which smelled of a minty analgesic cream the driver and housekeeper, Jean, used on her splotched, arthritic hands. Freezing air would stream in as Jean dangled a cigarette out the window and drove with one hand, commenting on the foul snow banks.

"She smoked in the car?"

"Uh-huh."

"Wow."

Luke was indifferent toward Blake in the van, barely acknowledging his presence. But when they entered the house through the large archway, paid for by the medical and legal judgments rendered by Luke's parents, he would surreptitiously take Blake's hand and lead him down to the basement.

While Blake flipped through discarded *House and Garden* magazines, Luke would paint a toboggan or sand down a skateboard. Blake grew accustomed to Luke's sloe-eyed stare, and the foamy brain that had such a thick, sentimental crust, and made Luke swallow tears when he saw a bird dragging its wing around the backyard. Eventually they would connect the old Nintendo machine to the television and play Mario Brothers, perched on a tan leather sofa, legs curled under an afghan. As Luke pinioned from right to left, elbows out, Blake would look up the sleeve of his T-shirt to the enticing dark patch of hair in his armpit.

Deputized to Luigi, Blake found death quickly in balls of fire or in the jaws of carnivorous plants, while Luke's triumphant and coruscating Mario flew over yawning gorges, hacked dragons to pieces, and rescued princesses.

After three or four rounds, Luke would declare, in a self-consciously hollow voice, that he was sick of video games and preferred to watch TV. Despite the laboring furnace, they could credibly enlist the services of a blanket, under which they would privately grope each other. It was always cold in the basement; everyone complained about it.

The possibility of discovery increased the tension. They were alert to the possibility of Jean coming down the stairs with a pale blue duster in hand. It was gripping to maintain the facade of normalcy as long as possible, going through preliminary motions, tucking in the blanket and bringing out the Masseur-In-A-Box portable massage pad from beneath the sofa—a black polystyrene thing with metal rods running lengthwise across it.

The Masseur-In-A-Box had several settings. It could go very fast, bringing them to a climax in a matter of seconds, or slowly, with an interval of ten or fifteen seconds, as it cycled down the length of the pad. Luke's preferred setting was "Rolling Shiatsu," because it prolonged the experience. There was a small black device attached to the pad where the settings could be chosen. Blake liked to abandon control to Luke. Would he be selfish or generous? Blake wondered, his throat dry with anticipation.

"So what happened in the end?"

"Luke went to college in Canada and we lost touch."

The main course arrived.

"Bon appétit," Blake said. He vigorously sawed off a piece of steak and started chewing. "Well, I wouldn't say this is *rare*."

He put down his fork and made a cupped gesture of futility with his hand.

"Would you like to try mine?" Richard said. "It might be different."

"It looks worse."

Blake renewed his carving.

"I'm a food brat. I apologize."

"That's okay."

For dessert, they shared a piece of carrot cake, and then Richard excused himself, figuring he would give Blake the opportunity to pay. As he went toward the restrooms, he had a feeling of contentment. Soft candlelight bathed the attractive couples leaning toward each other across the tables as Wu-Tang Clan's *36 Chambers* pulsed from the speakers.

When he returned to the table, Blake stood up.

"My turn," he said. "Be right back."

Richard watched as Blake headed in the direction of the bathroom, his broad back emphasized by the undersized polo shirt he wore, the neat fade of his hair indicative of a recent visit to the barbershop. Richard looked out the window and saw two men licking ice cream cones, swooping and maneuvering to catch errant streams, their hands coming together in a gentle grip as they walked off.

"One bill or two?" the waiter said, appearing beside him.

"One."

The waiter went away again. Several minutes passed. Wondering where Blake was, Richard again looked toward the far end of the restaurant. What else was back there? A tiny faux market selling a brand of lobster oil made at the restaurant. It was dark and boarded-up now. Perhaps the food didn't agree with Blake. Richard hoped nothing was wrong with the steak. Had it been too rare after all?

In another minute, the waiter was there again.

"We're still not ready."

The waiter bounded off with a look of annoyance. Richard couldn't decide what would be more embarrassing: greeting Blake after such a long trip to the bathroom, or telling the waiter each time he came for the check that Blake was still back there?

The waiter skidded past again.

"My shift is over. I have to cash out."

"Right now?"

"Yup."

Richard reached into his wallet and handed over a credit card. The waiter swiped it through the machine and the receipt curled out immediately. He handed it to Richard and roared off without another word.

Blake came back to the table as the waiter was leaving.

"Where's the bill?"

"Taken care of," Richard said, with a sense of wobbling pride.

"I have cash."

Richard nodded but didn't say anything. Blake picked up the curling piece of paper, his lips moving silently as he calculated the numbers.

"Here."

He handed Richard some bills.

"Thanks," Richard said, putting the money in his pocket. Their shoulders gently knocking together, they went outside and walked down the block. Some light remained in the clouds. Couples hung about with their bicycles in the pleasant warmth and made conversation. It seemed the model of a functioning neighborhood, a progressive urban tableau, and Richard wanted to say look at us, we're part of this.

They climbed a set of stairs into Fort Greene Park. For a few intensely pleasurable, lingering, and uncertain moments, they sat on a bench, cowitnesses to the evening.

"I want to invite you over," Blake said finally. "But I have to get up very early tomorrow morning. Meeting."

"Sure," Richard said, disappointed but also understanding, because he felt entirely disposed to Blake at that moment.

"I am *genuinely* disappointed," Blake said, winding his fingers in Richard's.

"Well, so am I, but that's okay."

Blake squeezed his hand.

"You have nice hands," he said.

"Is this your MO? You compliment and then you leave? Blue-ball me with compliments?"

"I compliment and then I leave, disappointed."

They sat for another few minutes. When they stood up, Blake leaned forward and they kissed, this final contact almost cruel in the light of their impending separation, but Richard left the dimming park feeling assured. He walked home through the low organ hum of the sultry evening. When he arrived, he took the money out of his pocket and discovered that it amounted only to Blake's share.

THIRTEEN

The June days went past like clear windows, each one filled with a brighter picture of sun, cloud, and sky. In the budding skirmish of the heat, Anne and Richard continued their academic routine, beginning their research for the Clio Prize. Richard persisted in making an effort, though with increasing halfheartedness. Sensing this, Anne continued to praise him, but her praise had more to do with him as a person and rather obviously little to do with his scholarship. She said that he was dedicated, patient, and kind—things Patrick, for one, did not say of him. These were not unpleasant things to hear. But he remained firmly an assistant, not a contributor. Like those friends of Toller's who worked for powerful media figures as sorters of email, bookers of flights, filers of taxes, and impromptu babysitters, he orbited around true talent and made it possible for that talent to express itself.

He had always drawn a great deal of his self-esteem from his involvement with bickering ideas, ephemeral arguments, and paradigm shifts expressed in demure and now increasingly obscure forms of media. He was smarter than most, he'd always thought. But Anne no longer asked his opinion about what they were doing. She went up alone into a cloud of inventive scholarship and didn't come down again until it was time to leave the library.

Their habit was, when they finished, they would go to her apartment and cuddle on the leather sofa, before getting into bed and launching into the latest ungainly but high-spirited sexual encounter. There was something innocent and adolescent in the novice character of their movements, the fits of athletic clumsiness broken by slumps of reevaluation in which they paused and reset their positions, asking each other what worked best. The bed was like a drafting table and they were collaborating on a big project. Though they directed and trained each other, they did not talk about it afterward. Anne said she had not told anybody yet. It felt too delicate and refined to put into words, a shared conspiracy that might evanesce if exposed. When he heard this, Richard was relieved.

During those times they were not at the apartment or the library—or when Richard wasn't with Blake, under the guise of seeing his friends that Anne otherwise found conveniently intolerable— they went all over the city to eat, to places that were high on everyone's list. They waited in line for an hour until their patience snapped and they hissed that to wait for so long was undignified. They went to franchises: Peruvian rotisserie chicken on East Ninety-First Street and burger chains that defied expectations, and they trekked out to distant neighborhoods on Staten Island and to Queens for famed slices of pizza and acclaimed dumplings. They had the duck at Mission Chinese, the blood sausage at Estela, the chicken-liver pâté sandwich at Saltie. They ate with the dedication of food pilgrims whose time was limited, frantic, and exalted.

Based on the photographic evidence posted online, this seemed to be how most of his friends and acquaintances spent their time, and Richard felt the reassurance of conformity. He had the impression that he had become one of those people whom he had used to meet up with back home when he was still living there, the people who had moved away and then would come back to visit, who had exciting metropolitan lives, with their tender condescension and their sympathy for his obscure, unfortunate singlehood, his residency in a backwater.

During these studious interludes and cuisine displacements led by Anne, Richard's phone became, more than it usually was, an instrument of anxiety—like a sensor designed to warn of an impending social earthquake. Occasionally he forgot to put it on silent, and the beep of an incoming message from Blake punctured whatever meal, conversation, or kiss was at hand. If Anne asked Richard with whom he was texting, and she usually did, with the appropriate tone for such distraction and rudeness, Richard blamed Patrick or his father. For the latter, he evoked a suffocating figure, a hound of concern, a man who had never gotten over the departure of his son from the household (actually, Richard's father was gently indifferent about what Richard was doing, now that their financial bond had been largely severed—his Unitarian tolerance was mixed with libertarian detachment). For the moment, this seemed to satisfy Anne's curiosity and put her off, but it was getting more and more difficult to account for his time and to parse out his schedule, to explain and justify his worried diversion, his constant checking of his phone and the balletic skitter of his fingers across the screen as he dispatched another frantic blast of text to Blake, or sometimes to Patrick.

What he felt for both of them, for Anne *and* Blake, was like a warm solvent that dissolved an armor he hadn't even known he was wearing. He felt soft, gentle, and undefended. His calendar had not been this full in years. It pulsed with precarious, often clandestine obligations, and the complications gave him a reassuring, bolstering thrill that he was an in-demand person, a desired, loved, and wanted individual. Like an addict, soothed by the chaos of heightened sensitivity, he was happy.

And beneath that, barely registered but inevitable, there was the threat, vague enough to be ignored or construed as a kind of nervous excitement, the tremor of guilt and fear.

He ignored any misgivings. Those glorious full months of early summer—he would remember how fine the weather was—were also filled with Blake. They too went all over the city. Blake was an enthusiast of the urban experience. He said that if you spent so much money to live in a place you might as well enjoy what it had to offer in the areas of food, culture, and recreation. They went to parks and movies or spent nonvocal hours together perusing bookstores, furniture stores, design stores, clothing stores.

This was not lying, Richard felt; it was not deception, spending time with Blake and not telling Anne, and the reverse. No, it was a kind of settling scores with his past, a long-delayed, retaliatory strike on the thinly populated years of his adolescence, the affective sparseness of his early twenties, the years of lying in bed alone at night while indifferent pornography played on the computer, the squalid spectator sport of watching friends and acquaintances drift in and out of love with the languorous motion of a dream techno dance, of tall sea grass swaying in a current. Like a defeated nation, surreptitiously rebuilding its arsenal, to strike back once and for all against the enemy that has cowed it, Richard felt he had been prepping himself for a great conquest of affection, the moment when he'd make his definitive stand against solitude and raid its most precious spaces. He'd been waiting for the moment when *he* would be the one to whom everything was given.

As for Anne and Blake, he gave back to both of them what they gave to him—friendship, romance, sex, or otherwise. No one was left out.

RICHARD WAS USUALLY PLEASED when Blake wanted to know something more about him—this was a sign of a growing connection, after all—but when, unexpectedly one day toward the beginning of July, Blake asked Richard to show him around the campus, Richard was taken by a sense of panic.

"It's not that interesting," he said, trying to indicate by his tone his profound disinterest in the idea, but not feeling quite comfortable enough with Blake yet to flat-out refuse.

"It's kind of funny I've lived here as long as I have and haven't once gone up to Morningside Heights, no?" Blake said. "Or maybe not. Supposed to be dull, but *so many parks*. I just want to see it because you spend so much time there."

"Is this some kind of lawyer talk?"

"What?"

"Can I see your firm then?"

"Sure, of course, I'll show you the firm."

"That would be nice . . . I guess," Richard said.

"All right, so, when to see the campus?"

That Saturday, Richard reluctantly found himself heading up-town on the 1 train with Blake. Wanting to know specifically whether or not she planned to be in the library, he'd texted Anne to see where she was spending the day. He thought he remembered, from a few weeks previous, her mentioning a golf date in New Jersey with her father, but he couldn't be sure. As was her sulky habit these days when he said he couldn't see her, she took a long time to respond to his question and then was noncommittal. He'd already refused her once that week, when she wanted to get together on Thursday, but having already promised Blake, he said an old friend from home was in town just for one night, and he couldn't say no to drinks.

In a series of ensuing texts Anne told him outright that she hated when they were not together, detested that space between their meetings where he could be off anywhere doing anything. He had this habit of saying "See you" when they parted, she said, and rolling his eyes in a wistful, resigned, acceding manner, as if to say there really was no telling when they would be with each other again. She felt that he was changing and growing distant. *Making plans*, with him, was like the leap of faith that Kierkegaard described, she said, the image of running toward the waves as they curled backward out to sea, in the hope, inevitably and eternally deferred, that they would turn back and embrace you.

The easy flow of Richard's time with Blake stood in pleasant contrast to Anne's analysis of their current dynamic, which felt annoyingly like a critical theory dissection of some obscure poet's last desperate work, though with actual genuine feeling coursing through it. He and Blake were not collaborating on anything except their own time together. There was no "prize" to be won in the future, like the Clio, except the prize of Blake himself, of the two of them out and about in the city, and at home. With Blake, it was easy and spontaneous, give or take an unsettling trip to campus.

As the train screeched ever closer to their destination, Richard was troubled by a sense of impending calamity. He wondered melodramatically if this was how young soldiers felt as they prepared in the moments before the start of a battle to launch themselves across a minefield.

"You're quiet," Blake said, with the mellow, inquisitive look on his face that Richard was starting to love.

"I need some coffee. One is not enough."

"We'll find you some then."

"There's no good coffee up here," Richard said, his nervousness giving his words a testy inflection.

Outside, the sky was paved over by cloud, and a slight breeze had arisen. The succulent emissions of a food truck formed a curtain through which they passed.

They walked through the gates and entered the campus.

"Well, here it is!" Richard said, like a game show host. "Satisfied?"

Blake looked around.

"How about coffee then?" Richard said, smiling anxiously.

"I want a few more minutes, mister."

Was Anne somewhere watching from high up in a window? Richard scanned the vicinity. She must have a sixth sense of his presence now. He sometimes felt linked to her in this way. It was superstitious nonsense but he couldn't deny the feeling.

"Where's your building?"

Richard pointed over toward what he thought might be the Economics Department.

"I want to see inside."

"It's probably locked."

"Let's try anyway."

Richard's throat was drying out and he swallowed with difficulty.

"Wait," he said as Blake forged across the quad. "It's over there."

Richard pointed in the opposite, accurate direction.

"Why did you tell me it was over there?" Blake asked, looking puzzled.

"It moved," Richard said. "It used to be over in that building, but it moved."

They walked up a set of stairs.

"Will anyone be here? I want to meet one of your colleagues."

"On a Saturday? Probably not."

With any luck, the department would be empty and they would be out of there in a few minutes. He hoped Blake would refrain from touching him, at least. They could otherwise pass as friends.

The first floor was quiet, yet Richard felt as though some high-pitched whine, the dangerous, glass-breaking bleat of a newly discovered insect, were consolidating all consciousness to its thin, vibrating form.

Down the hall, they turned a corner and approached the departmental administrator, Carol, who was seated at a desk opposite the elevators. She had a bleached-blond crew cut, a septum ring, and an aura of annoyance.

She didn't look up from her texting.

"Is Anne here today?" Richard asked.

Carol shook her head.

"I haven't seen her," she said.

"Thanks."

They continued down the hall.

"Who is Anne?" Blake asked.

"Anne," Richard said. "*An*tonella. Sometimes I call her Anne. My advisor."

"Okay."

"I hear my name," someone said.

Richard went a few feet forward, turned, and looked through an open doorway, into Professor Caputo's office. Antonella was sitting in his chair, wearing a forest-green turtleneck.

"Hi," Richard said. "You're here."

"Hi," said Antonella.

"What are you doing here?" Richard asked. "It's Saturday."

"Dima's away. I thought I would get some work done. My computer is infected with malware so I'm using Rino's."

Blake peered in from behind, his chin resting on Richard's shoulder. Antonella nodded in his direction.

"Blake, this is Antonella Bolongaro. Antonella, meet Blake."

"Pleasure."

"Nice to meet you."

"What are *you* doing here today?" she asked. "You should be having an overpriced brunch in Greenpoint or Fort Greene, whichever."

"We already have," Blake said, smiling.

"We're just looking around," Richard said, trying to maneuver his description into territory that was sufficiently vague but not over a cliff into conspicuous meaninglessness. He moved slightly to dislodge Blake's chin. "I thought I'd show Blake the department."

"What do you think, Blake?"

"Nice spot."

Antonella nodded.

"It could use some paint though," she said, looking disapprovingly at a dark spot high on the wall to her left, to which she pointed.

"Well, we'll leave you to it," Richard said, with manifest abruptness.

"So soon?"

He nodded.

"Before you go, I wanted to ask you something."

"What's that?"

Richard glanced at Blake, and Blake returned his glance with an even scrutiny. Was this the expression Blake employed in court when he wanted to intimidate a plaintiff?

"There was something familiar in one of the papers." Antonella put a finger to her lips before reaching into a leather attaché case canted at a dangerous angle on the edge of the desk. She briefly rifled around. "I don't think I have it with me."

Richard was immensely grateful, in that moment, for Antonella's disorganization. Someone with a firmer grasp on their papers might have noticed patterns and murky parallels between his work and Anne's. There certainly existed algorithms one could employ to pinpoint these sorts of dubious similarities, but Antonella was also fortunately too low-tech for that.

"Can you remember what it was?" he asked, striking a pose of innocent curiosity.

"You haven't recycled anything from earlier papers, have you?"

"Hmm," he said with raised eyebrows. "I don't *think* so."

"I know it can happen. When you're tired, you don't even realize it."

Richard shook his head.

"I really don't think so."

"You have to be very clear if you're quoting yourself," Antonella said. "I'm being direct. I know you know this, but just a friendly reminder."

"Of course, I'll be careful."

"Especially for the Clio Prize submission," she said. "Those judges won't be as forgiving as me for that kind of mistake."

"True."

She was staring at him and he suddenly felt quite sure that she knew everything; she was communicating with him, but across a plane of no judgment, a smooth zone of acceptance. Perhaps she forgave him and dismissed the potential drama of catching him as too exhausting. They were allies, after all, united in their obsolescence. And she had enough on her plate—not just academic duties but administrative responsibilities. No one bothered to appreciate Petrarch anymore, adjuncts were turning to prostitution and sleeping in their cars; the people's confidence in higher education had been destroyed; the philological method languished.

Richard's heart was pounding. Maybe it was nothing. Maybe she suspected no one. But what did she mean?

"What was that about?" Blake asked, as they went outside into a breeze and Richard wiped a trickle of sweat from his forehead, trying to maintain his composure.

"I don't know."

They walked over to the *Alma Mater* statue and sat down.

"Why was she wearing a turtleneck?"

Richard's phone buzzed and he slid it out of his pocket.

ARE YOU ON CAMPUS? Anne wrote.

He stared at the screen, wondering if she and Antonella were now in a conspiracy of direct communication about him.

"It *is* very nice here," Blake said, looking at the brick at their feet, a geometric pattern that extended out over the ground before descending into a shapely junction of cement paths and lawns, framed by a hazy sequence of Ionic columns.

"Yeah, it is," Richard agreed distractedly.

DID YOU JUST TEXT ME? Richard wrote back. **THE MESSAGE IS GARBLED.**

He glanced back toward the department.

I'M IN THE DEPARTMENT. ANTONELLA SAID YOU WERE JUST HERE.

"Let's go," Richard said, standing up. "Come on."

"Yes, sir."

He took Blake's hand.

"This way."

As they walked, he texted.

YES, BUT I'M ON THE TRAIN NOW. GOING TO LOSE RECEPTION.

They turned a corner and he glanced back to see Anne emerge from the department building and scan the immediate surroundings with rapid-fire jerks of her head.

"This is taking us away from the subway," Blake said.

"I want to walk for a bit."

Anne texted again.

ANTONELLA SAID THERE WAS SOMEONE WITH YOU. WHO WERE YOU WITH?

Richard put his phone away.

"That's the law library," he said to Blake, pointing to an imposing and dreary concrete structure. They passed brusquely out onto Amsterdam Avenue.

WHAT ARE YOU DOING? she wrote again. Richard turned off his phone. They took a circuitous path up to 125th Street, where they got onto the A train. His right eye twitched and fluttered, as if a speck of dust had landed in it. He felt awful.

"Where are you taking us?" Blake asked, his voice amused, sensing how flustered Richard was. Perhaps Blake attributed it to Antonella's suspicion, which *was* partly its cause, though it was heavily compounded by the guilt Richard felt at abandoning Anne.

"I just haven't walked up here in a while."

The train heaved loose and began to travel south.

"So what was Antonella talking about?"

"I use the same research twice, sometimes—in different papers. I quote the same scholars. I could have missed something."

Blake nodded quizzically.

"That doesn't seem like a big deal. Probably happens a lot."

"Yeah, just mental fatigue."

By the time they got off at West Fourth, Richard's mood was black. They moved down the truculent gauntlet of Sixth Avenue, passing the IFC.

"Look, you like that director, right?" Blake said, pointing toward the roster of films playing that afternoon. It was an Antonioni matinée. "You were just talking about that film."

A film could be an escape from the weekend revelry of the surrounding streets, and also a reason to cite for not responding to Anne's texts. But hearing all the *buon giorno*s and *che*s and *fatto*s and *sua*s would remind him of what he'd done, would peck at his brain, he feared, like a decrypted message reminding him that he'd run away from Anne, left her bewildered and abandoned on campus.

"I don't really feel like a movie," he said. "Is that okay?"

"It's not a big deal," Blake responded in an even voice. "There's that bookstore on Bleecker I like. Want to go there?"

"Sure."

They were at the bookstore a few minutes later. Blake browsed in the nonfiction section while Richard turned on his phone to numerous messages from Anne. They followed an ascending arc of anxiety and accusation.

He could probably make up some excuse not to stay the night at Blake's. Since they'd spent the whole day together, it was possible Blake wouldn't be too upset. But Richard didn't want to leave Blake. He had such an unsuspecting air as he flipped through a large hardcover book.

It all seemed horribly arbitrary. Richard was sure that Blake would find his decision to leave confounding. How would he explain it?

Without waiting for her reply, ignoring the presumptuousness of assuming she would still want to see him after what he'd done, Richard texted Anne: **JUST GOT OFF THE TRAIN IN BROOKLYN. SORRY WE MISSED EACH OTHER. CONFUSION. ARE YOU BUSY TONIGHT?**

FOURTEEN

Courtney and Leslie's relationship was entering a new, serious phase, and Richard felt the approach of his inevitable displacement. He had the impression of being nudged, gently pushed to one side. They were always preparing food in the kitchen together now, expertly chopping tofu into cubes while wearing matching gingham aprons with SLOPPY written across the front in blocky blue letters. Richard usually watched from the sofa, a hint of cloistered tension in the air, sensing their irritation at his presence. The conversation between the three of them had taken on a tautness sprinkled with murmured, dainty remarks.

But along with this feeling of displacement, Richard had begun to envy the exclusive, dedicated, tight coupledom that Leslie had suddenly found for himself. Outwardly Richard threw his support behind a bohemian deconstruction of traditional relationship mores, and the necessity for gay people to break them, yet secretly he was old-fashioned and yearned for the stability and endurance of his parents' marriage and of the marriages he'd observed in the upper-middle-class milieu in which he'd been raised. He hadn't discussed exclusivity, or the lack thereof, with Blake since they'd started seeing each other. He hoped that conversation would happen soon, though he was scared to start it himself.

One day Courtney asked him if he wanted children, as she doused a bright green salad in homemade poppy-seed dressing.

"I'm not really sure," he said, which was true, and also he felt that to say no at that moment would have marked him out as a deviant.

"You've got to plan," Leslie said, rubbing Courtney's back. "You don't want to be caught unprepared."

Richard considered pointing out that Courtney was a barista and Leslie a failed doctoral candidate, that the estimated cost of raising a child in New York City would vastly outpace their combined earning power, and anyway wasn't it immoral to have children under the specter of climate change? But he decided against it. None of that would matter to them anyway. Furthermore, he felt it was unwise to provoke them. Lately, whenever he was in the apartment, he had the troubling sensation of being outnumbered.

HE PONDERED ALL THIS as he climbed the steps to meet Anne at the library. Inside, she was hunched forward at their usual spot, her glasses perched on her head. She didn't bother to look up when Richard sat down across the table.

Clearly she was still mad at him for the other day, when he had come to campus with Blake, even though he had found an excuse, a not very convincing one judging from Blake's expression—a leak from the apartment upstairs—to bolt and head over to Anne's apartment that same night. Plumbing issues had seemed more convincing than a human illness; perhaps this had been a mistake.

The subway was falling apart. It was increasingly frustrating to get anywhere in the city these days, but especially to get from Crown Heights to Manhattan. Richard had found her on the sofa, barely verbal and watching Netflix, when he arrived. After a few glasses of wine, things had relaxed a little, but in the morning her crabby mood returned and their oily brunch passed in almost complete silence.

Today, they were supposed to work all afternoon, and then go downtown and catch a film at the Angelika. Down the table, a group of physics students filled notebooks with cryptic sequences of numbers and symbols. On his left, two young men whispered about intergenerational poverty. The silence was full of accusation.

If she was mad at him, well, he was mad at her too. She wasn't innocent in all of this; she had hurt him before, exposing him to insult and teasing in front of Erin and Alicia, dismissing his ideas. She didn't know how condescending she could be. All this time, she had barely listened when he offered ideas and perspectives, only pretending to pay attention. But even that pretense of respect and consideration had fallen away, so that when he made a suggestion now she hardly even bothered to look up from her work. Before he had considered her to be merely distracted, enthralled by her own originality. Now it was clear to him that she ignored his ideas because she thought him an intellectual inferior, and that she disguised this conviction with insincere praise, though today she was obviously not in any mood to praise him.

He was still smarting about Le Goff. When he'd suggested they might incorporate the work of the medieval historian Jacques Le Goff into their latest paper, she'd just shaken her head. She hadn't even bothered to say no. He thought of it now as "the Le Goff incident."

Richard wanted her to believe that he was intelligent and capable. But even if, at that very moment, she were to say something complimentary, he would no longer believe her. She would only heighten his doubt. Instead of finding her praise flattering, he would be patronized; the candy-coated falsity of her words would annoy him.

She had never really bothered to ask him what was wrong, why he couldn't write, and though he would not exactly have been able to describe the feeling, the whoosh of irrelevance—like gravel sliding from a dump truck into a dead, dry pile—that had replaced an earlier, long-standing feeling of exultance or responsibility when he opened up his computer to write about Torquato Tasso or Guido Guinizelli, nevertheless he would have appreciated the question.

These days, even with her help, he asked himself with alarming frequency: What was the point of it all anyway? Somewhere, Anne must wonder that too. But maybe she was one of those people whose brilliance resides partially in their indifference or unawareness of obstacles that might distract or impede them, an inability to even imagine a credible refutation of their purpose.

That was a kind of ignorance.

Richard had once imagined her carrying the light of scholarship in the loutish darkness of twenty-first-century culture, but now he couldn't help but see a mere snob, a hoary elitist who belonged in another time. The library was full of young men and women of every race with beautiful soaring graphs on their computer screens, equations that seemed to offer a mysterious key to things, pointed to the origins and the ends of the universe, to multiple worlds, to problems that had once been intractable but now lay aloof and pliant as a bunch of sleeping house cats. They were building solid bridges and conquering resistant illnesses. What fulfillment, he thought, to know that you will go forth and affect life, instead of wasting your time in a remote corner of some library, choking on dust, escaping only to convene with other dowdy obscurantists for some ill-defined conference about discredited worldviews. He thought back to what Erin had once asked him: *Still solving world hunger through Neoplatonism?*

As if on cue, Anne bluntly asked him to get her a coffee. He shook his head.

"I'm working on something."

She raised her eyebrows. "What is it?"

"It's an article."

"You are? Since when?"

Richard shrugged. "Since recently."

If she got up and came around to the other side of the table, she would see that he had written only two lines. *As the episode of Pier delle Vigne demonstrates, in* Inferno *language is intimately linked to pain. Describing the work of the harpies . . .* It trailed off after that.

Anne lowered her head, but a moment later raised it again. She dug out something from her bag.

"I brought us a snack," she said, handing him a large cookie in wax paper.

"Thank you," he said, nodding as he took it, and immediately lowering his eyes back to the screen.

"You're not going to eat it?"

"Not right now. I'll eat it later."

"I have other food. Let me know if you're hungry."

"I will."

It was awful the way you could dislike, even briefly hate, someone you really cared about. He felt a spreading disgust at his own capriciousness. She was trying.

Several more minutes passed in silence.

"I'm sorry I'm being a bitch," she said finally.

Richard looked up.

"It's not you," he said, exhaling. "I'm sorry I'm being an asshole."

"Maybe it's both of us. Do you want to get out of here?"

Her eyes were glassy with suppressed hurt. At the gentle tone of her voice, he swallowed.

"We haven't been here for very long," he said. "Are you sure?"

"We deserve a break. Let's go downtown. I want to go shopping."

"Right now?"

"Why not?"

"We just got here."

"I can't focus. Let's come back another day."

He hesitated. He was about to tell her that he was in the middle of an elegant paragraph. But after all, he wasn't.

"Don't we have work to do?"

"I can finish it another time."

Her eyes had a frenzied glint.

"Okay. Whatever you say."

They took the train down to SoHo. The car was crowded, and the whole time Anne spoke loudly about what she wanted to buy, asking Richard what he needed in his wardrobe. He felt that the other people in the train, those without earphones to cocoon themselves, must find her irritating. With a low, tactful voice, he tried to answer her questions, hoping she would take the hint. But it was as though she wanted everyone to know what they were about to do: to go and spend money on frivolous things. Didn't she know this was something you did with discretion, especially in the early twenty-first century, when the American Dream had died?

Anne led the way when they emerged.

They walked several blocks west. Slender Europeans in leather jackets, Japanese and Korean women with furry purses, and chic black couples in bright pants crowded the sidewalks.

They went inside A.P.C.

"Hello," said an attractive young man, dressed in a creamily mono-chromatic sweater-and-shirt combo. "How are you today?"

"Fine," Richard said, vaguely recognizing him from one of the websites. They'd had a few nonstarter conversations.

What's up lol. My name is Jeremiah Park. I want to enjoy life and I want sex.

Richard walked down a rack, rubbing the arm of a navy-blue suede jacket between thumb and forefinger, glancing behind him. Jeremiah was a handsome, sweet-looking young man, with enviably glossy black hair. He was helping a pair of grim-faced Germans find a pair of shorts.

Judging by what I see here, we all feel the same way. So relieved everyone is so miserable. I'd hate to feel this way alone. LOL.

As Anne perused the women's racks on the other side of the room, Richard was overcome with a warm sympathy. He imagined that he could summon the lonely dark hours when this boy Jeremiah returned to his apartment alone after a thwarted night out. The innocent search for love, especially as it played out on the Internet, struck Richard in that moment as intolerably sad: clicking through reels of poignant smiles and precarious declarations—*I want a man who will rock my world!*—pictures of torsos and openmouthed dogs with hanging tongues. He thought of the widely employed defensive maneuver of sending a sassy, one-word question—*Hipster?*—or taking the defensive posture to its aphoristic limit and writing only *Hi.* Some risked long-winded confessional paragraphs that included obscure nuggets about their personal lives. These were cheery and inevitably concluded with the self-effacing acknowledgment of the unlikelihood of a reply, or a sense of hopeful resignation, or even a last-ditch compliment as they slipped beneath the surface, to the tune of *even if you don't write back, you're still one of the most beautiful guys I've ever seen.*

Richard experienced a wave of relief at having shut down his profile. It was miraculous that he and Blake had found each other on that godforsaken website.

Anne was motioning to him, holding up a pair of pants.

"What do you think?"

"Leather pants?" Richard said. "For me?"

"Why not?"

She was often offering him fashion advice. Did she think he was badly dressed? She herself had a flamboyant style that, though admirably original, made him think of Susan Sontag's "Notes on 'Camp.'"

"I'd prefer jeans."

"I'm going to hold on to them, just in case."

Richard went to the other side of the room and looked at a pair of black leather boots. Jeremiah Park covered his mouth as he yawned.

"What about this?" Anne said, loudly again, pointing to a caramel-colored suede bomber jacket.

"That's nice."

Richard looked at the price tag.

"It's twelve hundred dollars."

"That's fine."

"Anne," he said, but his attempt to dissuade her was halfhearted.

She took the jacket and continued down the rack.

"You would look great in all of this."

Richard glanced at Jeremiah Park again, now standing in a corner with his hands clasped together. Some lingering resistance began to crumble. He walked down the rack and put his hand on Anne's shoulder.

"What about for you?" he said. "Let's find something for you. We can try it all on at the same time."

She looked up at him and smiled.

"What do you think?"

"What do you need in your wardrobe right now?"

They took the items into adjacent changing rooms and tried them on, side by side. Soon they were spinning out scenarios and characters from the different items they pulled on and off, making each other laugh. They stepped out of the changing rooms and did mock runway walks. He was Fritz, Luther, Miguel, and Chandler; she was Valerie, Sido, Martha, and Paige. Unmoved by the spectacle, Jeremiah Park looked on.

Richard wondered how they had found themselves here, with these clothes, and about the potential of their connection, the future that formed when they were together, disordered but fertile. He could be numbed by her, deadened, but then life would spring out from between them, a refined, affronted color against a gray sky, like a flower growing from a heap of rocks, or a fox running past a cement wall.

FIFTEEN

Richard spent the week in the library with Anne, as she began to prepare her submission for the Clio Prize, and he cast around for his own topic. It was mid-July, the heat familiar and intense. Each day, when they were done at the library, they would go back to her apartment. Anne no longer seemed to care about the power bill or the New York City power grid—she ran the air-conditioning all day, even when they were gone. When they returned, the space was peaceful, humble, and glacial. If they felt particularly oppressed, they swam in the pool in her building or just disrobed and watched Netflix.

"You should move in," she said one early evening as they watched PBS. "It's so much better here than in Brooklyn."

"It *is* very nice."

"Yeah, is that really up for debate?"

"It's already crowded though, with Erin and Alicia."

He could obviously never live with those two.

"They're moving out," Anne said. "They're in Queens today actually, looking at a place. Besides, even if they don't, you can live in my room. There's plenty of space. And *I* wouldn't charge you, obviously. You're never going to rent in a better location."

"I can't just leave my place."

"Why not? It's a dump."

Richard frowned.

"I assume it's a dump," she said. "You've never let me see it after all."

"It's not that bad."

"Okay."

"It's not that bad, but it's also not worth seeing."

"You whine about the neighborhood and you hate your roommates. All you do is complain."

He took another bite of the sandwich they'd picked up at Eataly.

"There's a lease. I have to think about that."

"Right," Anne said, crossing her arms.

He reached over and rubbed her cheek.

"Don't be mad."

"I'm fine," she said. "*Fine.* Erin and Alicia are giving me some kind of vegetable facial treatment later."

"Well, that sounds nice."

She was silent.

"I'll think about it, okay?" he said.

"Fine."

FOR SEVERAL WEEKS ANTONELLA had been in Italy for the long-dreaded wedding of her cousin, but she had recently returned to New York and wanted to meet with Richard. Comforted by the ocean between them, now that she was back Richard was nervous again.

He told Anne they would need to differentiate their work more starkly.

"Maybe you should start writing your own stuff again then," she said, in one of her angrier moods. They were sitting on her couch again, eating from a charcuterie plate.

He hardly knew how to respond. In fact, he was speechless. She had struck him consciously in his most vulnerable place.

"I'm sorry," she said, seeing this. "I'm not in a very good mood."

"You know, it's not that easy for me," he said, managing to cough out some words. "I thought you knew that."

It was clear, by her unusual cowed expression, that she regretted her words.

"That was a terrible thing to say," she said. "I'm sorry."

His face was red with embarrassment.

On the way to the meeting, she tried to make up for it by sending him texts exhorting him not to feel guilty—citing the corrupt character of the academic establishment, the high instances of plagiarism, and the fact that the ideas expressed in her work were latent in him as well. It was simply that he'd not had time to express them.

Richard deleted these texts immediately.

He entered the campus wearing Converse high-tops, shorts, and a short-sleeve, button-down shirt adorned with a childish pattern of sailboats. It was an outfit meant to project a guileless innocence, but perhaps it only seemed immature.

"*Bentornata*," he said to Antonella as he entered her office. She stood up from the desk and gave him a hug.

"*Salve.*"

"How was Italy?"

"I saw my family but it was too hot in Naples. I'm always glad to be back in America."

"Really?"

"I'm used to the informality and convenience now," she said. "How are you?"

"The same old, really. I've been trying to exercise more."

"No jogging, I hope. Jogging has destroyed my knees."

She sat down again.

"It's swimming mostly."

"I don't like the public pools in New York, except that one off Riverside Drive."

She opened a plastic container of figs.

"I'm also trying to get more sleep," he said.

A glistening fig in hand, she nodded.

"Great, great."

Trying to gauge the expression on her face, he nodded in return. Was she angry or suspicious?

"I wanted to talk to you about your paper—the one on the *Modistae*."

"Sure." Did he sound agitated?

"There are so many beautiful parts to this paper, Richard," she said, flipping through Anne's latest masterpiece as if it were a contract. "You really have a passionate interest in this."

He nodded, somewhat relieved.

"I didn't know you were particularly interested in the *Modistae*."

A group of medieval speculative grammarians, the *Modistae* had indeed not been much on Richard's radar until Anne decided she wanted to write about them and apply their theories to Dante. Richard had to give himself a little credit: after she'd mentioned them he'd gone straight to the Wikipedia page, and then he'd transitioned to heavy scholarly works in the library. Martin of Dacia, Thomas of Erfurt, Siger de Courtrai. Their names were like Chiclets he moved around in his mouth, walnuts to crack between his molars.

"It was Thomas of Erfurt who first led me down that path."

"Are you going to submit this for the Clio?"

"I thought about it."

"I think it's a good idea. If you won that, it would help your job prospects. And there is the money, of course. You could go to Italy for the year—for a postdoc."

"It's very enticing," Richard said. He hesitated, and then leaned forward. "Don't you think . . . I mean, isn't Anne a more appropriate candidate? Maybe her work is a bit closer to this idea than mine?"

"You can both submit. Besides, I think her Clio topic is something else."

"Right."

He nodded, his brow wrinkled.

"How is Anne?" she asked. "Do you see her?"

"Yes, I see her often. I mean, we run into each other in the department all the time."

It was better, he thought, to be honest in as many ways as he could be. Open the valves wherever possible.

"Is she all right?"

"She's fine, I think. I mean, as far as I can tell. Why do you ask?"

"She has gained weight. You have too. *Ti sei ingrassato.*"

"I've *gained weight?*"

This seemed an outrageously tactless, and perhaps inappropriate remark. It occurred to Richard that he could probably take Antonella up on some kind of complaint if he wanted to.

"It suits you." Antonella nodded.

"Uh, thanks."

"Anne seems very tired though."

"Aren't we all . . . here in New York."

Antonella squinted.

"Actually, Richard, I am concerned that, if she is under pressure somehow, the work—"

"I can't imagine Anne's work suffering."

She paused.

"No, but your work is very similar. You must be careful."

"What do you mean?"

"Not to be . . . derivative. Not to put yourself at risk."

It was true, he thought, she really did hate Anne. And she didn't do a very good job of hiding it. Richard was nodding vigorously.

"I won't put myself at risk."

"There are certain types in the world, Richard. You are the generous type."

"That's nice of you to say."

"And then there are other types."

He nodded more slowly now.

"Don't worry about Anne," she said. "Write up the application proposal tonight and send it to me tomorrow. Focus on the area of syntax."

"I think that's a promising area," he agreed.

"Can you do that? Can you send me the proposal?"

Not knowing whether Anne would be free to help him, but agreeing anyway, Richard nodded.

"I'm very happy that you were able to start writing again, Richard. This has been a wonderful change. What's your secret? Do you have any tips I can offer to other students?"

Was it the most absurd question that had ever been posed to him? He smiled bashfully and shook his head.

"Organization, I guess," he said, going quiet. "Organization is key."

"Yes." She laughed. "But I was hoping for something more."

"Sorry to disappoint," Richard muttered, anxious to get out of there as quickly as he could.

HE WENT TO THE library. It was strange to be there without Anne. He was so used to her anchoring him in the space, contracting the room around her with the pull of her absorption, shielding him from the waves of distracting chatter, snack unwrapping, and the phones on the tables with their incessant seizures.

He reread the paper on the *Modistae* that had so impressed Antonella. Anne was still working on it—revising and expanding it in one direction—but of course it was already trenchant and tasteful. The particular area that Antonella wanted him to focus on was similar, but disparate enough to constitute another paper entirely. He decided to try to work on it himself.

He went to the website of the Clio Prize and read the requirements for the initial proposal. Most of the work had already been done; he could pull the bulk of the main text of the proposal from the paper itself. He opened a blank document on his computer and began to jot down notes. To his surprise, his thoughts arrived and settled in a reasonably brisk and efficient manner. He was reminded of his previous, successful academic career—when he'd been an accomplished undergraduate, and the early, hopeful days of graduate school.

For several hours he remained at the library. Though he did not write as quickly as he once had, to his relief he managed to complete the application by five o'clock that afternoon. He revised and corrected for another hour, and then he emailed the submission to Antonella.

Patrick was waiting for him outside, in high spirits. Professor

Mikhailkov had found him an office with a stained-glass window. Every time the professor came by, he offered Patrick a wine gum and praised him. He was fulfilling the role of a mentor, something Patrick had long been looking for in the university. Patrick was working long hours on his Russian, and it was improving markedly. They translated together, passing words back and forth like precious jewels, a vague smell—minty and analgesic—emanating from Professor Mikhailkov's hair, which seemed to shine even under dim light.

"I had another article accepted," Patrick said. "It's a contemporary art magazine. I'm thinking this could be a new angle for me."

"Oh wow."

"And the postdoc is pretty much locked in."

Richard pretended to listen, but he was distracted by what Antonella had said. He could not unburden himself to Patrick about Anne—especially now that Patrick was at the apex of his achievement and happiness as a student. Richard imagined revealing the truth and Patrick pushing him into Antonella's office, one hand on his shoulder, as in those black-and-white photos of downtrodden collaborators at the end of World War II. He was doing something wrong—though really, whom was he hurting? But Patrick would not see it this way.

"I broke up with Valdes."

Richard's attention was swiftly recaptured.

"When?"

"About three weeks ago," Patrick said, nodding.

"Why didn't you tell me?"

"You were busy. I was busy. I didn't want to talk about it at the time."

Maybe he didn't want me to know, Richard thought. Maybe he didn't want me to think he was free again.

"How are you feeling about it?"

"Fine," Patrick said. "I want to focus on the future."

It was another one of Patrick's bold maneuvers, Richard thought. He would have wallowed for weeks if not months after the breakup, smoking copiously and playing the same gooey melancholy songs, whereas Patrick—he was giving a quick summary of his activity since the breakup—had already blasted through a series of sentimental freshmen, several of whom, after they were crisply dropped, began to follow him around campus. Patrick dealt with this through a campaign of kindness, sitting the dejected suitors down in coffee shops, in one or another overly lit campus bar with wobbly patio furniture, and attempting to give them a roadmap out of their infatuation. Richard was troubled by a morbid empathy as he pictured these dazed, ambitious young men shuffling around campus, dismally resilient.

"You're sure *you're* okay?" Richard asked.

"Totally sure."

But how was Valdes? Did he go back through the messages he'd exchanged with Patrick, glancing with an entirely forced air of casualness at the radiant impassive screen of his phone, the textual history of their now-defunct relationship contained behind it like the bones of a saint in a glass box?

"That's my news," Patrick said. "How are things going with Blake?"

"They're great," Richard said. "He's great." Patrick was nodding, clearly waiting for more details. "I'm having dinner with his parents tomorrow night."

"Is it the first time you're meeting them?"

"Yup."

"Well, you'll get a good meal for once."

Richard might have amplified or embroidered the dinner plans, but he found that he no longer wanted to batter Patrick with the happy details of his time with Blake; the desire to retaliate was gone. Which was no conversational impediment. Patrick would surely be willing to go back to talking about his own life.

"Wait, though," Richard said. "Are you still living together? With Valdes?"

Patrick had left his apartment a few weeks earlier and moved in with Valdes, after Paul Michael sold the decaying brownstone and decamped to Alto Paraíso, a town in southern Brazil with the world's largest concentration of crystals. Patrick shook his head.

"Thankfully, no. It was us and then suddenly, like, all his friends from art school. Always coming in and out. There was no privacy. It was a nightmare. I couldn't fuck, I couldn't listen to music, and I couldn't cook."

"So where are you now?"

"In a sublet not far from here."

"Sounds grim."

"Grim enough—just a mattress on the floor and a hot plate."

"God."

"I'll be back in Brooklyn soon. Anyway, I needed a break from the vegetable pancakes and forty-year-old-men who still ride skateboards."

"Touché."

"Plus, I met someone who lives in Manhattan," he continued. "And I think he's husband material."

"Husband material?" Richard asked, nodding and trying to feign enthusiasm. "Who is he?"

He was a handsome advertising executive named Vladimir who

had contacted Patrick online. Aside from a substantial salary, Vladimir was blessed in real-estate terms—his family owned two apartments in the city.

"He's a *Republican*," Patrick said, barking out a laugh.

"That's okay."

"You think?"

"Well, maybe it's, like, cool to disagree politically with your significant other? Maybe it's more, um, more *open* than agreeing."

"I thought people got divorced over politics now."

Richard shrugged, thinking of himself and Blake, of Blake's profile and how it said that *Atlas Shrugged* was one of his favorite things. Richard wasn't about to pull out an Ayn Rand novel and read it on the subway, but of course Blake—conscientious, honest, kind—wouldn't hide it if he believed in it, would scrupulously claim it as a favorite thing on his profile along with Tennessee Williams and Marc Chagall, talk about it at a party even under the specter of obvious scorn. He was direct in his communication, measured in his criticism, open to dialogue. Perhaps he had picked up these traits from his parents, whether in the genes or in the raising. As he was meeting them in a matter of hours, Richard might possibly find out.

"I like that idea," Patrick said. "I don't know how true it is, but it's convenient for my current situation."

Ultimately, Richard didn't much care what Blake thought about Ayn Rand, if he was against affirmative action, pro-life, pro–death penalty, or anything else considered by Richard's circle to be an egregious moral or political infraction. None of it seemed to matter terribly when they were together; the world receded. Perhaps this was the true test of their compatibility?

Still, in Blake's presence Richard did feel the specter of improvement, the mechanism of judgment nudging him along toward some superior version of himself. With Anne, on the other hand, there was an equivalent freakishness: they were two animals of the same species who had sniffed each other out in the blind murk of a swamp, not even realizing or caring how dirty they were.

As for Patrick, despite his new Republican boyfriend, he did not allow differences to slide by so easily. His sense of right and wrong was consistently inflamed. Richard admired and was impressed by Patrick's moral certainty, but it also frightened him. He did not want to live in the classroom of Patrick, forever imbibing a moral lesson, did he?

SIXTEEN

Richard waited for the light to change. Across the street, Blake was standing beside a middle-aged couple in open trench coats, which fortunately didn't match, amid the human topiary of tourists and hot dog stands gathered near the Columbus Circle entrance to Central Park.

As though on some kind of bluff, with a handsome, disaffected, and perturbed expression, Blake was staring off in an easterly direction. He was probably hungry, Richard thought. A concerned crease bisecting her forehead, Blake's mother rubbed his arm.

Richard stepped off the curb, excited to begin this evening, even as it seemed to grow suddenly wider and denser—the approaching dwarf star of meeting and knowing Blake's parents. Blake spotted him and waved. There was something marionette-like about the way his arms and face, the entire exoskeleton of his mood, lifted and came alive. Both promising and frightening, it pointed to a feeling that deepened and a potentially harrowing responsibility. This was a significant step. Blake's expression of casual happiness, and Richard's own cheerful, measured smile as he crossed Fifty-Ninth Street, were at stark odds with the expectations and hopes they'd both placed on the meal.

Blake's mother had a thin, airy, dignified bone structure, little of which had been transmitted to Blake, Richard observed. Or had it been smudged into the rounder, beefier circle inherited from the man now standing to one side of Blake, unreadably absorbing Richard's approach? With a flare of worry, Richard wondered if Blake's father was the kind of patriarch who makes a hard point of his skepticism when an outsider tries to enter the family circle.

They were shaking hands. It was all so concrete now. They were saying how nice it was to meet him, and how much they'd been looking forward to it. Richard smiled at Blake, and Blake leaned forward and kissed him on the lips, answering an unvoiced question. When they pulled apart, Richard didn't look up to see the expressions on the faces of Blake's parents. He wondered if they were at a place where this simple exchange of affection was no longer charged, if it had ever been charged; if it felt of a piece with the flamboyant city where they'd found themselves, the tolerant commercial metropolis; if this was a defiant pose for Blake or merely a habit he'd fallen into. It was possible they'd seen Blake kiss a man before, maybe even on that block. Richard was suddenly jealous of a whole imaginary series of men who had preceded him on that very corner.

They started walking and soon took their seats in a busy, highly praised, and sought-after new restaurant two blocks south of Columbus Circle.

"Blake told us you don't cook," Sara, Blake's mother, said in neutral tones.

"Unfortunately, not really," Richard said.

"Takeout has gotten so much healthier though," she said, considering. "Do I sound like I come from the country?"

An elegant, retired professor of social work, she had a throaty laugh.

"Not at all."

"Blake was telling us about his Fresh Direct bill," Blake's father said. He was named Rick—a fleshy, jovial man in a blazer, also a lawyer. "I cook tempura these days. Cook, not eat. Sometimes I'll work hours on it, but then all that time standing over the pan—the oil kills my appetite."

"Blake is a wonderful cook. We sent him to cooking school in France," Sara said.

"He didn't tell me about that," Richard said, giving Blake a chastising smile.

"The way they treated the ducks was barbaric," Blake said, not looking up. "*Where* is the waiter?"

Blake had skipped lunch because of a meeting. His mood was tetchy.

"I love foie gras," Rick said.

"He used to make us pastries," Sara said.

"I've heard pastries are a challenge," Richard said, attempting to add something to this topic on which he was vastly uninformed. "But I can't say I have any firsthand experience."

"Mmm-hmm," Sara said. "We'd have a Ricard before dinner. Then we got out of the habit. But I love the idea of the aperitif."

They scanned the menus.

"You look hungry. Most of the young men look hungry in New York," she said. "Order something hearty."

"Mom—are you commenting on Richard's body?"

"Thank you," Richard said, feeling tension deflate within him. He'd assumed Blake's parents would be paying. Nevertheless, it was reassuring to have confirmation. "I will. This is lovely."

"Is there a one-child policy in this restaurant when it comes to waiters?" Blake said, looking over his shoulder again.

"Blake introduced us to sushi," Rick said, leaning close to the menu, open flat on the table. "I never ate this growing up. He has more discerning taste than we do."

"And more expensive."

"There's too much choice," Richard said.

"You always have this problem," Blake said.

Richard nodded. "It's true, I do."

Blake was unaware of this pressure to be open-minded and adventurous he exerted on Richard when they went out to eat. Richard didn't want to come off as squeamish, timid, or button-down, so usually he caved to Blake's badgering culinary permissiveness.

"Ask Blake," Rick said. "He's the expert."

"Well, I've eaten a lot of sushi in my life, in a lot of different countries," Blake said, with the pragmatic clout, the matter-of-factness, of a weather forecast.

The waiter came with the bottle of sake and they placed their orders.

"What did you do in the city today?" Richard asked.

"We went to the Museum of Arts and Design. Then lunch in the park."

"Tomorrow, shopping downtown. I'm looking for a new raincoat."

Richard's phone buzzed. He twitched.

"Settle down, partner," Blake said, noticing this. "Everything okay?"

"Definitely."

"You better not have seen a mouse."

"No, no," Richard said.

He slid the phone out of his pocket and glanced down.

WHERE ARE YOU? Anne wrote.

Why was she writing to him? She was supposed to be having Mexican with Erin and Alicia on the Lower East Side.

Vaguely annoyed, Richard put the phone away without responding. The tempura appetizer arrived.

"That's good," Blake said after taking a bite.

The phone buzzed for a second time.

MY PLANS FELL THROUGH.

Richard again slid the phone into his pocket, where it buzzed a few more times. He thought of excusing himself and calling Anne from the bathroom, but he was enjoying himself. Now that it had been established, the flow of the dinner felt effortless and self-sustaining, but it was necessarily precarious, requiring constant tweaks and adjustments. Furthermore: what would he say to her?

He was not about to be rude to Blake's parents.

While holding Richard in her affable gaze, Sara began explaining that both Rick and Blake suffered from a kind of hunger-induced melancholy.

"It runs in the family," she said.

A lack of food provoked not just irritation but profound existential dread. When a gnawing futility settled on them—a not infrequent occurrence—it was usually due to a lack of protein. Eggs and bacon would smother that voice for a while, steak convince them it was worth walking out of the house; a cheeseburger lay a sturdy plank over the abyss.

"Sensitive men. Something to remember when he's in a bad mood," she said, winking.

She spoke with palpable affection and concern. Richard smiled and glanced at Blake.

There was another round of buzzing. He glanced into his lap again. Anne wrote that Erin wanted Korean, but Alicia stuck to her guns about Mexican, and what started off as a minor disagreement then exploded into an argument about selfishness and privilege that left both of them crying. They were currently making up over tea, still at the apartment. Anne was desperate to get out.

ARE YOU OKAY? she wrote. **I'M STARTING TO WORRY.**

Richard felt the impoliteness of his divided attention waft from him like the smell of garlic.

A few seconds later:

PLEASE RESPOND.

He inhaled sharply. A zip of claustrophobic resentment went through his chest.

"Is everything all right?" Sara asked.

"Everything is fine, thank you."

"Everything will be fine if there's enough salmon in my maki roll," Blake said, clapping his hands together and rubbing.

Rick smiled.

"I'm the same way," Richard said, turning the phone off. "Hunger turns me into a monster."

Blake nodded knowingly.

The food soon arrived, and the restaurant grew louder. An atmosphere of urban inclusion and glitter prevailed. To Richard's delight and relief, he had a natural rapport with Sara and Rick. They were charismatically informal—evoking studies undertaken and abandoned, old habits, youthful sloth, misdirection, and marijuana use—and the questions they asked were considered but not intrusive. They wanted to know about his childhood and where he grew up, his parents and his family life, but their inquiries were gentle and open-ended, allowing him to determine the level of specificity in each response. Sara was especially pleased to hear that Richard's mother was a French teacher. Sara was a Francophile herself. She had been taking French lessons for years.

They had a skeptical attitude toward the city that Richard found refreshing and not unfounded. He agreed with many of their points but did not deny his abiding affection for the place. They asked him about his studies, and he described them in a broad sweep, briefly mentioning his paper on the *Modistae*, and then wondering if making a reference to such an obscure group had made him look ridiculous or pretentious.

"Tough job market in academia," Rick said, the only—modestly—inimical words he had uttered all evening, despite Richard's earlier worry.

"*Dad*," Blake said, shaking his head and rolling his eyes in one combined gesture.

"It's not easy," Richard said, clearing his throat. "It's a challenge. But I'm at a good school."

"You must work with some interesting people," Sara said.

"I do, yes."

The evening was concluded with a drink in the bar of Rick and Sara's hotel. When Richard left to go, they hugged him, and he felt that he had won them over.

Blake walked him to the subway.

"Your parents are wonderful."

"I'm lucky."

"A lucky boy."

Richard slid his hand into Blake's back pocket. Blake lightly knocked against him.

"I feel bad about my mood earlier—*God*, I revert with them sometimes. Plus I was starving."

"That's okay."

They walked quietly for a moment.

"So . . . you met them."

"I wonder what that means," Richard said coyly, smiling.

"What *does* that mean?"

They both wore quizzical, amused faces. The streets were calmly alive with pedestrians.

"Well," Blake said, his expression turning sly. "For me, it means that I'm only dating you."

Richard turned to him and smiled.

"It means the same for me."

Was this statement true? For a moment he thought of Anne. He decided it was.

"I have the contract right here," Blake said, pretending to pull a document from the breast pocket of his jacket. "I'll need you to sign."

Richard snickered.

"I'm not kidding."

"Um . . ."

They kissed, squeezed each other for a moment, and Blake told Richard to text when he got home. Richard descended into the subway.

There were no free seats on the train, but that was okay. He was in a daze of contentment. He swayed with the motion of the car and stared at an advertisement for blemish reduction, and then at one of two muscular black men with no shirts on, exhorting him to get tested for venereal diseases. The train lurched from side to side, accelerated, and then came to an abrupt halt. An unintelligible voice made a rambling announcement. He was so happy contemplating the evening with Blake and his parents, the fact that Blake was a man who wanted a monogamous relationship, who had a good job, who treated him decently, and whose parents had just taken him out for dinner, that he forgot, for several stops, that he had left his phone off.

When he turned it on, there was a long chain of messages from Anne, leading up to:

WHERE ARE YOU? ARE YOU OKAY? I DON'T KNOW WHAT TO DO. I'M LOSING MY MIND.

He went outside and hailed a cab. He texted her from the cab.

I LOST MY PHONE. JUST GOT IT BACK. I'M COMING OVER.

When he arrived at her building, the doorman called up to the apartment but there was no answer. Richard had him try again a minute later, but still nothing. He went outside and texted her.

I'M DOWNSTAIRS.

He went back inside and was about to show the doorman her texts when the phone on the desk rang.

"I'll send him right up, " the doorman said, motioning for Richard to go ahead.

When he knocked on the door, a small croaking voice from inside told him to enter. Anne was on the sofa, wrapped in blankets. It was cold in the apartment, as if she'd been running the air-conditioning all day on high. An empty bottle of red wine stood on the table. There was a towel beside her.

"I threw up," she said, pointing at the bottle.

"Do you want water? Aspirin?"

She didn't answer.

"Tea?"

"I can't drink anything. I'll be sick again."

He sat down on the sofa, crossed one leg over the other, and looked at her. Her eyes were red and inflamed.

"I'll make tea."

He stood up again and went to the kitchen.

"Where are Erin and Alicia?" he said with his back to her. "Why are you all by yourself?"

He plugged in the electric kettle, trying to calm his growing annoyance. The night had gone so well up to this point.

"They went for Indian."

"They left without you?"

He shook his head, struggling not to harden against this drunken, histrionic display.

"I told them to. I didn't want to go."

"Okay."

"Can you stay here tonight?"

She was mumbling. He opened the cupboard and examined the boxes of tea.

"Yes, I can."

"Why don't you want to live here?"

"I kind of do live here," he said, picking out a chamomile. "I'm here all the time."

"It's not the same."

"Anne, let's not talk about this now. You're drunk."

"I have been working hard," she said. "I've been working hard for both of us."

He came back to the sofa.

"I know you have."

"I need to sleep."

She put a hand to her forehead.

"Good idea. Let's go to bed."

He helped her up and they went into the bedroom. While she stood motionless, eyes closed and arms raised as though she were a small child in a doctor's office, he removed her clothes.

She crawled into bed and Richard got in after her without undressing. The combination of his clothes with their city odors and street particulates, and the clean, detergent-smelling sheets of the bed, produced a sense of nesting and mixture. He put his arm up above her, resting it gently against the top of her head.

The water started to boil.

"Shit."

"It will turn itself off," Anne murmured, rubbing her cold bare toes against his sock feet.

"Why did you get so upset tonight?" he asked.

"You didn't answer me."

"I don't always see my messages right away," he said.

And, he wanted to add: I was having a lovely meal. I was having a great time. He swallowed at this thought.

She shifted.

"I didn't know where you were. People die in this city all the time. Someone might have pushed you onto the subway tracks."

"That never happens."

"Yes, it does happen."

"Okay, it does," he said. "But it didn't tonight."

"It probably happened to someone."

She nuzzled herself against him, and he wrapped his arm around her, feeling the doughiness of the two of them pressed together in the sheets. The warmth of the bed was soon homey and enfeebling. When it became uncomfortable, he shifted and awkwardly peeled off his clothes. Anne snuggled into the crook under his arm and began to snore, an acidic puff issuing from her mouth.

Spending time with her had initially seemed a minor pantomime to perform in exchange for her assistance. Now, along with conspiracy and entrapment, they had a flesh solidarity. Their bodies were familiar to each other, their tissues accustomed to the warm traction and transitions from smoothness to friction. They were sentimental and tender to each other's limbs and bones, a freckle on Anne's clavicle, a bowtie of veins on Richard's arm. Tonight, this open gash in her armor, this abrupt collapse into vulnerable disorganization, pierced him.

It wasn't possible for Richard to imagine destroying someone. If she found out about Blake, what would Anne do to herself? The outcome veiled itself in metaphor: he imagined her back on the sofa again, wrapped in a blanket, surrounded by a debris field of soggy Kleenex and empty wine bottles.

But it was so ridiculous. Who hadn't spent a night alone with a phone entombed in silence, or an uninteresting movie, or a clutch of indignant articles, or a listless blur of pornography? You went to sleep and the next morning it was another day. She was like Patrick: preposterously strong, crashing through the world and shoving people aside and controlling things.

This disinterred similarity made Richard blink with affection as he stared at the ceiling. Her calmed, steady breathing filled the room. The annoyance that had ripened into worry subsided again into the same sweet, complaisant burden that he'd felt earlier that evening as Blake's face lit up in a blaze of expectation and welcome, when he'd spotted Richard crossing the street toward him.

SEVENTEEN

There was a one-bedroom on the edge of Clinton Hill Blake wanted Richard to see. On a Saturday afternoon toward the end of July, when Anne was visiting a cousin in Baltimore, they spent an hour perusing furniture and interior stores on Atlantic Avenue, and then walked up Lafayette Street and turned right onto Clermont, continuing until they found the address.

Richard loved the neighborhood—the people were so good-looking, and there was something of the ideal progressive future in it. The leafy brownstone quadrants appeared placid and gorgeous against the clear blue sky. To boot, the restaurant where they'd eaten their first steak together was close by.

His hand on a greasy banister, Richard followed Blake up a flaking staircase. The apartment was predictably small, and crowded with junky furniture and appliances. There was a brick fireplace, non-functioning yet charming. They walked around in a state of quiet appraisal. The unit had a built-in washer and dryer, and the kitchen was tiny but recently renovated.

"Can you see yourself here?" Blake said.

Richard stepped toward the window. A fringe of leaves shielded the living room from the neighbors across the street. He *could* see himself here—retreating from Manhattan at day's end, looking forward to coming home and drinking gin and tonic with Blake on the stoop, having gentle and trifling conversation, and watching Netflix. Even the prospect of paying bills with Blake had, in that moment, an oddly promising feel.

Of course, he spent a significant portion of his nights at Anne's place these days—but that seemed, in this new apartment miles away, less an obstacle than an alternate reality.

"Yes, I can. Can you?"

"I think I can."

"I think I can too."

They laughed.

Afterward they sat at a nearby coffee shop, crowded with young families. Blake outlined the down payment and the rent. Though not unexpected, the numbers were staggering.

"We should keep looking, of course," he said, his eyes on the papers. "Maybe we'll find something better. But I love this neighborhood."

Richard nodded, turning slightly to face the open door. Confronted so directly with the financials, and the speed with which all this was happening, he was beginning to feel light-headed. He wondered if Blake might adjust their shares of the rent to reflect the stark differences in their income levels, but he doubted it. Was that unfair of Blake? Was that unfair of Richard to want Blake to? Perhaps Blake, now vaguely aware of Richard's delicate financial situation, believed that subsidizing the rent might damage their relationship. He was—of course—sensible in that way. Or maybe he believed the specter of this gay domesticity would be enough to snap Richard into shape financially?

Was that all it took?

"Considering where we are, the numbers aren't that bad," Blake said.

"Not bad at all, I guess," Richard said, his teeth clicking together.

They each paid for their coffee and walked down to Fort Greene Park. Clouds drifted across the steep sky. There was an empty spot in the grass overlooking an open expanse, where a game of soccer was being played. Richard sat down, closed his eyes, and let the sun warm his face.

"Can I ask you something?" Blake said.

Richard inhaled.

"Go ahead."

"Did you actually like that place? I sensed some hesitation. I want to make sure we're on the same page."

Richard had to make it work. Moving out and getting away from Leslie and Courtney, and not just that, but *living with Blake*, was what he wanted. He had to make it work.

"Yes, Counselor. I did like it."

"Good," Blake said. "I wanted to make sure. I'm relieved. I know this is maybe a little fast, but I think we're ready."

"Me too."

Blake grabbed his hand and squeezed.

The next day Richard went to see Antonella to ask if the department could give him any more money. She wasn't encouraging.

"I thought—I just read in the *Times* that the endowment has been doing very well on the stock market."

"You can see the state of my office," Antonella said. "I don't know where the money goes, but it's not coming here."

Richard clasped his hands together and closed his eyes.

"I wish I could do more to help," she said. "I really do."

"I understand."

"In Italy my friends never work. They stay in school or they move back in with their parents. There is no money, and somehow the system keeps going."

Once you finally did get out of school, she said, you had to leave: in Italy you could only move up the academic ladder through sexual favors.

Richard nodded but he wasn't really listening. Birds chirped in a tree beside the window. Down below, the students in their clumps seemed annoyingly privileged and unfairly prosperous.

"Your proposal for the submission to the Clio Prize was excellent," she said. "If the paper itself is of the same high quality, you have a good chance. You must keep going."

On the way home, despite this discouraging conversation, he imagined himself on a podium swept with floodlights as he accepted the Clio Prize. Anne and Blake were both in the audience, but on separate sides of the room, clapping.

COURTNEY WAS LEANING OVER a steaming kettle when Richard arrived home, her face dripping. With her fingers, she squeezed and prodded at recalcitrant pores.

"Ariel came by and I gave him your check," she said.

"Thanks for doing that."

"Have you thought much about where you'd like to go next?"

"Travel, you mean?" he said.

"Oh," she said, wiping her face. "No. When the baby comes, I meant. Where you want to live. Your next apartment."

"Right." He nodded. "Yeah, I've been thinking about it a bit."

"I know it's still a few months away. I was just wondering, with how hard it is to find a place to live in New York, I assumed you'd have started looking."

"I think I'd like to stay around here."

She nodded encouragingly while saying, "Prices are really going up around here. Do you think you can afford it?"

"I don't know. I hope so."

"You'd have to find some roommates, probably."

"Probably."

He frowned.

"I'll let you know if I hear of anything."

"Thanks, Courtney."

She wiped her face with a towel.

"Uh, how are you feeling about everything?" he asked.

"I can't wait, Richard. I really can't wait. I think this baby will solve a lot of my personality issues."

She turned placidly back to the kettle. Richard went into his room, closed the door, and sat down on the bed. He put his face in his hands.

HE MET ANNE FOR lunch the following day at a small restaurant near her apartment. The older waiters with their tranquil but precise locomotion circulated around the cramped space, emitting a dusty, restful, and established superiority.

He asked Anne how it was going with Erin and Alicia.

"They just moved out. They're in Queens now. I'm all alone in that big apartment."

She picked up her sandwich and took a bite, then patted her lips with a napkin.

"I meant what I said, you should move in."

"I can't just leave."

"Why not?" she said, exasperated.

Richard took another bite of the sandwich, an oily soppressata, but said nothing. He was picturing the apartment in Clinton Hill, with the fringe of leaves over the window.

"Why would you imprison yourself in that place?" she insisted.

"I'll think about it," he said. "I *do* think about it."

"You've said that before."

"I mean it this time."

"Well, that's good to hear." She sipped her spritzer, looking at him over the rim of the glass. "You can't keep living with those two. Why would you stay?"

"I'm not planning to stay forever. It's just for now."

Fortunately, Anne had an imminent appointment at the dentist. They went outside and parted ways with a brusque kiss.

ON THE WEEKEND RICHARD went to SoHo with Blake. They were browsing at McNally Jackson, in the magazine section. The aisles were crowded with tourists and people from the neighborhood dressed in weekend slovenly precision. Anne had asked him to come over but he let her messages go unanswered, feeling resentful for the pressure she'd put on him the day before at lunch.

Blake said he'd spoken to the landlord, who had yet to check the references, but otherwise it was looking good.

"That fast?" Richard said, again beset by the sense of anxiety that had become as familiar as his own heartbeat.

"Efficiency of the private sector," Blake said.

"Ha."

It was all happening at a disturbingly fast pace. If you had asked him a year ago whether the speed of such a potential arrangement—moving in with a handsome, lawyerly man in one of the most sought-after neighborhoods of Brooklyn—would have made him anxious, he'd have laughed scornfully. But now that it loomed in front of him, Richard was uneasy. In his swiftness and certainty, his sincerity and generosity, and his open communication, Blake was so unlike the majority of young men he had met and dated in New York, those curatorial souls who could never find the ideal arrangement of things, like a decorator forever tormented by the misalignment of a portrait above the fireplace.

Frankly, sometimes Richard wasn't sure he wanted to spend his life with a man anyway. Men were on the whole essentially incompetent when it came to taking care of you—at least, he was eager to believe this at that moment, despite all evidence to the contrary where Blake was concerned—and would always, now that Grindr had been invented, be tempted to go onto their phones and seek out a bigger dick. It was the same as checking the weather. They always said they were *happily partnered* and yet you could tell by the green dot in the corner they'd been online only ten minutes ago, or within the last forty-five minutes, or were online *at that very moment*. It was a nightmare of infinite choice, a menu without end.

And yet Blake had decided on him; he was ready to close the menu.

"An efficient landlord is a good thing," Richard said, clearing his throat.

"Oh, he's efficient."

Richard smiled.

"You don't sound very jazzed about it," Blake said. "I'm sensing hesitation again."

"No, no," Richard said. "I'm definitely happy about it."

"Okay," Blake said, with a sort of half smile.

Blake went back to reading a copy of *VMAN*. He stared at a young man with full lips, wearing one leather glove and a bright green speedo. He put the magazine back on the shelf, frowning.

"Are you really sure?"

"Yes," Richard insisted. "I really am."

"I don't know if I believe you."

Blake looked like he was gearing up for a cross-examination. Richard inhaled.

"What do you mean?"

"You're distracted," Blake said. "I mean, like, *all the time*. I don't know where you are. Where do you disappear to? I mean *that* literally. And aren't we beyond the phase of leaving each other hanging by text?"

Richard was taken aback, having long convinced himself that his clandestine moves were effective, that Blake did not miss him when he was with Anne, nor did she miss him when he was with Blake.

"Is that why you want me to move in?" Richard said, attempting a playful tone. "To keep an eye on me?"

"You're being cagey." Blake's voice was unaltered. "You don't have to play games with me." He took Richard's hand. "I told you, I'm all in."

"I'm all in too. I didn't realize . . . I should try to communicate better."

"I thought we'd be spending more time together at this point. I mean, shouldn't we be spending more time together?"

There was a brief silence, and then Richard confirmed: "Yes."

"I know I've been busy. But I'm willing to make time if you're willing to make time," Blake said. "Didn't I say that?"

"I'm willing to make time—of course I am."

Blake exhaled. "I felt like I needed to say that. I don't want us to be living together but then never see each other, or some stupid situation like that."

"No, of course not."

"We go days apart. Don't you think that's weird?"

"I guess?"

"You don't have a day job."

Richard frowned.

"That's not what I meant." Blake grabbed his arm. "I love what you do. I mean that you could do your work at my place. Or we could go to a coffee shop or something. We could work together."

"It's hard for me to concentrate if I'm not in the library."

"I could bring my work to the library."

"But that's so inconvenient for you."

"This is what I'm saying," he said, putting his hands on Richard's shoulders. "I don't mind making the effort."

"Right, I get it."

"And I want *you* to not mind doing that for *me*."

Blake was plaintive and unblinking.

"I *don't* mind."

Richard reached for Blake's hand. At the klutzy sensitivity, the superabundance of mirror neurons that showed on Blake's face whatever emulsion of testosterone and cortisol splashed from his glands, Richard felt a slip in his gut.

"I want to be around you as much as possible," Richard said.

Blake nodded eagerly.

"I think you're just hungry," Richard said. "I think you need something to eat."

"Probably," Blake said, and smiled.

They walked west, not able to decide where to go but figuring they would come upon something. The crowds seemed to grow ever more dense.

"This neighborhood on a Saturday, ugh."

"I know," Richard said, looking in the windows of a shop where black neoprene fabrics clung to headless mannequins.

They made their way along Prince Street, stopping at a traffic light. Richard's phone vibrated. He glanced down at it.

I SEE YOU, Anne wrote.

As if he'd been alerted to the presence of a sniper, he scanned the street.

"What's wrong?" Blake said.

"I thought I saw someone I know."

The light changed and they crossed the intersection. It was then Richard saw Anne, approaching from Crosby Street. She locked eyes with him. It was too late to walk away now. He felt submerged in a woozy fatigue.

"I decided to have a very late breakfast at Sant Ambroeus," she announced, coming directly toward Richard, her words blaring in his ears. She raised her sunglasses onto her head and smiled.

By the angles involved, Blake was for an instant excluded.

"Anne," Richard said, both introducing her and addressing her. He felt he might have been yelling; it was as if he had lost control of his voice.

"This is Blake," he said, stepping backward to open up a space for Blake again.

"Hello, Blake," Anne said, looking up at the person who had caused, she must certainly have noticed, Richard to make this discreet but accommodating adjustment in his position.

231

They shook hands. Then she looked at Richard, who, for no reason at all, nodded.

"I decided to get some fresh air," she said. "I've been a bit sick, Blake. But don't worry, I'm long past being contagious."

"Okay," Blake said. "We're having a casual Saturday morning."

Richard flinched at his use of the first-person plural, a word that in another situation would have pleased him.

"Why don't you join me for a very late breakfast?" Anne suggested. "Sant Ambroeus isn't far." She looked at Blake. "Are you hungry?"

Blake looked at Richard, eyebrows raised.

"I actually am hungry."

"Do you like Sant Ambroeus?" Anne asked him.

"I've never been," Blake said.

"In that case, we have to go."

"Let's go then." Blake looked at Richard. "If that works for you?"

"Sure," Richard said, having no other option, and struggling against a sense of dread.

A MAN IN A beautiful green suit took them to a table.

"Are you really hungry?" Richard asked Blake quietly as they sat down. "We don't have to stay."

Though he had no idea how he would extricate them.

"Am I really hungry?" Blake said. "I'm starving. And we're already here. Why leave?"

A droplet of sweat went down the side of Richard's face.

"Are you okay?" Blake asked, frowning.

"I'm just hot. It's hot in here." Blake put a hand to Richard's forehead, a gesture that Anne observed pointedly. "Really, I'm fine."

"It's not that hot in here," Blake said. "The air-conditioning is perfect."

"He's right. It's really not," Anne said. "The air-conditioning is some of the most perfect in the city, I think."

"Can you take something off?" Blake said, eyeing him up and down in a vaguely flirtatious manner. "I guess not."

"I'll be okay," Richard said, continuing to sweat.

For a moment Richard closed his eyes and pretended that he was somewhere else. A waiter approached. Sensing him, Richard opened his eyes and looked up. Like a car on film when the film is reversed, the waiter's voice seemed to retreat as he asked for their orders.

Anne chose the Norwegian eggs Benedict and a coffee. The waiter turned to Richard, and Richard avoided his gaze by looking at the menu. All of the options were faintly sickening.

"I'll have the artichoke salad."

Blake ordered a crostino Milanese and a cappuccino.

"Anything to drink?" the waiter asked Richard.

"A cappuccino."

"You're getting the *salad*?" Anne said when the waiter left. "Is that going to be enough?"

"It's fine," he said, slightly delirious.

"You know how you are when you don't get enough protein," Anne said.

Blake snorted.

"At least I'm not dining alone," she said to Blake. "I hate doing that."

"Personally, I don't mind it," Blake said. "Sometimes when I do it, I feel like I'm in a movie. It can be glamorous."

"If you want anything else, go ahead," Anne said. "It's my treat."

"What's the occasion?" Blake asked.

"Oh, running into you."

"That's nice."

Richard sensed a befuddled skepticism emanating from Blake, who kept looking at his water and nodding.

"And please order something else," Anne said. "Or you'll make me feel like a glutton."

Blake glanced at Richard opaquely. He turned back to Anne.

"I can't eat any more than what I've ordered," he said, his smile constricted.

"You're not on a diet or anything?" she said.

Blake shook his head.

"We could split the ricotta," Richard said, disgusted, in fact, by the idea of ricotta at that moment.

"No thanks," Blake said.

Richard glanced toward the veiled freedom of the street.

"How do you two know each other?" Anne said after a pause, her eyes wide, involuntarily expectant.

Richard felt like something large and underwater had begun moving toward him.

"Through friends," he said. Blake turned toward him.

"Which friends?" Blake asked, jokingly but with a hint of irritation. The question arched tensely over the hysteria gathered beneath, like a concert tent inflated with gas.

"Well—"

"How do *you* two know each other?" Blake asked Anne, turning toward her.

"School," Richard said.

"That's right, school," Anne said, her tone of voice slightly altered.

"Everyone is so well dressed here," Richard said, as a man in a blue topcoat and red suede ankle boots went past. "It's all of a style. How would you describe it?"

"Have you met Antonella?" Anne asked Blake.

As he considered the question, a perplexed crinkle appeared on Blake's forehead, as though he'd come across some not immediately soluble piece of information.

"Sorry, I'm getting a bit thrown by the name overlap. You know Antonella too? Are you in the same program?"

"More or less," Richard said.

"Yes, we're in the same program," Anne said. "You seem to know a lot about it."

"Richard has told me about it."

"Are you thinking of going for your doctorate?"

Blake shook his head. "Can you excuse me for a moment?" he said.

"Where are you going?" Richard asked.

"To the bathroom. I'll be right back."

Blake moved off. Anne looked at Richard.

"Who is he?"

"He's a friend of mine."

"You've never mentioned him to me before."

"Do I have to mention every single person in my life?"

"Does he know *anything* about me?"

"What are you talking about? Why do you always have to interrogate me?"

"That's your response for everything."

His phone buzzed.

WHO IS SHE? Blake wrote.

As the waiter passed, Anne flagged him down and ordered a cocktail.

"You're drinking?"

"Yes, I suddenly feel like I need a drink," she said. "Who are you texting?"

"I'm leaving if you don't calm down," Richard said, putting the cappuccino to his mouth. He'd already had too much caffeine. His hands were shaking but he couldn't stop. He needed to do something, to commit himself to some definitive action, not just sit there and endure the tremors of his body.

"You're threatening to leave now?" Anne said. "What's wrong with you? We're having brunch."

"I'm not *threatening* anything. But I am going to leave if you don't relax. You're stressing me out."

She shook her head. For a minute they didn't speak. The waiter came back with her cocktail and a basket of bread.

"Could you please toast this?" she said to him. "I always take my bread toasted."

Blake returned to the table.

"Where's the bread going?" he asked.

"The bread will be back in a moment," Anne said. She took a long sip of her cocktail. "I hope you're not gluten free."

"I'm not."

"I love that you can still run into people in a city as big as New York," Anne said, with a stiff smile.

"We probably hang out in the same neighborhoods," Blake said, considering. "There's always some other explanation."

"Do you live in Manhattan?"

"Brooklyn."

Richard's fingers were quivering. He was about to pick up his cappuccino again and then decided against it.

"What neighborhood, exactly?"

"Clinton Hill."

"It's nice there."

"We like it."

We.

But he could be talking about anybody, Richard thought. *We* does not have to mean *us*, me and Blake.

"What do you like about it?" she asked.

Blake mentioned a favorite restaurant, the coffee shops, the bookstore, the nearby market.

Anne nodded. She said there was a disgruntled eccentric, a once-famous actor who was always talking loudly on his phone at the end of her block. That was the main attraction.

"Everything okay?" Blake said to Richard.

"Maybe we should all get cocktails?" Richard suggested.

"Excuse me for a moment," Anne said.

She got up and went toward the bathroom. Blake watched her go, and then turned toward Richard.

"Is she a little strange?"

Richard shrugged.

"Why did you say we met through friends?" Blake asked.

"Those websites embarrass me."

"Everyone is online."

"I'm old-fashioned."

Richard's phone buzzed.

WHO IS HE? Anne wrote.

Richard put the phone back in his pocket.

"Are you okay?" Blake said. "Are you upset about something?"

"No."

"What's wrong then?"

"Nothing."

"Do you want to go?"

"I don't know."

"You look pale."

"I'm fine. I've had too much coffee."

"Is it her?"

Richard shook his head. His phone continued to buzz.

"I need to go to the washroom," he said. "Just give me a second. I'll be right back."

"Go ahead," Blake said, frowning. "But get back before her. I don't want to be alone with her."

Richard left the table. The bathrooms were at a fortunate remove from the seating area. Anne was standing in the corner, her phone at eye level.

"What is going on?" she asked.

"You're behaving like a child."

"By taking you and your 'friend' "—she made air quotes with her fingers—"out to lunch?"

"We can pay for our own food. Why are you making such a fuss? Don't talk so loudly."

"I'm *not* talking loudly. Why are *you* whispering?"

He wiped his forehead with the back of his hand. "It's so hot in here. I can't breathe in this fucking place."

"The air-conditioning is perfect in here."

"Stop saying that."

"You're still sweating."

"I'm sweating because *you're* stressing me out."

"You're making things up. What is going on?"

"Nothing."

"This is stupid. Erin and Alicia moved out. I'm all by myself. I'm *alone*. Where have you been? Something is going on."

Her lip was trembling. She looked as if she might start to cry.

"I haven't been doing anything," he said. "I've been busy. I've had things to do."

"You were busy and you weren't doing anything? How is that possible?"

He put his hands on her shoulders.

"We can't be together all the time."

"Why *not?*"

"Some parts of our lives are separate. They have to remain separate, for our own good."

"What parts?"

"Stop being unreasonable."

"You're twisting things."

She was like a child who could not calm herself down. She was flapping her arms as she spoke.

"I'm not twisting things."

"I don't want us to be separate," she said.

"We both have *lives*, Anne."

"We have a *life, together*."

They did have a life together, a life that seemed governed by a rule of inversion, whose weight seemed to increase in direct proportion to the flippancy with which he treated it.

"I'll come by later, okay? I'll stay tonight. I promise. You won't be alone tonight."

"So I'm supposed to go home now, while you go with him? When will you come home? I'm supposed to wait? What, and watch Netflix?"

Richard's stamina was beginning to flag. He had so little energy left to obfuscate. It was like with lawyers who defended child molesters, he thought. How could they do it? How could he be doing this to her?

Resignation came over him.

"Can we go back to the table?"

He was exhausted and needed to sit down.

"No," she said.

"We left him there."

"He can wait all day."

"You're impossible."

"Are you two sleeping together?"

He felt like he might faint. "Stop being so aggressive."

"I'll tell him," Anne said, her eyes tearing up. "I'll tell him what we've been doing. I'll tell everyone what happened."

"Don't say that."

He wrapped his arms around her, squeezing. He put his lips to her forehead. "Stop it," he said.

"I don't care anymore," she said.

She exhaled hot blasts of air against his chest, shuddering.

"Don't say that."

"You can't do this," she said.

"You're right," he said, squeezing her tighter. "I can't."

"You can't."

"Anne, I'm not going to leave you."

A man wearing a tie clip walked by and glanced at them before heading into the bathroom.

"This is embarrassing. We should stop," Richard said. She didn't say anything. "I'll come and stay."

"You'll stay?" she said, shaking. "You'll move in?"

She was looking up at him, and he nodded, desperate to stop this display. She hugged him tightly again.

"Good."

"We all need to calm down," he said. "Relax."

She looked at him like an angry child.

"Promise you'll relax?" he tried again.

"Okay."

She took in a deep, jagged breath.

"Good," he said.

"I'll be all right in a minute."

"Okay," he said. "You'll be all right."

"I need a minute."

"Promise you'll be calm at the table?" he said.

"Yes, I promise." She nodded and went into the bathroom. Richard returned to the table, where the main courses were already waiting. Blake was on his phone, looking bored and annoyed.

"How is it?" Richard asked.

"It *smells* good," Blake said, sipping his cappuccino impassively. "But I haven't tried it yet. I'm not a Neanderthal. I was waiting for you two. It's probably cold by now."

"Sorry," Richard said, taking his seat. "She's not feeling well today."

"Yeah?" Blake said, barely able to mask his indifference.

"You should start. Go ahead."

"Actually, I think I'll wait for her."

They said nothing more for a moment. Richard breathed in through his nose, and out through his mouth.

Looking refreshed if puffy under the eyes, Anne came back to the table and sat down. She unfolded her napkin on her lap and began to slice up the eggs Benedict on her plate.

"Sorry to keep you waiting," she said, not looking up.

Blake nodded. They ate in silence for a while, then Anne took in a deep breath, seemed to steady herself, and looked at Blake.

"I didn't ask you what you do," she said.

"I'm a lawyer. I work at a law firm."

"That's interesting work."

"It can be."

Anne nodded.

"And, uh, do you study the same authors as Richard?" Blake said.

"Yes."

"Dante . . . ?"

"Yes, a lot of Dante."

"Ah."

Blake sighed.

"Are you a reader, Blake?"

"Sure. Not like him," Blake said, resting a hand on Richard's shoulder for a moment. "But I do read."

Even as the conversation seemed to flow again, all Richard wanted was for a knife to come down through the table and cut the room—the world—into two distinct, quarantined halves.

"Actually, I have something for you to read," Blake said to Richard.

"What is it?"

"I got it earlier when we were at McNally Jackson."

Richard always hesitated when a *nonreader* recommended a book to him. Not that Blake was a *nonreader* exactly, but all of the books in his apartment were fairly mainstream—a few classics, probably left over from college, popular science texts about concentration and the link between abortion and crime, a fashionable anthology of postmodernism, several hardcover coffee-table books. In the heaviness between them, this worry on Richard's part about Blake's reading tastes felt like a comical but almost welcome distraction.

"After you read it, we can discuss what you think." He removed a large volume from his bag. Taking the square, thick object in hand, Richard nodded. It was *Atlas Shrugged*.

"Oh!" he said, trying to strike a futile balance between skepticism and enthusiasm, while also trying not to look at the book as if it were some sort of rodent. He couldn't meet Anne's eyes. She would surely find Ayn Rand—this gesture of Blake giving him Ayn Rand to read—absurd. The expression on her face would be scornful and amused.

"She does seem to be popular in certain quarters," he heard her say. "But I've never read her."

There was no obvious judgment in her voice.

"Yes, she does," Richard said, his face tingling.

"Is she a touchstone for you?" Anne asked Blake.

"I read her now and then," he said.

"Can I see the book?"

"Here."

Richard handed it to her.

"That's heavy. No one writes books like this anymore."

She opened the flap and read the opening lines. Richard searched her face for the inevitable mockery.

"I'll give it a try," he said.

"So much enthusiasm," Blake said.

"Where's the waiter?" Richard continued, betting that petty impatience about food in the early twenty-first century was righteous and ominous enough to interrupt almost any conversation, no matter the topic.

"What's wrong?" Anne asked.

"My food is . . ."

It was a salad, so he couldn't say it was *cold*. It was disorganized? What could he say?

"Actually, it's fine," he said.

Anne handed the book back to him.

"I'm sure it will be fodder for interesting discussion," she said.

"At least someone appreciates a good book," Blake said, shaking his head at Richard.

"You hardly ate a thing," Anne said to Richard. "Let's order you dessert."

"I can't eat anymore," he said.

From the table, her glass rose like a transparent satellite dish transmitting a message. She must have been circulating through the streets and preparing her intervention, he thought; she must have been lying in wait.

"I want to celebrate. It's a celebratory dessert."

"Celebrate what?" Blake said.

"Meeting you. Today."

She looked at Richard.

"Shouldn't we celebrate?"

Blake looked at Richard.

"Here." She positioned the menu so that they could read it together. "What would you like?"

"I don't know," Richard said.

"How about a *Toscano*?" Blake said, pointing and shrugging. "Gin seems like a good idea."

Richard couldn't hear what Blake was saying. Sounds retreated, evanesced. The men in hunting jackets, the women in blouses and cashmere sweaters took on an alien, algorithmic quality as they sat eating, drinking, and talking. It seemed to him that everyone had a life that was impregnably arranged, sensible and candid, anchored by necessary journeys and destinations, while his own was spectacularly fraudulent and estranged.

"Good choice," Anne said.

She called the waiter over and with a heavily accurate Italian accent ordered the *torta di frutta*.

"Do you have roommates?" Blake asked when the waiter left.

Ready to spring, sounds veered back and crouched.

"I did," Anne said. "They just moved out. Now the apartment is finally free. And ready."

"Ready?"

"For someone else to move in."

She looked at Richard with a gentle smile.

"But having an apartment to yourself is the dream," Blake said. "Isn't it?"

"Not for me." She shook her head. "Not at all. I don't like to live alone."

"Who do you have in mind?" Blake asked.

Richard wished then for someone in the restaurant to start dramatically choking.

"I've been trying to get this one to move in for a while," she said, nodding toward Richard.

Blake's eyes widened.

"It seems like I've finally convinced him."

"We'll have to fight over him then," Blake said, smiling mordantly and possessively.

Anne laughed, but her voice paused in the air.

"What do you mean?"

"I think I beat you to it," he said.

Her eyebrows lifted and her face opened.

"I don't get the joke," she said.

"I'm not joking," Blake replied.

She shook her head again. Her face was like a clamshell, ready to recede and bathe in salt water.

"Richard is moving in with me," Blake said.

The clamshell closed. Anne reddened, as if the joke that everyone around her had instantly perceived still hovered at an intractable remove. This incomprehension was something Richard had never seen on her face before.

Blake turned to Richard, who was pale. Blake linked their arms and said, "*We're* going to live together."

"This is embarrassing," Anne said. "I'm still not understanding."

Her voice had turned to a mincing professional discretion stretched over a gaping wound.

"We're moving in," Blake said. "What's not to get?"

"*You're* moving in together?"

"Yes."

She turned to Richard, though she was still speaking to Blake.

"How long have you been planning on moving in with Richard?"

Her face was beginning to lose its battle with distress.

"I can explain," Richard said.

"Maybe you should," Blake said, his face also waiting on the edge of something. "I think one of us is very confused. Actually, *both* of us . . . we're both very confused."

"Richard and I have been planning to move in together," Anne said.

"Is that so?"

". . . to move to the next step in our relationship," she continued.

She spoke as if everything that Blake had just said had been erased from the air in which it traveled.

"Your *relationship*?"

"Anne, stop talking," Richard said.

"No, go on," Blake said. "*What* are you talking about, Anne?"

"I never said I'd move in with her. I never said that."

"You just said it ten minutes ago," Anne replied.

"What is this?" Blake said to Richard. "Could you *please* tell me what's going on here?"

"Nothing," Richard said. "Nothing is going on."

"You told me you were moving in," Anne said, her words barely audible. "You just told me."

Her face was a mask over flailing arms and legs.

"I said before that I'm not going to make any rash decisions. I'm sticking to that."

"Could you please explain?" Blake said. "What you mean by 'rash decisions'? What do you mean you told her you were *moving in*?"

Anger and disappointment were spreading across Blake's face.

"We've been talking about it for months," Anne said, her eyes starting to water. "It's not a rash decision. Stop saying that."

The waiter brought the bill. He was briefly ignored, until Anne handed over her credit card. Blake stood up.

"Please sit down," Richard said.

Blake's head seemed to move out from his body in the manner of an ostrich or a giraffe, a sudden, righteous extension.

"I don't think so."

His angry dignity struggled against a coarse loss.

"Wait," Richard said.

He looked around the restaurant, as though a solution, a sensible course of action, could be discovered there—in among the graceful eaters, the two men with their tie clips over minestrone, now chatting with espresso cups in hand, the famous young male singer, ostensibly straight, who kept glancing their way, the blond ponytailed woman in her preposterous jodhpurs—if only he looked hard enough.

Blake went toward the bathroom, almost knocking the table over in the process. Richard got to his feet. He caught up to Blake at the bathroom door, grabbing him by the arm, but Blake shook off his hand.

"What the fuck is this? *What* is she talking about?" Blake's face was mottled with anger.

"I told you. Nothing. I don't know what's wrong with her."

"But who *is* she?"

"I've mentioned her to you. I'm sure I have. I told you. She's a colleague, she's in my program."

"No, you haven't. I would have remembered an overweight red-head who clearly has some deranged suburban hetero fantasy about you."

"Why are you being unreasonable?"

"Stop saying that. You think it's *unreasonable* that what she's saying—what *you've* said to *her*, apparently—upsets me? What's wrong with you? Who the fuck is she?"

Richard cast around in his mind for a response, but found nothing.

"I don't know. She's someone I know."

"What kind of an answer is that?"

Richard felt utterly vacant, as if even the simplest words were beyond his capacity. "She's lonely and desperate."

"Obviously, but there's more going on than that."

Richard was sweating again.

"What am I supposed to do if she has feelings for me?"

"She has more than feelings for you. She thinks you're going to *move in* with her."

"She's delusional."

"She made that up?"

"I might have said that I'd move in with her, at one of her low points."

"Why would you say something like that?" Blake's voice was flat but throbbing.

"I didn't know what else to do. She was suffering."

"She said you've been talking about it for months."

"It was once, maybe twice."

"Have you been leading her on?" Blake folded his arms. "Tell me the truth."

Richard was briefly unable to speak. He saw Blake in the courtroom, in a dark blue suit, handsome and effectual, volleying questions at a witness.

"I don't know what goes on in her mind."

"You must play some part."

"What?"

"You're supposed to move in with me," Blake said, his voice aggrieved, but also angry and darting, like a wasp caught in a small space. "If you didn't want to, you should have been honest."

"I want to move in with *you*," Richard said, grabbing his crossed forearms.

Blake didn't say anything. He seemed to be calculating, to be near one or several conclusions.

"I was scared," Richard said, beginning to sense irreparable damage being done.

"Scared of what?"

"Of things that would happen. Of things going badly."

He tried to put his arms around Blake, but Blake brushed him off again and shook his head. He reached into his pocket, took out his wallet, and removed some cash.

"Give this to Anne. I don't want her paying for me."

"Where are you going?"

"I'm going home."

"I'll come with you."

"No, you won't."

"Don't say that."

"I need to think."

"Come on. Let's talk."

"Not now."

Richard grabbed his arm again, but instead of flinching, Blake deftly and gently took the hand and removed it, leaving it hanging in the air.

What was happening? Richard thought. He had always wanted a young man to say to him: Move in with me, let's live together. I want to see you when I go to sleep, and I want to see you when I wake up.

"You need to figure this out," Blake said, gesturing toward the table.

He slid past. Richard watched him move with nimble resignation through the restaurant. As composed as any other diner, he opened the front door and disappeared out onto the street.

For a moment Richard stood still, not wanting to set time moving again. If he shifted even an inch, the sinister ripple of disturbed molecules would irreversibly alter the world.

A man appeared in a blue corduroy suit. Richard stepped aside to allow him entry into the washroom. When he returned to the table, he had the sense that Anne would be gone too, that the restaurant would be empty, or newly filled with strangers, one life built on the erasure of the old, Aperol spritz and buttered bread in different hands, as if they'd never even sat there together.

But she was still there, wiping her eyes with a napkin.

EIGHTEEN

Richard went home with her. The entire brief cab ride they were silent. When they arrived, he moved to follow her into the building, but she stopped in front of the doors.

"Can I come up?"

She shook her head.

"I don't know what just happened," he said.

"Richard, come on."

She had a look of almost enjoyable mockery on her face.

"Can I try and explain?"

She shook her head again.

"Can we talk later then? Tonight?"

"I don't know. Probably not."

She wasn't crying now; he wondered if she would cry the moment she stepped inside; or if she wouldn't cry at all. It was horrible to hope for the former. Or perhaps it wasn't.

"Tomorrow?"

"I'm going inside now."

What if Erin and Alicia appeared? he thought suddenly, with a sensation of solid threat. If they found out what happened, they would probably assault him. Maybe he would deserve it.

"What are you going to do for the rest of the day?" he said frantically. "Are you going to take a bath?"

"Yes, I'll probably take a bath."

Her voice was utterly flat.

"That's good. That's a good idea. Maybe I'll do that too."

"Just go," she said.

So he did.

On the subway, he had to grip the filthy silver pole tightly to stop from toppling over. There was the sensation of living in a performance with all the other passengers that would abruptly fail and collapse into anarchy if even one tiny movement was not properly executed, one innocuous breath forgotten, or if an oblivious gesture faltered.

Leslie and Courtney were on the couch when he arrived home. His loathing for the apartment and their presence had not diminished, yet it felt like a fortress in the newly intense assault of impressions that the street had unleashed on him. An obtuse blur of comfort and affection was settled on their faces. They appeared oblivious to the ominous sensorium they, and everyone else, were living in.

Leslie motioned to a bottle of wine on the table.

"Cab sauv?"

Richard looked at them as if they were insane and shook his head.

"It's a little early, don't you think?" he said, bitterly enjoying turning the tables on them and expressing disapproval of their behavior.

"Hey, Richard," Leslie said. "Do you remember my friend Joe?"

"*Joe?*" he said, impatiently holding back a fusillade of acid remarks. "I think so."

In fact he did have a fuzzy memory of an anthropologist friend of Leslie's, or someone like that. "Why?"

"His lease is up around September or October. I think he'll be looking for a roommate. He and Jessica are getting divorced. She's moving to California."

"Where does *he* live?"

"Spanish Harlem."

Richard, his back turned, rolled his eyes at the suggestion of this far-distant neighborhood as the next logical housing destination for him.

"Great. Thanks, Leslie. I'll keep it in mind."

"It's good to get out in front of stuff like this. The summer is passing us by."

"Yes, it is."

"Are you sure you don't want a drink?" Courtney said.

Richard strode haughtily across the room.

"I don't want a drink." His fist clenched involuntarily. "I'm going to take a shower and then have a nap."

It was a signal to them that they would have the apartment to themselves again. It was a signal for them to leave him alone.

"We just want you to make sure you end up in a good place next."

"Your concern is noted."

"No sweat. We hate to do it, but you know—" she said.

He looked at Courtney and was struck by the realization that she did, after all, have the belly of a pregnant woman. When had that happened?

"Of course."

He went into his room, closed the door, and sat cross-legged on the bed. With its unadorned walls, the fake gleam of the parquet floor, and the window with its muffled alley light, Richard's bedroom was the proverbial Craigslist horror show. It was a room that he had always hated in a building that he had always hated. He'd always *wanted* to be out of here. And now, one way or another, he would be. But whenever he'd pictured himself gone, he'd pictured himself with Blake, or Anne. And somehow he'd also pictured himself with this gloomy room to go back to.

THREE DAYS LATER HE went to Sheep's Meadow to celebrate the acceptance of Patrick's thesis revisions. As a pretext for a gathering this seemed a bit of a stretch, but Richard had barely left the apartment since the brunch disaster, and he wasn't about to reject an invitation from people who, it seemed, actually *wanted to see him.*

The young men were stretched out on blankets, resembling wayward Athenian philosophy students in a neoclassical tableau. The blue sky was festooned with the ghost fleet of cirrus clouds. Thin towers rising south of the park looked like the denatured fingers of an elderly hand of great wealth. It was one of those impromptu delirious gatherings in the open air that young, vaguely creative people hope to have with other young, vaguely creative people when they come to New York.

Except it seemed that everyone was leaving New York.

Barrett and Amir were graduating in the spring and choosing, for their internships, between San Francisco, London, and Ho Chi Minh City. Toller was thinking of selling his loft and relocating to Santa Fe. And Patrick was leaving soon enough to take up the postdoc in California.

Richard shuddered at this talk. Wasn't New York supposed to be the ultimate destination?

Toller unzipped a leather duffel bag and removed bread and cheese and a bottle of champagne. Richard's contribution was a baguette. To purchase this conduit of bread had seemed a major endeavor. Every action undertaken these last few days had felt slow, uncanny, and weighted, like the viscous delay of a game of tennis played at one-quarter speed.

He'd been obsessively checking his phone—he *hated* that thing—for any signs of contact from Anne or Blake, but of course there had been none.

"Is there any brie with this baguette?" Patrick asked. "Butter?"

"No, sorry," Richard said.

"Who's surprised?" Patrick laughed.

Richard was too distracted to be piqued by this comment. On top of all his present chaos, he felt a silencing depression at the thought of Patrick's impending move. He tried to focus on its purportedly short-term character. How long would he last out there in San Francisco anyway?

Toller asked Richard how things were going with Blake. Richard said things were going well.

"Two toasts then—to Richard's happiness and Patrick's departure."

Patrick frowned.

"Patrick's *success*."

They all leaned away as Toller tried to uncork the bottle.

"You're scaring me," Amir said.

"It's fine."

"Let me do it. You have no wrist strength."

"What are you implying?"

Amir took the bottle and pointed it toward a group of distant children. The cork flew through the air.

"Why didn't we go to a bar?" Toller said as he spilled the champagne into plastic flutes. "Someone else would have poured for us. A hot waiter, for example."

"It's beautiful here."

"But the new skyscrapers are so ugly."

"Skyscrapers are usually banal. That's what my architecture friends say, anyway."

"I hate having sticky hands," Toller said.

Barrett was lying on his back at the edge of the blanket. He sat up as he was handed a glass of champagne.

"Will this interact with my headache medication?"

"I'm so relieved it's over," Patrick said of his thesis defense. "And now"—he paused theatrically—"the rest of my life."

Part of Richard was genuinely happy for Patrick, but the majority of him, as usual, was impatiently drawn back to his own problems. He wondered what Blake was doing. Was he driving along a highway with the images of trees and dispersed rural shapes reeling like badly Xeroxed images across the windshield? Was he at the beach in a tiny swimsuit? Had he booked a room in a house on Fire Island? Doubtful, you had to do that far in advance. Did he have his face in someone's crotch? Was he back on the apps, offering himself up on the steaming bazaar of New York's sexual marketplace, face angled for a hint of wholesome depravity, chest hair exposed, height and weight listed, desires and attitudes crisply evoked among the gaudy confetti of so many willing and available men?

He had to remind himself that it had only been three days.

Richard took out his phone and scrolled—back, back, back— through his text conversations with Blake. He had often thought that all it would require for him to develop into a great cook, or a really great handyman, or any of those other skills so vital for the proper running of the world, and for which he had demonstrated such an abominable lack of ability, was the necessity of a loved one—a defenseless or at the very least vulnerable young man who depended on him for his food or his shelter. This would have spurred him to become a competent, domestically minded person. His own welfare was clearly not enough.

If Blake welcomed him back, he thought, an annihilating wave of disinfectant would sweep the new bathroom, the kitchen attain a level of sterilization to satisfy even the most compulsive of germophobes. He'd decontaminate the fridge with something brutally effective but environmentally sound, sanitize the cupboards, wash the sheets, and dry them with Bounce to make them soft and smell like flowers. It was so pleasant to sleep on soft, fragrant sheets. Gleaming floors and elaborate cooked meals, things that Patrick had cooked in the past, but beyond even those recipes, noble standard-bearers but nothing too original, would proliferate. He saw himself familiarized with *Larousse*, mastering absurd French dishes that called for weeks-long marinating and other extravagant techniques, reproducing the maniacal courses served in noted restaurants around the world that were photographed in magazines.

He would pay the rent ten times over—both of their shares; given time, he would find the money. He would discover a way to take utter and complete care of Blake, to liberate Blake from his legal responsibilities and allow him to pursue his acting, to give them both a glittering life of curated abundance, of careless outlays, of trips to Montauk, Palm Springs, and Mexico City, of expensive Latvian blankets, Turkish towels, and Japanese toothpaste.

He took a gulp of champagne and, struck by an idea, surreptitiously began downloading or redownloading every single app he could think of. Searching for Blake, he scrolled through the horny un-differentiated mass of the city. The closest guy, who reappeared across several of the apps, was a wiry dancer who asserted his modesty but did splits upside down in a leotard, the camera focused on his clenched buttocks.

The dancer sent Richard a message:

> You look like you're from
> another time. Send nudes.
> Let's go from there.

Richard continued to scroll. The faces and torsos and crotches pro-liferated. Where would it all lead? It was madness, he thought. All this flesh was madness.

"What are you doing over there?" Patrick asked.

Richard looked up.

"Nothing."

He put the phone back in his pocket.

"Mind joining the conversation?"

"Sure."

"Anyway," Toller said, responding to Patrick's earlier remark. "*You'll* be fine. It's *our lives* that are the problem."

"Our lives are fine," Amir said, indicating himself and Barrett.

"Mine and Richard's then," Toller said, and proceeded to describe his recent thwarted ambitions across a variety of media. He had just completed a one-act play called *One-Act Play for a Suicide*, but no one was interested in it.

"It's so hard to break in," Toller said, taking a drink. "I mean, even with all the people my father knows. Maybe it's a style thing?"

"Do you feel like your work lacks grit somehow?" Amir toyed with him.

Richard gripped the phone in his pocket, wishing for one of Blake's cheerful strings of emoticons, or one of the impromptu, interrupting texts that seemed Anne's own special and, he felt at that moment, charming habit to send.

"But grit isn't fashionable anymore. No one is interested in the poor. We've known for a long time that they, like, won't inherit the earth after all. I mean, seriously, do we *want* the poor to inherit the earth? *Hello*, Stalin!"

"I disagree. Everyone is interested in the poor."

Barrett mentioned several crowd-sourcing ventures he wanted to pursue.

"What about law school?" Toller said. "You spent all that time studying for the LSAT at my apartment."

"I didn't say law school was out of the picture," Barrett snapped.

Richard wrapped his arms around his legs and squeezed himself—the sun was bright, but he felt cold—thinking that Barrett and Amir were making the appropriate moves to stave off future ruin. And what had he done? Learned Italian.

"Otherwise," Amir said pensively. "I either want to go into international development—or yes—become a lawyer and defend the disenfranchised."

"I had those dreams once," Toller said. "But then I realized how much I like social chaos."

"How can you say that?"

"It's like in the seventies people went out all the time. Maybe the streets were full of potholes, but it certainly made for some great black-and-white photography."

Barrett and Amir rolled their eyes.

"What do you want to do?" Barrett asked Richard.

"Teach and do research, I guess."

"You *guess*," Barrett said.

"Like, on Dante?" Amir asked. "Do people still do that?"

The question was so evenly put—posed with such a radiant impartiality—that Richard wanted to reach out and hug him.

"For the time being," he said.

After the picnic, they went en masse to Toller's loft for a more expansive party. People began to arrive almost immediately. Vladimir, Patrick's new boyfriend, met them there.

With his pitiless brow, perfect blockade of teeth, and cheekbones smoothed to a poreless glisten, Vladimir was undeniably handsome, but he was also a terrible dancer—even worse than Blake, Richard thought affectionately now, with satisfaction scrutinizing him as he gyrated. On top of that, Vladimir wore in Richard's opinion terrible clothing: a pastel-blue shirt, chinos, and aerodynamic Nikes.

But then, at the end of this pesky line of reflection, Richard could only conclude that all this squareness in dress and manner was likely proof of nothing except that *Patrick really did love Vladimir for who he was.*

Toller came and stood beside him.

"What do you think of Vladimir?" he asked.

"Does it matter what I think?"

"No, I guess it doesn't."

Toller moved off and a few minutes later Patrick was beside him.

"Everybody seems to be figuring things out," he said sunnily.

"What do you mean?"

"Well, Toller will probably get one of his plays produced at some point and Barrett and Amir are both getting into law school, I'm sure."

"Good for them."

"Try and be less obviously bitter. People don't like bitterness."

"You never used to give me that kind of advice."

"Well, we're getting older."

People were lighting cigarettes, and the air was thick and milky with curving smoke. Nearby, Barrett danced opposite a muscular boy in a tank top. They maintained competitively intense and blank stares, their bodies set like contrasting morphs in a physiology textbook.

"Toller invited too many people again," Patrick said, sipping his beer. "I wish he would curate more."

Richard nodded but said nothing.

"Are you mad at me?"

"I'm not mad at you," Richard said. "But I'd prefer that you weren't leaving."

"Want to get some fresh air?"

They squeezed out of the crush of people and went toward the front door. When they were outside, Patrick lit another cigarette. Richard felt nervous. He could feel a weight like a large open hand pressing down on his chest, a mix of nerves and exhilaration.

"Where's Blake tonight?" Patrick asked.

"Blake's working," Richard said. He paused. "I think *he's* mad at *me*."

"That's too bad."

"Can I have a cigarette?"

"Of course."

"Thanks."

"I won't be smoking in San Francisco," Patrick said, handing the pack to Richard. "I don't want to get punched in the face."

As Richard inhaled, he knew almost immediately that it was a mistake to draw in so much smoke. A wave of nausea passed over him, and he leaned against the building.

"I hope I don't hate San Francisco."

"*You'll* love San Francisco," Richard said, slowly regaining his equilibrium. "*You'll* be fine. What am *I* going to do?"

A car went past, the driver bopping his head to a heavy bass line.

"You're fine," Patrick said with a chill elegance. "You'll survive."

"Yes, but *how?*"

"Stop asking yourself that. Anyone would worry."

"It's a legitimate question."

Patrick raised an eyebrow and looked at Richard.

"What's wrong?"

They were both silent for a moment.

"Everything."

"I'm going to ask you a question," Patrick said. "Sound okay?"

"I guess so."

"Who was that girl at Toller's last party?"

Richard frowned. Part of him did want Patrick to ask him this question, knew it was coming. Part of him wanted to create a detailed map and express everything in a neutral schema of columns and numbers. Part of him wanted it to be perfectly clear.

"What woman?"

"That woman you were with."

"Anne?"

"If I knew her name I wouldn't be asking."

"She's a friend from school."

"Right," Patrick said, glancing down from his height of six foot three and a half. It was an obnoxious height, Richard thought.

"Is that all?"

"Is that all, what?"

"Is that why Blake is mad?"

"No," Richard said, dumbstruck as always by Patrick's sonar-like ability to identify what lurked in his mind, to keenly perceive him, to *see* him.

"I sincerely hope you're not bisexual."

Richard twitched. A bird landed on a branch across the street, and he stared hard with an accusatory expression, his face hot.

"Did you really just say that?"

"If you want a husband, which is what you've always wanted, a girlfriend is not going to help."

"She's *not* my girlfriend."

Did Patrick pay closer attention than Richard gave him credit for? Maybe he was not as bound up in his own narcissism as Richard had always thought.

"Fine then," Patrick said. "What do you guys do?"

"What, like, during the day?"

"Yeah."

"We study together. Sometimes we eat together."

"She takes you out?"

"It's mostly a dutch thing."

"You need to be careful," Patrick said. "You know how you confuse women."

"I have a female friend, and suddenly I need to be careful? That sounds pretty retrograde."

"Don't be vague."

Richard felt himself gathering energy. A defensive bitterness propelled him.

"If *you* were getting the attention, we'd be laughing."

Patrick frowned.

"I think you should consider her feelings a little more," Patrick said. "You could hurt someone."

"I don't see where you're going with this. I do think about her feelings."

"Do you? And why are you getting so upset?"

"You're seriously asking me that, when *you're* attacking *me*?"

"I'm not *attacking* you." Patrick lit another cigarette. "I'm curious."

"'Who is she?' 'Are you bisexual?'"

"Relax. Jesus."

Richard rolled his eyes.

"So you get to have all this—Vladimir, San Francisco—and what do I get? Am I supposed to just hang around and listen to your drama forever?"

He was almost yelling, and Patrick's head snapped back, but he stopped himself from actually taking a step away from Richard. As the cigarette burned in his hand, Patrick raised it to his mouth. He had a look of stung disbelief on his face, an expression that, though it quickly turned to derisive incredulity, could not hide the slash of Richard's words.

"I've spent hours listening to you," Patrick said. "Years."

"The amount of time you've spent listening to me is nothing compared to the time I've spent listening to you."

"You've been measuring, is that it? Counting it up? Sounds fun."

"It's uncountable, actually."

Patrick exhaled.

"We better change the subject," he said. "I don't like this." Richard shrugged.

A rigid silence came over the street.

Everyone was so angry with him, Richard thought. Was it really so terrible, what he had done?

Maybe it was terrible. He did feel sick with himself, disgusted, as if, like pigeons on a derelict building, lies were roosting all over him. He wanted to brush them off. He had deceived Anne; he had deceived Blake; and he had deceived Patrick, who had always seen right through him—Patrick, who was not dependent on him, who had a full life separate from him, who could have severed all their ties without any material loss to himself, yet still loved him.

"All right," Patrick said. "We don't have to talk about this. So you're moving in with Blake, right?"

"I'm not sure now."

"Are you having second thoughts?"

"Not second thoughts. I've never felt this way about someone."

"Then I really am happy for you."

Patrick spread his arms out and motioned for Richard to step forward. Richard shook his head, but Patrick kept his arms open, insisting. There was a moment of hesitation, but then Richard came forward and wrapped his arms around Patrick's broad body, leaning his forehead against Patrick's shoulder. For a moment, he felt that they were tangibly, intuitively connected, their chests opposite walls that curved around the same chamber, arcing over a shared, precious space.

"You'll have to come out to San Francisco," Patrick said, rubbing his back. "We can go to the two good gay bars that are left."

"Maybe I should move out there too. I'm not sure I like it here anymore."

Richard could feel both of their hearts beating.

"You're going to move in with Blake. You don't actually want to leave."

"I don't know."

Richard exhaled but didn't say anything. "Your future is full of plans," Patrick said. "Instead of repeating 'What am I going to do?' repeat 'I'll be fine.'"

"Maybe."

"You don't believe me?"

"Well, I don't doubt you."

"Then what's the problem?"

Richard felt he had to try to block the panic and sickness, to contain it. If he did not, it would overwhelm him.

"I want you to know something, but you have to promise to forgive me first."

"I can't do that," Patrick said without a beat.

Richard sighed.

"Why do you have to be so difficult?" But there was little recrimination in his voice, just fatigue. "Why can't you be supportive?"

"What is it?" Patrick said, rubbing his back again. "I need to know what to forgive you for."

"Remember when I couldn't write?"

"Your writer's block. Of course I remember."

"That took me a long time to get over."

"Mm, that was rough."

"It *was* rough—it really was."

Patrick's sympathy was calming, but still there was the combative feeling that Richard could not vanquish, an anger that would not disperse.

"But you got over it."

"Yes, well. I'm *getting* over it," Richard said.

"Good, that's good."

"I've been getting help with it."

"Everyone needs another set of eyes."

"It was a little more serious than that, you know? It wasn't just, 'I need another set of eyes.' It wasn't like I could just go to the Writing Center. I was suffering."

"I know that, Richard."

"If you knew, then why didn't you do anything?"

With this accusation, Richard felt a burst of righteous anger. It was as if he'd suddenly realized, after a period of troubled amnesia, that a terrible wrong had been done to him.

"I didn't know you needed *my* help." Richard nodded at the ground, not meeting Patrick's eyes. There was an uncomfortable silence. "So how did you get over it then?" Patrick said. "What was the solution?"

"I asked for help."

"Who from? Antonella?"

"It wasn't Antonella."

Richard tried to think of some other suitable person, but his mind would provide no plausible scenario. He suddenly felt weak and unable to sustain the charade.

"Who was it then?" Patrick asked.

"Someone else in the department."

"Okay, what was the formula? What did you do?"

"Nothing. We didn't do anything. We just worked together."

"Like what, a group paper?"

"No, yes—I got help. We helped each other. It was sort of like—it was a collaboration."

He was starting to sweat. He hoped Patrick could not tell.

"This all sounds a little vague," Patrick said, his brow furrowed.

"I didn't know what to do," Richard said. His throat was drying out; he wanted another cigarette. "I needed the money from the foundation."

"I'm not getting a good feeling from this."

"I know—I shouldn't have done it."

"What did you do, Richard?"

Richard didn't say anything.

"What did you do?"

Patrick stopped the rubbing motion. Richard looked up at him with a pathetic expression, like a dog kicked in the face.

"I handed in someone else's work. I didn't know what else to do."

Patrick's arms fell away. He was silent a moment.

"There were lots of things you could have done."

"Like what?"

"Ask for help."

"Do I have to spell it out all the time?"

"Don't try to blame *me* for this."

Richard was angry again.

"I'm not blaming *you*. This has nothing to do with *you*. But you get pretty wrapped up in your own life."

"Maybe I do, but that doesn't change anything about what you did."

"It has nothing to do with you."

"Yes it does," Patrick said.

"How?"

"It has to do with my whole life, my whole academic career."

Richard frowned. "You're being dramatic."

"Do you want me to tell you it's okay?" Patrick said. "Just invalidate everything *I've* worked hard for?"

"I didn't say that."

"It would mean that all the work I've done—all the years I've spent, all the reading, all the writing and thinking, means nothing."

"It wouldn't mean that."

"It doesn't because I don't absolve you."

"*You* don't *absolve* me?"

"No."

"It's up to you?"

"Well, why did you tell me? You don't care what I think?"

Of course he cared what Patrick thought. He cared *too much* what Patrick thought. What Patrick thought could paralyze him; what Patrick thought could reduce him to a state of incoherent paralysis.

"I always care what you think. I've always been terrified by what you think."

"Now *you're* being dramatic."

But it wasn't drama. Richard was being truthful.

"I'm sorry."

"I'm not going to let this go," Patrick said.

"Never mind," Richard said. "I don't think I can deal with you right now."

"With what?"

"Your sanctimonious tone."

"Fuck off."

Patrick tossed his cigarette away, nodded cuttingly, and strode toward the door of the building. Richard watched him go. For a moment he stood in front of the building with a stripped sense of exposure. Then he turned and started walking.

Along the street, voices floated out from open windows. The neighborhood seemed full of parties. Fresh and miraculously cool, the soft air drifted. Richard told himself that he was happy that he did not have a bag; he tried to buoy himself by noting that he had not forgotten anything inside and did not have to go back to Toller's apartment, that the drunken faces that had greeted Patrick as he stormed in would not turn to appraise him.

But the world itself had been transformed to ensure a space for judgment to be exacted on him. The entire city was a courtroom. Just as he'd feared, Patrick had condemned him.

He took out his phone.

HOW WAS YOUR DAY? I MISS YOU. PLEASE ANSWER.

NINETEEN

Lying in bed, Richard observed that it had been too long since he changed the sheets. The amount of time he'd been spending there in the last few days clearly meant he should have been doing laundry more often. When he inhaled, he brought in the smell of sweat.

Shapes appeared as the ceiling went in and out of focus. He rubbed his eyes, finally persuading himself to take a shower.

An hour later, when he was dressed and outside, he walked down the humid arcade of the block. Branches and leaves clustered over, like the extended arms and hands of an audience applauding a performance.

Around eleven o'clock, he was sitting in an unfamiliar coffee shop with a latte. As he looked vacantly out the window, his phone buzzed.

HELLO, Blake wrote.

Richard supposed it could be considered a response to the text message he had sent the other night, though so much time had passed, perhaps he could think of it as Blake reaching out.

He shifted in his chair and began crafting his response. It had now been two weeks since he had last seen Blake at Sant Ambroeus and it was the first time Blake had responded to any of his texts.

HOW ARE YOU? he wrote.

The minutes passed. Richard stared at the phone. There was no response.

CAN I BUY YOU DINNER? he tried again.

MAYBE A COFFEE, Blake replied after a moment.

It was a disheartening suggestion. Richard felt immediately that it wasn't the coffee of idle, mending conversation, but that of a steaming propellant, grabbed in a hurry. Did Blake picture ending things definitively and quickly and then leaving with the remains of his latte in a to-go cup?

But then Richard was hit with a burst of die-hard enthusiasm, envisaging that he would persuade Blake to let him move in after all. The scenario was glowing: they rendezvoused and their intimacy overflowed any difficulties. They had a cathartic discussion about what had happened and began making renewed plans for their future together. He would treat Blake and remind Blake—convince him—that he was not a bad person. They would put everything back the way it had been.

HOW ARE YOU? Richard wrote again, gallantly ignoring the fact that he'd already asked that very question, and that it had been ignored. **IT'S A WARM DAY, BUT SO HUMID.**

A few hours later—Richard was back in bed—the phone shook with a response.

It turned out that Blake wasn't in the city. For the past three days he'd been in Pennsylvania, interviewing clients with two other lawyers from the firm, but he was currently on his way back to Brooklyn.

THAT'S GOOD. GOOD TO SLEEP IN YOUR OWN BED AGAIN.

YUP.

Richard decided that he would surprise Blake upon his return. He got up, put on his shoes, and walked all the way to Blake's favorite Korean-barbecue spot, placing an order for a bucket of chicken wings, half sweet-and-sour, half spicy. Then he proceeded to the organic grocery store down the block from Blake's studio and bought two bottles of Brio, the syrupy bitter Italian soft drink they both liked.

With the bucket of fried chicken in a plastic bag between his feet, along with the bottles of Brio, he waited on the stoop of Blake's building. The humid pollinated evening hung listlessly on the street. He sat there and nodded at the people who went in and out of the building. How long would it take Blake to get back from Pennsylvania? The expected window of arrival came and went, and he waited. Was there another way into the building? Maybe Blake had slipped inside without his seeing.

Richard went around the building; there wasn't any other way in. Keeping the front door in view, the cooling meal swinging from his hand, he walked up and down the block. The sky faded to a thin contusion.

He decided to text.

HOW WAS THE TRIP? MAKE IT BACK YET?

Blake responded twenty minutes later. By that time Richard was back sitting on the stoop.

NIGHTMARE. WE HAD TO TAKE GEOFF TO THE HOSPITAL. TURNS OUT HE HAS A KIDNEY STONE. WE FINALLY JUST LANDED.

OH NO! I'M SORRY TO HEAR THAT, Richard wrote, not knowing or caring who Geoff was, and trying to mask his irritation at this medically triggered delay.

When Blake finally arrived he had a quizzical look on his face as he approached the entrance to the building. Richard rose stiffly.

"What are you doing here?" Blake asked.

"I'm the bringer of chicken," Richard said, lifting the plastic bag almost to eye level.

Blake's expression turned skeptical.

"You're looking for somewhere to eat that?"

"Mm. Otherwise I'll just be eating on your stoop."

"Okay, I guess I've got plates inside. One of the few things I haven't packed up yet."

"Perfect."

Richard followed as Blake dragged his suitcase inside.

"How was Pennsylvania?" he asked once they were in the apartment, while Blake set out plates. Stacked against the walls, most of Blake's belongings were in cardboard boxes. Dust balls had accumulated in the corners of the once fastidious space.

Under a floor lamp dimmed to low intensity, they sat on pillows.

"Tiring."

"Where is the case now?"

"Um," Blake said, inhaling with a hint of exasperation, as if he really didn't care to discuss it. Richard could tell in his face that he was exhausted, and in other circumstances he would have said don't bother, I can tell you don't feel like talking about it; let's discuss something else. But he worried that if they didn't continue on this trajectory, they might not get onto another one, that recrimination and complaint would rise to fill the space.

"The other side keeps bringing up silly objections," Blake said. "Which the judge seems to think warrant consideration. It's going to be a long haul."

"That sounds annoying."

Blake nodded.

"How are your parents?"

"Fine. They're in Maine."

"Good for them—escaping this weather."

"Yup."

They gnawed at the chicken in their fingers. It was easier to eat than to speak.

"Is the chicken as good as usual?"

"It's good."

"I noticed a new smoked meat place, um, down the block on my way over," Richard said.

"Oh yeah, where?"

"Down the block. I forget the name now."

It was alienating and strange for the conversation to be so awkward, but maybe it was better than silence.

Blake's eyes moved around the room, as if curious about the design of the space.

"Can we talk?" Richard finally said.

Blake raised his eyebrows in mock-surprise.

"Go ahead, talk."

"Well . . . uh, I need you to talk as well."

"I'm talking."

"You're *hardly* talking."

"Tell me what to say."

"Come on, Blake. I'm sorry. Anne needed me. I didn't know what to do. You saw what she was like."

There was a metallic taste in his mouth. He took a swig from the bottle of Brio.

"I imagine it would be strange, what you're doing," Blake said.

"What do you mean?"

"Richard, it has to be *something*."

"Why do you want to know?"

It was a stupid question, an artless attempt to deflect from all the wretched detail so close at hand.

"I just can't really imagine what it's like, with her. Just her trying to jump you . . . or something? That's about as far as my mind goes. Based on what I've seen of your interactions."

"Don't be cruel. It's not like that."

"Does she read Dante at breakfast?"

Blake snorted. Richard closed his eyes and exhaled.

"It was a mistake. I led her on because I didn't want to hurt her feelings."

"Did you *sleep* with her?"

His mouth opened haltingly.

"Yes."

Blake nodded.

"I thought so," he said, with a tired, absent look in his eyes. "I've never slept with a woman."

Richard didn't say anything.

"Should I be jealous? Am I allowed to be angry about that?"

"I don't know," Richard said "What do you *want* me to say?"

"Is it easier to talk to her than to talk to me?" Blake asked.

"No."

"Do you need her?"

"Where are you getting this?"

"I'm trying to understand," Blake said.

"You already understand me. You already know me."

Richard reached out and took Blake's wrist in his hand. Surprisingly, Blake didn't pull away.

"That's what you need to understand," Richard said. "I want to move in with you. I want to live with you. I don't want to live with *her.* I needed her help; that's it. She needed my help. It's not like with you."

It was dramatic scenes like this that Richard had imagined for himself as a teenage boy, lonely in bed. But the imagined feeling had been so different then. There had been a swell, not this threatening quiet between words. Not this solvent taste in his mouth. Not the potential for fatal rejection and the possibility of a still, solitary aftermath.

"Move in with me? I don't know if that's still a good idea."

"Let's not lose this. I don't want to lose this."

Blake shook his head.

Richard leaned forward. "Is this because I can't cook?" he said, holding up a piece of chicken.

Blake rolled his eyes but was unable to resist the flicker of a droll smile.

"I hope you're joking."

"I'm not funny?"

"I'm not sure this is a good idea, starting this up again."

Richard nodded slowly and said, "Okay."

He bit through the chicken's greasy skin. He felt his eyes must look glistening and slippery, as if they might start furiously spinning in their sockets like the numbers of a slot machine.

"Don't you think?" Blake said. "Don't you think it's a bit fast after everything that happened?"

"No."

Blake shrugged. Richard glanced around at the boxes. He was desperate.

"You're going to have a lot of room in that place."

"Hardly," Blake said. "It's not that big."

"I'll help you move in anyway," Richard said.

"You don't need to do that. I certainly don't expect you to."

"I'm going to help you. I'm going to make it up to you."

Blake sighed. He reached out and put his hand on Richard's leg.

"Your leg is warm. You have good circulation."

Richard took Blake's hand again. They remained linked for a moment, and then Blake pulled back.

"A moving company is taking most of my stuff over to the new place tomorrow, but there will be some odds and ends."

"So I can help?"

"Come over in the evening," Blake said.

At this assent and invitation from Blake, this voluntary if reticent opening, Richard felt revived, almost physically enlarged. After these last few sad, limp weeks, hope prodded him again.

"You can help me take the last things over," Blake said.

TWENTY

With the last of Blake's belongings in a series of duffel bags, Blake and Richard took a livery cab over to the new apartment. Sitting at the window, surveying the August night full of the voices of people wandering in the soft purr of the humid streets, they drank kombucha from the bodega while Blake maintained a prudent physical distance. Hoping the evening would continue in this fashion, Richard was disappointed when Blake said he had work to do and went into the bedroom, in the corner of which he had installed a small desk. Richard got out his computer and began to read, resigned to his solitude.

But an hour later Blake wandered out again, complaining that he found it impossible to concentrate with the heat. It's because of me, Richard thought. Blake poured himself some iced tea and sat down on the sofa near to Richard and asked what he was working on.

"I'm reading about the *Modistae*, those medieval grammarians I told you about."

"That again?"

"Yup."

A pleasant hour passed. To Richard's relief, he felt them falling back into old conversational patterns. Then Blake suggested they go out. They put on their shoes and walked around the neighborhood, ultimately choosing to sit down for beers on a patio. A while later, they parted on the street with a long hug and Richard walked home happily.

The next day he woke up early to a text from Blake, suggesting that they go to the beach together. Pleased and surprised in his grogginess, Richard responded that he was up for whatever Blake had in mind.

Blake rented a Zipcar, picked up Richard at his apartment, and they drove out to Fort Tilden. For several hours they swam in the ocean, gawking at young men and dodging the seaborne garbage, Richard wearing the red swimsuit Anne had bought for him in Montreal. Water beading on their shoulders, applying and reapplying sunscreen, they took pictures of each other with their phones. It was the most intimate touch they'd had in some time. They were submerged in intense heat, healthy young men, the slender bending columns of their bodies quietly flourishing amid a thriving panoply of beach towels, umbrellas, and coolers.

Richard felt exhausted and happy when they returned to the apartment with banh mi sandwiches and Cokes they'd picked up on the way back. Unwrapping the sandwiches on the coffee table, they sat on the sofa and watched *Nights of Cabiria* on Blake's computer. Blake's tanned legs, one stretched out and the other tucked beneath him, seemed the most perfect, beautifully formed limbs Richard had ever seen. He wanted to stick his tongue in Blake's ear but held himself back.

Instead of turning his way with knowing eyes when the movie was over, as Richard had been hoping he would, Blake stood up from the sofa and walked over to the closet. He extracted a pile of bedding and handed it to Richard.

"You're welcome to crash on the couch. I know it's late."

"Thanks," Richard said, hiding his disappointment. "But I can just get an Uber, or walk."

"It's too far to walk now. Besides, it's a really comfortable couch."

"All right." He smiled. "If you insist."

Blake nodded and looked away.

"Good night," Blake said.

Blake went into the bedroom and closed the door. The light under the door persisted for some time, and then went out.

A WEEK OF ODD maneuvers followed. Richard slept in his own bed only twice, opting for Blake's couch instead. During the day, when Blake was at work, they texted frequently. Although Blake tried to maintain some distance, as though Richard were a houseguest he didn't know very well, they couldn't help being in close proximity. As such encounters proliferated, Richard could feel their natural chemistry slowly eroding Blake's resolve, the artificial and inversely sexy formality of this prescribed distance, this role-playing at withholding that began to imbue their every movement, eye contact, or avoidance of contact with tension and the potential for a turbulent physical resolution.

By the following weekend, they'd had sex on the couch a few times. Richard loved the once again familiar frame of Blake's face looking up at him from the pillow when he climbed on top of him, the faraway ecstatic distraction in his eyes. Things seemed to shift, if not back to where they had been before, then forward into a new zone, a place both scarred and reinforced by their recent troubles. The apartment had the feeling of a vulnerable yet cherished redoubt where retreating forces would stop to regroup before pressing forward again, a welcome lull in the artillery barrage from which a new advance could be planned.

One night Blake said, "I want you to sleep beside me."

Amid the cheerful disorder—his stuff was still in piles and

boxes—and a thunderstorm outside, they drank an expensive bottle of red wine that Blake's parents had given to him the day he was hired by the firm. They discussed the furnishings and decorative schemes Blake had been considering.

Maybe it was best that the destructive brunch at Sant Ambroeus had happened, Richard thought later as Blake snored beside him; that he had been forced to break with Anne, that she had been freed from him. It was better in the long run for her, for both of them. He was still texting her once every few days, but she never replied.

Of course, there was the matter of school and the money from the foundation. It seemed a light and irrelevant question for the time being. He could tell Antonella that his block had returned. She was obliged to help him. They would have to deal with it somehow. Maybe if he stood on his head. Perhaps he would give it all up and learn to cook and be Blake's live-in husband. He wasn't really worried about Anne telling Antonella, or anyone else, what they'd done. He had never believed that she would, for the simple fact that she would be implicated in any confession, and that whatever happened, she did not want to hurt him. He did not want to hurt her either. He was happy.

A week after Blake had invited Richard to sleep in his bed again, they were standing in line at a restaurant in Williamsburg. Content to have Blake a foot away, to have their hips and arms brushing against each other, Richard felt generously disposed to everything in his vicinity. It was going to be a bit of a wait, the maître d' in her mesh top had informed them. Never mind. In the unexpected breeze, it was pleasant to be outside. Anne found slow-moving restaurant lines intolerable, Richard thought. They'd have left by now and gone somewhere else, tension in the air. But today, calmed by sex perhaps, Blake was patient.

They were both dressed in cotton pants and T-shirts, the luminescence of the season on their skin. Despite the summer reaching its kindled apex, Blake still had an appetite for heavy, expensive dishes. These dishes went well with alcohol, and desserts like grapefruit Pavlova or peanut butter ice cream sandwiches reliably followed. Like a person suffering a manic episode who decides to buy a ski hill or several horses, Blake's potential outlays had the power to bankrupt those around him, namely Richard. Anne was no longer there to shoulder a good portion of his food costs, and the next installment from the foundation was still a month away, but Richard—for the time being anyway—found that he didn't seem to care. Even though, instead of withdrawing twenties from the ATM, he now went to Duane Reade or CVS, bought gum or floss, and added five dollars cash back on top of the purchase; and even though it was now routinely as expensive to eat in the first half of the day as in the second, he was still in the phase of being gently ecstatic, of being quietly thrilled, to go anywhere with Blake.

The cost of brunch could be worried about later. He was living in a condition of deferral, a state of dazed suspension in which Blake could hardly do wrong.

"This is my treat," Blake said.

"What's the occasion?"

"You took me out the first time we ate together."

The commanding professional who would spread his largesse, demonstrate his generosity, and *take care of the meal* was somewhere in there, Richard had always suspected. He'd been eager for this person to surface ever since they'd met. What else was the point in working that horrible lawyer's job except to be able to *pay for stuff*?

"I remember. The diner. I was such a high roller then."

"I thought it was very . . . chivalrous. It impressed me that you were willing to take that risk on me."

"*I* took a risk and in return *you* lied to me and told me you were an administrative assistant." Richard was smiling.

"I told you why I did that," Blake said, not taking Richard up on this line of teasing.

Richard rubbed his chin on Blake's shoulder. The line moved forward and then a pompous crew-cut waiter sat them at a minuscule table near the door, where the noise level was deafening.

The restaurant was a tin-ceilinged space of competing rustic and industrial tendencies. They ordered mimosas and Richard adjusted his position on the tiny, uncomfortable chair.

"Fucking brunch," Blake said, shaking his head at the menu. "Brunch is the reason no one can afford to buy an apartment in this city."

They drank, chatted, ordered a second round of mimosas, and soon their meals arrived. Once Blake had settled the bill at the chaotic server's station, they walked outside. The afternoon was elegantly warm. Richard was dozy from the food and slightly drunk.

"Do you want to go into the city and window shop?" Blake said. "I have to go to Bloomingdale's."

Normally Richard would have resisted a trip into the city on the weekend, but he didn't want to part from Blake.

"Sure."

They soon found themselves on the L train, which shuddered and lurched, as if sickened by its burden. A baby wailed at the other end of the car.

"What do you honestly think of children?" Blake said, staring at the baby. Richard was awakened from his state of aimless passivity. He let a moment go by without answering.

"They're fine."

"Do you *want* children?" Blake clarified.

"Maybe. I haven't thought too much about it, honestly."

"And what would your conclusion be if you *did* think about it?"

"I could probably be pushed toward wanting kids," Richard said, the words drifting out.

"You think?" Blake said, one eyebrow raised, but smiling.

"I think it's possible."

Children had never been a part of the elaborate future fantasy Richard had spun in his mind, which was perhaps unsurprising considering his supposed inability to take care of himself or others. But now, he imagined a circular kitchen table with a small flower in a cloudy vase standing at the center. Outside, the light was fading. A child screamed and spilled apple juice; another began whipping skeins of spaghetti attached to its fork, leaving a spray of pinpricks on the wall behind its head, like the aftermath of a violent acupuncture treatment. After bathing and putting the children to bed, he and Blake would climb into bed themselves, consult each other about the dangers, responsibilities, and possibilities of their life together, and then turn off the light, anxious and exhausted but with the security of an exclusive personal alliance to fall back on.

Not being a parent himself, Richard suspected that he might be leaving out certain fundamental elements. Children were an important experience: some said the most important. As with most important experiences, the division of labor was crucial. Blake would have to do the cooking, for example.

"Bracing enthusiasm," Blake said, but he was still smiling.

Richard shrugged as the train paused and then set off again.

"It's better than a no," he offered.

"That's true," Blake said. "Just give me some time. It's my job to convince people of my point of view."

Despite his undeniable qualms about giving himself over to the care of a child, Richard felt lifted on a wave of togetherness, on the potential for cooperation to redraw his life, on the hovering apparition of a long union with Blake.

They got off the subway at Fifty-Ninth Street and made their way to Bloomingdale's. Primed by the mimosa, Richard felt mellowly transported in time by the sleek onyx walls, the powdery blues and fuchsias, and the checkered floor. Like many of his peers, he loved the peppy gaucherie of the 1980s. They weaved in and out of brassy, indistinguishable boutiques. Retail sentries in business slacks and kohl makeup looked on with bored expressions. Richard recalled the beautiful transvestite Octavia St. Laurent from *Paris Is Burning*, strolling through in her summer whites, trying on perfume.

When Blake was finished, they left Bloomingdale's and walked toward Madison Avenue. It was bright and hot. Grit swirled off the pavement.

"Let's go to Barney's," Blake said. "It will be cool in there."

On Madison, men in linen pants and leather moccasins strolled the sidewalks beside women in silk blouses, distressed jean shorts, and gold-rimmed aviators. As they approached the entrance to Barney's, Richard glanced across the street. His brain registered something familiar. He did a double take, thinking he saw Anne.

As they walked over to a rack of sunglasses, he felt the room shift frequencies.

He stood still for a moment. Then he said, "I'm going to find the bathrooms," hoping Blake would not want to follow.

"Text me," Blake said, trying on a pair of glasses, "I'll tell you where I am." Richard stepped into the elevator and went up two floors. He walked around to the escalator and took it back down to the ground floor. He peered around a corner, scanning for Blake in the vicinity of where they'd separated. Two tall, handsome men with punctilious beards—they appeared to work in the men's shoe section, based on the way they were standing—glanced up at him; he smiled and they nodded in return, acknowledging him but retaining their modish distance. Blake was nowhere to be seen. Locating the nearest exit, Richard hurried out onto the street and walked quickly back in the direction of Madison.

He crossed to the east side and went north. Then he crossed back and walked down the west side, but he didn't see Anne anywhere. He stood and scanned the intersection. What was he doing? What would he say to her? Words were not the purpose. It was instinct: an arcane, remote but imperative guide, a preverbal assertion of need. To be close to that perception again, the hand that reached out and took hold of the world, cradled it and laid it out before him, the longing for that connection across the table in the library, the hushed rapport with the mind he'd grown used to observing and cherishing.

His phone buzzed in his pocket.

I FOUND THE BEST PAIR OF SUNGLASSES, Blake wrote. **COME LOOK!**

Richard sent back a smiley face wearing sunglasses.

BE RIGHT THERE!

After one last scan of the street, he headed back toward the entrance.

Maybe it was no one.

TWENTY-ONE

Blake took a week off from work. Instead of leaving the city they decided to have a "staycation." Richard was disappointed, and also relieved. He had no money for any kind of trip. In any case, he was looking forward to spending time with Blake after the recent near-obliteration of their relationship.

They trekked up to the Met to look at the French Impressionist paintings. They went to the Guggenheim and the Whitney and to galleries in Chelsea and on the Upper East Side. They drove up to Hudson and Beacon and spent the days perusing bookstores and antique shops. They went to the beach.

As August waned, days relaxed their borders and spilled into each other, filled with meals and pictures. Things spread out, hot and exhausted and satisfied. The slackening in time was echoed by slackening boundaries—open doors and windows and minimal clothing on the citizens of the city, drafts that had been kept in dark, still places, the cool snout of air-conditioning that poked over the sidewalk from the open doors of boutiques. Richard felt hot and sweaty and attractive, sheltered from responsibility and the self-scrutiny of solitude.

But when Blake went back to work, Richard again became listless and reluctant to face the Clio submission alone. It was almost due: at the beginning of September, when classes started again. In the afternoons he went to the library and tried to work on it, to summon that happy, anxious energy of composition, of thoughts and ideas locking together, which had once occurred with regularity in his mind.

His strategy was to extract ideas from Anne's last paper, organize them into bullet points, and compel them to form something novel—a fresh perspective, arranged on the screen with a velvety rationality. But nothing would come; the proposal, which he had managed to complete, had been just a tease of competence. Thomas of Erfurt and Martin of Dacia remained elusive. After days of fruitless effort, the dexterity of her thought, the subtlety of her readings, and the elegance of her style crushed him. A manacled wreckage of disjointed and digressive statements, at stark odds with the reasoned, dignified analysis that had preceded it, was all that he could produce. It was strange to think that he had once been able to do this, or even wanted to.

Still, he told himself it was better that Anne was not there.

He had grown dependent on her. It was crucial that he emerge from her shadow, find his way back to where he'd been before his mind had grown recalcitrant and indifferent. But when he left and went out into the neighborhood, past the restaurants where they had eaten together and the patios where they had shared pitchers of sangria, he felt regret.

He wondered where she was, what she was doing, if she thought about him.

AS THE DEADLINE APPROACHED, each time Richard left the library his sense of solitude and incompetence rose to a pitch. If he was honest with himself, all he wanted to do was to go back to his own apartment and lie down on his bed and not worry about anybody else, even if Leslie and Courtney happened to be perseverating in the kitchen about Lamaze class or the baby yoga they'd signed up for, reminding him gently that a new roommate was in the offing and asking him where he planned to move. They seemed to spend their days accomplishing nothing, yet in the meantime they were poised to achieve the fact of building a family and a life together.

At the end of the day, when Blake got home from the law firm, Richard suspected that his own comparatively rested face must be a galling sight after nine-plus hours of work on the island of Manhattan. It occurred to him that he was, in fact, more at ease when Blake was not there, when Blake was still at the office tangled in precedents and torts, with the expectation that his warm person would soon return, bringing competence and a smile.

The approach of evening made Richard apprehensive. They had established what on the outside appeared to be a cozy domestic equilibrium, but an imbalance in competence was on vivid display, and Richard's insecurities flared.

The worst instance came one day when, at Blake's request, Richard went to the Pathmark to buy fish. Blake arrived home, took a deep breath, and said:

"It's gone bad. Can't you tell?"

"It's bad?"

"You can't tell when a fish is bad?"

"I guess not. I can't smell anything at Pathmark."

It was raining and windy out. Blake had gotten soaked on the walk from the subway. They opened the windows to air out the smell, and he was annoyed at being cold. He wrapped a blanket around his shoulders.

"I wish we had a bathtub," he said. "There's a bathtub at my old studio."

They ordered an expensive, artisanal pizza in place of the fish and ate it in silence.

But Blake's patience, or his indulgence of Richard's ineptitude, was a kind of solid, and despite these small idiocies on Richard's part, he typically made an effort to dampen Richard's ensuing anxiety.

"I'll teach you my tricks," he said. "Soon you'll be making me bouillabaisse."

"Maybe."

They drank, and in the analgesic flow of the wine Richard's worries subsided, and he fell into bed with a brackish combination of alcohol and dehydration in his body, picturing his future competence, though his sleep was often shattered by dreams of deficiency and abandonment.

It was a feeling he'd never had with Anne, who saw him clearly for what he was, and who had seen him for who he was, he suspected, ever since she'd appraised him across the room at the departmental wine and cheese, the first time they'd really spoken. At the idea of him standing in an apron, holding a spatula, she would laugh dryly but sympathetically; she would not be too surprised to find that he'd purchased a rotten fish.

Richard had reached the vaunted destination—he was living with a man in one of the most sought-after neighborhoods in Brooklyn—but what he could not stop picturing was some faraway station of disclosure and repentance. He longed to unburden himself about everything he'd done in the past few months, but he feared that the results, as with Patrick, would be disastrous. They hadn't spoken since the terrible night of the party, and now Patrick was living thousands of miles away. Of course, part of the reason they had yet to speak was that nothing had changed. Richard had not apologized for what he had done. Now and then he had the urge to reach out, but the idea of prostrating himself before Patrick filled him with resentment and sometimes anger.

He was not absolved.

ONE WEDNESDAY, A FEW days into September, Richard was sitting at the kitchen table when Blake arrived home.

"Was it a good day?"

"It was long," Blake said, putting his bag down on a chair.

"Poveretto."

"Happy it's over," Blake said, slumping onto the sofa and resting his sock feet on the coffee table. "Glad to be home. What about you? What were you writing?"

"I was looking over my submission for the Clio."

"And . . . ?"

"Hoping it's good," Richard said, knowing full well it was not, knowing full well that "submission" was a generous term for the hash of notes he had accumulated.

"I'm sure it's *good*. Give yourself some credit."

"What about you?"

"We always talk about me."

"No we don't."

"Let's talk about you."

"I hate talking about myself."

"No one really hates talking about themselves."

"Stop being argumentative," Richard said, smiling, but finding himself vaguely irritated. "You're at home now. You're not at work anymore."

"I'm not being argumentative," Blake said. "Even though—yes, I know—I'm disagreeing with you. We're just trying to talk."

It was the rocks Blake was placing one by one on his chest—that was the problem. It was the fact that these questions—having to account for his day, being asked to describe, and therefore relive, the hours of lonely frustration at the library—could feel like a show trial.

Blake walked over and wrapped his arms around Richard from behind. Richard tried to relax his body, to become receptive to Blake's touch.

"We don't have to talk about your day."

Blake squeezed tighter, and Richard suddenly felt so guilty about being irritated that he couldn't bring any words to his lips. He exhaled, and the feeling passed.

"I'm starting not to care about the case though." He wandered to the fridge. "I'm going to make us something to eat."

"I should have made something."

"We both know that's beyond you."

Richard frowned.

"But you can still be useful. Find me some ingredients."

Blake rattled off a list. Richard gathered the ingredients and put them in a disordered pile beside the stovetop. Even with the list, and Blake's supervision, he was unsure about what to do. After all, he was constitutionally unable to prepare his own food unless it came in a package and contained over half of his daily salt requirement. The sooner everyone realized this, the better.

Blake stepped in and began the next stage.

"While you're doing that," Richard said, brightening at his own idea, "I'll get Häagen-Dazs at the bodega. Or Ben and Jerry's. Or both. They have both."

"You sure you don't want to stay and watch? Learn something?"

Richard shook his head.

"Okay, fine," Blake sighed.

When Richard returned, the apartment was full of smells and Blake had set a place for him at the table.

"I have a proposal," Blake said as he put the food on the table. It was spaghetti Bolognese, Richard saw.

"Cooking lessons?"

"Well, that too. Actually, that's a good idea, but no. I have friends in town from Portland next week. I want to invite them over. Is that okay?"

"Sure," Richard said, even then feeling a tinge of annoyance at whatever expectations would flow from agreeing to this meeting. "Why wouldn't it be? I'd love to meet them."

"With their kid."

Richard nodded. "Yup, that's totally fine by me."

"Great," Blake said, and they sat down to a dinner prepared in its totality by Blake.

Agreeing to meet Blake's friends—and their child—was a far cry from actually meeting them, of course. Between now and then, there was a yawning gap to cross. When they came, Richard would have to convince them that he actually belonged there with Blake in that apartment, in that neighborhood, in that arrangement with all its promise, all its twenty-first-century suggestion of triumph and justice and possibility, of everything he was tasked with living up to. Nevertheless, Richard was relieved to see that Blake was happy, convinced of his enthusiasm, and unaware of the hesitation and ambivalence, even dread, that this approaching event had inspired in him.

TWENTY-TWO

Richard went down the steps of the library after yet another attempt to get the Clio paper into shape. It was a bright, limpid day. Students in their druidic formations went past, carrying heavy backpacks, tense young personalities full of summer punditry. Soon the relative remoteness and sluggishness of these dog days would cede to a phalanx of new personalities, tender freshmen, green but cunning, charged with the excitement and danger of potential academic and sexual exploits. But Richard knew the campus would still feel desolate to him, now that Patrick was not walking its halls and pathways.

He went out toward Broadway and when he turned south, he saw Anne walking in his direction. It took him a moment to register that things were, of course, different now, that this previously routine scenario of the two of them together on that street, bumping into each other in the vicinity of campus, might have a new temperature. It was the first time he'd seen her since the brunch at Sant Ambroeus. When the fact of this separation did finally clarify itself, he was pressed by a feeling. He had the urge to move. Where? Toward her?

She looked up and saw him.

"You're here?"

He shrugged. "I was at the library."

"You were?"

"Yeah."

She nodded. He stretched out his arms and put his palms up, narrowing his eyes. "You haven't answered any of my texts."

She shook her head.

"If you want to be rude, then by all means."

Flung out from genuine emotion, the words left his mouth before he could think. It was only on seeing her now that her neglect or indifference assumed its full sting. Before, having her out of sight, it had been easier to assume he didn't miss her.

"The responsibility always falls on me," she said.

"The martyrdom too."

She rolled her eyes.

"I didn't mean that," he said.

She nodded ironically.

"You never mean what you mean."

"I'm sorry. About everything that happened."

"You've said that."

"I'll keep repeating it."

"Please don't."

"Well, I miss you."

"You're repeating yourself again."

"I miss swimming with you." He stepped forward without meaning to. "And I miss talking with you."

Seeing her at the edge of campus, only a few hundred feet from where everything had begun, he felt again the gravity of her presence, the tremendous threat and promise of her personality. He was both happy and frightened; he wanted simultaneously to demolish and maintain the distance between them.

Her face softened.

"Look, I do want you to know," she said. "What I said before, about telling everyone. I didn't mean it."

This had never been his main worry. Nevertheless, he was relieved to have her say out loud that she didn't intend to destroy him.

"I still need you, Anne."

"I'm supposed to meet with Antonella," she said. "I have to go."

"Can we just talk?"

"About what? What is there to talk about, Richard?"

"I don't know. I just want to talk with you."

"Do you need my help again?"

"No, that's not why I want to talk."

"Isn't it?"

"I just want to communicate with you."

He wanted to do something, to hug her or otherwise to touch her, but she was already walking away. He watched her disappear into the campus.

To restrain his drifting thoughts, Richard decided to see how far he could walk. He went down Broadway and then crossed over to Central Park West. He went across the park and down Fifth Avenue and it was several hours before he gave up and got onto the subway. When he finally reached the apartment, Blake was at the kitchen table, leaning over his computer.

"There are some leftovers in the fridge," he said. "Fish tacos. I already ate. I have to keep working."

Richard kissed him on the top of the head and took the food into the bedroom. While he ate he tried to find something to watch online but nothing stemmed his distraction.

Troubled by a sense of distance from Blake, of hiding something, he decided to go out again. The night was pliant and hushed. He walked all the way to his own neighborhood, to the block of besieged lawns and half-benighted trees, currently bisected by a spurt of garbage. A wet, plasmic smell hung in the air.

It was an odd feeling to be living there and to miss it anyway: the nondescript building that hid a flight of stairs perfectly designed to film a blonde being chased by a serial killer; the air that bulged with multifarious air fresheners; the floor that was a puzzle of aquamarine tiles, separated by blackened grout.

Several of the familiar antique cars hid their faded vitality under stiff tarps, dusted with pollen. He went around the building and looked down the alley. The light was reassuringly off in his bedroom. Near the end of the block, candles glowed in the window of Sloppy. The houses were still, the closure of the sealed windows and doors tepidly formal through the mist and the hanging glow of the streetlights. He already felt the benevolent tug of a previous life, the calm sterility of his lonely days with Leslie, patiently tilled and infertile, before the spores of Anne and Blake floated by and took hold.

He went inside and climbed the coiling stairs, prepared for the spectacle of Courtney and Leslie cooking, watching a documentary, or otherwise blissfully conjoined in mind if not—he hoped—in body.

When he opened the door, the apartment was dark. He stepped inside and turned the light on. The drying rack was full of dishes; the dish towel hung on the oven door, and on the counter there was a half-full bottle of wine. They weren't at home.

He considered sitting on the sofa, turning on the television. But the space hardly felt like his own after its long annexation. He didn't want to be caught there when Courtney and Leslie returned. He went into his bedroom and closed the door. Perhaps they would somehow remain away the entire night.

He sat on his bed and looked at his phone. He decided to text Blake.

I NEEDED SOMETHING AT MY PLACE. THERE NOW. I'M PRETTY TIRED. THINK I'M GOING TO STAY HERE TONIGHT.

Blake responded almost immediately.

IS EVERYTHING ALL RIGHT?

Richard inhaled. Even the rapid response felt oppressive.

EVERYTHING IS FINE!

Blake responded with a frowning emoticon.

I'LL SEE YOU TOMORROW, Richard wrote, along with a heart emoticon.

BLAKE'S FRIENDS, WHOM BLAKE knew from law school, came over the next night. Richard was sent out for another bottle of wine before they arrived. When he returned they were all seated around the coffee table.

Upon entering Richard waved, and the two men waved back. They were both wearing jeans and oxford shirts, one red and one blue, over broad, trim bodies. He had to admit that they were quite handsome, intimidatingly so. Just as he'd feared. Between them, a toddler in a red cardigan struggled to its feet, locked eyes with Richard, and burst into tears.

"Say hi," one of the men said. The toddler's crying turned into a scream. "Hey, what's wrong with that guy? Look, he brought wine."

"Tell us what's wrong," the second man said, catching a tear on the tip of his finger and displaying it to the toddler. The toddler tried to swat it away.

"Nice to meet you. I'm Richard."

"He doesn't like strangers."

"Ah."

"I'm Ramon and this is Jeff," Ramon said.

Richard leaned forward and they shook hands. There was a heavy but expectant silence.

"How old is . . . ?"

It was the only question Richard could think to ask.

"Tarquin is two."

"But he tests at a three-year-old level."

"Almost four, if we're being honest."

"He's probably the smartest person in the room," Blake said, winking.

He can't even feed himself though, Richard thought. Then again, neither can I.

"We do yoga together now," Ramon said, looking at Tarquin, who had climbed down from the sofa. "He loves it."

Tarquin glared up at him as if he were talking gibberish.

"And classical music, Kindermusik. Tarquin follows along like he's conducting. Put something on."

Jeff fiddled with his phone.

"What should I play?"

"Just pick something. But not Mahler. Mahler sends him into a rage."

"No American composers either, remember."

"Except Charles Ives," Ramon corrected him. "Or Philip Glass."

"That's true."

The Well-Tempered Clavier started from the speakers.

"A child prodigy, appropriate choice."

"Come on, Tarquin!"

They swung their arms above their heads. Tarquin looked back and forth between them, squinting angrily.

Another couple who dress alike, Richard thought. With the same haircut even. They were probably wearing each other's clothes—they definitely could, they were about the same size. They might work at the same law firm, he thought. They probably had the same fitness regimen, did CrossFit together. They probably met at CrossFit.

"So how did you two meet again?" Ramon asked, his eyes still on the child.

"I told you," Blake said, with comic exasperation. "Online."

"Which site?"

"OkCupid."

"I know a few people who've had luck on that one," Ramon remarked.

"Dating in New York is tough."

"Yeah, we're both kind of like *phew*," Jeff said, looking at Ramon, who nodded.

"We met here," Ramon said to Richard, who came over from the kitchen counter with long-stemmed glasses. "And then we moved out to Portland together."

Richard nodded and started pouring the wine.

"Look at him go," Blake said.

Tarquin was waddling down the hall. They all followed him with their eyes. Richard had no desire to discuss where he and Blake had met, or anything else about their relationship. It suddenly seemed utterly juvenile in comparison to what Jeff and Ramon had. They had made a move together; they had a family together. They probably owned a house. These were real adults.

Richard felt like a child, like a fraud. It was a relief that Tarquin was there to divert their attention.

"What do you think he's going to do in there?" Richard asked, as Tarquin stopped in front of the bedroom, grasped the doorknob with a pudgy hand, and proceeded inside.

"Take everything in."

Richard waited for someone to get up and retrieve him, but no one moved.

A moment later, Tarquin emerged with Richard's iPad in hand. He put a corner into his mouth.

"It's Steve Jobs!" Jeff said.

"Don't call him *that*," Ramon said.

When Tarquin saw that he had everyone's attention, he squealed and ran back toward them, dragging the edge of the iPad against the floor.

Richard tensed. He could not afford to have it repaired, let alone replaced, and he certainly did not want to get stuck with the awkward task of pursuing Blake's friends over it.

"Okay, you've had your fun," Jeff said. "Now give it back."

Tarquin took a step forward and placed the iPad on the floor, keeping his eyes on Richard, as though feeding a dangerous animal. Richard took the iPad, wiped down the corner with the hem of his shirt, and inspected it for damages. Ramon leaned toward him.

"Could you say thank you?" he said. "We're trying to teach him manners."

LATER, AFTER THEY'D GONE, Blake was cleaning the dishes.

"Wasn't Tarquin cute?"

303

"Sure," Richard said.

"*Sure?*"

"Yup, just sure."

"So I guess my strategy to make you like kids isn't working so far?"

"Not really."

"Are you in a bad mood or something?"

Richard tingled with resentment at this comment. There was an inherent reduction implied by it, as if everything that this night pointed to was a mere mood. It was a petty and legalistic view on Blake's part. But that legalistic view of things *was* petty. Did Blake actually know him at all?

"I don't think they liked me, and honestly I didn't like them either."

"Sure they liked you."

"I thought they were really rude. And their kid was weird."

"Now you're just being a jerk."

"He was a monster. Admit it."

Richard was joking, but only half joking.

"He's just a kid," Blake said, turning off the faucet. "His behavior wasn't out of the ordinary."

"That whole experience was kind of painful, honestly. They were snobs."

"You're not even trying, you know that?"

"I feel like you want the entire world from me," Richard said. He was sitting on the sofa, staring at the floor.

Blake sighed.

"I ask so little from you," he said. "You don't see that? I really ask so little."

What did it mean that Blake thought the pinching off of his life, the closing down of his freedom, the sapping of his will, could equate to so little?

"It's my *life*, Blake."

"Richard, I let you move back in. What about *our* life?"

It seemed a myth, the sacrifices and compromises everyone spoke of as if they were sacred totems. But it was infinitely more than that—it was imprisonment and effacement. If you made a wrong step, you could find yourself locked in for years. What was all this effort for? Washing the dishes and watching Netflix and pretending to share, which you could never do enough of, that never amounted to what it was supposed to be, that never fulfilled the arbitrary requirement, that as often as not left you empty?

"I'm exhausted," Blake said, standing at the sink, staring down into the sudsy water. "I'm going to bed."

TWENTY-THREE

The Clio deadline was a day away, and even though it seemed too far-fetched even for her to accept, Richard considered claiming sickness or otherwise inventing another excuse to avoid seeing Antonella. But then, as the meeting approached, he had a moment of aberrant courage and resolved to send her the wreck of what he had written. An hour later, however, in yet a further instance of raw and pinched clarity, he changed his mind again and instead decided to be forthright.

"I don't have anything for you."

They were sitting in her office. Orientation games were going on outside, the new freshman class cheerfully corralled and directed.

"Is it the same problem as before?"

Richard nodded.

"But you've been doing remarkable work. You've been on track. What happened?"

"The pressure of the submission, maybe. It just came back all of a sudden."

"I don't know what I can do, Richard. I might be able to get you another few days. The real deadline is coming again soon though, the foundation deadline, and I have no control over that."

"I know."

She tore the seal on a granola bar and nibbled at the tip, staring at him with her abyss-like brown eyes.

"There must be therapy for this," she said.

He didn't say anything.

"Have you spoken to Anne?" she asked. She bit off a chunk of the granola bar and chewed.

"I saw her a few days ago."

"Her Clio submission was very impressive. She may be able to help."

Richard nodded.

"She submitted already?"

"Yes, and I think you should talk to her. She knows this material better than anyone. And she has a fine mind for composition."

Richard tried not to smile. There was something pleasing—pleasingly tidy, pleasingly ironic—about being sent back to Anne. It made him feel as if he were sitting at a control panel somewhere, pressing buttons. It had the deep precision of physics, like the beautiful curve of a wave that travels across a pool, hits a wall, and starts back the way it has come.

"That is a good idea," he said, nodding seriously so as to temper his smile. "I'll get in touch."

"Let me know how it goes," she said. "We'll figure this out."

Dazed by the meeting with Antonella, Richard walked outside. The street air had the frenzied slackening and expectation of after-work. As he went down the slope of Broadway, he felt a sense of total defeat, which was almost a relief. Pedestrians moved around him, coding plans into their phones, sloshing coffee onto their fingers, and contentiously discussing public figures, or openmouthed and nodding with impatient agreement. He felt that he belonged to a world completely separate from the one they belonged to, that he was visiting from somewhere else entirely.

There was a young man limping in his direction, exasperatedly negotiating the uneven pavement with crutches and making hissing comments to himself. It was Barrett. His slanted carriage added a startled vulnerability to his handsome face.

"I can't fucking *deal* with this anymore," he said as they hugged. "At first it was kind of fun, now . . ." He lifted a crutch forlornly. "Want to get drunk with me?"

Richard looked at the time on his phone. He would be late getting home if he had a drink with Barrett. Blake would wonder where he was. It would add to the already palpable strain in the apartment. But at this thought, he felt a lurch of resentment toward the responsibility to which he now felt hostage, and the decision was made.

"I'll have a drink with you," Richard said, nodding.

They started walking at a slow pace.

"What happened?"

"I slipped going down into the subway," Barrett said.

"I'm sorry."

At a nearby bar that smelled stale but had a run-down charm, an almost comically attractive man in a black polo shirt, his rampant yet controlled hair curled over in a wave, came to the table and took their order. He smiled knowingly at Barrett.

"I *think* we met online," Barrett said when the waiter walked away.

"Nice muscles."

"That's an understatement."

A pitcher of beer was soon brought to the table.

"Should we cheers?"

"To what?" Richard said.

Barrett's eyes made a contemplative arc in the air.

"Getting to know each other better."

He fixed Richard with a serious expression and then burst into laughter.

"I hate that the summer is basically over. I hate the darkness. You can already tell it's coming. Last winter I almost killed myself *without* a broken leg, but then I was lucky enough to find a stash of Xanax." He took a large sip of beer. "So what's up with you?"

Richard momentarily considered, then decided against describing recent events. What would he say, that he'd driven away all those people he cared about most in New York—Blake, Anne, and, as Barrett surely now knew, Patrick? Barrett was a straightforward person, averse to pointless complications. Like Blake, he would become a useful instrument of adjudication, massaging disputes with the pressure of abstract rules, breaking disagreements, allocating blame and money, and not wasting his time discussing the vague pap of the human imagination. Also, Richard was afraid of how close Barrett and Patrick had become. Perhaps Barrett already knew everything; perhaps Barrett knew about Richard's deceptions. But this worried him strangely little. It was much more that Richard did not want to start a discussion that might reveal Barrett was aware of developments in Patrick's life of which he, Richard, was now ignorant.

"I moved out of my apartment," Richard said. "I'm living with Blake now." Richard's formally moving in hadn't been discussed yet, but it was the de facto state of things, and this rounding-up was easier than explaining the fuzzy middle ground that they currently occupied.

"Congratulations. Where's the new place?"

"Clinton Hill."

"You should have a housewarming."

"Maybe we will."

Even as he said this, Richard somewhere knew it would never happen.

"Amir and I just took in his cousin. He's working for some demented producer who keeps throwing leather backpacks at him. He's so worried they'll fire him he goes into Ambien comas and posts gibberish on Facebook. Are *you* in therapy?"

"Not yet." Richard sipped his beer. "Does it help?"

"Can't say. I usually always feel the same."

"Me too," Richard agreed grimly.

He ran his hand along the pitted surface of some worn oak molding. "You're the perfect type to go," Barrett said. "I always kind of picture you in a bean bag chair with your legs tucked under you, books, and you like eating Kraft Macaroni and Cheese Dinner or something."

It was a dubiously accurate image.

"Did Patrick tell you that?"

"Not exactly. Well, yes."

"I wish he would shut his mouth sometimes," Richard said. He felt a gratifying blast of anger along his arms.

"It's always affectionate."

"I'm sure. What else did he say?"

"He said you're polite on the outside and scathing on the inside; full of one-liners but too polite to use them until afterward."

Barrett poured himself another glass of beer. Perhaps Barrett didn't know the details of Richard's break with Patrick. It was after all a characteristic of Patrick's maddening dignity that he would keep this salacious information to himself.

"What have you heard from him in San Francisco?" Richard asked.

"He seems to like it."

"They all do."

"Vladimir has been out there a few times. It's pretty annoying."

"I haven't heard from Patrick in a while."

"He said *you* haven't been in touch."

"*I* haven't been in touch?"

Barrett shrugged.

"Maybe I *should* get in touch and tell him what an asshole he is," Richard said. The moment the word left his mouth, he regretted it.

"Why would you do that?"

Richard looked toward the bar, his face burning. He shook his head.

"I wouldn't do that. I would never do that."

The waiter returned and passed Barrett the bill. There was a phone number written on it in red pen. Barrett tilted his head to one side and sighed heavily.

"I'd sit on it," he said. "But just for tonight."

When Richard got home, he could tell that Blake was in a bad mood. The apartment was dark except for a light over the table. Blake was sitting there with his laptop and a stack of documents.

"You smell like smoke," Blake said. His hands were poised on the keyboard.

Richard took off his shoes and walked into the kitchen. He leaned down and wrapped his arms around Blake from behind.

"I did smoke a cigarette."

"Who with?"

"Only one though. With Barrett. I saw him on campus."

Richard stood up straight and rubbed his face with both hands.

"I didn't think you were going to be so late," Blake said.

"Neither did I."

"Are you tipsy?" Blake asked.

"I drank some beer. I guess I'm a bit drunk. Nothing some bread and water won't fix."

"There's part of a baguette left from the meal, which of course I ate alone." Blake's voice was taut.

Tired from the beer, the agitation of his meeting with Antonella, and the long day in general, Richard sighed.

"I'm sure I told you I might be late."

"I still had to eat alone."

"What should I say?"

"It's depressing coming home to an empty apartment."

"I know, I'm sorry. Didn't I say that already?"

"Then, you know—why not be here? It would be nice to *eat* together, you know?"

Richard swallowed as he imagined this scene replaying itself, the stress of watching the clock wherever he was, of cutting short any spontaneous engagement and rushing home through the twisted intestine of the transit system, worried that he would find Blake sitting at this very table, illuminated by the overhead light that cast the rest of the kitchen into darkness, like some interrogator in a basement jail. It was not a scenario whose gloomy power was neutralized by his love for Blake. It was a goal imposed on him that he would never reach, a test that he was compelled to take repeatedly but would always fail.

"Yes," he said, exhaling. "I understand that."

"At the end of the day I want to see you."

"Can't I have a drink with a friend?"

"Oh my God—don't make me feel like I'm holding you hostage."

Blake stood up and went to the kitchen. He had an agitated expression on his face.

"Are you hungry?" he asked. "I'll make you something."

What is he doing? Richard wondered with annoyance.

"You don't have to do that," he said.

"I'll make you a fried-egg sandwich."

"No, don't."

"I want to."

Blake opened the fridge and leaned into the beaming chill. Richard poured himself a glass of water and sat down with it at the table.

"Do you need me?" Blake asked.

Richard tensed. The question was insurmountable. It was impossible to arrange the potential responses in their proper order. They all struggled at once to get out and in the process choked off any escape, like people trying to flee a burning house. What was the symmetry that would explain everything? What was the design that would leave Blake unhurt—only crediting the rightness of the answer? Yes, he needed Blake; yes, he felt as though he wanted to get up and leave.

Blake turned on the burner and cracked an egg into a frying pan, where it sizzled and bubbled.

"Yes, I need you," Richard said. Blake sliced two pieces of bread and inserted them into the toaster. "Why are you so needy today?"

"I'm not needy. I just want you there."

"There?"

"*There*," Blake said impatiently. "*With* me."

"When am I not there? I'm there. I'm here right now."

"You're not open. You're opaque, actually."

Blake was shaking his head, and Richard frowned. He raised an eyebrow, staring at the table.

"Is this about your friends?"

Blake flipped the egg and sprinkled it with pepper, not answering. He put the two pieces of toast on a plate, and then angled the fried egg on top.

"Why are you cooking? Is this another dig at me?"

"Sometimes I think you've never heard a single word I've said to you," Blake said, putting the plate down in front of Richard. With a knife and fork, Richard began slicing up the fried egg sandwich. The yoke burst and spread across the plate. "Are you unsatisfied?"

"Everybody is unsatisfied," Richard said. "Everybody around here anyway. Everybody in this city."

"Not everybody," Blake said. "Jeff and Ramon aren't unsatisfied."

"They don't live here. And they probably are."

"I don't think they are."

"They were unsatisfied with me. They were judging me. So were you."

"Why are you doing this?"

"What do you want?" Richard asked, putting the knife and fork down on the plate.

"I want what they have—what Ramon and Jeff have."

"That awful kid?"

"Not the kid. Maybe the kid. Whatever it is they have. The peace."

They stared at each other across the thickening neutrality of the table.

"I thought you wanted that too," Blake said.

IN THE QUIET THAT followed their argument, Richard said he was going to sleep at his place. He washed the dish and put it in the drying rack. Blake sat down with an air of rumination at the kitchen table, his computer and a stack of documents at hand. He told Richard to text when he got home. Richard kissed him on the top of the head and left.

He walked the entire way, the sidewalk piebald with shadow. Save for a lone young man who went along the curb with his phone close to his face, a gleam on his bearded skin, Richard's street was deserted when he arrived. But there were lights on in the building.

He went inside and climbed the stairs to the apartment. Their door closed, a fan rotating audibly inside the room, Leslie and Courtney were already asleep. He got into bed and turned off his light, spreading his limbs out in the empty bed.

He didn't respond to Blake's message the next morning asking if he'd arrived home safely, and he didn't answer any of the other more worried and impatient texts that continued to arrive intermittently throughout the day. If he answered, a predictable conversation would follow: he would have to explain why he hadn't yet acknowledged and replied. They would need to address their conversation from the night before. It would mean Richard would have to admit he had no clue what he wanted anymore.

Until Blake had calmed down, until there was some air to breathe between them, he would leave it a little while longer.

His phone rang several times, but he didn't pick up. An email came to his inbox. He left it unanswered. It went on like this for several days, as Richard deferred to an equivocal but considered neglect. His guilt increased, but he also felt distant from any move to respond. Finally the guilt seemed to reach a plateau, and then to settle. As he realized he was not going to respond, it was accompanied by a feeling that he identified as relief.

The messages eventually stopped, but then after a pause of several days, in which it was starkly obvious to Richard what a terrible thing he'd done, another text from Blake arrived saying:

I SEE YOU'RE ACTIVE ON FACEBOOK SO AT LEAST I KNOW YOU'RE STILL ALIVE.

But no more texts came after that.

TWENTY-FOUR

Orientation was over and the semester was under way a week later.

That week—which had started slowly and densely, like the inertial rumble of an old locomotive gripping iron tracks—accelerated and became headlong and reckless as the second and final Clio deadline arrived. The air of the campus seemed to twitch and plunge with the excitement and promise of the freshmen students. It was the optimistic end of school: the beginning.

For Richard, there was little point in being on campus. He could have done this—his ritual of sluggish stagnation—anywhere; he could have been at home, in the irritating nest with Courtney and Leslie. He did not admit to himself that the reason had to be the possibility of running into Anne. Of course he had not reached out to her at Antonella's behest. And now that she'd submitted her Clio, she was probably taking a break, had other things to do, or she had decided to avoid the library because she didn't want to see him. In any case, there was no sign of her in the streets, in the library, or on his phone, though she took her place in the throng of ghosts that drifted around the campus now—a clutch of notables, the wraith of Patrick, the looming specter of Antonella, Richard's own ectoplasmic prolific former self.

Maybe it was best that she wasn't there. Even though Anne had observed him for months in his inert, parasitic mode, he felt that he must look worse now, more frustrated and impotent, flat and beset, sitting there all day in the light of the computer screen, running his hands through his hair with nervous flicks. He rarely typed a word, though his curled index finger hung just above the keyboard for long stretches.

Then one day she appeared on the other side of the table as Richard stared futilely off into space. Her presence was so familiar, he did not immediately react. When he looked up he expected it to be one of the new undergraduates who had begun colonizing the library and crowding him.

He straightened up in his seat.

"Hi," he said.

"Can I sit here?" she asked.

"Go ahead." He nodded.

"I'm not disturbing you?"

"No," he said.

She pulled out her laptop. He wondered if she was there to talk but soon the familiar look of gathered focus entered her eyes. He wondered if she had come with the express purpose of interrupting him, of spreading a wrecking static into the room. They sat there not speaking for a long time, and though Richard was now doubly unable to concentrate, the familiar sense of reassurance, the comfort at having her across the table from him again, returned along with her presence.

Eventually, when he couldn't stay there or silent any longer, he suggested they get coffee. A moment of hesitation was evident, but she agreed. They went to Starbucks, paid separately, and brought their iced Americanos back to the steps of the library. They looked out over the campus, where a humid film had settled.

"How are Erin and Alicia?" he asked.

"They're fine. Still in Queens. I see them once in a while. How are Leslie and Courtney?"

"They're fine too. Her belly keeps growing. I'll have to move soon, but I haven't done anything about it."

"I'm not surprised."

"You're not?"

"Not really."

"Yeah, well."

He thought he saw her conceal a smile. For a moment, they sipped their coffees in silence. A group of slim, sinewy runners went past in a pneumatic trance.

"What are you working on these days?" he tried.

"I had an abstract accepted to a conference in Houston. Pietro Aretino."

"Ah, interesting."

"What are you working on?" she asked, though he was sure that she knew the answer. They were doing a dance.

"I'm still working on the Clio submission," he said. He glanced at her to gauge her reaction.

"And?"

"I'm already late, but I got an extension. I'm going to be late again."

She nodded but didn't say anything.

"I'm trying to use that idea you had about the *Modistae* and jump off from there. I hope you don't mind."

She sighed. "I don't mind, Richard."

THAT NIGHT HE LAY in bed absorbed by what it was like being there with her, in the library, what an odd, out-of-date person she was, how she remained indifferent to the tragic—or entertaining—distraction of the present. Maybe he'd been wrong in thinking that what Blake did was so noble, the defense lawyer guaranteeing a fair chance for the persecuted, and that what he and Anne did together was so pointless.

He decided to text her.

IT WAS GOOD TO SEE YOU TODAY.

He hardly expected a response, certainly not one in the middle of the night, but she replied almost immediately.

I CAN'T SLEEP.

NEITHER CAN I. WHY CAN'T YOU SLEEP?

NOISE.

I FORGOT TO TELL YOU THAT I SAW ANTONELLA. SHE TOLD ME YOUR CLIO SUBMISSION WAS A MASTERPIECE.

THAT'S NICE OF HER TO SAY.

Richard hesitated.

I MISS YOU, he wrote.

She didn't reply.

MAYBE I'LL SEE YOU IN THE LIBRARY AGAIN. I'M THERE ALL THE TIME.

IT WAS GOOD SEEING YOU.

He decided to be direct.

I NEED YOUR HELP, ANNE.

?

THE CLIO. CAN I SHOW YOU WHAT I'VE WRITTEN?

He put down his phone, then picked it up again. He scrolled back to the beginning of their conversation and read through it once more. He was happy to be texting again; it felt good to be in a back-and-forth with someone he cared about, to be connected in the city, in the austere silent middle of the night.

SEND ME WHAT YOU HAVE AND I'LL TAKE A LOOK.

THANK YOU.

And suddenly there they were: back at the library in their usual places. He brought out his laptop and for a while sat there in silence across from her as she worked with a glare on her face. He thought about getting a newspaper from the rack of world newspapers—they seemed to have everything—but then decided just to sit and wait in silence, like a penitent.

When she began her critique she was initially cold, almost scolding him, but her arctic formality eventually softened.

"There's a lot of good stuff in here," she said, not able to fully suppress her enthusiasm and, he found himself hoping, her affection.

He came around and sat beside her, listening with flattering scrutiny as she outlined a revised structure for the submission. She even praised some of the points he'd made.

Maybe she did think he was stupid, he thought, but that was okay. He *was* stupid, compared to her. She did not mean, and had never meant, to hurt him. She abhorred the idea of doing harm to anyone; she was practically a Jain in this respect. It was miraculous that she even tolerated his presence after what he'd done, let alone agreed to help him.

By late afternoon, she had finished.

"I did what I could with it," she said. "It's not perfect."

"Whatever you did, I'm sure it's a vast improvement."

"There wasn't much time. It was a lot of work," she said. He nodded sheepishly. "And now I'm hungry."

"Would you believe it, I'm hungry too?"

"I have an idea. Let's go to Sabarsky's."

There was a hint of her old enthusiasm.

"I like that idea."

"We'll take a cab."

It felt good to her, he sensed, to reassert herself over him like this.

"Okay, let's go."

They got into a cab and drove across Central Park, looking out their opposite windows as the trees and the buildings beyond them floated by. The restaurant was full when they arrived.

"I guess it's always high tourist season here."

Anne suggested they kill time by looking at the paintings upstairs. She bought the entrance tickets and they climbed the wrought-iron staircase to the second floor.

There was something appropriate to where they there—all the traumas hermetically sealed and made quiet in harrowing tableaus along the wall, a cool space of empty but freighted air between them and what they looked at. Richard felt calmed. It was usually galling when someone talked through an exhibit, and even then a trip to the museum often left him with the impression that he'd failed in the pursuit of judgment or at least understanding. Like a canny dog that gets loose and knows you're trying to reattach the leash, there was a feeling but it continually absconded, scampering away at each approach. But as they moved from Klimt to Schiele to Kokoschka—they paused decorously before each canvas—Anne's informed, nonpedantic commentary filled the room with an unusually pleasing hum. The drunk murdered the prostitute, the bloated industrialist traded on the lives of the poor, the Freikorps soldier rampaged through the streets. She knows so much, he thought.

When they went down to the restaurant, he saw himself in a long mirror, walking behind her. Reflected with him was the dark wood paneling, the tables with their marble tops, and the waiters in white aprons, all of it made to resemble fin de siècle Vienna.

One of the black-and-white-attired waiters came to the table.

"The Hungarian beef goulash, please," Richard said.

Anne ordered trout crepes and wine.

"I won't be able to eat it all," she said when the waiter left. "We haven't shared a dish for a while. You should have some."

It occurred to Richard that she had not asked him if he was still living with Leslie and Courtney, and he wondered if she thought he was living with Blake. He felt relieved that he could tell her truthfully that he was still at the old apartment.

"The coffee is good here. They bring it on a silver tray."

An elegant elderly couple, wearing identical tortoiseshell eyeglasses, sat down in the next booth. The waiter came back with the wine and poured them each a glass.

"Are you glad to have your space back?" he asked. "Now that Erin and Alicia are in Queens?"

"I'm living all alone."

"It's everyone's dream to get rid of their roommates."

"Not mine."

"No, I guess it isn't."

She smiled at him.

"I thought you didn't need me anymore," she said. "I guess I was wrong."

"I guess you *were* wrong. You're not often wrong."

He smiled.

"You can still move in, you know?" she said quietly. "I still want you to. There's even more room for you, now that Erin and Alicia are gone. It would be a home at my apartment."

It was an acute, provoking keyhole break in her armor, opening out onto the expanse of loneliness that she carried around inside of her, the inadvertent sequestration caused by her intellectual talent, the strangeness and originality of her person forming an accidental abyss that engulfed her.

He felt like he was crouching and peering through the keyhole, the shadows and lights of something moving on his face. This miserable admission, that in spite of everything he'd done she wanted him to move in again, her inscrutable debasement and the decision to forgive him, took on a quiet glow, like an elevated act of sacrifice.

"I know it would," he said, his throat catching. "I know that it would be a wonderful home."

The food arrived, and for several minutes they ate in a mechanical, abashed silence. Even as she waited for him to speak, he didn't know what else to say.

"Would you really still want me there?"

"Yes," she said—too quickly, he thought. He watched her arm move through the air as she poured him more wine. Amid the bulging emotion of the room, it was a gesture whose impartial practicality was almost radiant. Her voice quavered. "You can come whenever you want."

After the meal, they hugged each other on the street, and then she walked off toward Madison—she had an appointment—leaving him with a clenched feeling in his hands, as if he wanted to say something more before she dematerialized into the city. As in a paralytic dream, the words were impossible to extract.

He crossed the avenue and went into the park. He walked down an empty path in a vague diagonal toward the towers that rose in the southwest. When he reached Columbus Circle, he pulled out his phone

I'LL COME TONIGHT.

TWENTY-FIVE

He met with Antonella in her office two days later.

"The submission is good," she said. "And I want to underline that I'm so happy you managed to work through these latest difficulties. But it's . . . well, perhaps not as good as your previous work."

"No?"

He tried to calm his face.

"Your other work had a real elegance." She paused, weighing her thoughts. As if on rungs of growing consideration, her eyes climbed to the ceiling.

"This is competent, but not elegant."

He nodded seriously.

"Is it ready to submit though?"

He felt a great impatience to conclude the discussion.

"I've marked up a few things. Once you address those issues, I think you can submit. I have to say, I don't expect you to win the Clio with this, especially now that it's late, but I can write the paper to the foundation now."

Below the window, a group of students marched past, protesting something. Lively chanting could be heard.

"I appreciate your honesty."

"I don't need to see it again," she said, raising her eyebrows, and clearly making an attempt to be reassuring. But her words were like a cup of hot water tossed into an inexorably cooling bath. "Go ahead and submit."

Anne had tried to help him, but even she had been unable to raise the termite-ridden sticks of his thoughts into a gleaming cathedral.

"I will."

"Is everything else all right? You're over your problem?"

"Yes, I'm over it now, I think. Everything should be fine."

"I hope you will let me know if that changes."

"I will."

"And make sure you focus on yourself, Richard. That's the first step to getting healthy again."

"I'll submit this afternoon," he said.

"Wonderful, Richard. *Complimenti*. I'm so happy for you."

He wondered what Antonella honestly thought of him, apart from what she was supposed to think of him as one of her students. Did she see through him? Did she wonder what he was doing there, in that city? A succession of do-gooder mayors had shoved all the junkies and pimps off the streets, banned smoking and trans fat, and put bike racks on every corner, but anyone with half a brain knew it was more of a jungle than ever. He'd always thought that he blended in, that the base unreliability of his character was hidden. But he was beginning to suspect that anyone with a more than averagely penetrating stare, and especially anyone who had the opportunity to observe him for more than a brief moment, could perceive his foundational weakness.

AUTUMN BECAME WAXY AND veiny over the sidewalks. As Anne and Richard resumed their routine in the library and she began TA-ing a class, a pedagogical spectacle she enjoyed, there was a genuine healing that seemed to take hold between them. They did not talk about Blake, or what had happened. Blake had made no further attempts at communication. Neither had Richard.

It was a somber relief that he had never shown Blake the apartment he shared with Leslie and Courtney, despite all of Blake's good-natured curious insistence. Now it would be unlikely, close to impossible, for Blake to knock on the door, to seek Richard out if only to confirm in person that he was alive, had not been taken hostage by his roommates, or left the city without telling anyone. Scenarios revolved in Richard's mind: Blake employing his legal skills to comb records, enjoining friends who worked for Google or Facebook to scour the Internet in search of traces, suggestive evidence, or emphatic specks—power bills, phone bills, Amazon orders—in order to track Richard down. Richard did sometimes imagine Blake successful in his search. He saw Blake climbing the gloomy stairs and knocking on the door of the apartment. Richard stepped out onto the landing, trying to explain what he himself didn't fully understand, annoyed at Leslie and Courtney, who listened with the giggly complicity of couples humorously aroused by the romantic travails of single friends.

Richard already looked back, was trying to look back, on his time with Blake, so brief and so recently concluded, as belonging to another life, as though he was historically evaluating a younger self, objectively examining another person moving under a cloud or a bright sky of ignorance, unaware of whatever the future might happen to be, though the future was all along inexorable.

HE TOOK WALKS ALONG the Hudson with Anne. They loitered in shops and galleries. They went out to eat in the neighborhood, by candlelight. They began to settle into a life together.

Every time he was about to see her, he anticipated the feeling of sinking into himself without regret or hesitation. He looked forward to being unjudged, relinquishing control, to the prospect of Anne wielding her expertise and authority as manager and dispenser of the money, her ownership of the apartment, her jurisdiction over where he slept, ate, and bathed.

Richard finally put his bed and his desk on Craigslist. The rest of what he did not need or want he left on the curb. Predictably, a white van pulled up, a compact woman in a pink cardigan got out, lifted the entirety into the back of the vehicle—curtains, nicked chest of drawers, speckled mirror—and drove away.

When he told Leslie and Courtney, they could not disguise their palpable relief at finally having him gone.

"Come and visit us, Richard."

"Are you going to be close by?" Leslie asked.

"I'll be living in Manhattan," Richard said, visibly satisfied at revealing his upscale destination. "I'm in the West Village, actually."

"Very fancy."

"I got a good deal," he said. "No roommates or anything."

With the remainder of his belongings, he took a livery cab over to Anne's apartment. They had a happy night and woke up on a white sheet flattened out beneath them like a trampled meringue.

Erin and Alicia came over for dinner a few days later—Anne ordered Indian—and even they seemed amenable to this new reality. Their formerly confrontational posture had metamorphosed into a gentle bemusement and acceptance.

"Cheers," Anne said, and they raised their glasses. "Is it nice to be back in Manhattan?"

"So nice."

"What's so bad about Queens?" Richard asked. "Everyone loves Queens."

"Nothing," Alicia said, looking around. "We just miss our old nest."

"Though it has changed," Erin remarked.

She was obviously referring to Richard's presence in the apartment. He considered pointing out that preferring Manhattan to Queens did not square with their politics. But he was happy enough for them to all get along, so he decided against it.

"Everyone is moving to Queens," he said.

Anne went to the bathroom. When she came back she was looking at her phone. She was oddly silent.

"What is it?" Richard asked.

"I won the Clio Prize."

He stood up and hugged her. Only a few weeks had passed since the deadline, but in his new circumstances, Richard had hardly—if at all—thought about the Clio. It was part of some other life, some other rancorous, unstable period.

And then, suddenly, here it was again.

"Congratulations!" he said.

"Thank you. Wow."

"This is great news."

Erin and Alicia clapped.

"But I'm sorry you didn't win."

"Are you serious?" he said, shaking his head. "You deserve it."

Even as he said it, he was conscious of how quickly he'd leapt from his seat to offer his congratulations. Had he become too good at mimicking these kinds of emotions? Did he really mean it?

He did believe that he meant it; he was happy and pleased. It was the right and good thing to relish Anne's achievement, to celebrate her expertise.

"Let's make a toast," Alicia said. "To Anne becoming a famous scholar."

"She's a brain on the make," Erin said. "Aren't you glad you'll be able to say you knew her when you were young?"

They each took a sip of wine, while Anne beamed.

"It's like an auction," Erin said. "Offers will be coming in from all over."

"All the best schools will want her."

"Where would you like to go?"

"We'll see," Anne said. "Maybe Oxford? That's where the manuscripts are."

"England would be nice."

"Or California."

"Or here," Richard said.

"Cluck, cluck," said Alicia. "Enough with the flattery! I forgot to tell you both. There's a demonstration tomorrow on campus. Are you coming? We're protesting the right to publish sexual fantasies about our professors in the student press. They're cracking down."

"I'll think about it," Richard said.

"Come on," said Alicia. "Stand up to censorship!"

"I want to see you chant!"

They had cookies for dessert. When Erin and Alicia had gone, Richard stood at the kitchen sink washing the dishes, while Anne dried them beside him. Adrift in thought, Anne hummed to herself with a soft smile on her face. Even this mellow and proud distraction, after good news, struck him. She had never been even slightly demonstrative about her own success. Now she was unable to tamp down a buzz of accomplishment; she was thrilled. He smiled down at the soapy water, happy for her too.

TWENTY-SIX

The latest installment from the foundation came into Richard's account late in the fall. He felt flushed and secure. He became a coffee shop regular again, at a place a few blocks away from Anne's apartment called Slouch. The staff dressed with bucolic cheer, oftentimes in overalls and railroad caps, and there was always chirpy electronic music on the speakers. Their shared sartorial preferences, neighborhood, routine, and in all probability dull or stressful jobs, testy coworkers, depleted bank accounts, and lofty ambitions ostensibly united them but did not inspire them to conversation. Every time he made his way there, he passed a ragged-looking man sitting cross-legged on the sidewalk holding a sign that read, in black marker, FUCK EVERYONE IN THE WEST VILLAGE. But still, he went often enough that soon he began to feel at home.

He also felt at home in Anne's apartment, in the surrounding blocks with their boundless provision of culinary and retail choice, in the boutiques filled with silk dresses and in the bodegas overflowing with fashion magazines and bundles of lilies. He and Anne both loved all of this; they shared a deep affection for the city, especially in its deluxe versions, and they went out and walked it together, just as they had done before.

The question of their future did assert itself. As they were lying in the wreckage of their hangovers one morning, Anne turned to him and said:

"What if I get a job in another city? Will you come with me?"

"You don't want to leave New York," he said.

"I don't *want* to leave New York, but I may not get a job here."

He was staring at the ceiling.

"Do you need to get one?" he asked.

He was picturing them in another kind of life—a life that was safe and vivid, frivolously arranged, and flavorful. He saw them drinking martinis in an elevated bar, carving into some newfangled meat, trying on clothes, Antonella and the Clio Prize dim silhouettes in their past. It was a city made for people with nowhere to be, when you got down to it.

"I *want* to get one."

"What about when *I* get a job?"

"We'll look for you too, obviously. We'll find jobs in the same place. We won't settle."

He got out of bed and looked out the window. It was snowing beautifully, like a mammoth cloth shredded by moths. Women with long silken hair, in black tights and furry boots, moved along the sidewalk in animated pairs, resembling a seductive alpine patrol force.

If they moved to a small college town, she said, maybe she could buy a big gabled house. There would be room for friends and visitors, a bucolic update of Peggy Guggenheim's Venetian palazzo.

"I'll go wherever you go," he said.

He meant it. He had grown to believe that this tolerant communion, this forgiving harmony in which he was never compelled into a dishonest and untenable competence, would persist wherever they went together. She knew him, and she would never grow impatient searching for what was not there. "And I'm going to start writing again. I'm going to come out of this," he contemplated.

"Of course you will."

ONE DAY AROUND LUNCHTIME Richard found himself in Midtown. He was going to meet Anne after an appointment she had, but he was early. It was cloudy, dry, and cold, winter coming into focus. At his hairline there was a slim film of moisture and he felt damp under his coat. He went to a cafeteria-style place, dimly lit as if the day were somnolent, the frothy curved residuum of discarded cappuccinos scattered across the tables like a halfhearted installation. The spontaneous organization of the city went on under a palsied sky, the logistical and spatial negotiations dense and cryptic. He watched delivery trucks and couriers pass by and solemn young editors who wore sober, determined expressions, wrapped in scarves against the cold air. He ordered a cappuccino and sat down at a table beside the window.

When he thought of the streets of Manhattan, he pictured stratified crowds of commuters surging between tall buildings, dressed in precise and disheveled overcoats, covertly racing each other to the subway with overstuffed briefcases. He saw himself on a different, less crowded street, walking straight-backed and trying to keep up as he did a series of double takes, while oblivious young men went past in sneakers and T-shirts. It was a vision at odds with the present cold, the scouring wind that sheared between buildings, and the salt that spread underfoot, eating up cars and shoes. Somewhere in Brooklyn Leslie and Courtney pushed around a stroller big enough to be an armored personnel carrier.

He was about halfway through his cappuccino when the street transformed into a stage, pedestrians receded into the mental shorthand of type, and cars turned into inert props. Blake was sitting in the window of the restaurant across the street.

He was with someone. Not someone: it was Patrick. Richard was immediately filled with shocked affection. Patrick, whom Richard had not spoken to for months, was trying to make Blake understand why he had gone out one night and never come back. Patrick, who understood him best of all, Patrick was on the verge of convincing Blake to understand him and to forgive him. Benevolence radiated out across the newly dramatic street. Despite the estrangement, in a gorgeous gesture Patrick had flown in from San Francisco to fix Richard's life. Who had told him what had happened?

It wasn't Patrick. It was a guy named Josh. Richard remembered the face: high, flat forehead, deep-set eyes, a histrionic, self-obsessed theater person. He was from Blake's Tennessee Williams group, a few years older than Richard. Josh turned to look out the window. It wasn't Josh. It was a Josh-like someone, with a higher, flatter forehead, larger, deeper-set eyes.

Richard stood up to get a better look. A waiter came to their table and Blake pulled out a credit card. Richard watched as Blake inserted it into a machine.

Richard had tried to convince himself that what he had with Anne was best: you chose someone who was an impenetrable mystery, but whose elusiveness did not tug at you; their distance gave you space to breathe and abide in a sphere of possibility, whereas the gravitational panic he felt for Blake was a precarious compound that would darken and decompose until it had burned away the surface of the earth and killed everything it touched.

Then, as Richard watched, Blake became something else entirely, and he felt a haunted sense of a life that continued on a track from which he had diverted, a track that he was not suited to follow, or likely was incapable of following, or from which he had simply fallen and then lost sight of. The self he had struggled to conjure his entire life, whole and capable, appeared like a hummingbird that paused in the air, displayed its brilliant throat, and retreated in a blur.

A group of people entered the café, their voices an indolent roar arriving from somewhere else. Richard walked to the door, the muffled convection of the coffee cup against his hand. He pictured himself crossing the street and tapping on the window of the opposite restaurant. Blake looked up and locked eyes with him through the glass.

Richard stepped outside. He imagined that Blake and the guy were newly obsessed with each other, that they worked on opposite sides of the park and traveled across town on their lunch breaks to see each other, enduring exasperating traffic complications just for a few minutes in each other's company: it was the acute, extraordinary dawn of the relationship. Every gram of matter was suffused with the expectation or aftermath of contact, flesh was the absolute element, and the thick materiality of everything that would eventually decay was the greatest blessing and not the worst joke.

The man reached out and gripped Blake's hand, and Blake shook his head, laughing, as if he were being asked to tango in some ridiculous setting. They stood up, and Richard saw that they were dressed almost identically—in pea coats and monochromatic scarves, with briefcases. They gathered their belongings and walked outside. They stood talking in the soft, centrifugal drifts of snow.

In front of his dowdier establishment Richard stood perfectly still.

He almost said something; he almost raised his hand and crossed the street. He watched Blake and the young man step across the slush and the garbage, two appropriate candidates for a long life together. They went off down the street and disappeared around a corner.

When they were gone, Richard walked east to meet Anne.

ACKNOWLEDGMENTS

Thanks:

To my family, for their forbearing and steadfast support; to my friends, far and wide, for comfort and critique; to the wonderful team at Frances Goldin, who helped shepherd this book into the light of day, but especially to my agent, Caroline Eisenmann, who, in her infinite wisdom, saw the potential in an early manuscript and made all this happen; to the dedicated people at Simon & Schuster, who have handled this book with such care, but especially my editor, Zack Knoll, of whom too many kind and admiring words cannot be said.

ABOUT THE AUTHOR

JAMES GREGOR holds an MFA in fiction from Columbia University. He has been a writer in residence at the Villa Lena Foundation in Tuscany and a bookseller at Shakespeare and Company bookshop in Paris. James was born and grew up in Canada. *Going Dutch* is his first novel.